英 *Make Me High* 系列

108課綱、全民英檢初級適

U0022203

基礎英文字彙力

2000

隨身讀

三民英語編輯小組 **彙整**

📱 APP 🎧 音檔

三民書局

序

英語 Make Me High 系列的理想在於超越，在於創新。
這是時代的精神，也是我們出版的動力；
這是教育的目的，也是我們進步的執著。

針對英語的全球化與未來的升學趨勢，
我們設計了一系列適合普高、技高學生的英語學習書籍。

面對英語，不會徬徨不再迷惘，學習的心徹底沸騰，
心情好 High！
實戰模擬，掌握先機知己知彼，百戰不殆決勝未來，
分數更 High！

選擇優質的英語學習書籍，才能激發學習的強烈動機；
興趣盎然便不會畏懼艱難，自信心要自己大聲說出來。
本書如良師指引循循善誘，如益友相互鼓勵攜手成長。
展書輕閱，你將發現⋯⋯
學習英語原來也可以這麼 High！

使用說明 ▶▶▶

符號表

符號	意義
[同]	同義詞
[反]	反義詞
～	代替整個主單字
-	代替部分主單字
< >	該字義的相關搭配詞
( )	單字的相關補充資訊
▲	符合 108 課綱的情境例句
💡	更多相關補充用法
__ / __	不同語意的替換用法
__ / __	相同語意的替換用法

略語表

1. adj. 形容詞
2. adv. 副詞
3. art. 冠詞
4. aux. 助動詞
5. conj. 連接詞
6. n. 名詞
   [C] 可數
   [U] 不可數
   [pl.] 複數形
   [sing.] 單數形
7. prep. 介系詞
8. pron. 代名詞
9. v. 動詞
10. usu. pl. 常用複數
11. usu. sing. 常用單數
12. abbr. 縮寫

電子朗讀音檔下載方式

請先輸入網址或掃描 QR code 進入「三民・東大音檔網」。
https://elearning.sanmin.com.tw/Voice/

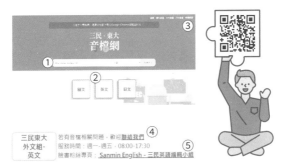

① 輸入本書書名即可找到音檔。請再依提示下載音檔。

② 也可點擊「英文」進入英文專區查找音檔後下載。

③ 若無法順利下載音檔，可至「常見問題」查看相關問題。

④ 若有音檔相關問題，請點擊「聯絡我們」，將盡快為你處理。

⑤ 更多英文新知都在臉書粉絲專頁。

英文三民誌 2.0 APP

掃描下方 QR code，即可下載 APP。

Android

iOS

開啟 APP 後，請點擊進入「英文學習叢書」，尋找《基礎英文字彙力 2000》。

使用祕訣

① 利用「我的最愛」功能，輕鬆複習不熟的單字。

② 開啟 APP 後，請點擊進入「三民／東大單字測驗」用「單機測驗」功能，讓你自行檢測單字熟練度。

目次

嗨！你今天學習了嗎？
一起使用進度檢核表吧！
學習完一個回次後，你可以在該回次的◯打勾。
一起培養基礎英文字彙力吧！

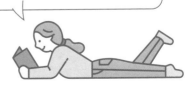

我的進度檢核表，
學習完成就打勾！✓

Level 1	① ② ③ ④ ⑤ ⑥ ⑦ ⑧ ⑨ ⑩
	⑪ ⑫ ⑬ ⑭ ⑮ ⑯ ⑰ ⑱ ⑲ ⑳
	㉑ ㉒ ㉓ ㉔ ㉕ ㉖ ㉗ ㉘ ㉙ ㉚
	㉛ ㉜ ㉝ ㉞ ㉟ ㊱ ㊲ ㊳ ㊴ ㊵

Level 2	① ② ③ ④ ⑤ ⑥ ⑦ ⑧ ⑨ ⑩
	⑪ ⑫ ⑬ ⑭ ⑮ ⑯ ⑰ ⑱ ⑲ ⑳
	㉑ ㉒ ㉓ ㉔ ㉕ ㉖ ㉗ ㉘ ㉙ ㉚
	㉛ ㉜ ㉝ ㉞ ㉟ ㊱ ㊲ ㊳ ㊴ ㊵

Unit 1

1. **a** [ə] art. 一 (個)

   ▲ Judy is a hard-working student.
   Judy 是一位勤奮的學生。

   an [æn] art. 一 (個) (用於母音開頭的名詞前)

   ▲ There is an orange on the table. 桌上有一顆柳丁。

2. **become** [bɪ`kʌm] v. 成為 (became | become | becoming)

   ▲ Mary wants to become a teacher after graduating from college. Mary 大學畢業後想當老師。

   💡 become of... …情況如何

3. **choose** [tʃuz] v. 選擇 <from>；選舉 <for, as> (chose | chosen | choosing)

   ▲ The guests can choose what they like from the menu.
   客人可以從菜單中任選他們喜歡的。

4. **church** [tʃɝtʃ] n. [C] 教堂

   ▲ I go to a Catholic church every Sunday morning.
   我每個週日早上都會去天主教堂。

5. **computer** [kəm`pjutɚ] n. [C] 電腦

   ▲ My computer has an Internet connection.
   我的電腦有網路連結。

6. **fast** [fæst] adv. 快速地

   ▲ A dog ran fast toward the mail carrier.
   有一隻狗快速地衝向郵差。

fast [fæst] adj. 快速的

▲ Kevin is the fastest runner in his school.
Kevin 是他們學校跑得最快的人。

7. **health** [hɛlθ] n. [U] 健康

▲ My eighty-year-old grandfather is still in good health. 我八十歲的祖父身體仍然很硬朗。

8. **home** [hom] n. [C][U] 家

▲ There's no place like home.
【諺】金窩銀窩不如自家窩。

💡 be/feel at home 感覺自在

home [hom] adv. 回家；在家

▲ Leo ran into an old friend on his way home from work. Leo 在下班回家的路上碰見一位老朋友。

home [hom] v. 集中注意力於… <in on>

▲ The news report homes in on the problems of climate change. 這篇新聞報導主要在論述氣候變遷的問題。

home [hom] adj. 家庭的，家裡的；國內的

▲ Oliver wrote his home address on the envelope.
Oliver 在信封上寫下他家的地址。

9. **knife** [naɪf] n. [C] 刀 (pl. knives)

▲ The knife is too blunt to cut meat.
這把刀太鈍了不能切肉。

knife [naɪf] v. 用刀砍或刺 [同] stab

▲ It was reported that a woman was attacked and knifed when she was walking along a dark street.

根據報導，一個女人在黑暗街道上走的時候受到攻擊並被砍殺。

---

10. **later** [ˈletɚ] adv. 待會兒，稍後

▲ I think we can deal with the issue later.
我覺得我們稍後再處理這個議題。

---

11. **middle** [ˈmɪdl] adj. 中間的；中等的

▲ The middle desk is empty, so you can sit there.
中間的位子是空的，所以你可以坐那裡。

middle [ˈmɪdl] n. [sing.] 中間

▲ Don't park the car in the middle of the road.
不要把車停在路中間。

♥ in the middle of nowhere 杳無人煙之處

---

12. **not** [nɑt] adv. 不是；沒有

▲ You are not young anymore. 你不再年輕了。

---

13. **over** [ˈovɚ] prep. 在…上方；超過 [反] under

▲ There is a helicopter flying over the city.
有一架直升機正飛過城市上方。

over [ˈovɚ] adv. 結束；從一地 (邊) 到另一地 (邊)

▲ What do you usually do when school is over for the day? 學校放學後你通常做些什麼事呢？

---

14. **person** [ˈpɝsn̩] n. [C] 人 (pl. people)

▲ Bill is a nice person, and we all like him.
Bill 是個和善的人，我們都喜歡他。

💡 in person 親自，直接

15. **place** [ples] n. [C] 地方；名次
   ▲ It was awful that the taxi driver took me to the wrong place. 計程車司機把我帶到錯誤的地點，真是糟糕。
   💡 take the place of... 取代…
   place [ples] v. 放置 [同] put
   ▲ My mom placed a large vase on the table.
   我媽媽把一個大花瓶放在桌子上。

16. **slow** [slo] adj. 緩慢的 [反] quick, fast
   ▲ Slow and steady wins the race. 穩扎穩打事必成。
   slow [slo] v. 變慢 <down>
   ▲ Please slow down; I can't keep up with you.
   請慢一點，我跟不上你的腳步。
   slow [slo] adv. 緩慢地 [同] slowly
   ▲ You should drive slower through the small town.
   在這小鎮開車時，你應該要減速慢行。

17. **talk** [tɔk] v. 說話 <to>；談論 <about>
   ▲ Andy has talked to his girlfriend on the phone for an hour. Andy 已經跟他女友講電話講了一個小時了。
   talk [tɔk] n. [C] 交談 <with> [同] conversation
   ▲ Ida had a long talk with her teacher about her schoolwork. Ida 與老師長談關於學業的事。

18. **television** [ˈtɛləˌvɪʒən] n. [C][U] 電視 (機) <on> (abbr. TV)

▲ The author has appeared several times on television.
這位作家在電視上出現過幾次。

19. **the** [ðə] art. 這 (個)，那 (個)；這些，那些
▲ Could you pass me the magazine?
你可以將那本雜誌遞給我嗎？

20. **there** [ðɛr] adv. 在那裡，往那裡；有 (表示存在) (～ is, are, was, were 等)
▲ How long will it take us to get there?
到那要花我們多久時間？

21. **top** [tɑp] n. [C] 頂端；上衣
▲ There is a flag at the top of the mountain.
這座山的頂端有一面旗子。

💡 on top of 除⋯之外還 (尤指令人不快的事)
top [tɑp] adj. 頂端的；最重要的，最成功的
▲ The swimming pool is on the top floor of the hotel.
游泳池位於飯店的頂樓。

top [tɑp] v. 放在⋯的上面 <with>；超過
▲ The cake was topped with some strawberries and cherries. 這個蛋糕的上面放了一些草莓和櫻桃。

22. **train** [tren] n. [C] 火車
▲ Joseph goes to work by train every day.
Joseph 每天都搭火車去上班。

train [tren] v. 訓練
▲ All the new employees have to be trained before

doing their jobs.

所有的新員工在進行工作前都必須要先受訓。

trainer [`trenɚ] n. [C] 教練

▲ Phoebe hired a trainer to help her work out at the gym. Phoebe 在健身房僱用教練來幫她健身。

---

23. **turn** [tɝn] v. 轉彎；轉變 <into>

▲ Please turn left at the next crossing.

請在下一個十字路口左轉。

turn [tɝn] n. [C] 轉彎；順序

▲ The path took a sharp turn to the right.

那條小路往右急彎。

♥ take turns 輪流

---

24. **well** [wɛl] adv. 很好地

▲ I'm surprised that Jack speaks Japanese so well.

我很驚訝 Jack 日語說得這麼好。

well [wɛl] adj. 健康的 (better | best)

▲ I hope you can get well soon. 我希望你能早日康復。

well [wɛl] n. [C] 井

▲ There is a well in Mr. White's backyard.

White 先生的後院有一口井。

---

25. **woman** [`wumən] n. [C] 女人 (pl. women)

▲ Today, many women use skincare products to have fair skin.

現今許多女性會使用保養品以擁有白皙的皮膚。

Unit 2

1. **angry** [ˈæŋgrɪ] adj. 生氣的 <at/with sb, at/about sth>
   (angrier | angriest)
   ▲ Oliver was angry with me for forgetting his birthday.
   Oliver 對於我忘記他生日這件事對我感到生氣。

---

2. **baby** [ˈbebɪ] n. [C] 嬰兒
   ▲ Mandy is expecting a baby in June.
   Mandy 六月要生產。

---

3. **back** [bæk] adv. 向後地；回到原處
   ▲ Jimmy kept looking back to see if anyone was
   following him.
   Jimmy 一直向後看，想知道是不是有人在跟蹤他。

   back [bæk] n. [C] 背部；後面 [反] front
   ▲ I've got a pain in my back. 我背痛。
   ● turn sb's back on... …背棄…

   back [bæk] v. 使後退；支持 <up>
   ▲ My father tried to back his car into the garage.
   我爸爸試著倒車進入車庫。

   back [bæk] adj. 後面的 [反] front
   ▲ Children should sit in the back seats.
   小孩應該坐在後座。

---

4. **bug** [bʌg] n. [C] 小蟲子；(電腦應用程式中的) 缺陷
   ▲ My goodness! There is a bug on your arm.
   天啊！有隻小蟲在你的手臂上。

bug [bʌg] v. 煩擾 (bugged | bugged | bugging)

▲ The noise from next door is bugging me.

鄰居家傳來的噪音正煩擾著我。

---

5. **class** [klæs] n. [C] 班級；階級

▲ Zack is the tallest student in my class.

Zack 是我們班最高的學生。

class [klæs] v. 把⋯分類 <as>

▲ Irish coffee is classed as an alcoholic drink.

愛爾蘭咖啡被分類為酒精類的飲品。

---

6. **clear** [klɪr] adj. 清楚的；清澈的

▲ Please make your point of view clearer.

請將你的觀點說得更清楚一點。

clear [klɪr] v. 清理，清掃

▲ Joe mopped the floor, and his sister cleared the table.

Joe 拖地，而他妹妹清理桌子。

clear [klɪr] adv. 不靠近地

▲ Please stand clear of the stove. 請不要站在火爐旁邊。

---

7. **dark** [dɑrk] adj. 黑暗的 [反] light；(顏色) 深的 [反] light, pale

▲ After the sunset, it started getting dark.

夕陽西下後，天色漸漸變暗了。

dark [dɑrk] n. [U] 黑暗

▲ The child is afraid of the dark. 那個小孩怕黑。

💡 in the dark 蒙在鼓裡，渾然不知

---

8. **first** [fɝst] n. [C] 第一個人或事

▲ Ken was the first to reach the finish line.
   Ken 是第一個抵達終點線的人。

   first [fɝst] adv. 第一，首先

▲ My family comes first, and my work second.
   我的家庭第一，而工作第二。

   first [fɝst] adj. 第一的，初步的

▲ This was Lily's first visit to Paris.
   這是 Lily 第一次來巴黎觀光。

   🔍 in the first place 首先 | for the first time 第一次

9. **help** [hɛlp] v. 幫忙

▲ Please help me do the dishes. 請幫我洗碗。

   🔍 cannot help + V-ing = cannot help but + V 不得不…

   help [hɛlp] n. [U] 幫忙；[sing.] 幫手

▲ Ted finally finished the job with the help of his
   friends. Ted 最後在朋友的幫忙下完成這個工作。

10. **house** [haʊs] n. [C] 房子

▲ Mr. Wang decided to buy the house because it was in
   a good location.
   王先生決定要買這房子是因為它的地點很好。

   house [haʊz] v. 收容，為…提供空間

▲ The museum houses some of Vincent van Gogh's
   paintings. 這博物館收藏了一些梵谷的畫作。

11. **job** [dʒɑb] n. [C] 工作

▲ Besides his full-time job, Lucas does some odd jobs

in the evening for some extra money.

除了全職工作之外，Lucas 晚上還打一些零工賺外快。

12. **light** [laɪt] n. [C] 燈；[U] 光
   ▲ Gary turned off the lights before leaving the office.
   Gary 離開辦公室前關掉電燈。

   light [laɪt] adj. 明亮的 [反] dark；輕的 [反] heavy
   ▲ The big window makes the living room light.
   這個大窗戶讓客廳很明亮。

   light [laɪt] v. 點燃 (lighted, lit | lighted, lit | lighting)
   ▲ Jake lit a cigarette and started to read a newspaper.
   Jake 點燃一根菸，然後開始看報紙。

   light [laɪt] adv. 輕裝地
   ▲ Nowadays, more and more people like to travel light.
   現今有越來越多人喜歡輕裝旅行。

13. **lot** [lɑt] n. [C] 許多；一塊地
   ▲ It costs a lot of money to build the bridge.
   造這座橋要花很多錢。

14. **mind** [maɪnd] n. [U][C] 頭腦，心思
   ▲ My grandfather still has a clear mind even in his
   nineties. 我的祖父九十幾歲仍然頭腦清楚。
   ♥ keep/bear sb/sth in mind 記住…
   mind [maɪnd] v. 介意；注意
   ▲ Do you mind if I sit here? 你會介意我坐在這裡嗎？

15. **near** [nɪr] prep. 在…附近

▲ The White family lives near an MRT station.

White 一家人住在捷運站附近。

near [nɪr] adj. 接近的

▲ Leo and Maria will get married in the near future.

Leo 和 Maria 在不久的將來會結婚。

near [nɪr] adv. 接近

▲ The ship came near to the shore. 船駛近了岸邊。

near [nɪr] v. 接近

▲ The train is nearing the station. 火車正駛近車站。

---

16. **right** [raɪt] adv. 向右地；正好，恰好

▲ Turn right and you'll see the post office on your left.

向右轉你就會看到郵局在你的左手邊。

right [raɪt] adj. 右邊的；正確的 [同] correct [反] wrong

▲ Lauren had a tattoo on her right arm.

Lauren 的右手臂有一個刺青。

right [raɪt] n. [U] 右邊；正義

▲ Chinese is written from right to left.

中文是從右到左書寫的。

---

17. **sea** [si] n. [C][U] 海，海洋 [同] ocean

▲ It is dangerous to go swimming in the sea.

在海裡游泳很危險。

---

18. **see** [si] v. 看見；理解 (saw | seen | seeing)

▲ I saw my mom talking to a stranger in the doorway.

我看見我媽媽在門口和一位陌生人說話。

💡 see sb off 為…送行

19. **subject** [ˈsʌbdʒɪkt] n. [C] 主題；科目
   ▲ The subject for discussion today is climate change.
   今天要討論的主題是氣候變遷。

20. **tell** [tɛl] v. 告訴；分辨 (told | told | telling)
   ▲ Excuse me, could you tell me the way to the museum? 不好意思，你能告訴我去博物館的路嗎？
   💡 tell sb/sth apart 分辨

21. **this** [ðɪs] pron. 這，這個
   ▲ Please make sure this won't happen again.
   請務必確保這不會再發生了。
   this [ðɪs] adj. 這，這個
   ▲ Do you know how much this ring cost?
   你知道這個戒指要花多少錢嗎？
   this [ðɪs] adv. 這麼，如此
   ▲ No kidding. The apple was this big!
   沒開玩笑。那顆蘋果有這麼大！

22. **tree** [tri] n. [C] 樹
   ▲ Louis used to climb the tree when he was a child.
   Louis 孩提時常爬這棵樹。

23. **trip** [trɪp] n. [C] (短程的) 旅行
   ▲ Charles hopes to take a trip around the world one day. Charles 希望有一天能環遊世界。
   trip [trɪp] v. 絆倒 <on, over>

▲ Don't trip over that wire. 別讓那條電線絆倒了。

24. **use** [juz] **v.** 使用，利用
　▲ Hebe used her old jeans to make a fashionable handbag.
　　Hebe 用她的舊牛仔褲做了一個時髦的手提包。
　♥ used to 過去常做
　use [jus] **n.** [U] 使用 <in, out of>；[C] 用途
　▲ Keep your children away from the machine when it is in use. 當機器在運轉時，讓你的孩子遠離它。

25. **weather** [ˋwɛðɚ] **n.** [U] 天氣
　▲ What's the weather like in Sydney? = How's the weather in Sydney? 雪梨的天氣如何？
　♥ weather forecast 氣象預報 | be/feel under the weather 身體不適的
　weather [ˋwɛðɚ] **v.** 平安度過 (困境)；受到風雨侵蝕
　▲ The small business weathered the depression.
　　這小型企業平安度過經濟蕭條期。

◆━━━━━━━━◆━━━━━━━━◆

Unit 3

1. **above** [əˋbʌv] **prep.** 在…之上 [同] over [反] below
　▲ The helicopter was flying above the city.
　　這架直升機在城市上空飛行。
　♥ above all 最重要的是
　above [əˋbʌv] **adv.** 在上方 [反] below

▲ Far above I saw an airplane flying east.

我看見在極高處有一架飛機往東飛去。

above [ə`bʌv] adj. 上述的

▲ For the definition of the term, please refer to the above paragraph.

關於這個詞語的解釋，請參考上一段。

---

2. **along** [ə`lɔŋ] prep. 沿著

▲ Mr. Smith took a walk along the lake.

Smith 先生沿著湖邊散步。

along [ə`lɔŋ] adv. 向前；帶著…一起

▲ The children walked along and chatted happily.

這些孩童邊走邊開心聊天。

💡 all along 一直，始終

---

3. **appear** [ə`pɪr] v. 出現，露面 [反] disappear；似乎

▲ Shelly stopped appearing in public after her accident.

Shelly 在意外後不再公開露面。

---

4. **both** [boθ] pron. 兩者 <of>

▲ Both of the sisters are smart and beautiful.

這兩姊妹都很聰明、漂亮。

both [boθ] adv. 兩者

▲ You and Allen are both from Canada, aren't you?

你和 Allen 都是來自加拿大，不是嗎？

both [boθ] adj. 兩者的

▲ The kid had some candies in both hands.

這小孩兩手都拿著糖果。

5. **call** [kɔl] **v.** 打電話給；給⋯取名
   ▲ Call me when you hit the road.
   你出發時打個電話給我。
   💡 call for sth 需要⋯ | call sth off 取消⋯
   call [kɔl] **n.** [C] 打電話；叫喊
   ▲ Give your grandmother a call before you visit her.
   在你拜訪祖母前先打電話給她。

6. **cost** [kɔst] **n.** [C] 費用，價格；成本 (usu. pl.)
   ▲ The house was built at a cost of three million dollars.
   這棟房子的造價是三百萬美元。
   💡 at all costs 不惜任何代價
   cost [kɔst] **v.** 花費；使付出代價 (cost | cost | costing)
   ▲ The orange juice cost NT$100.
   這杯柳橙汁要一百元新臺幣。

7. **drive** [draɪv] **v.** 開車；迫使 (drove | driven | driving)
   ▲ Jude drives to work every day.
   Jude 每天都開車去上班。
   drive [draɪv] **n.** [C] 駕車的路程；[U] 決心，魄力
   ▲ Would you like to go for a drive today?
   你今天想要去開車兜風嗎？

8. **eat** [it] **v.** 吃 (ate | eaten | eating)
   ▲ My father is not used to eating out.
   我父親不習慣外食。

9. **he** [hi] pron. 他 (用於代替男人、男孩或雄性動物)

▲ Mr. Jones is an English teacher, and he's very popular with his students.

Jones 先生是位英文老師，而且他很受學生歡迎。

him [hɪm] pron. 他 (用於代替男人、男孩或雄性動物)

▲ Mr. Williams is very intelligent, and we often turn to him for advice.

Williams 先生很有智慧，我們常常向他尋求建議。

his [hɪz] pron. 他的 (用於代替男人、男孩或雄性動物)

▲ Ken's colleagues threw him a farewell party on his last working day.

Ken 的同事在他工作的最後一天幫他辦一個歡送會。

himself [hɪm`sɛlf] pron. 他自己，他本人

▲ It seems that Caleb is very confident in himself.

Caleb 似乎對自己很有自信。

---

10. **nature** [`netʃɚ] n. [U][C] 大自然 (also Nature)；天性 <by, in>

▲ The theme of the poem is to praise the beauties of nature. 這首詩的主旨是在讚嘆大自然之美。

---

11. **north** [nɔrθ] n. [U] 北方 (also North) (abbr. N) (the ～)

▲ Keelung is in the north of Taiwan.

基隆位在臺灣北部。

north [nɔrθ] adj. 北方的，北部的 (also North) (abbr. N)

▲ We decided to visit the north coast.

我們決定造訪北海岸。

north [nɔrθ] adv. 向北 (also North) (abbr. N)

▲ This train is heading north. 這是北上列車。

---

12. **now** [naʊ] adv. 此刻，現在

▲ Tina is cleaning the bathroom upstairs now.
Tina 現在正在樓上打掃廁所。

● every now and then/again 偶爾

now [naʊ] n. [U] 此刻，目前

▲ Now is the time to sell the house.
現在該是把房子賣掉的時候了。

---

13. **only** [`onlɪ] adv. 僅，只

▲ We took part in the activity only for fun.
我們參加這個活動只是為了好玩而已。

● not only...but (also)... 不但…而且…

only [`onlɪ] adj. 唯一的，僅有的 (the ~)

▲ Seth is the only child in his family. Seth 是家中獨子。

only [`onlɪ] conj. 不過，只是 [同] except (that)

▲ I would like to help, only I have something urgent to
do. 我想要幫忙，只是我有緊急的事要做。

---

14. **park** [pɑrk] n. [C] 公園

▲ Most of Taiwan's dog parks are in northern Taiwan.
臺灣大多數的狗狗公園位於北部。

park [pɑrk] v. 停車

▲ It is illegal to park in the red zone.
在紅線區域停車是違法的。

---

15. **small** [smɔl] adj. 小的，矮小的 [反] big；不重要的

▲ This white sweater is too small for Kyle.

這件白色毛衣對 Kyle 來說太小了。

small [smɔl] n. [U] 後腰部

▲ Lena had a scar on the small of her back.

Lena 在後腰部有一個傷疤。

small [smɔl] adv. 小，不大

▲ The label on the wine is printed very small.

這瓶酒上面的標籤字體印刷得非常小。

16. **smell** [smɛl] n. [C] 氣味；[U] 嗅覺

▲ These organic apples have a distinctive smell.

這些有機蘋果有一種獨特的氣味。

smell [smɛl] v. 發出…氣味；嗅，聞

▲ I think the stinky tofu smells awful.

我覺得臭豆腐的味道很可怕。

17. **team** [tim] n. [C] 隊，組

▲ A basketball team can send five players to play on the court each time.

一支籃球隊一次可以派五位球員在場上比賽。

team [tim] v. 組成一隊，合作 <up>

▲ The two scientists teamed up to carry out the experiment. 這兩位科學家合作進行實驗。

18. **thing** [θɪŋ] n. [C] 東西；事情

▲ What is that black thing on your face?

你臉上那黑色的東西是什麼？

💡 for one thing 一方面

19. **through** [θru] prep. 通過；整個…之中
   ▲ The train is going through a tunnel.
   火車正在通過隧道。

   through [θru] adv. 完成；完全地
   ▲ I read through the entire newspaper in one morning.
   我一個早上就把報紙全看完了。

20. **to** [tu] prep. (方向) 朝，向；(時間) 距，到
   ▲ It will take about 15 minutes to walk from here to the
   museum. 從這走到博物館大約要花十五分鐘。

21. **type** [taɪp] n. [C] 類型 <of>；[U] 印刷字體
   ▲ There are various types of hats to choose from in the
   store. 這間店裡有各式各樣的帽子可供選擇。

   type [taɪp] v. 打字
   ▲ Please type this letter by noon.
   請在中午以前把這封信打好。

22. **want** [wɑnt] v. 想要
   ▲ Brian desperately wanted a new smartphone as his
   birthday gift.
   Brian 非常想要一支新的智慧型手機作為生日禮物。

   want [wɑnt] n. [U] 缺少，不足
   ▲ Some refugees in the country died for want of food.
   這個國家的一些難民因缺乏食物而死亡。

23. **warm** [wɔrm] adj. 暖和的；熱情的

▲ The climber kept rubbing his hands to keep them warm. 登山客不斷摩擦他的手以讓它們暖和。

warm [wɔrm] v. 使變暖和 <up>

▲ Patricia warmed the room up by turning on the electric heater. Patricia 開電暖爐讓房間暖和起來。

💡 warm up 熱身；熱鬧起來

24. **wear** [wɛr] v. 穿戴著；磨損 <away> (wore | worn | wearing)

▲ Margaret wore a pink dress and a diamond necklace to her friend's wedding. Margaret 穿著粉色洋裝、戴著一條鑽石項鍊去參加朋友的婚禮。

💡 wear sth out 用壞…，磨損… | wear off 逐漸消失

25. **will** [wɪl] aux. 將要，將會

▲ The weather forecast says that the storm will come tomorrow. 氣象預報說暴風雨明天會來。

will [wɪl] n. [U][C] 意志；意願

▲ Those who have strong wills don't give up easily. 那些有堅強意志力的人不會輕易放棄。

Unit 4

1. **beautiful** [ˋbjutəfəl] adj. 美麗的

▲ The girl is so beautiful that many boys adore her. 這位女孩如此美麗，以致於很多男孩愛慕她。

2. **behind** [bɪ`haɪnd] prep. 在後面
   - ▲ The child was hiding behind a big tree.
     那孩子躲在一棵大樹後面。
   - **behind** [bɪ`haɪnd] adv. (遺留) 在後面
   - ▲ Mr. Anderson left a large fortune behind after he died. Anderson 先生死後留下一大筆財產。

3. **buy** [baɪ] v. 買，購買 [反] sell (bought | bought | buying)
   - ▲ I bought a used car from Tom at a low price.
     我用低價跟 Tom 買二手車。
   - ♥ buy sb off 買通… | buy into sth 完全相信…
   - **buy** [baɪ] n. [sing.] (划算或不划算的) 買賣
   - ▲ The dictionary is a good buy at $3.
     這本字典真划算，才三美元。

4. **center** [`sɛntɚ] n. [C] 中央，中心點；(某一活動的) 中心
   - ▲ The actress was the center of attention at the party.
     那女演員是宴會上眾所矚目的焦點。
   - ♥ in the center of sth 在…的中心

5. **change** [tʃendʒ] n. [C][U] 改變；零錢
   - ▲ The manager made some changes to the proposal in the meeting. 經理在會議中對提案做些改變。
   - ♥ for a change 為了轉換氣氛
   - **change** [tʃendʒ] v. 改變；變成 <into, to>
   - ▲ The small town has changed a lot over the past ten years. 這小鎮在過去十年間改變很大。

💡 change sb's mind 改變主意

changeable [`tʃendʒəbl] adj. 善變的 [反] reliable

▲ The weather in the United Kingdom is very changeable. 英國的天氣反覆無常。

---

6. **clean** [klin] adj. 乾淨的；公正的，光明正大的 [反] dirty

▲ Mrs. Collins always keeps her house clean and tidy. Collins 太太總是把家裡保持得很整潔。

clean [klin] v. 清理，打掃

▲ My roommate and I take turns cleaning the bathroom. 我室友和我會輪流打掃廁所。

💡 clean sth out 把⋯完全掃除

clean [klin] adv. 完全地，徹底地

▲ I'm terribly sorry that I clean forgot our meeting. 很抱歉我完全忘記我們會面的事了。

clean [klin] n. [sing.] 打掃，清掃

▲ The basement is very dirty and needs a good clean. 這地下室很髒，需要好好打掃了。

---

7. **deal** [dil] n. [C] 交易

▲ I know where to get a good deal on new cars. 我知道哪裡可以買到便宜的新車。

💡 no big deal 沒什麼了不起

deal [dil] v. 處理 <with> [同] handle (dealt | dealt | dealing)

▲ You should deal with the problem as soon as possible. 你應該要盡快處理這個問題。

8. **deep** [dip] adj. 深的 [反] shallow；深切的，強烈的
   ▲ There are a variety of creatures in the deep sea.
   在這深海裡有各式各樣的生物。

   deep [dip] adv. 深地，向下延伸地
   ▲ To look for her car key, Pamela thrust her hand deep into her handbag.
   為了找車鑰匙，Pamela 將手深入到包包底部。

9. **dry** [draɪ] adj. 乾的，乾燥的 [反] wet；枯燥的 (drier | driest)
   ▲ These tea leaves should be kept in a cool, dry place.
   這些茶葉必須保存於涼爽、乾燥的地方。

   dry [draɪ] v. (使) 變乾
   ▲ Debra likes to hang her laundry outside to dry in the sun instead of using a dryer. Debra 喜歡將衣服晾在外面讓太陽曬乾，而不是使用烘乾機。

10. **fish** [fɪʃ] n. [C][U] 魚；魚肉 (pl. fish, fishes)
   ▲ The fish in the lake are of many varieties.
   這湖裡的魚種類很多。
   🕯 be like a fish out of water 不知所措

   fish [fɪʃ] v. 釣魚，捕魚 <for>；間接探聽 <for>
   ▲ The fishermen are fishing for trout in the river.
   這些漁民正在這條河裡捕鱒魚。

11. **good** [gʊd] adj. 好的，有益的 [反] bad, poor；令人滿意的 (better | best)
   ▲ Taking more exercise is good for your health.

多做運動對你的健康有好處。

good [gʊd] adv. 很好地

▲ The job applicant did pretty good in the interview.

這位求職者在面試中表現良好。

good [gʊd] n. [U] 好處，益處；正直的行為

▲ Frank should quit drinking for his own good.

Frank 應該要為自身健康而戒酒。

💡 it's no good + V-ing …是沒有用的

---

12. **hard** [hɑrd] adj. 硬的 [反] soft；困難的 [同] difficult [反] easy

▲ The meat is still hard because it is frozen.

這肉因為是結凍的還很硬。

💡 be hard on sb 對…苛刻的

hard [hɑrd] adv. 努力地；猛烈地

▲ Angela failed the exam because she didn't study hard. Angela 因為沒有努力念書而考試不及格。

---

13. **however** [haʊ`ɛvɚ] adv. 然而，可是 [同] nevertheless；無論如何 [同] no matter how

▲ I intended to visit you last Saturday. However, a friend of mine called on me.

我原本打算上週六去看你。然而，我有個朋友來訪。

---

14. **little** [`lɪtl] adj. 年幼的；很少的 (less, littler | least, littlest)

▲ The little girl was crying loudly on the street.

這小女孩在街上大哭。

little [ˋlɪtl̩] adv. 稍微地

▲ Rosa is a little worried about the exam results.
   Rosa 有點擔心考試的結果。

💡 little by little 逐漸地

little [ˋlɪtl̩] n. [sing.] 少量，少許

▲ Mr. Cole left little of his wealth to his children.
   Cole 先生將很少的財富留給他的孩子。

---

15. **of** [ɑv] prep. …的；離…

▲ You can find the meanings of words in a dictionary.
   你可以在字典裡找到字的定義。

---

16. **paper** [ˋpepɚ] n. [U] 紙；[C] 報紙 [同] newspaper

▲ The boy made a plane with recycled paper.
   這男孩用回收紙做飛機。

paper [ˋpepɚ] v. 用壁紙貼 [同] wallpaper

▲ Maggie and her husband are busy papering the living
   room. Maggie 和她丈夫正忙於在客廳貼壁紙。

---

17. **people** [ˋpipl̩] n. [pl.] 人；[C] 民族

▲ Thousands of people came to the open-air concert.
   好幾千人來聽這戶外音樂會。

people [ˋpipl̩] v. 居住於 <by, with> [同] inhabit

▲ The island is peopled by two aboriginal tribes.
   兩個原住民部落居住在這島嶼上。

---

18. **poor** [pʊr] adj. 貧窮的 [反] rich；粗劣的，不好的 [反]
   good

▲ The goal of the organization is to help many poor people around the country.
這個組織的目標是要幫助這國家許多貧窮的人。

19. **run** [rʌn] **v.** 跑步；(機器等) 運轉 (ran | run | running)

▲ Cindy ran up to me, saying hello.
Cindy 跑過來跟我打招呼。

💡 run across sb 偶然遇到⋯

20. **study** [ˋstʌdɪ] **n.** [U] 學習；[C] 研究，調查 <on, into> (pl. studies)

▲ The following are some tips on improving study skills. 以下是一些可以增進學習技巧的訣竅。

study [ˋstʌdɪ] **v.** 學習；研究 (studied | studied | studying)

▲ Stacey has been studying Russian for two years but has learned very little.
Stacey 學了兩年俄文但懂得很少。

21. **way** [we] **n.** [C] 路，路線；方法

▲ Jim saw a car accident on his way home.
Jim 回家的途中目睹了一場車禍。

💡 by the way 順便一提 | give way 屈服，讓步

22. **week** [wik] **n.** [C] 週

▲ Mrs. Carter goes grocery shopping about twice a week. Carter 太太一週約採買雜貨兩次。

23. **wide** [waɪd] **adj.** 寬大的 [同] broad [反] narrow；(範圍、

知識等) 廣大的

▲ Mary stared at Jerry with wide eyes.

Mary 睜大眼瞪 Jerry。

wide [waɪd] adv. 大大地

▲ The dentist asked Ruby to open her mouth wide.

牙醫要 Ruby 把嘴巴張大。

---

24. **world** [wɝld] n. [sing.] 世界，地球 (the ～)

▲ Tourists from all over the world came to the town to attend the jazz festival.

來自世界各地的旅客來到這個城鎮參加爵士樂慶典。

---

25. **writer** [`raɪtɚ] n. [C] 作者，作家 <of, on> [同] author

▲ Agatha Christie is a well-known writer of detective fiction. 阿嘉莎克莉絲蒂是偵探小說的名作家。

Unit 5

1. **ability** [ə`bɪlətɪ] n. [C][U] 能力，才能 (pl. abilities)

▲ It is said that cats have the ability to see in the dark.

據說貓能在黑暗中看見物體。

---

2. **airport** [`ɛr,port] n. [C] 機場

▲ Jack saw his uncle off at the airport.

Jack 到機場為他叔叔送行。

---

3. **art** [ɑrt] n. [U] 藝術 (作品)；美術

▲ Carl enjoys going to the museum to look at art.

Carl 喜歡到博物館去欣賞藝術品。

4. **at** [æt] prep. 在…地點；在…時刻

▲ There was a long line at the bank counter in the morning. 早上銀行的櫃檯前大排長龍。

5. **blue** [blu] adj. 藍色的；憂鬱的 [同] depressed

▲ The day is bright and sunny with not even a cloud in the blue sky. 陽光燦爛，藍天裡一片雲都沒有。

blue [blu] n. [C][U] 藍色

▲ Aaron often dresses in blue because it is his favorite color.

Aaron 常穿藍色衣服，因為那是他最喜歡的顏色。

6. **build** [bɪld] v. 蓋，建造 <of> (built | built | building)

▲ Many houses in Japan are built of wood.
日本許多房屋是木造的。

💡 build on sth 以…為基礎

7. **child** [tʃaɪld] n. [C] 兒童，小孩 (pl. children) [同] kid

▲ I liked playing hide-and-seek when I was a child.
我小時候喜歡玩捉迷藏遊戲。

8. **close** [kloz] adj. 接近的 <to>；親密的，親近的 (closer | closest)

▲ Please give me a table close to the window.
麻煩給我靠窗的座位。

close [kloz] adv. 靠近地 <to> [同] near

▲ I feel uneasy when people stand too close to me.

當其他人站得太靠近我時會讓我感到不自在。

close [kloz] v. 關上；不營業，關門 [同] shut [反] open

▲ Please close the door when you leave.

你離開時請把門關上。

close [kloz] n. [sing.] 結尾，結束

▲ The concert came to a close with an encore.

演唱會是以安可曲作為結束。

---

9. **country** [ˋkʌntrɪ] n. [C] 國家 ；[U] 鄉下 (the ～) [同]
   countryside

   ▲ Canada and Mexico are the countries that border the
   United States. 加拿大和墨西哥是與美國交界的國家。

---

10. **doctor** [ˋdɑktɚ] n. [C] 醫生 [同] doc；博士

   ▲ If you feel sick, you should see a doctor.

   如果你覺得不舒服就該看醫生。

---

11. **door** [dor] n. [C] 門

   ▲ Anita ran to answer the door as soon as she heard
   someone ringing the doorbell.

   Anita 一聽到有人按門鈴就跑去開門。

   💡 shut the door on sth 使…成為不可能

---

12. **excellent** [ˋɛkslənt] adj. 優秀的，傑出的

   ▲ Ethan's excellent skills in basketball attracted the
   coach's attention.

   Ethan 傑出的籃球技巧引起教練的注意。

---

13. **explain** [ɪkˋsplen] v. 解釋，說明 <to>

▲ Megan explained to the host that she had been delayed by a traffic jam.

Megan 向主人說明她是因交通阻塞才延誤的。

---

14. **heart** [hɑrt] n. [C] 心臟；內心

▲ Joe's heart beat very fast when he was asking Ann out. Joe 在邀 Ann 外出時心跳得非常快。

💡 break sb's heart 令⋯心碎

---

15. **in** [ɪn] prep. 在⋯之中，在⋯之內；在⋯期間

▲ Gina looked at herself in the mirror.

Gina 看著鏡中的自己。

in [ɪn] adv. 朝裡面 [反] out；在家裡 [反] out

▲ Roger saw a recycle bin and threw his bottle in.

Roger 看到資源回收桶就把他的瓶子朝裡面丟進去。

in [ɪn] adj. 流行的

▲ Torn jeans are in now. 破損的牛仔褲現在正流行。

---

16. **make** [mek] v. 製作；造成，引起 (made | made | making)

▲ Melody can make delicious chocolate brownies.

Melody 會做美味的巧克力布朗尼。

💡 make it 成功 | make sth up 編造⋯

---

17. **need** [nid] v. 需要 [同] require

▲ Everyone needs air and water to survive.

每個人都需要空氣和水才能生存。

need [nid] n. [U][sing.] 需要，需求；[pl.] 需要物 (～s)

▲ The severely injured man is in need of medical treatment. 這位受重傷的男子需要醫治。

💡 meet/satisfy a need 滿足需求

need [nid] aux. 必須

▲ You needn't worry; Gloria will deal with the problem. 你不必擔心，Gloria 會處理這個問題。

needless [`nidlɪs] adj. 不必要的

▲ Nora didn't prepare for the math test. Needless to say, she failed it.
Nora 沒有為數學考試做準備。不用說，她考不及格。

---

18. **out** [aut] adv. 向外，外出 [反] in

▲ Mr. Moore went out for a drink after dinner.
Moore 先生晚餐後外出喝酒。

💡 out of control 失去控制 | out of date 過時

out [aut] prep. 向外

▲ The cat jumped out the window. 貓從窗戶跳出去。

out [aut] adj. 偏遠的；(產品) 上市的

▲ It is too late to travel to the out islands now.
現在去偏遠的離島太晚了。

out [aut] n. [sing.] 藉口

▲ The knee injury gave Albert an out to take a day off.
膝傷讓 Albert 有請一天假的藉口。

out [aut] v. 公開 (名人) 同性戀身分

▲ The Hollywood star has been outed recently.
那位好萊塢明星最近被揭露是同性戀者。

19. **real** [ˋrɪəl] adj. 現實的，真實存在的；真的 [反] fake

▲ Magic doesn't exist in the real world.
魔法在真實世界中是不存在的。

20. **road** [rod] n. [C] 道路，馬路

▲ Tim helped an old lady cross the road.
Tim 協助一位老婦人過馬路。

21. **show** [ʃo] v. 出示；顯示 (showed | showed, shown | showing)

▲ Show your driver's license, please. 請出示駕照。

💡 show off 賣弄，炫耀 | show up 出現

show [ʃo] n. [C] 戲劇，表演；展覽

▲ The magician disappeared from the stage at the end of the show. 魔術師在表演的最後從舞臺上消失。

💡 on show 在展出 | show business = show biz 演藝圈

22. **soon** [sun] adv. 不久，很快

▲ I didn't expect you to get here so soon.
我沒想到你這麼快就到這裡。

💡 as soon as... 一⋯就⋯ | as soon as possible 盡快 | sooner or later 遲早

23. **tea** [ti] n. [U][C] 茶

▲ The hostess poured tea for everyone in the room.
女主人為房間裡的每個人倒茶。

24. **very** [ˋvɛrɪ] adv. 非常，很

▲ Joey likes to play soccer very much.

Joey 非常喜歡踢足球。

---

25. **white** [hwaɪt] adj. 白色的；(面色) 蒼白的
  ▲ The bride looked stunning in the white wedding gown. 穿著白紗的新娘看起來很漂亮。

  white [hwaɪt] n. [U] 白色；[C] 白人 (also White)
  ▲ The color white symbolizes innocence and purity.
    白色象徵天真和純潔。

Unit 6

1. **already** [ɔl`rɛdɪ] adv. 已經
  ▲ I have already seen the movie before.
    我之前已經看過這部電影了。

---

2. **and** [ænd] conj. 和；然後，接著
  ▲ Joan and Amy are good friends.
    Joan 和 Amy 是好朋友。

---

3. **attack** [ə`tæk] n. [C] 攻擊 <on>；(疾病等) 突然發作
  ▲ The soldiers made a sudden attack on the enemy.
    這些軍人對敵軍發動突襲。
  ● come under attack 遭受攻擊

  attack [ə`tæk] v. 攻擊；抨擊，批評
  ▲ Our army attacked the enemy during the night.
    我軍夜襲敵軍。

---

4. **away** [ə`we] adv. 去別處；離…多遠 <from>

▲ My father is away on a business trip.
我父親出差去了。

💡 right away 立刻

---

5. **between** [bə`twin] prep. 在…之間

▲ There are some differences between British English and American English.

英式英語與美式英語間有若干差異。

between [bə`twin] adv. 在…中間

▲ The workshop includes two speeches with a lunch break in between.

這個研討會包含兩場演講，中間有一個午餐休息時間。

---

6. **bread** [brɛd] n. [U] 麵包

▲ My mom bought some freshly baked bread at the bakery. 我媽媽在麵包店裡買了一些新鮮出爐的麵包。

---

7. **case** [kes] n. [C] 實例，案例；盒子

▲ The police are looking into the robbery case.
警方正在調查這起搶案。

💡 (just) in case 以防萬一 | in any case 無論如何

case [kes] v. (為做壞事等) 探勘，探路

▲ The burglar had cased the store before he committed the theft. 這名竊賊在行竊前先探勘這間店。

---

8. **cut** [kʌt] v. 切，割；減少 (cut | cut | cutting)

▲ The cook cut the onion and carrot into small pieces.
廚師將洋蔥和胡蘿蔔切成小塊。

💡 cut sth down 縮減… | cut sth off 切斷…；停止…

cut [kʌt] n. [C] 傷口；削減

▲ Billy came home with many cuts on his arms.
Billy 手臂傷痕累累地回家。

---

9. **different** [ˋdɪfərənt] adj. 不同的 <from, to> [反] similar

▲ Zack is very different from his twin brother.
Zack 跟他的雙胞胎弟弟差異很大。

---

10. **dream** [drim] n. [C] 夢 <about>；夢想 <of>

▲ Abby had a dream about her Prince Charming last
night. Abby 昨晚做了關於白馬王子的夢。

dream [drim] v. 夢見 <about>；夢想 <of, about>
(dreamed, dreamt | dreamed, dreamt | dreaming)

▲ Tina sometimes dreams about being attacked by a
bear. Tina 有時會夢見被熊攻擊。

---

11. **every** [ˋɛvrɪ] adj. 每個

▲ Cindy goes to school by bus every day.
Cindy 每天都搭公車去上學。

💡 every now and then/again 偶爾

---

12. **exercise** [ˋɛksɚˌsaɪz] n. [U] 運動；[C] 習題，練習

▲ The doctor advised that Tom do exercise regularly.
醫生建議 Tom 要規律做運動。

exercise [ˋɛksɚˌsaɪz] v. 運動；運用

▲ My aunt exercises for one hour each day to remain
healthy. 我嬸嬸每天運動一個小時以保持健康。

13. **experience** [ɪk`spɪrɪəns] n. [U][C] 體驗，經驗 [反] inexperience

▲ The job didn't need any previous work experience.
這份工作不需要任何工作經驗。

experience [ɪk`spɪrɪəns] v. 體驗，經驗

▲ The Jacksons experienced some difficulties when they first moved to the United States.
Jackson 一家人剛搬到美國時經歷了一些困難。

experienced [ɪk`spɪrɪənst] adj. 有經驗的 <in>

▲ The researcher is very experienced in financial analysis. 這位研究人員對於財務分析很有經驗。

---

14. **follow** [`falo] v. 跟著，跟隨；跟隨而來

▲ While Joanna was walking in the dark alley, she noticed a man following her.
當 Joanna 走在暗巷時，她注意到有個男人在跟蹤她。

♥ as follows 如下

---

15. **give** [gɪv] v. 給與，交給 <to> (gave | given | giving)

▲ The gentleman gave some money to the poor man.
這位紳士把一些錢給這窮人。

♥ give up 放棄 | give in 讓步

---

16. **group** [grup] n. [C] 群體

▲ The volunteers are from different racial groups.
這些義工來自不同的種族團體。

group [grup] v. (使) 分類 <together, round>

▲ The roses on exhibition are grouped together by

colors. 展覽中的玫瑰按顏色分類。

---

17. **hide** [haɪd] **v.** 把…藏起來；隱瞞 (消息) <from> (hid｜
hidden｜hiding)
   ▲ Mrs. Benson hid her son's present to give him a
   surprise on his birthday. Benson 太太把她兒子的禮
   物藏起來，為了在他生日當天給他驚喜。

---

18. **history** [ˋhɪstərɪ] **n.** [U] 歷史；歷史學
   ▲ Our city has a rich history. 我們的城市歷史悠久。

---

19. **mean** [min] **v.** 意思是；有意，打算 (meant｜meant｜
meaning)
   ▲ The phrase "to have a green thumb" means "to be
   good at making plants grow." 「有綠手指」這個詞語
   是指「擅長讓植物生長」的意思。
   mean [min] **adj.** 卑鄙的；吝嗇的 [同] stingy
   ▲ It's mean of you to speak ill of your friend.
   你說朋友的壞話很卑鄙。

---

20. **more** [mor] **adj.** 更多的 [反] less
   ▲ Would you like some more tea? 你還要一些茶嗎？
   more [mor] **pron.** 更多的事 [反] less, fewer
   ▲ I'm curious about your date last night; please tell me
   more. 我對你昨晚的約會很好奇，拜託多跟我說一點。
   more [mor] **adv.** 更多
   ▲ Can you walk more quickly? We're going to be late.
   你能走快一點嗎？我們要遲到了。

💡 the more...the more... 越…就越…

---

21. **mother** [ˋmʌðɚ] n. [C] 母親

▲ Every mother loves her children.
每個母親都愛她的孩子。

22. **red** [rɛd] adj. 紅色的；(臉等) 變紅的 (redder | reddest)

▲ Jim painted the window frame red.
Jim 將窗框漆成紅色。

red [rɛd] n. [U][C] 紅色

▲ Traditionally, Chinese brides often dressed in red.
傳統上，中國新娘通常穿紅色禮服。

23. **salt** [sɔlt] n. [U] 鹽

▲ The chef added some salt to the soup after tasting it.
主廚嘗過湯頭後在裡面加了一些鹽。

salt [sɔlt] v. 給…加鹽

▲ Remember to salt the fish before you roast it.
記得在烤魚之前先抹鹽巴。

salt [sɔlt] adj. 含鹽的

▲ Sam ordered some salt peanuts to go with his beer.
Sam 點了一些鹽花生配啤酒。

24. **student** [ˋstjudn̩t] n. [C] 學生

▲ My sister is a medical student. 我姊姊是醫學院學生。

25. **who** [hu] pron. 誰

▲ Who is the red-haired girl standing by the door?

站在門邊那個紅髮女孩是誰？

Unit 7

1. **bank** [bæŋk] n. [C] 銀行；河岸
   ▲ Tammy opened an account with the bank.
   Tammy 在這家銀行開戶。
   bank [bæŋk] v. 把錢存入銀行 <with, at>
   ▲ Mr. Jones always banks with Hope Bank.
   Jones 先生總是把錢存入 Hope 銀行。
   💡 bank on sb/sth 依賴…，指望…

2. **break** [brek] n. [C] 中斷；中間休息
   ▲ There has been no break in the rain for days.
   已經連續不停下了好幾天的雨。
   break [brek] v. 破碎，弄斷；打破 (broke | broken | breaking)
   ▲ Nelson broke his leg in the baseball game.
   Nelson 在棒球比賽中摔斷了腿。
   💡 break down (車輛等) 故障 | break up with sb 與…分手

3. **check** [tʃɛk] v. 檢查 <for>；核實，得到資訊
   ▲ After you finish the test, be sure to check the answers for mistakes.
   你做完試卷後一定要檢查答案有沒有錯誤。
   💡 check in/into sth (在飯店等) 辦理入住手續 |

check out (在飯店等) 辦理退房手續

check [tʃɛk] n. [C] 檢查；帳單 [同] bill

▲ The worker gave the machine a thorough check.
這工人把機器徹底檢查一遍。

---

4. **choice** [tʃɔɪs] n. [C][U] 選擇；[sing.][U] 選擇範圍

▲ It's difficult for Andy to make a choice between the
two cars. Andy 要在這兩輛車上做選擇是很困難的。

💡 have no choice but to V 別無選擇只好⋯

choice [tʃɔɪs] adj. 上等的，優質的

▲ The choice rib-eye steak is very tender and juicy.
這塊上等的肋眼牛排非常鮮嫩多汁。

---

5. **death** [dɛθ] n. [U][C] 死亡

▲ Louisa miraculously escaped death in the plane
crash. 在墜機事件中，Louisa 奇蹟似地死裡逃生。

💡 put sb to death 把⋯處死

---

6. **drop** [drɑp] v. 滴落 <from, off>；(使) 落下 (dropped |
dropped | dropping)

▲ Sweat dropped from the farmer's forehead.
汗從農夫的額頭流下來。

💡 drop out 中斷，退出 | drop by sb 拜訪⋯

drop [drɑp] n. [C] 滴 <of>

▲ Some drops of rain fell on the leaves.
一些雨滴落在樹葉上。

---

7. **eye** [aɪ] n. [C] 眼睛

▲ The baby fell asleep soon after he closed his eyes.
嬰兒閉上眼睛後很快就睡著了。

💡 catch sb's eye 引起…的注意 | keep an eye on... 注意…

---

8. **family** [ˋfæməlɪ] n. [C][U] 家人，家庭 (pl. families)；(動植物的) 科

▲ Wendy's family often gets together during holidays.
Wendy 的家人通常在假日時會聚在一起。

---

9. **for** [fɔr] prep. 給；為了 (目的、用途等)

▲ Someone left a message for you at the front desk.
有人在櫃檯留了訊息給你。

for [fɔr] conj. 因為，由於 [同] because

▲ Ashley couldn't go swimming with us, for she had something important to do. Ashley 無法跟我們一起去游泳，因為她有重要的事要做。

---

10. **friendly** [ˋfrɛndlɪ] adj. 友善的，親切的 <to, towards> [反] unfriendly (friendlier | friendliest)

▲ Ruby is very friendly to all the people around her.
Ruby 對身邊的人都很親切。

💡 be friendly with sb 和…交好

---

11. **fruit** [frut] n. [U][C] 水果 (pl. fruit, fruits)

▲ Which fruit would you prefer? Apples or oranges?
你比較喜愛哪種水果？蘋果還是柳丁？

💡 the fruit(s) of sth …的成果

12. **hope** [hop] v. 希望

▲ I hope that I can do well on the test.
  我希望我考試能考得不錯。

hope [hop] n. [U][C] 希望 <of, for>

▲ Charles had hopes of studying abroad after graduation. Charles 希望畢業後能出國念書。

♥ in the hope of... 希望…

---

13. **important** [ɪm`pɔrtn̩t] adj. 重要的 <to>

▲ My family is very important to me.
  我的家人對我來說很重要。

---

14. **keep** [kip] v. 保持；保留，保存 (kept | kept | keeping)

▲ Roy drank three cups of coffee to keep awake during the all-day meeting.

  Roy 喝了三杯咖啡以在這整天的會議中保持清醒。

♥ keep on V-ing 繼續做… | keep up with sb 跟上… | keep sb from V-ing 使…不能做…

keep [kip] n. [U] 生計，生活費用

▲ Mrs. Mitchell asked her grown-up son to get a job and earn his keep.

  Mitchell 太太要她成年的兒子找個工作自謀生計。

---

15. **know** [no] v. 知道，了解；認識 (knew | known | knowing)

▲ Do you know when Uncle Ben will arrive?
  你知道 Ben 叔叔什麼時候會到嗎？

known [non] adj. 聞名的 <for, as>

▲ Taipei 101 is known as the tallest building in Taiwan. 臺北 101 以臺灣最高的建築物聞名。

16. **life** [laɪf] n. [U][C] 生命；生活 (pl. lives)

▲ Hundreds of lives were lost in the terrible accident.
數百人在這場恐怖的意外中喪生。

🕯 bring sth to life 使⋯鮮活起來 | come to life 有生機 | for life 終生

17. **must** [mʌst] aux. 必須；一定 (表推測)

▲ Everyone must obey the law. 每個人必須遵守法律。
must [mʌst] n. [C] 必須要做的事，必不可少的事物

▲ Visiting the Statue of Liberty is a must when you go to New York City.
你去紐約市一定要去參觀自由女神像。

18. **next** [nɛkst] adj. 下一個的

▲ The rock band will give a concert tour in Europe next month. 這搖滾樂團下個月會在歐洲進行巡迴演出。
next [nɛkst] adv. 接下來

▲ First, melt butter and chocolate in the pan. Next, add two eggs to the mixture. 首先，在鍋中融化奶油和巧克力。接下來，加入兩個蛋到混合物中。

🕯 next to 在⋯的隔壁；幾乎⋯；僅次於⋯

19. **night** [naɪt] n. [C][U] 夜晚 [反] day

▲ We have to find a place to stay for the night.
我們必須找地方過夜。

💡 night after night 每晚 | night owl 夜貓子

20. **school** [skul] n. [C][U] 學校；上學期間

▲ Mr. Hill drives his children to school every day.
Hill 先生每天都開車送孩子去學校。

school [skul] v. 訓練，培養；教育

▲ The workers were schooled in communication skills.
這些員工被培訓溝通技巧。

schooling [ˋskulɪŋ] n. [U] 學校教育

▲ It was surprising that the learned man didn't receive much schooling. 這位學識淵博的人沒有接受太多學校教育，真是令人驚訝。

21. **start** [stɑrt] v. 開始 [同] begin；創辦

▲ More and more people today start to bring their own shopping bags with them.
現今有越來越多人開始攜帶自己的購物袋。

💡 to start with 首先 | start on sth 開始進行 | start over 重做

start [stɑrt] n. [sing.] 開頭，開端

▲ Eric didn't get along with Scott from the start.
Eric 從一開始就跟 Scott 不合。

22. **successful** [səkˋsɛsfəl] adj. 成功的 <in>

▲ Joe was successful in persuading his mother to change her mind. Joe 成功地說服他媽媽改變心意。

23. **sun** [sʌn] n. [sing.] 太陽 (the ～)；陽光 <in>

▲ There is nothing new under the sun.

【諺】太陽底下沒有新鮮事。

sun [sʌn] **v.** 曬太陽，做日光浴 (sunned | sunned | sunning)

▲ Brenda sunned herself on the beach.

Brenda 在沙灘上曬太陽。

---

24. **up** [ʌp] **adv.** 向上；(價值等) 增高地 [反] down

▲ The birds flew up into the air. 小鳥群飛上了天空。

💡 up and down 上上下下地；來回地

up [ʌp] **prep.** 在…上面 [反] down；沿著，順著 [反] down

▲ There is an attic up the stairs.

這樓梯上面有一個閣樓。

up [ʌp] **adj.** 向上的 [反] down

▲ Lisa took the up escalator to the Men's Department.

Lisa 搭著往上的電扶梯到男裝部。

up [ʌp] **v.** 提高，增加 (upped | upped | upping)

▲ The store upped the sale prices to make more profits.

這間店提高售價以獲取更多利潤。

up [ʌp] **n.** [C] 興盛，繁榮

▲ Mr. Morgan's business has had its ups and downs over the years.

Morgan 先生的事業這幾年經歷了盛衰起伏。

---

25. **what** [hwɑt] **pron.** 什麼

▲ What had happened before we arrived at your place?

我們到達你家之前發生了什麼事？

💡 What about...? …如何？(提供建議) | What if...? 要是…會怎麼樣？

what [hwɑt] adj. 多麼

▲ What a beautiful place! 多麼漂亮的地方啊！

Unit 8

1. **act** [ækt] n. [C] 行為 <of>；(戲劇或歌劇的) 幕

▲ John was awarded a medal for his act of courage.
John 因為他英勇的行為而獲頒獎牌。

act [ækt] v. 行為，舉止 <like>；採取行動

▲ Even though Mark is 18 years old, he still acts like a child.
雖然 Mark 十八歲了，他行為舉止像個孩子一樣。

2. **after** [`æftə] prep. 在…之後 [反] before

▲ Mr. Reed went to work after breakfast.
Reed 先生吃完早餐後就去上班了。

💡 after all 畢竟 | one after another 陸續地

after [`æftə] conj. 在…之後 [反] before

▲ David went to bed soon after he brushed his teeth.
David 刷了牙不久後就上床睡覺了。

after [`æftə] adv. 之後，後來 [反] before

▲ Thomas will visit his grandparents tomorrow or the day after. Thomas 明天或後天會去看望祖父母。

3. **animal** [`ænəml̩] n. [C] 動物

▲ The charitable organization aims to help stray animals. 這個慈善機構目標是幫助流浪動物。

---

4. **black** [blæk] adj. 黑色的；黑人的

▲ Ida looked slim in the black dress.
Ida 穿這件黑色的洋裝看起來很苗條。

black [blæk] n. [U] 黑色；[C] 黑人 (also Black)

▲ People often dress in black when attending funerals.
人們去參加喪禮時通常會穿黑色衣服。

---

5. **born** [bɔrn] adj. 天生的

▲ Michael Jordan is a born sportsman.
麥可喬登是天生的運動員。

---

6. **cold** [kold] adj. 寒冷的 [反] hot ；冷淡的 <toward> [反] warm

▲ Put on your coat; it's freezing cold outside.
穿上你的外套，外面非常冷。

cold [kold] n. [U] 寒冷；[C] 感冒

▲ There was a poor beggar standing outside in the cold.
有個可憐的乞丐站在寒冷的戶外。

---

7. **cookie** [`kʊkɪ] n. [C] 餅乾 [同] biscuit

▲ My mom bakes cookies for us every weekend.
我媽媽每個週末都烤餅乾給我們吃。

---

8. **course** [kors] n. [C] 課程 <on, in>；[sing.] 過程，進展

▲ Patty took a course in American literature this semester. Patty 這個學期修了美國文學課程。

course [kɔrs] v. 奔流，奔湧 <down>

▲ Tears coursed down Mina's cheeks as she read the touching story.

Mina 在讀這感人故事時，淚水從她臉頰滾落。

---

9. **east** [ist] n. [U] 東方 (also East) (abbr. E) (the ～)

▲ Hualien is in the east of Taiwan. 花蓮位在臺灣東方。

east [ist] adj. 東方的，東部的 (also East) (abbr. E)

▲ We'll travel around the east coast of Australia during summer vacation.

我們暑假期間會去澳洲東海岸旅遊。

east [ist] adv. 朝向東方 (also East) (abbr. E)

▲ According to the map, you should drive east for three miles and turn north.

根據地圖，你應該往東開三英里後轉彎向北。

---

10. **example** [ɪg`zæmpl] n. [C] 例子；典範 <of>

▲ This is a classic example of where most students make their mistakes.

這是一個學生會犯錯的經典例子。

💡 for example 例如 | follow sb's example 仿效⋯

---

11. **fat** [fæt] n. [U] 脂肪，肥肉

▲ Barbara cut some fat from the meat before cooking it. Barbara 在烹煮前先將這塊肉的一些肥肉去除。

fat [fæt] adj. 肥胖的 [反] thin (fatter | fattest)

▲ Having too many sweets makes people get fat easily.

吃太多甜食容易讓人發胖。

12. **full** [fʊl] adj. 充滿的 <of>；完整的
   ▲ The tank is full of water. 水箱裝滿了水。

13. **interested** [ˋɪntrɪstɪd] adj. 感 興 趣 的 <in> [反]
   uninterested, bored
   ▲ George is interested in studying marine creatures.
   George 對於研究海洋生物有興趣。

14. **just** [dʒʌst] adv. 正好；只是 [同] only
   ▲ The flat is just right for a family of four.
   這間公寓正好適合一家四口。
   💡 just now 剛才 | just in case 以防萬一
   just [dʒʌst] adj. 公正的，正義的
   ▲ It is a just decision made by the just man.
   這是這個正義的人所做出的公正決定。

15. **leave** [liv] v. 離開；留下 (left | left | leaving)
   ▲ Sylvia left without saying goodbye to the host.
   Sylvia 沒向主人道別就走了。
   💡 leave sth behind 留下…
   leave [liv] n. [U] 休假
   ▲ Anna had two weeks' paid leave.
   Anna 有兩個禮拜的帶薪假。
   💡 annual/unpaid/sick/parental/maternity leave 年 / 無薪 /
   病 / 育嬰 / 產假

16. **look** [lʊk] v. 看 <at>；看起來

▲ The kids are looking at the flying clouds in the sky.
孩子們正看著天空中的浮雲。

💡 look like 看起來像 | look after 照顧 | look forward to V-ing 盼望…

look [lʊk] **n.** [C] 看，注視 <at>

▲ Do you want to have/take a look at my paintings?
你想看看我的畫嗎？

---

17. **main** [men] **adj.** 主要的

▲ Dora wrote down the main points of the speech in her notebook. Dora 在筆記本上寫下演講的要點。

main [men] **n.** [C] (輸送水、煤氣等的) 主要管線

▲ The earthquake caused the gas main to burst.
地震造成這條煤氣管線破裂。

mainly [`menlɪ] **adv.** 主要地 [同] primarily

▲ The film festival was mainly funded by the government. 電影節主要是由政府資助。

---

18. **man** [mæn] **n.** [C] 男人；[U] 人類 (pl. men)

▲ The man in a black suit is my brother.
那個穿黑色西裝的男人是我哥哥。

man [mæn] **v.** 為…配備人手 (manned | manned | manning)

▲ Fire stations are usually manned around the clock.
消防局通常全天候都有配備人手。

---

19. **money** [`mʌnɪ] **n.** [U] 錢，金錢

▲ Jane spent a lot of money on clothes.

Jane 花了很多錢在衣服上。

💡 make/earn money 賺錢

20. **open** [`opən] adj. 開著的；開放的，可用的 [反] closed, shut

▲ It was strange that my neighbor left the front door open. 我鄰居的前門大開很奇怪。

open [`opən] v. (使) 開始；打開

▲ The new shopping mall is due to open this Friday.
那間新的購物中心預計本週五開幕。

💡 open sb's eyes (to sth) 使⋯認清 | open the door to sth 使⋯成為可能

21. **serious** [`sɪrɪəs] adj. 嚴重的；認真的 <about>

▲ Bullying has become a very serious problem in high schools. 霸凌在中學已經變成很嚴重的問題。

seriously [`sɪrɪəslɪ] adv. 嚴重地；嚴肅地，認真地

▲ The man was seriously injured in the car crash.
那名男子在車禍中受重傷。

22. **story** [`storɪ] n. [C] 故事；新聞報導

▲ Mr. Brooks reads a bedtime story to his daughter every night.
Brooks 先生每晚都讀床邊故事給他女兒聽。

💡 end of story 就是這樣，沒什麼好說了

23. **that** [ðæt] conj. (用以引導子句，常可省略)

▲ Gina said (that) she would give you a call today.

Gina 說她今天會打電話給你。

that [ðæt] pron. (用來當關係代名詞)；那，那個

▲ George Bernard Shaw is one of the greatest dramatists that have ever lived.

蕭伯納是歷史上最偉大的劇作家之一。

that [ðæt] adv. 那麼

▲ Sorry, I can't wait that long.

不好意思，我等不了那麼久。

that [ðæt] adj. 那個 (pl. those)

▲ Who is that girl in a pink dress?

那個穿粉色洋裝的女孩是誰？

---

24. **when** [hwɛn] adv. 何時

▲ When did Edward quit his job?

Edward 是何時離職的？

when [hwɛn] conj. 做⋯的時候，當⋯時

▲ Wilson danced with joy when he heard the good news.

Wilson 聽到這個好消息時整個人手舞足蹈起來。

when [hwɛn] pron. 何時

▲ Since when did you begin to study French?

你何時開始學法語的？

---

25. **where** [hwɛr] conj. 在⋯的地方

▲ Mrs. Foster put the medicine where her children couldn't reach.

Foster 太太把藥放在孩子拿不到的地方。

where [hwɛr] adv. 哪裡

▲ Where will you spend your winter vacation?
你要去哪裡過寒假？

where [hwɛr] pron. 哪裡

▲ Where are you from? 你是哪裡人？

where [hwɛr] n. 哪裡 (指來源)

Unit 9

1. **able** [`ebl̩] adj. 能夠的 [反] unable；聰明能幹的

▲ Ms. Ross is able to speak five languages.
Ross 小姐會說五種語言。

2. **about** [ə`baʊt] prep. 有關，在⋯方面；在⋯四周 [同] round, around

▲ The book is about child development.
這本書是關於孩童發展。

about [ə`baʊt] adv. 大約，差不多 [同] roughly, approximately；四處 [同] around

▲ Paul broke up with his girlfriend about one month ago. Paul 大約是一個月前跟他女友分手。

3. **across** [ə`krɔs] prep. 穿過，橫越；在⋯的另一邊

▲ The local people built a bridge across the river.
當地人在河上造了一座橋。

across [ə`krɔs] adv. 從一邊到另一邊，橫過

▲ There isn't a bridge, so we'll have to swim across.

這裡沒有橋，所以我們得游過去。

4. **ago** [ə`go] adv. 以前，之前

▲ A long time ago, there lived a monster in the castle.
很久以前，這個城堡裡住了一隻怪獸。

5. **camera** [`kæmərə] n. [C] 照相機

▲ Don't forget to take a digital camera with you when
you go on a school outing.
你去校外教學時別忘了要帶數位相機。

6. **each** [itʃ] pron. 每個

▲ Each of the boys has a cap on. 每個男孩都戴著帽子。
each [itʃ] adj. 每個

▲ There are trees on each side of the street.
這條街兩側都有樹。
each [itʃ] adv. 各自

▲ The teacher gave his pupils a pencil each.
老師給每個學生一枝鉛筆。

7. **easy** [`izɪ] adj. 容易的 [反] hard, difficult ；安逸的 [反]
hard (easier | easiest)

▲ The question was so easy that Ben answered it right
away. 這個問題如此簡單以致於 Ben 立刻就回答。

♥ take it easy 休息；放輕鬆 | go easy on sb 寬容對待⋯

8. **either** [`iðə] adv. 也 (用於否定句)

▲ Kelly doesn't like seafood and her sister doesn't,
either. Kelly 不喜歡海鮮，且她妹妹也不喜歡。

either [ˈiðɚ] pron. 兩者中任何一方

▲ Either of the books will do.

(兩本中) 任何一本書都可以。

either [ˈiðɚ] adj. (兩者中) 各方、任一

▲ Coke and Pepsi are both fine with me. Bring me either one.

可口可樂和百事可樂我都可以。隨便拿一罐給我。

either [ˈiðɚ] conj. 不是⋯就是⋯ <or>

▲ Either Jason or Kevin should be responsible for the accident.

不是 Jason 就是 Kevin 要為這個意外事件負責。

---

9. **face** [fes] n. [C] 臉；表情

▲ There is a birthmark on Jessica's face.

Jessica 的臉上有一個胎記。

💡 face to face 面對面 |

in the face of sth 不顧⋯；面臨 (負面情況)⋯

face [fes] v. 面對，面臨

▲ The scientists are faced with new challenges.

這些科學家正面臨新的挑戰。

10. **far** [fɑr] adv. 遠地，遙遠地；遠遠，非常

▲ Ryan had to drive far to his uncle's farm.

Ryan 必須開很遠的路到他叔叔的農場。

💡 so far 到目前為止 | go too far 做得太超過

far [fɑr] adj. 遙遠的 (farther, further | farthest, furthest)

▲ My hometown is not far from Taipei.

我的家鄉離臺北不遠。

---

11. **find** [faɪnd] v. 發現，找到；認為，發覺 (found | found | finding)

▲ Dennis found his wallet under the sofa.
Dennis 在沙發底下找到他的皮夾。

💡 find sth out 查明⋯，找出⋯

find [faɪnd] n. [C] 發現物

▲ The archaeological finds will be displayed in the museum. 這些考古的發現將會在博物館展出。

---

12. **grass** [græs] n. [U][C] 草

▲ Cattle are feeding on the grass. 牛群在吃草。

---

13. **head** [hɛd] n. [C] 頭；智力

▲ Joyce shook her head to show her disapproval of the plan. Joyce 搖頭以表示不贊同這個計畫。

💡 come into sb's head 浮現腦海 | keep sb's head 保持冷靜

head [hɛd] v. 朝某特定方向前進 <for, toward>

▲ Sophie headed for her bed as soon as she got home.
Sophie 一到家就朝她的床走去。

---

14. **hold** [hold] v. 抓住；舉行 (held | held | holding)

▲ The old couple held hands while walking.
這對年老的夫妻走路時手牽手。

💡 hold sth back 阻擋⋯；抑制 (情感) | hold on 持續；不要掛電話

hold [hold] **n.** [sing.] 抓，握 <on>

▲ The beggar kept a tight hold on the bill a passerby had given him. 那乞丐緊緊握住路人給他的紙鈔。

---

15. **it** [ɪt] **pron.** 它 (指無生命的物品、動植物、性別不詳的幼孩等)；這，那 (用來做主詞或受詞)

▲ The fax machine is out of order, and I'll have it fixed today. 傳真機壞了，我今天會找人修理它。

its [ɪts] **pron.** 它的

▲ The dog waved its tail at the boy.
這隻狗對男孩搖尾巴。

itself [ɪt`sɛlf] **pron.** 它自己，它本身

▲ Strangely, the cellphone switched itself off.
好奇怪，這支手機自行關機了。

---

16. **kill** [kɪl] **v.** 殺死，使致死；停止，終止

▲ The Anderson family was killed in a severe earthquake. Anderson 一家死於一場大地震。

kill [kɪl] **n.** [sing.] 被捕殺的動物

▲ The lion swiftly seized its kill and ran away.
獅子迅速抓住牠捕殺的獵物就跑走了。

killer [`kɪlɚ] **n.** [C] 殺人者，凶手；致命疾病

▲ The killer was put in prison for twenty years.
那位殺人凶手要入獄二十年。

💡 serial killer 連環殺手

---

17. **live** [lɪv] **v.** 居住；生存

▲ Billy lives with his grandfather in the cottage.

Billy 和他爺爺同住在這個村舍裡。

💡 live on sth 依靠⋯生活；吃⋯生存 | live through sth 經歷 (困難的狀況)

live [laɪv] adj. 活的；現場播出的

▲ It is a thrilling experience to see a live bear.
看見活生生的熊是個刺激的經驗。

living [ˈlɪvɪŋ] n. [C] 生計，收入

▲ The old lady made a living by selling flowers.
那名老婦人藉由賣花維生。

---

18. **may** [me] aux. 可以 (表示允許) [同] can；可能 [同] might

▲ "May I come in?" "Yes, you may."
「我可以進來嗎？」「可以。」

---

19. **member** [ˈmɛmbɚ] n. [C] 會員；成員，一分子

▲ The swimming pool is for club members only.
這個游泳池僅供俱樂部會員使用。

---

20. **modern** [ˈmɑdɚn] adj. 現代的 [同] up-to-date

▲ The Internet has played a significant role in modern life. 網路在現代生活中扮演著重要的角色。

---

21. **music** [ˈmjuzɪk] n. [U] 音樂

▲ Listening to classical music helped Joan relax after work. 聽古典樂幫助 Joan 在下班後放鬆。

💡 be music to sb's ears 對⋯是中聽的話 | face the music 勇敢面對批評或處罰

22. **news** [njuz] **n.** [U] 新聞；消息 <of, on, about>

▲ Mr. Roberts watches the seven o'clock news on TV every day. Roberts 先生每天收看七點鐘的電視新聞。

💡 break the news to sb 透露壞消息給…

newscast [`njuz͵kæst] **n.** [C] 新聞廣播或節目

▲ The weather forecast appeared at the end of the newscast. 氣象預報在新聞節目的尾聲出現。

23. **play** [ple] **v.** 玩 <with>；參加 (遊戲、比賽等)

▲ The girl played with her dog in the park.
這女孩在公園和她的狗玩。

play [ple] **n.** [C] 戲劇，劇本

▲ Maggie played a leading role in the school play.
Maggie 在學校的戲劇中扮演要角。

24. **water** [`wɔtɚ] **n.** [U] 水

▲ Ella drinks a glass of water right after she gets up in the morning. Ella 早上一起床就喝一杯水。

💡 pour cold water on/over sth 潑…冷水

water [`wɔtɚ] **v.** 給…澆水

▲ Mr. Cruz waters the lawn almost every day.
Cruz 先生幾乎每天都給草坪澆水。

25. **young** [jʌŋ] **adj.** 年輕的，年幼的

▲ Although Lucy is young, she is mature and wise.
雖然 Lucy 很年輕，她成熟又聰慧。

young [jʌŋ] **n.** [pl.] 年輕人 (the ~)

▲ The young should be taught to respect the elderly.

年輕人應該要被教導要尊敬老年人。

Unit 10

1. **as** [æz] conj. 像⋯一樣；當⋯時
   ▲ Jose kept changing jobs as his brother did.
   Jose 像他哥哥一樣一直在換工作。
   🕯 as if/though 彷彿，好像
   as [æz] adv. 像⋯ (一樣)
   ▲ Victoria's skin is as white as snow.
   Victoria 的肌膚像雪一樣白皙。
   🕯 as...as possible 盡可能地⋯
   as [æz] prep. 作為
   ▲ Adam used his umbrella as a weapon when he was
   attacked by a stranger on the street.
   Adam 在街上受到陌生人攻擊時拿傘當武器。

2. **bad** [bæd] adj. 壞的，不好的 <for> [反] good (worse |
   worst)
   ▲ Drinking too much alcohol is bad for health.
   飲酒過多有害健康。
   🕯 feel bad about sth 對⋯感到難過或羞愧 | go from
   bad to worse 每況愈下

3. **believe** [bɪ`liv] v. 相信
   ▲ Don't believe everything you hear.
   別相信你所聽到的每件事。

💡 make believe 假裝 ｜ believe it or not 信不信由你

believable [bɪˋlivəb!] adj. 可信的

▲ I think what Vincent said is quite believable.
我覺得 Vincent 說的話可信度很高。

4. **body** [ˋbɑdɪ] n. [C] 身體；屍體

▲ My body felt tired after a long day's work.
在工作了一整天之後，我覺得身體很疲累。

💡 body and soul 身心；全心全意

5. **but** [bʌt] conj. 但是

▲ I am old, but you are still young.
我老了，但是你還年輕。

but [bʌt] prep. 除…之外

▲ Nobody but Ruby saw Diane leave.
除了 Ruby 之外，沒有人看見 Diane 離開。

💡 anything but 絕不 ｜ nothing but 只有

but [bʌt] adv. 只是，僅僅

▲ Johnny is but a little child; don't be so hard on him.
Johnny 只是個小孩子，不要對他這麼嚴苛。

6. **chocolate** [ˋtʃɔklɪt] n. [U][C] 巧克力

▲ Lauren had a chocolate bar as a snack.
Lauren 吃一條巧克力棒當點心。

7. **earth** [ɝθ] n. [U][sing.] 地球 (also Earth)；[U] 土壤 [同] soil

▲ The earth is the 3rd planet from the sun.

地球是從太陽數來的第三個行星。

---

8. **enjoy** [ɪn`dʒɔɪ] v. 喜愛，欣賞；享有
   ▲ We don't like Gary because he enjoys making fun of others. 我們不喜歡 Gary，因為他喜愛取笑別人。
   enjoyment [ɪn`dʒɔɪmənt] n. [U] 愉快，樂趣
   ▲ The noise from next door spoiled Amy's enjoyment of the music.
   隔壁傳來的噪音破壞了 Amy 欣賞音樂的樂趣。

---

9. **even** [`ivən] adv. 甚至，連；更加
   ▲ Even small children can finish the work with ease.
   就連小孩都能輕鬆完成這項工作。
   💡 even if/though... 即使… | even so 即使如此
   even [`ivən] adj. 平坦的，平滑的 [反] uneven；相等的
   ▲ The road is not even and needs to be resurfaced.
   這條馬路不平而需要重鋪。
   💡 break even 收支平衡 | get even with sb 對…報復
   even [`ivən] v. 使相等，使平衡 <up>
   ▲ You bought the food, so if I buy the wine, that will even things up.
   你買了食物，所以如果我買酒的話，那就扯平了。
   💡 even sth out 使…均等

---

10. **expensive** [ɪk`spɛnsɪv] adj. 昂貴的 [反] cheap
    ▲ That house is too expensive for Robin to afford.
    那房子對 Robin 來說太貴了而負擔不起。

11. **finally** [ˈfaɪnl̩ɪ] adv. 最後，終於 [同] eventually

▲ After a long search, Martha finally found the letter.

Martha 找了很久，最後終於找到了這封信。

12. **food** [fud] n. [U][C] 食物，食品

▲ The Italian restaurant is famous for its delicious food.

這間義式餐廳以它美味的食物聞名。

13. **front** [frʌnt] adj. 前面的 [反] back

▲ Terry is very short, so he often sits in the front row of the classroom.

Terry 很矮，所以他經常坐在教室的第一排。

front [frʌnt] n. [C] 前面 (usu. sing.) [反] back；鋒面

▲ Gloria got on the bus and sat in the front.

Gloria 上公車，然後坐在前面的位子。

💡 in front of sb/sth 在⋯前方；在⋯面前

14. **hear** [hɪr] v. 聽見 ; 聽說 <about, of> (heard | heard | hearing)

▲ Molly heard her husband singing in the shower.

Molly 聽見她丈夫洗澡時在唱歌。

💡 hear from sb 收到⋯的消息

hearing [ˈhɪrɪŋ] n. [U] 聽力；[C] 聽證會

▲ The study indicates that bats and owls have good hearing. 研究指出蝙蝠和貓頭鷹有良好的聽力。

15. **island** [ˈaɪlənd] n. [C] 島

▲ Iceland is an island country. 冰島是一個島國。

16. **land** [lænd] `n.` [U] 陸地；土地

▲ The sailors spotted land in the distance.
水手們在遠方發現了陸地。

land [lænd] `v.` (使) 降落 [反] take off；落在 [同] drop

▲ The plane crashed when it attempted to land in the storm. 飛機試圖在暴風雨中降落時墜毀。

---

17. **machine** [mə`ʃin] `n.` [C] 機器

▲ Today, people have all kinds of machines to make their lives easier.
今日，人們有各式各樣的機器讓他們的生活更便利。

💡 fax/washing/sewing/vending/answering machine
傳真 / 洗衣 / 縫紉 / 販賣 / 答錄機

machine [mə`ʃin] `v.` 用縫紉機縫製

▲ Denise is busy machining the hems of the dress.
Denise 正忙著縫製洋裝的摺邊。

---

18. **move** [muv] `v.` (使) 移動；搬家

▲ Natalie moved around in a wheelchair after losing her legs. Natalie 失去雙腿後藉由輪椅移動。

movement [`muvmənt] `n.` [C] 移動，動作；(有特定目的的) 運動

▲ The class closely observed the yoga teacher's movements. 整個班級都在仔細觀察瑜伽老師的動作。

---

19. **number** [`nʌmbɚ] `n.` [C] 數字；號碼

▲ Three and five are both odd numbers.
三和五都是奇數。

🔥 a number of sth 幾個…

number [ˋnʌmbɚ] v. 給…編號

▲ The assistant numbered all of the files carefully.
這助理仔細地將所有的文件編號。

---

20. **order** [ˋɔrdɚ] n. [U] 順序 [同] sequence；[C] 訂貨 <for>

▲ The information is arranged in order of importance.
這些資訊是依重要性次序而編排的。

🔥 in order to... 為了 | make sth to order 訂製…

order [ˋɔrdɚ] v. 命令；訂購

▲ Ralph ordered his dog to come over, and it obeyed right away.
Ralph 命令他的狗過來，然後牠就立刻服從命令。

---

21. **public** [ˋpʌblɪk] adj. 大眾的；公共的 [反] private

▲ The opinion poll has reflected the public views about the new economic policy.
意見調查反映了大眾對新的經濟政策的看法。

public [ˋpʌblɪk] n. [U] 社會大眾 (the ～)

▲ The library is open to the public.
這間圖書館開放給社會大眾。

🔥 in public 公開地

---

22. **reason** [ˋrizn] n. [C] 理由，原因 <for, behind>

▲ The reason for Gilbert's resignation was that he had cancer. Gilbert 辭職的原因是因為他罹患癌症。

🔥 by reason of 因為

reason [ˋrizn] v. 推理，論論

▲ Some people reasoned that the business closed down because of poor management.

一些人推論這間公司是因經營不善而倒閉。

💡 reason with sb 與⋯講道理

23. **several** [`sɛvərəl] adj. 幾個的，數個的

▲ The flood victims had to live in the shelter for several months.

那些水災災民必須住在收容所好幾個月。

several [`sɛvərəl] pron. 幾個，數個

▲ Several of the guests at the party were strangers to us. 舞會裡有幾個客人我們不認識。

24. **time** [taɪm] n. [U] 時間；[C] 次數

▲ It is just a matter of time before we achieve our goal.

我們實現目標只是時間早晚的問題。

💡 in time 來得及 | on time 準時地

time [taɪm] v. 為⋯設定時間

▲ The bomb was timed to explode at 7 o'clock.

炸彈設定在七點鐘爆炸。

25. **without** [wɪð`aʊt] prep. 沒有

▲ Zoe went to work without make-up this morning.

Zoe 今天早上沒化妝就去上班了。

without [wɪð`aʊt] adv. 沒有

▲ Since there was no cheese left, we had to do without.

由於起司用完了，我們只好將就不用它了。

Unit 11

1. **bridge** [brɪdʒ] n. [C] 橋
   ▲ The locals must cross the bridge to go to the neighboring village.
   當地人必須過那座橋才能到鄰村。
   bridge [brɪdʒ] v. 在…上架橋；消弭
   ▲ The man cut down a tree to bridge the river.
   男子砍倒一棵樹在河上架橋。

2. **car** [kɑr] n. [C] 汽車；車廂 [同] carriage
   ▲ The boy is too young to drive a car.
   這男孩太年輕不能開車。

3. **ever** [ˋɛvɚ] adv. 曾經；從來
   ▲ Do you ever play chess? 你曾經玩過西洋棋嗎？
   💡 ever since 從那以後一直 | as ever 同往常一樣

4. **fight** [faɪt] v. 戰鬥 <with, against>；打架 <with>
   (fought | fought | fighting)
   ▲ The soldiers fought fiercely against their enemies.
   士兵與他們的敵人激戰。
   💡 fight a losing battle 打一場沒有勝算的仗
   fight [faɪt] n. [C] 打架；吵架
   ▲ Last night, there was a fight outside the nightclub.
   昨晚，夜總會外面有人打架。

5. **fun** [fʌn] n. [U] 開心；樂趣

▲ The girls had a lot of fun singing and dancing.
女孩們又唱又跳很開心。

💡 make fun of sb/sth 取笑；拿…開玩笑

6. **future** [ˈfjutʃɚ] n. [C] 未來 (the ∼)；前途

▲ The company is going to move into a new building in the near future. 這公司在不久的將來要搬進新大樓。

future [ˈfjutʃɚ] adj. 未來的

▲ Tina met her future husband at a party.
Tina 在派對上遇見她未來的丈夫。

7. **green** [grin] adj. 綠色的；缺乏經驗的

▲ The mother asked her son to eat more green vegetables. 媽媽要她兒子多吃綠色蔬菜。

💡 have a green thumb 善於種植花木 | be green with envy 嫉妒

green [grin] n. [U] 綠色；[C] 草地

▲ Green is the color of nature. 綠色是自然的顏色。

green [grin] v. 綠化

▲ The mayor plans to green the streets by adding planter boxes. 市長計劃增加種植箱來綠化街道。

8. **grow** [gro] v. 生長；種植 (grew | grown | growing)

▲ Mosquitoes grow in swamps. 蚊子生長在沼澤地。

💡 grow up 長大成人 | grow into... 逐漸成長…

9. **here** [hɪr] adv. 在這裡

▲ The Lins have been living here for more than five years. 林氏一家人已經住在這裡超過五年了。

💡 here and there 到處

here [hɪr] n. [U] 這裡

▲ The lighthouse is 50 miles away from here.
燈塔離這裡有五十英里。

10. **high** [haɪ] adj. 高的；(比一般標準) 高的 [反] low

▲ The highest mountain in the world is Mount Everest.
世界上最高的山是聖母峰。

high [haɪ] adv. 高高地，在高處 [反] low

▲ The boy kicked the soccer ball high into the air.
那個男孩把足球高高地踢入空中。

high [haɪ] n. [C] 最高水準

▲ June's rainfall hit a record high.
六月的降雨量達到創紀錄的最高點。

11. **idea** [aɪˋdɪə] n. [C] 主意，想法；[U] 了解，知道 <of>

▲ Sam is a man of ideas. Sam 有很多點子。

💡 have no idea 不知道

12. **late** [let] adj. 遲的 <for>；晚的

▲ Hurry up, or you'll be late for school.
趕快，否則你會上學遲到。

late [let] adv. 遲到 [反] early；晚地

▲ Because of the heavy rain, the bus came half an hour late. 由於大雨，巴士遲到半小時。

13. **meat** [mit] n. [U] 肉類

▲ Hannah is a vegetarian. She doesn't eat meat at all.
Hannah 吃素。她完全不吃肉。

14. **most** [most] adv. 最 [反] least；最多

▲ I trust you the most out of all my friends.
在我所有的朋友中，我最信任你。

most [most] pron. 最多；大部分 <of>

▲ Of all the strawberry pickers, Jimmy picked the most strawberries in the least amount of time. 在所有摘草莓的人中，Jimmy 在最短的時間內採摘了最多的草莓。

most [most] adj. 最多的；大部分的

▲ Whoever gets the most answers right will get first prize. 答對最多的人就得到第一名。

💡 make the most of/get the most out of sth 盡量利用⋯

15. **newspaper** [`njuz,pepɚ] n. [C] 報紙 [同] paper；報社

▲ Have you read today's newspaper?
你讀過今天的報紙了嗎？

16. **old** [old] adj. 老的 [反] young；⋯歲的

▲ I helped the old man cross the street.
我幫助那位老人過馬路。

17. **plan** [plæn] n. [C] 計畫 <for>

▲ Fred is making plans for the summer vacation.
Fred 正在做暑假計畫。

plan [plæn] v. 計劃；打算 (planned | planned | planning)

▲ If we plan carefully, we can complete the work on time. 如果我們仔細計劃，我們可以準時完成工作。

18. **problem** [`prɑbləm] n. [C] 問題；數學習題
   ▲ The company eventually solved the financial problem. 那家公司終於解決了財務問題。
   ♥ have problem V-ing... 做…有困難

19. **so** [so] adv. 如此，那麼；也一樣
   ▲ It was so hot that I couldn't sleep last night.
   昨晚如此熱以致於我無法入睡。
   so [so] conj. 為了，以便；所以
   ▲ The teacher spoke clearly so that his students could understand him.
   那位老師說得很清楚以便他的學生們能了解他。

20. **test** [tɛst] n. [C] 測驗；檢查
   ▲ The students had a math test yesterday.
   學生們昨天有個數學測驗。
   test [tɛst] v. 測驗 <on>；試驗 <on>
   ▲ The teacher tested his students on English.
   那位老師測驗學生的英文。

21. **they** [ðe] pron. 他們
   ▲ They are coming back soon. 他們快要回來了。
   them [ðɛm] pron. 他們
   ▲ Mark couldn't find his pens. He forgot where he had put them.

Mark 無法找到他的筆。他忘記把它們放在哪裡。

their [ðɛr] pron. 他們的

▲ The mother gave her sons their new pants.
媽媽給兒子們他們的新褲子。

theirs [ðɛrz] pron. 他們的

▲ My bike is black, and theirs are yellow.
我的單車是黑色，而他們的是黃色。

themselves [ðɛm`sɛlvz] pron. 他們自己 <by>

▲ The boys finished their homework by themselves.
男孩們自己做完他們的功課。

---

22. **too** [tu] adv. 太；也

▲ The dress is too tight for you.
這洋裝對妳來說太緊了。

---

23. **until** [ən`tɪl] conj. 到…為止

▲ I'll wait here until school is over.
我會在這裡等到放學為止。

until [ən`tɪl] prep. 直到…

▲ Jack was single until recently.
Jack 直到最近才脫離單身。

💡 not until 直到…才…

---

24. **work** [wɝk] n. [U] 工作；[C] 作品

▲ After work, Andy likes to go for a drink.
Andy 喜歡下班後去喝一杯。

work [wɝk] v. 工作；有效，起作用

▲ The laborer works 8 hours a day.
這位勞工一天工作八小時。

💡 work at/on sth 致力於…，改善…

25. **yet** [jɛt] adv. 尚 (未)；仍然
▲ The task is not yet finished. 這工作尚未完成。
yet [jɛt] conj. 然而，但是
▲ The question seems simple, yet I can't figure out the answer. 這個問題似乎很簡單，但我無法找出答案。

Unit 12

1. **age** [edʒ] n. [U][C] 年紀 <at>；[U] 法定年齡 <for>
▲ Mr. Wang has a daughter at your age.
王先生有個和你同年紀的女兒。
age [edʒ] v. 衰老
▲ The man aged quickly after the death of his wife.
男子在他妻子死後一下子衰老了很多。

2. **area** [ˋɛrɪə] n. [C] 地區；領域 <of>
▲ There are few bookstores in this area.
這個地區書店很少。

3. **city** [ˋsɪtɪ] n. [C] 城市 (pl. cities)
▲ Manila is the capital city of the Philippines.
馬尼拉是菲律賓的首都城市。

4. **do** [du] aux. (助動詞)

▲ What do you do? 你做什麼工作？

do [du] v. 做，執行 (did | done | doing)

▲ The student hasn't done her homework yet.
這學生還沒完成她的功課。

💡 have nothing to do with... 與…無關

---

5. **fall** [fɔl] n. [U] 秋天；[C][sing.] 降低 <in> [反] rise

▲ Fall comes after summer. 秋天在夏天之後到來。

fall [fɔl] v. 落下 <from>；跌倒 (fell | fallen | falling)

▲ An apple fell from the tree. 一顆蘋果從樹上落下。

💡 fall apart 散掉；破裂 | fall behind 落後

---

6. **file** [faɪl] n. [C] 文件夾；檔案

▲ The document can be found in the file under "D."
文件在標著 D 字母的文件夾中可以找到。

file [faɪl] v. 把…歸檔 <away>；提出

▲ Please file away these documents.
請把這些文件歸檔。

---

7. **glass** [glæs] n. [U] 玻璃；[C] 玻璃杯

▲ The boy threw a rock and broke the glass window.
男孩丟了一顆石頭，打破了玻璃窗。

---

8. **ground** [graʊnd] n. [sing.] 地面 (the ~) <on>；[U] 土地

▲ The little girl sat on the ground crying.
小女孩坐在地上哭。

💡 get (sth) off the ground (使) 開始；(使) 成功進行

ground [graʊnd] v. 禁足；使停飛

▲ The parents grounded their son for a week.
那對父母禁足他們的兒子一個禮拜。

9. **half** [hæf] **n.** [C][U] 一半 <of> (pl. halves)

▲ The mask covered the top half of the woman's face.
面具遮住了女子臉部的上半部。

half [hæf] **adv.** 一半地；部分地

▲ The bottle is half full. 這瓶子半滿。

💡 half dead 累個半死

half [hæf] **adj.** 一半的

▲ Half the students are in the classroom.
一半的學生在教室裡。

10. **hand** [hænd] **n.** [C] 手；[sing.] 幫忙 <with>

▲ Peter held his grandma's hand when they crossed the
road. Peter 在過馬路時握住他奶奶的手。

💡 at hand 在手邊 | on the other hand... 另一方面…

hand [hænd] **v.** 將…遞給 <to>

▲ Bob read the menu and handed it to his friend.
Bob 看了菜單，然後將它遞給他的朋友。

💡 hand sth in 提交… | hand sb/sth over 移交…

11. **interest** [ˋɪntrɪst] **n.** [sing.] 興趣 <in>；[U] 利息

▲ Katie has always had a great interest in biology.
Katie 一直對生物學很有興趣。

interest [ˋɪntrɪst] **v.** 使…感興趣

▲ What interests the tourists most is the history of the
city.

使遊客們最感興趣的是這個城市的歷史。

---

12. **last** [læst] n. [sing.] 最後的人或事物 (the ～) [反] first

▲ Rachael is always the last to leave the office.

Rachael 總是最後離開辦公室的人。

💡 at last 最終 | to the last 直到最後一刻

last [læst] v. 持續

▲ The weather forecast says that the rain will last until the end of this week. 氣象預報說雨會持續到這週末。

last [læst] adv. 最後地 [反] first；最近

▲ Although the runner came last in the race, everyone still applauded her.

雖然這位跑者得最後一名，所有人仍為她鼓掌。

💡 last but not least 最後但同樣重要的

last [læst] adj. 最後的 [反] first；上一個的

▲ The meeting will be held on the last day of July.

會議將在七月的最後一天舉行。

💡 the last time 最後一次

---

13. **left** [lɛft] adj. 左邊的 [反] right

▲ People drive on the left side of the road in Britain.

在英國人們開車靠左邊行駛。

left [lɛft] n. [U] 左邊 [反] right

▲ Nancy was sitting on her sister's left.

Nancy 坐在她姊姊的左邊。

left [lɛft] adv. 向左地 [反] right

▲ Turn left at the next corner. 在下個街角左轉。

---

14. **let** [lɛt] v. 讓，允許 (let | let | letting)

▲ The father doesn't let his son drive his car.
這位父親不讓他兒子開他的車。

♥ let sb down 使⋯失望 | let sb go 放⋯走，讓⋯自由

15. **media** [ˋmidɪə] n. [sing.] 媒體 (the ~) <in>

▲ The news of the United States presidential election campaigns was widely reported in the international media.
美國總統選舉活動的新聞在國際媒體間被廣泛報導。

16. **much** [mʌtʃ] adj. 很多的 (more | most)

▲ Jimmy doesn't drink much milk.
Jimmy 喝的牛奶不太多。

much [mʌtʃ] pron. 很多

▲ Much has changed since you left.
自從你離開後，很多事物都變了。

much [mʌtʃ] adv. 非常

▲ Cindy likes sports very much. Cindy 非常喜歡運動。

17. **never** [ˋnɛvɚ] adv. 從未

▲ Judy has never seen such beautiful roses.
Judy 從未見過如此美麗的玫瑰花。

18. **picture** [ˋpɪktʃɚ] n. [C] 圖畫 <of>；照片 <of>

▲ The artist is painting a picture of the beautiful countryside. 這位藝術家正在畫美麗鄉間的圖畫。

♥ get the picture 了解情況

picture [ˈpɪktʃɚ] v. 想像

▲ No one can picture how terrible it would be to get lost in the mountains.

沒人可以想像在山裡迷路會是多麼可怕。

---

19. **popular** [ˈpɑpjələ] adj. 受歡迎的 <with, among> [反] unpopular；普遍的

▲ This song is popular with young people.

這首歌受到年輕人歡迎。

---

20. **probably** [ˈprɑbəblɪ] adv. 很可能

▲ The old stadium will be replaced, most probably by a modern shopping mall.

這座舊體育館極有可能被一座現代化購物中心取代。

---

21. **something** [ˈsʌmθɪŋ] pron. 某事物

▲ Something in the refrigerator smells rotten.

冰箱裡某個東西聞起來發臭了。

💡 have something to do with sth 與…有關 | something for nothing 不勞而獲

---

22. **think** [θɪŋk] v. 想，考慮 <about>；認為 (thought | thought | thinking)

▲ Allen was thinking about what would be the best way to learn English.

Allen 在想什麼會是學英文最好的方法。

💡 think twice 深思熟慮 | think highly of sb 對…評價高

---

23. **with** [wɪθ] prep. 和…一起；用

▲ Zack lives with his family. Zack 和家人一起住。

24. **year** [jɪr] n. [C] 年

▲ Diana plans to travel abroad every other year.
Diana 計劃每隔一年就到國外旅遊。

💡 all (the) year round 一整年 | year after year 年復一
年 | leap year 閏年

25. **you** [ju] pron. 你 (們)

▲ I wish you good luck. 祝你好運。

your [juɚ] pron. 你 (們) 的

▲ Is this your bike? 這是你的腳踏車嗎?

yours [jurz] pron. 你 (們) 的

▲ The white bag is mine, and the black one is yours.
白色的袋子是我的,而黑色的是你的。

yourself [juɚ`sɛlf] pron. 你自己

▲ Be careful with the scissors, or you may hurt
yourself. 小心使用剪刀,否則你可能會傷到你自己。

yourselves [jur`sɛlvz] pron. 你們自己

▲ The man told the boys, "Take the money and buy
yourselves some ice cream."
男子告訴男孩們:「拿錢去給你們自己買些冰淇淋。」

Unit 13

1. **all** [ɔl] adj. 全部的,整個的

▲ Ben worked on his English report all day.

Ben 整天都在做他的英文報告。

all [ɔl] adv. 完全地

▲ The desk was all covered with dust.

桌子上覆滿了灰塵。

all [ɔl] pron. 全部；唯一

▲ That's all. 那就是全部了。

---

2. **almost** [ˈɔl,most] adv. 幾乎，差不多

▲ Ted was almost home when his car ran out of gas.

Ted 幾乎快到家時車子沒油了。

---

3. **always** [ˈɔlwez] adv. 總是；一直

▲ Wendy always goes to school at 7 a.m.

Wendy 總是在早上七點去上學。

---

4. **book** [bʊk] n. [C] 書

▲ Danny borrowed three books from the library.

Danny 向圖書館借了三本書。

book [bʊk] v. 預約，預訂.

▲ Iris booked a seat on the next flight to Paris.

Iris 預訂了下一班飛往巴黎的機位。

💡 be booked up 被預訂一空

---

5. **color** [ˈkʌlɚ] n. [C][U] 顏色；[U] 色彩，生動

▲ What color shall we paint the fence?

我們要把圍牆漆成什麼顏色？

color [ˈkʌlɚ] v. 著色

▲ The girl drew a star and colored it yellow.

女孩畫了一顆星星並把它塗成黃色。

---

6. **drink** [drɪŋk] v. 喝;喝酒 (drank │ drunk │ drinking)
▲ Polly felt thirsty and drank two glasses of water.
　Polly 覺得口渴,喝了兩杯水。
drink [drɪŋk] n. [C][U] 飲料;酒
▲ Ray's favorite drink is Coke.
　Ray 最喜歡的飲料是可口可樂。

---

7. **enough** [ɪˋnʌf] adv. 足夠地
▲ The boy is old enough to go to school.
　那男孩年紀夠大,可以去上學了。
enough [ɪˋnʌf] adj. 足夠的
▲ Dora stayed up very late and didn't get enough sleep.
　Dora 熬夜到很晚,睡眠不足。
enough [ɪˋnʌf] pron. 足夠
▲ Did you have enough to eat? 你東西夠吃嗎?

---

8. **god** [gɑd] n. [C] 神
▲ Apollo is an ancient Greek god of knowledge.
　阿波羅是古希臘學識之神。
goddess [ˋgɑdɪs] n. [C] 女神
▲ Mazu is considered to be a goddess who protects fishermen. 媽祖被認為是一位保護漁民的女神。

---

9. **happy** [ˋhæpɪ] adj. 幸福的 , 快樂的 [反] sad (happier │ happiest)
▲ Bill was happy to see his old friends at the reunion.

Bill 很開心在聚會中看到老朋友。

---

10. **healthy** [ˋhɛlθɪ] adj. 健康的 ; 有益健康的 (healthier | healthiest)

▲ The old man is healthy because he eats right.
這個老人因為飲食適當所以很健康。

---

11. **inside** [ˋɪnˋsaɪd] prep. 在…裡面 [反] outside

▲ There is candy inside the box. 這個盒子裡面有糖果。

inside [ˋɪnˋsaɪd] adv. 在裡面 [反] outside

▲ It was raining, so Ariel decided to wait inside.
天空下著雨，所以 Ariel 決定在裡面等。

inside [ˋɪnˋsaɪd] n. [C][sing.] 內部，裡面 (the ～) <on>
[反] outside

▲ The outside of the house looks fine, but it looks shabby on the inside.
房子外部看起來很好，但裡面看起來破破爛爛的。

💡 inside out 裡面朝外地

inside [ˋɪnˋsaɪd] adj. 內部的，裡面的 [反] outside

▲ The guest would like an inside seat.
這位客人想要裡面的座位。

---

12. **interesting** [ˋɪntrɪstɪŋ] adj. 有趣的 [反] boring, uninteresting

▲ The interesting speech attracted the attention of the audience. 那場有趣的演講吸引了聽眾的注意力。

---

13. **into** [ˋɪntu] prep. 進入，到…裡面；朝著…的方向

▲ The secretary knocked at the door and walked into the manager's office.

祕書敲了敲門，然後走進經理的辦公室。

14. **learn** [lɚn] v. 學習；聽說，獲悉 [同] discover

▲ It's never too late to learn. 【諺】活到老學到老。

15. **library** [ˋlaɪˌbrɛrɪ] n. [C] 圖書館 (pl. libraries)

▲ John borrowed a magazine from the library.

John 從圖書館借了一本雜誌。

16. **list** [lɪst] n. [C] 名單，清單 <of>

▲ The hostess is making a list of the guests.

女主人正在擬賓客名單。

list [lɪst] v. 列出

▲ The candidates' names are listed alphabetically.

候選人的名字按字母順序列出。

17. **long** [lɔŋ] adj. 長的；長時間的 [反] short

▲ The table is two meters long and one meter wide.

這桌子兩公尺長，一公尺寬。

long [lɔŋ] adv. 長久地，長時間地

▲ I am sorry to keep you waiting long.

抱歉讓你久等了。

● as long as 只要

long [lɔŋ] v. 渴望

▲ Romeo longed to see Juliet again.

Romeo 渴望再見到 Juliet。

18. **love** [lʌv] n. [U] 愛 [反] hate, hatred；[C] 情人
   ▲ There is no substitute for a mother's love.
   母愛無可取代。
   💡 fall in love with... 愛上…
   love [lʌv] v. 愛 [反] hate；喜愛
   ▲ Leo loves Emma so much that he would like to marry her. Leo 如此愛 Emma 以致於想跟她結婚。

19. **movie** [`muvɪ] n. [C] 電影 [同] film
   ▲ The old lady seldom goes to the movies.
   這位老太太很少看電影。

20. **on** [ɑn] prep. 在…上面；有關
   ▲ Don't sit on that broken chair.
   不要坐在那張壞掉的椅子上。
   on [ɑn] adv. 繼續；開著
   ▲ Never give up; keep on trying.
   絕不要放棄，繼續嘗試。

21. **player** [`pleɚ] n. [C] 運動員；演奏者
   ▲ A volleyball game is played by two teams of six players. 一場排球賽由兩隊各六名球員參賽。

22. **rest** [rɛst] n. [C][U] 休息；[U] 剩餘部分 (the ～) <of>
   ▲ The doctor told the patient to get a week's rest.
   醫生告知病人休息一週。
   rest [rɛst] v. 休息；倚，靠 <on>
   ▲ Since Bella was tired, she stopped and rested for a

while. 因為 Bella 累了，所以她停下來休息一下。

💡 rest in peace 安息

23. **second** [ˋsɛkənd] adj. 第二的；第二名的

▲ Charlie's first child is a girl, and his second one is a boy.
Charlie 的第一個孩子是女孩，而第二個孩子是男孩。

💡 second to none 最好的

second [ˋsɛkənd] n. [C] 秒 (abbr. sec.)；片刻

▲ The commercial lasts 45 seconds.
廣告持續了四十五秒。

second [ˋsɛkənd] adv. 第二

▲ Daniel finished second; it was Eden that came in first. Daniel 得了第二名，而 Eden 是第一名。

24. **special** [ˋspɛʃəl] adj. 特別的；專門的

▲ This is a very special case, not an ordinary one.
這是一件非常特殊的案子，不是普通的案子。

25. **take** [tek] v. 拿；帶 (某人) 去 (took | taken | taking)

▲ The woman took her purse and stood up.
女子拿了錢包，然後站了起來。

💡 take sth off 脫掉… | take (sth) over 接管…

Unit 14

1. **any** [ˋɛnɪ] pron. 任何一個 <of>；一些，若干

▲ The mayor didn't answer any of the questions.
市長沒回答任何一個問題。

any [ˋɛnɪ] adj. 任何的；一些的，若干的

▲ Can I borrow one of your pens? Any pen will do.
我可以跟你借一枝筆嗎？任何筆都可以。

any [ˋɛnɪ] adv. 稍微

▲ Is Felix any richer than his brother?
Felix 稍微比他哥哥富有嗎？

---

2. **be** [bi] v. (表示人或事物的狀態) 是；(表示時間或方位)
(was, were | been | being)

▲ Elsa is a student. Elsa 是學生。

be [bi] aux. 正在；被

▲ The boy is singing. 男孩正在唱歌。

---

3. **coffee** [ˋkɔfɪ] n. [U] 咖啡

▲ Let's discuss this matter over a cup of coffee.
我們邊喝杯咖啡邊討論這件事。

---

4. **down** [daʊn] adv. 向下 [反] up；(坐、躺、放) 下 [反] up

▲ The elevator is going down. 電梯向下。

down [daʊn] prep. 向下 [反] up；沿著 [反] up

▲ Grace fell down the stairs and broke her leg.
Grace 摔下樓梯，跌斷了腿。

down [daʊn] adj. 向下的 [反] up；情緒低落的

▲ Let's take a down escalator to the first floor and then
an elevator to the basement parking lot. 讓我們搭向
下的手扶梯到一樓，然後乘電梯到地下室停車場。

down [daʊn] n. [C] 失敗

▲ The old man has experienced ups and downs of life.
這老人經歷了人生的浮浮沉沉。

down [daʊn] v. 擊敗；一口氣吃或喝下

▲ The guest team downed the host team 3-2.
客隊以三比二擊敗東道主隊。

---

5. **end** [ɛnd] n. [sing.] 結尾 <of> [反] start, beginning；[C] 末端

▲ Those workers felt exhausted at the end of the day.
在一天結束時，那些工人覺得筋疲力盡。

💡 in the end 最後 | make ends meet 使收支平衡

end [ɛnd] v. (使) 結束 [反] start, begin

▲ World War I ended in 1918.
第一次世界大戰在 1918 年結束。

💡 end up 最後處於、成為 | end in sth 以…作為結果

---

6. **father** [ˈfɑðɚ] n. [C] 父親

▲ Ian is the father of three children.
Ian 是三個孩子的父親。

---

7. **feel** [fil] v. 感覺到；認為 (felt | felt | feeling)

▲ As the earthquake struck, Jade felt her house shaking. 地震發生時，Jade 感覺到她的房子在搖。

💡 feel like sth/V-ing 想要…；想做…

feel [fil] n. [sing.] 觸感 <of>

▲ Jacob loves the feel of cotton against his skin.

Jacob 喜愛棉貼著他皮膚的觸感。

8. **heavy** [ˋhɛvɪ] adj. 沉重的 [反] light ；嚴重的 (heavier | heaviest)
   ▲ The girl's schoolbag is so heavy that it hurts her back. 女孩的書包如此沉重以致於她背痛。

9. **kind** [kaɪnd] adj. 仁慈的，友好的 <to> [反] unkind
   ▲ The villagers are very kind to strangers.
   村民們對陌生人都很友好。
   kind [kaɪnd] n. [C] 種類 <of> [同] sort, type
   ▲ Jeff likes this kind of trees. Jeff 喜歡這種樹。
   💡 one of a kind 獨一無二

10. **language** [ˋlæŋgwɪdʒ] n. [C][U] 語言
   ▲ Can you speak a foreign language fluently?
   你能流利地說一種外語嗎？
   💡 sign/native/body language 手語 / 母語 / 肢體語言

11. **large** [lɑrdʒ] adj. 大的 [反] small
   ▲ This box is too small; we need a larger one.
   這個箱子太小了，我們需要一個大一點的。

12. **many** [ˋmɛnɪ] adj. 很多的 [反] few (more | most)
   ▲ Do you have many friends here?
   你在這裡有很多朋友嗎？
   many [ˋmɛnɪ] pron. 很多人或事物 <of>
   ▲ Not many of the children have learned to read.

這些孩子們當中學會閱讀的人不多。

13. **market** [`mɑrkɪt] n. [C] 市場
   ▲ Kane bought fruit and vegetables at the market.
   Kane 在市場買了水果和蔬菜。
   market [`mɑrkɪt] v. 出售；推銷，行銷 <for>
   ▲ The store markets many kinds of electrical goods.
   這間商店出售多種電器商品。

14. **matter** [`mætɚ] n. [C] 事情；[sing.] 麻煩事 (the ~)
    <with>
   ▲ The two brothers don't like to talk about money
   matters. 這兩兄弟不喜歡談論錢的事情。
   💡 as a matter of fact 事實上 |
     no matter what/when/why 不管什麼 / 何時 / 為什麼
   matter [`mætɚ] v. 重要，有關係
   ▲ It doesn't matter where the candidate is from.
   這位候選人從何出身無關緊要。

15. **million** [`mɪljən] n. [C] 百萬 (pl. million, millions)
   ▲ There are more than twenty million people in
   Taiwan. 臺灣有超過兩千萬人。

16. **morning** [`mɔrnɪŋ] n. [C][U] 早上
   ▲ Kelly goes jogging in the park every morning.
   Kelly 每天早上都去公園慢跑。
   💡 from morning till night 從早到晚

17. **mountain** [`mauntṇ] n. [C] 山

▲ Mount Everest is the highest mountain in the world.
聖母峰是世界上最高的山。

---

18. **national** [ˈnæʃənl] adj. 國家的，全國性的
   ▲ This event was reported in the national newspapers.
   這個事件在全國性的報紙中有報導。

---

19. **pass** [pæs] v. 通過 (考試)；(時間) 過去
   ▲ The students have to work hard to pass the exam.
   學生們要用功才能通過考試。
   💡 pass away 去世 | pass out 昏倒
   pass [pæs] n. [C] 通行證，出入證；考試及格 <in> [反]
   fail
   ▲ Passengers have to present their boarding pass before
   getting on a plane.
   上機前，乘客必須出示他們的登機證。

---

20. **pet** [pɛt] n. [C] 寵物
   ▲ Martin keeps three pets, including a dog, a cat, and a
   rabbit. Martin 養了三隻寵物，包括一隻狗、一隻貓和
   一隻兔子。
   pet [pɛt] v. 撫摸 (petted | petted | petting)
   ▲ The farmer petted the cow. 農夫撫摸那隻乳牛。

---

21. **practice** [ˈpræktɪs] n. [U] 練習；實行
   ▲ It takes a lot of practice to master a language.
   多練習才能精通語言。
   practice [ˈpræktɪs] v. 練習；從事 <as>

▲ The musician practices for hours every day.
這位音樂家每天練習好幾個小時。

💡 practice law/medicine 開業當律師 / 行醫

---

22. **rise** [raɪz] n. [sing.] 上升 <in> [反] fall；增加，上漲 <in> [同] increase [反] fall

▲ The scientists found a sudden rise in sea levels.
科學家發現海平面突然上升。

💡 on the rise 在上升 | give rise to sth 引起…

rise [raɪz] v. 上升 [反] fall；增加 <by> [同] go up [反] fall (rose | risen | rising)

▲ The sun rises in the east. 太陽從東邊升起。

---

23. **safe** [sef] adj. 安全的 <from> [反] unsafe

▲ The children are safe from danger while they are in this room. 孩子們待在這房間裡很安全。

💡 safe and sound 安然無恙

safe [sef] n. [C] 保險箱

▲ Jenny's money and jewelry were kept in the safe.
Jenny 的錢和珠寶都存放在這個保險箱裡。

safeguard [`sef͵gɑrd] v. 保護，捍衛

▲ The new regulations safeguard consumer rights.
這些新法規保護消費者權益。

---

24. **we** [wi] pron. 我們

▲ We are so pleased that you are able to come.
你能來，我們太高興了。

us [ʌs] pron. 我們

▲ Last night, Nelson treated us to dinner.
Nelson 昨晚請我們吃晚餐。

our [aʊr] pron. 我們的

▲ We sold our house three years ago.
我們三年前賣了我們的房子。

ours [aʊrz] pron. 我們的 <of>

▲ Lara is a colleague of ours. Lara 是我們的同事之一。

ourselves [ˌaʊrˈsɛlvz] pron. 我們自己

▲ We have bought ourselves a new car.
我們給自己買了一輛新車。

---

25. **why** [hwaɪ] adv. 為什麼

▲ Why did Oliver move to London?
Oliver 為什麼搬去倫敦？

why [hwaɪ] n. [C] 原因

▲ Mark knows little about the whys and wherefores of the problem.
Mark 不太知道是什麼原因導致這個問題。

Unit 15

1. **because** [bɪˈkəz] conj. 因為

▲ The climbers sat down for a rest because they were so tired from walking.
因為登山者們走得太累，所以他們坐下來休息。

💡 because of sb/sth 因為…，由於…

---

2. **day** [de] n. [C] 一天；[C][U] 白天 [反] night
   ▲ There are 365 days in a year. 一年有三百六十五天。

3. **dog** [dɔg] n. [C] 狗
   ▲ The dog barked at the stranger.
   那隻狗對著陌生人吠叫。
   ♥ a dog's life 悲慘的生活

4. **fresh** [frɛʃ] adj. 新鮮的；新的
   ▲ It is best to eat fruit when it is fresh.
   水果最好趁新鮮時吃。
   ♥ a fresh start 嶄新的開始 | be as fresh as a daisy 精神
   飽滿

5. **from** [frɑm] prep. (表示來源) 從；從…開始
   ▲ "Where are you from?" "I'm from Australia."
   「你來自哪裡？」「我來自澳洲。」

6. **get** [gɛt] v. 獲得，得到；收到 (got | got, gotten |
   getting)
   ▲ Patrick finally got his driver's license.
   Patrick 終於得到駕照了。
   ♥ get along (with sb) (和…) 和睦相處 | get away with
   sth 做 (錯事) 而未被懲罰或發覺

7. **great** [gret] adj. 大量的；偉大的
   ▲ Over the past five years, the improvement in the
   couple's relations has been very great.
   在過去五年間，這對夫妻的關係已大大改善了。

great [gret] n. [C] 偉人，名人

▲ Kobe Bryant was one of the NBA's all-time greats.
科比布萊恩是 NBA 有史以來的名人之一。

8. **knowledge** [ˋnɑlɪdʒ] n. [U] 知識；知道 <of>

▲ Knowledge is power. 【諺】知識就是力量。

9. **less** [lɛs] pron. 較少量 <than> [反] more

▲ To lose some weight, Adela exercises more and eats less than usual.
為了減重，Adela 比平常運動多並吃得較少量。

less [lɛs] adv. 較少地 [反] more；不如 <than> [反] more

▲ If you tell the truth, your mother will worry less.
如果你說實話，你媽媽會少擔心點。

♥ more or less 大致上；差不多

less [lɛs] adj. 較少的 [反] more

▲ To prepare for the exam, the student spent less time playing online games.
為了準備考試，那位學生花較少的時間玩線上遊戲。

♥ no less than 至少

less [lɛs] prep. 減去，除去 [同] minus

▲ The clerk gave Belinda her money back, less the $10 deposit that she had paid. 除去她已支付的十美元訂金，店員把 Belinda 的錢還給她。

10. **level** [ˋlɛvl] n. [C] 級別 <at>；水準

▲ The course can be taken at four different levels.
這個課程分為四個不同的級別。

level [ˋlɛv!] adj. 平坦的；相同高度的 <with>

▲ The land is not level; it slopes gently toward the sea.
  這片土地不平坦；它緩緩朝大海傾斜。

---

11. **line** [laɪn] n. [C] 線；行，排 <of>

▲ The teacher drew a straight line on the blackboard.
  老師在黑板上畫了一條直線。

line [laɪn] v. 沿…排列成行 <with>

▲ The country road is lined with maple trees.
  這條鄉間小路兩邊楓樹成行。

💡 line (sb) up (使…) 排隊

---

12. **low** [lo] adj. 低的，矮的 [反] high；(程度) 低的 [反] high

▲ The house has a low roof. 這間房子的屋頂很低。

low [lo] adv. 低地

▲ The sun sank low behind the mountains.
  太陽下山了。

low [lo] n. [C] 低點；(人生的) 低谷，低潮 <of>

▲ To our surprise, the temperature reached a new low
  in Taipei yesterday.
  使我們驚訝的是，臺北昨天的氣溫達到新低。

---

13. **mouth** [maʊθ] n. [C] 嘴，口

▲ The man was so hungry that he put much food in his
  mouth at once.
  那男子如此飢餓以致於他一次把很多食物放入嘴裡。

💡 keep sb's mouth shut 保持緘默 ｜ make sb's mouth
  water 使…垂涎欲滴

mouth [maʊθ] v. 用口形默示

▲ Cara mouthed the words "thank you" silently.
Cara 用口形默示：「謝謝你」。

---

14. **museum** [mju`ziəm] n. [C] 博物館

▲ The foreign tourist is going to visit the National Palace Museum.
這個外國觀光客將要去參觀國立故宮博物院。

---

15. **oil** [ɔɪl] n. [U] (食用) 油；石油

▲ Maggie put some olive oil in the pan and fried an egg. Maggie 在平底鍋裡放了一些橄欖油煎蛋。

oil [ɔɪl] v. 給⋯上油

▲ The machine needs oiling once a month.
這臺機器一個月需要上油一次。

---

16. **once** [wʌns] adv. 一次

▲ The cleaning lady comes once a week.
打掃阿姨每週來一次。

🔎 at once 馬上；同時 | once in a lifetime 千載難逢地 | once upon a time 很久以前

once [wʌns] conj. 一旦⋯就

▲ Once the boy gets to sleep, he doesn't wake up easily. 那男孩一旦睡著，就不容易醒來。

once [wʌns] n. [U] 一次

▲ I tried stinky tofu, but once was enough for me.
我試了臭豆腐，但對我來說一次就夠了。

---

17. **point** [pɔɪnt] n. [C] 觀點，論點；[U] 重點，目的 <of, in>

▲ The researcher made several interesting points in her report. 那位研究人員在報告中提到幾個有趣的論點。

💡 to the point 切中要點的

point [pɔɪnt] v. 指，指向 <at>；瞄準，用⋯對準 <at>

▲ It is impolite to point at others.
用手指著別人是不禮貌的。

💡 point sth out 指出

18. **power** [ˋpaʊɚ] n. [U] 影響力；政權

▲ Toby has little power over his sister; she does whatever she wants.
Toby 對他妹妹沒什麼影響力，她想做什麼就做什麼。

power [ˋpaʊɚ] v. 為⋯提供動力，驅動

▲ This car is powered by electricity instead of gasoline.
這輛車是由電而不是汽油驅動的。

19. **ready** [ˋrɛdɪ] adj. 準備好的 (readier | readiest)

▲ The meeting will begin soon, but the manager isn't ready yet. 會議即將要開始了，但經理還沒準備好。

ready [ˋrɛdɪ] v. 使做好準備 <for> [同] prepare (readied | readied | readying)

▲ The fighter aircraft was readied for battle.
戰鬥機已做好戰鬥準備。

20. **rock** [rɑk] n. [C] 石塊；[C][U] 岩石

▲ The protesters shouted slogans and threw rocks at the police.

抗議者呼喊口號並向警方丟石塊。

rock [rɑk] v. (使) 搖動；使震驚 [同] shock

▲ The old man rocked back and forth in the chair.
老人坐在椅子上前後搖動。

---

21. **save** [sev] v. 拯救 <from>；儲存

▲ The firefighter bravely saved a little boy from the fire. 消防隊員英勇地從火場中救出一個小男孩。

💡 save sb's life 救⋯的性命 | save up (sth) 存 (錢)

savings [`sevɪŋz] n. [pl.] 存款

▲ The couple spent almost all their savings on the apartment.
那對夫妻花了幾乎所有的存款買那間公寓。

---

22. **say** [se] v. 說，陳述；顯示，指示 (said | said | saying)

▲ The boy believed anything his father said.
男孩相信他爸爸說的任何事。

---

23. **season** [`sizn̩] n. [C] 季節；時節，季

▲ There are four seasons in a year. 一年有四季。

💡 in/out of season (蔬果) 當季的 / 不當季的

---

24. **strong** [strɔŋ] adj. 強壯的；強烈的

▲ The strong man easily lifted the heavy box.
那個強壯的男子輕易地抬起沉重的箱子。

---

25. **than** [ðɛn] conj. 比

▲ Ella sings better than I do. Ella 唱得比我好。

than [ðɛn] prep. 比

▲ Adrian left home earlier than usual.

Adrian 比平常早出門。

Unit 16

1. **bring** [brɪŋ] v. 帶來 (brought | brought | bringing)

   ▲ Adam's new job brought him a handsome income.

   Adam 的新工作給他帶來不錯的收入。

   💡 bring about sth 導致… | bring sth back 帶回…

2. **by** [baɪ] prep. 被，由；以 (方式)

   ▲ The article was written by a student.

   這篇文章是由一位學生寫的。

   by [baɪ] adv. 經過

   ▲ The house shook whenever a train went by.

   每當火車經過時，那房子就震動。

3. **famous** [ˋfeɪməs] adj. 著名的，有名的 <for>

   ▲ The Chinese restaurant is famous for its Peking duck.

   那間中式餐廳以其北京烤鴨聞名。

4. **hair** [hɛr] n. [U][C] 頭髮

   ▲ Jane is going to have her hair cut. Jane 要去剪頭髮。

   hairdo [ˋhɛrˌdu] n. [C] (尤指女子) 髮型 [同] hairstyle

   ▲ Fanny has a new hairdo, and it looks terrific.

   Fanny 換了新髮型，很好看。

   hairstyle [ˋhɛrˌstaɪl] n. [C] 髮型

▲ The girls kept teasing the boy's new hairstyle.
女孩們一直取笑男孩的新髮型。

5. **how** [haʊ] adv. (指方法) 如何，怎麼；(指數量或程度) 多少

▲ How did Ivan solve the difficult problem?
Ivan 怎麼解決那個難題的？

6. **name** [nem] n. [C] 名字，名稱

▲ What is Ben's family name? Ben 姓什麼？

● by the name of sth 被叫做⋯ | in the name of sb 以 (某人) 的名義；在 (某人) 名下

name [nem] v. 給⋯取名，為⋯命名

▲ The street was named after the famous writer.
那條街以那名作家的名字命名。

7. **nothing** [ˋnʌθɪŋ] pron. 沒有東西，沒有事情

▲ Grace has done nothing all day.
Grace 整天什麼事也沒做。

● have nothing to do with... 與⋯無關

nothing [ˋnʌθɪŋ] n. [C] 不重要的人或事物

▲ The young man is a nothing, namely a useless and worthless person.
這個年輕人微不足道，只是個無用且無價值的人而已。

8. **online** [ˋɑn͵laɪn] adj. 網上的 [反] offline

▲ More and more people prefer online shopping to in-store shopping.

比起店內購物，越來越多人更喜歡網上購物。

---

9. **part** [pɑrt] **n.** [C][U] 部分 <of>；[C] 角色 <of> [同] role
   ▲ The best part of the vacation is the delicious food.
   這趟假期最棒的部分是美食。
   💡 for the most part 多半，通常 | take part in sth 參加…
   part [pɑrt] **v.** (使) 分開
   ▲ The two classmates parted at the school's front gate.
   那兩個同學在學校大門口分開。
   💡 part with sth (不情願地) 放棄，捨棄

---

10. **pick** [pɪk] **v.** 挑選，選擇 <as>；摘，採
   ▲ Why did the manager pick Hazel as his secretary?
   經理為什麼選 Hazel 做他的祕書？
   💡 pick on sb 對…刁難挑剔 | pick sb up (用交通工具)
   接… | pick sth up 撿起…；學會
   pick [pɪk] **n.** [U] 挑選，選擇
   ▲ There are some books on the desk; you can take your
   pick. 桌上有一些書，你可以自己挑選。

---

11. **plant** [plænt] **n.** [C] 植物；工廠
   ▲ Many animals eat plants for food.
   很多動物以植物為食。
   plant [plænt] **v.** 種植
   ▲ Mrs. Brown is going to plant some vegetables in the
   yard. Brown 太太要在院子裡種一些蔬菜。

---

12. **program** [`prog ræm] **n.** [C] 節目；計畫

▲ Cartoons are many children's favorite TV programs.
卡通是許多孩子最愛的電視節目。

program [`progræm] v. 為…程式設計，編制程序
(programmed | programmed | programming)

▲ The robot is programmed by the computer software.
這個機器人按照電腦軟體編制的程序運作。

programmer [`proˌgræmɚ] n. [C] (電腦) 程式編制員，
程式設計師

▲ A programmer's job is to write computer programs.
程式編制員的工作是寫電腦程式。

---

13. **put** [pʊt] v. 放置 [同] place (put | put | putting)

▲ The man put the wallet in his pocket.
男子把錢包放進口袋。

💡 put sth away 把…收起來 ｜ put sth out 撲滅…

---

14. **report** [rɪ`pɔrt] n. [C] 報告 <on, about>；報導

▲ The student had to write a report on modern poetry.
那位學生必須寫一篇現代詩的報告。

report [rɪ`pɔrt] v. 報告 <on>；報導

▲ Dennis will report on his progress in the weekly
conference this Friday.
Dennis 將在本週五的週會中報告他的進度。

---

15. **rich** [rɪtʃ] adj. 有錢的，富有的 [反] poor；豐富的 <in>

▲ The rich man leads a life of luxury.
這位有錢人過著奢侈的生活。

16. **seed** [sid] n. [C][U] 種子；[C] 原因，根源 <of>

▲ The farmer planted sunflower seeds in his field.
農夫在他田裡種下向日葵的種子。

17. **sell** [sɛl] v. 賣，出售 <to> [反] buy (sold | sold | selling)

▲ Leo sold his old scooter to his neighbor.
Leo 將他老舊的摩托車賣給他的鄰居。

18. **short** [ʃɔrt] adj. 短的 (長度) [反] long；短的 (時間)，短暫的 [反] long

▲ Lara put on the short skirt instead of the long one.
Lara 穿上短裙而非那條長裙。

💡 be short of sth …短缺 | in short 總之

19. **since** [sɪns] conj. 自從…；因為，既然

▲ Pat and I have been good friends ever since we first met. Pat 和我自從初次見面就成了好朋友。

since [sɪns] prep. 自從…

▲ Susan has been sick in bed since last Sunday.
Susan 自從上週日開始就臥病在床。

since [sɪns] adv. 此後，從此

▲ Edward moved to New York two years ago, and his parents haven't seen him since. Edward 兩年前搬到紐約，自從那時起他父母就沒見過他。

20. **some** [sʌm] adj. 若干，一些

▲ Marian saw some birds on that branch.
Marian 看到那樹枝上有一些鳥。

some [sʌm] pron. 一些，幾個

▲ You have a lot of apples; please give me some.
你有很多蘋果，請給我幾個。

21. **spend** [spend] v. 花 (錢) <on> ；花費 (時間) <V-ing, with, on> (spent | spent | spending)

▲ Pearl spent most of her money on books.
Pearl 把她大部分的錢花在買書上。

22. **still** [stɪl] adv. 還是；儘管如此

▲ Does your back still hurt? 你的背還痛嗎？

still [stɪl] adj. 靜止的，不動的

▲ The little girl sat still while her mother was brushing her hair.
當小女孩的母親在幫她梳頭髮時，她坐著不動。

23. **third** [θɝd] adj. 第三的

▲ It is the little boy's third birthday.
這是小男孩的三歲生日。

third [θɝd] n. [C] 三分之一 <of>

▲ Two-thirds of the students passed the exam.
三分之二的學生通過了考試。

third [θɝd] adv. 第三

▲ Jack finished third in the big race and received the prize money of NT$30,000. Jack 在這場關鍵的比賽中獲得第三名並得到了新臺幣三萬元的獎金。

24. **those** [ðoz] pron. 那些

▲ Heaven helps those who help themselves.

【諺】天助自助者。

those [ðoz] adj. 那些

▲ The company is planning to set up some new branches in those urban areas.

這公司正計劃要在那些城鎮區域設立新的分部。

25. **together** [tə`gɛðɚ] adv. 一起 [反] alone, separately;同時

▲ Several teenagers went to the movies together.

幾個青少年一起去看電影。

💡 put sth together 組合… | together with... 連同…

Unit 17

1. **also** [`ɔlso] adv. 也

▲ Ping-Pong is also called table tennis.

乒乓球又叫桌球。

2. **before** [bɪ`for] prep. 在…前面 [反] after ；在…之前 [反] after

▲ The woman stood before the mirror to check her hair.

女子站在鏡子前檢查她的頭髮。

before [bɪ`for] conj. 在…之前 [反] after

▲ Rachel hadn't waited long before her friend came.

Rachel 沒等多久她的朋友就來了。

before [bɪ`for] adv. 以前

▲ Kim has never eaten mangoes before.

Kim 以前不曾吃過芒果。

---

3. **big** [bɪg] adj. 大的 (bigger | biggest)

   ▲ The refrigerator is too big to fit into the space.
   這臺冰箱太大而無法塞入這個空間。

---

4. **certain** [ˋsɝtn̩] adj. 確定的 [同] sure；某個

   ▲ The diligent student is certain that he will pass the exam. 這位勤奮的學生確定自己會通過考試。

   ♥ make certain 確定，確保

   certain [ˋsɝtn̩] pron. 一些，若干 <of>

   ▲ Certain of those present were students; the others were teachers. 一些出席的人是學生，其它是老師。

   certainly [ˋsɝtn̩lɪ] adv. 當然，確實

   ▲ These books are certainly not Kim's; I am very sure about that. 這些書確實不是 Kim 的，我很確定。

---

5. **have** [hæv] aux. (與過去分詞構成完成式) 已經；曾經

   ▲ The workers have just finished the job.
   工人們剛剛已經完成這個工作。

   have [hæv] v. 有；吃，喝 (had | had | having)

   ▲ Lester has his own reason to do so.
   Lester 這麼做有他自己的原因。

   ♥ have to V 必須…，不得不…

---

6. **least** [list] adv. 最少，最小 (the ~) [反] most；最不 (the ~) [反] most

   ▲ John talks (the) least. John 話最少。

least [list] pron. 最少，最小 (the ~)

▲ The least Tara can do is give the beggar some money. 給乞討者一些錢是 Tara 最起碼能做的事。

least [list] adj. 最少，最小 (the ~)

▲ Beth has the least money of us all.
在我們當中，Beth 的錢最少。

---

7. **no** [no] adj. 沒有；禁止

▲ There is no milk left. 沒有牛奶了。

no [no] adv. 不 [反] yes

▲ Marcus wanted to give the girl a ride, but she said no.
Marcus 想讓那個女孩搭便車，但她說不用。

no [no] n. [C] 否定，拒絕

▲ Vivian gave a definite no to the idea.
Vivian 對這個想法明確表示否定。

---

8. **off** [ɔf] adv. 離開，遠離；去掉，移開

▲ The manager is off to San Francisco next Monday.
經理下週一要離開去舊金山。

off [ɔf] prep. 離開，遠離；去掉，移開

▲ The driver was stuck in a traffic jam the moment he was off the highway.
駕駛一離開高速公路就遇上塞車。

off [ɔf] adj. 離開的；休假的，不上班的

▲ It's very late now; Judy must be off.
現在時間很晚了，Judy 一定是離開了。

---

9. **office** [ˋɔfɪs] n. [C] 辦公室

▲ The manager is making calls in his office now.

經理現在在他的辦公室裡打電話。

10. **past** [pæst] adj. 過去的；以前的

▲ Yvonne has been absent from work for the past three days. Yvonne 過去三天都沒上班。

past [pæst] n. [sing.] 過去

▲ You should not worry about your past.
你不該擔心你的過去。

past [pæst] prep. 經過；(時間) 晚於

▲ Zoe walks past the bakery on her way to school every day.

Zoe 每天上學的路上都會經過這間麵包店。

past [pæst] adv. 經過

▲ As Alice drove past, she waved at her friends.
Alice 開車經過時向她朋友揮手。

11. **pay** [pe] v. 付款，付費 <by, for>；支付…報酬 (paid | paid | paying)

▲ The customer paid by credit card.
那位顧客用信用卡付款。

♥ pay for sth 為…付出代價 | pay off 取得成功；償清債務

payment [`pemənt] n. [C] 支付的金額；[U] 付款 <in>

▲ The customer will pay for the cellphone in twelve monthly payments.

這位顧客將以十二個月分期付款來支付這支手機。

12. **raise** [rez] v. 舉起；飼養

▲ The mayor raised his hand to wave to the crowd.
市長舉起手向群眾揮手。

raise [rez] n. [C] 加薪

▲ The hard-working employee was given a raise.
那位勤奮的員工得到加薪。

13. **reach** [ritʃ] v. 抵達；達到

▲ What time will the climbers reach their destination?
登山客何時會抵達他們的目的地？

reach [ritʃ] n. [U] 伸手可及的距離

▲ Don't put the medicine within reach of children.
不要把藥放在孩子們拿得到的地方。

14. **really** [ˈriəlɪ] adv. 真正地；非常 [同] extremely

▲ Do you really mean it? 你是當真的嗎？

15. **river** [ˈrɪvɚ] n. [C] 河，江

▲ There is a bridge across the river. 河上有一座橋。

16. **service** [ˈsɝvəs] n. [C] 公共服務系統；[U] 服務，接待

▲ The postal service provides mail processing and
delivery services for individuals and businesses. 郵政
服務系統為個人和公司提供信件處理和遞送服務。

17. **ship** [ʃɪp] n. [C] (尤指航海的) 大船

▲ The sailors are boarding the ship that will sail soon.
水手們正登上不久將啟航的船。

ship [ʃɪp] v. 運輸，運送 (shipped | shipped | shipping)

▲ These packages will be shipped to Vancouver in a week. 這些包裹將在一週內被運送到溫哥華。

---

18. **side** [saɪd] n. [C] 面 <of>；旁邊 <by>

▲ The student didn't answer the questions on the other side of the exam paper and thus failed the test.
這位學生沒有翻到考卷背面作答因而考試不及格。

💡 side by side 肩並肩地 | take sb's side 支持…

---

19. **someone** [`sʌm,wʌn] pron. 某人 [同] somebody

▲ Someone left this letter for Bertha.
某人留了這封信給 Bertha。

someone [`sʌm,wʌn] n. [C] 重要人物，有名氣的人

somebody [`sʌm,bɑdɪ] pron. 某人 [同] someone

▲ Somebody is knocking on the door. Go answer it.
某人在敲門。去應門。

---

20. **song** [sɔŋ] n. [C] 歌曲

▲ The singer is singing a pop song on stage.
歌手正在舞臺上唱著一首流行歌曲。

---

21. **store** [stor] n. [C] 商店；儲存量 <of>

▲ Quinn bought a pair of jeans in the clothing store.
Quinn 在服裝店買了一條牛仔褲。

store [stor] v. 儲存，儲藏

▲ Thousands of books are stored in the library.
數千本書被儲存在這間圖書館裡。

---

22. **these** [ðiz] pron. 這些

▲ Are these yours or Jane's? 這些是你的還是 Jane 的？

these [ðiz] adj. 這些

23. though [ðo] conj. 雖然，儘管 [同] although

▲ Though it was raining, the two baseball teams still kept playing.

雖然在下雨，這兩支棒球隊仍然繼續打球。

💡 as though 好像，似乎

though [ðo] adv. 不過，可是

▲ It is hard work. Cathy enjoys it, though.

這工作很辛苦。不過 Cathy 喜歡。

24. under [`ʌndə] prep. 在…下面 [反] above；少於，低於 [反] over

▲ A submarine travels under the water.

潛水艇在水面下航行。

under [`ʌndə] adv. 在…下面 [反] above；少於，低於 [反] over

▲ The fisherman dived in and stayed under as long as he could. 漁夫潛入水，盡可能停留在水面下。

25. whether [`hwɛðə] conj. 是否

▲ Debby doesn't know whether her brother will go to Paris or not. Debby 不知道她哥哥是否會去巴黎。

💡 whether...or... 無論是…還是…

Unit 18

1. **air** [εr] n. [U] 空氣；乘坐飛機 <by>

   ▲ Air is a mixture of gases that we cannot see.
   空氣是一種我們看不見的氣體混合物。

   air conditioner [`εr kən,dɪʃənɚ] n. [C] 冷氣機，空調設備

   ▲ An air conditioner can keep the air in a building cool.
   冷氣機可以讓建築物裡的空氣保持涼爽。

2. **although** [ɔl`ðo] conj. 雖然，儘管 [同] though

   ▲ Although the worker was tired, he kept on working.
   雖然那個工人很累，但他卻繼續工作。

3. **around** [ə`raʊnd] prep. 四處，周圍 [同] round；在…附近 [同] round

   ▲ Many people want to travel around the world.
   很多人想要環遊世界。

   around [ə`raʊnd] adv. 四處，周圍 [同] about；附近

   ▲ The rumor has been spread around. 謠言已四處散布。

4. **business** [`bɪznɪs] n. [U] 買賣 <with>；[C] 公司

   ▲ The company does business with Russian customers.
   這家公司跟俄國客戶做買賣。

   💡 be none of sb's business 與…無關

5. **come** [kʌm] v. 來 [反] go；到達 (came | come | coming)

▲ There is a bus coming. 一輛公車來了。

💡 come from sth 來自… | come up with sth 想出… | come about 發生

---

6. **during** [ˋdʊrɪŋ] prep. 在…期間

▲ During the past ten years, the scientist has been working on his research.

在過去十年期間，這位科學家一直在做他的研究。

---

7. **egg** [ɛg] n. [C] 蛋；(鳥類的) 卵

▲ The girl prefers scrambled eggs to fried eggs.

女孩喜歡炒蛋勝於煎蛋。

---

8. **if** [ɪf] conj. 如果；是否

▲ If it is sunny, we'll go mountain climbing.

如果天氣晴朗的話，我們會去爬山。

💡 if necessary 如果有必要的話 | even if 即使

---

9. **new** [nju] adj. 新的 [反] old；不熟悉的，生疏的 <to>

▲ Irene is always open to new ideas.

Irene 對新觀念總是態度開明。

newlywed [ˋnjulɪ͵wɛd] n. [C] 新婚者 (usu. pl.)

▲ The newlyweds went to Japan on their honeymoon.

這對新婚夫婦去日本度蜜月。

---

10. **or** [ɔr] conj. 或者，還是；否則

▲ Which do you like better, tea or coffee?

你比較喜歡茶還是咖啡？

💡 or so 大約

11. **outside** [`aʊt`saɪd] prep. 在…外面 [反] inside

▲ Janice is waiting outside the classroom.
　 Janice 正在教室外面等。

outside [`aʊt`saɪd] adv. 在外面 [同] outdoors

▲ It is raining outside. 外面在下雨。

outside [`aʊt`saɪd] adj. 外面的，戶外的 [反] inside

▲ The people in the small village still use outside toilet.
　 這個小村莊裡的人仍使用戶外廁所。

outside [`aʊt`saɪd] n. [C] 外面 (the ~) <of> [反] inside

▲ The outside of the castle was painted blue.
　 城堡外面被漆成藍色。

12. **piece** [pis] n. [C] 片；一張，一件 <of>

▲ The glass broke into pieces when it fell on the floor.
　 玻璃杯掉到地上，破成碎片。

💡 be a piece of cake 很簡單 | in one piece 平安無損

piece [pis] v. 拼湊 <together>

▲ Kelly is trying to piece fragments of the letter
　 together. Kelly 正試著把信件的碎片拼湊起來。

13. **possible** [`pɑsəbl] adj. 可能的 [反] impossible

▲ It is possible for the students to finish their
　 homework today.
　 學生們今天做完他們的功課是可能的。

14. **restaurant** [`rɛstərənt] n. [C] 餐廳

▲ Mr. Williams took his wife out for dinner at an Italian restaurant.
Williams 先生帶他太太去一家義大利餐廳吃頓晚餐。

15. **science** [ˋsaɪəns] n. [U] 科學
▲ In recent years, development in science and technology has brought prosperity to humans.
近幾年,科技的發展已為人類帶來繁榮昌盛。

16. **sentence** [ˋsɛntəns] n. [C] 句子;判決,判刑
▲ The student couldn't find the topic sentence in the first paragraph. 學生在第一段裡找不到主題句。
sentence [ˋsɛntəns] v. 宣布判決 <to>
▲ The robber was sentenced to two years in prison.
這個強盜被判兩年徒刑。

17. **set** [sɛt] v. 放,置;使成為某狀態 (set | set | setting)
▲ The teacher set the book on the desk.
老師把書放在桌上。
💡 set...free 釋放… | set sth up 創立…
set [sɛt] n. [C] 一組,一套 <of>
▲ Anna gave the newlyweds a set of cutlery as a present. Anna 送新婚夫婦一套餐具作為禮物。

18. **share** [ʃɛr] v. 分享,共用 <with>;分配 <among, between>
▲ Bess likes to share her thoughts with her friends.
Bess 喜歡和她的朋友們分享她的想法。

share [ʃɛr] n. [sing.] 一份 <of, in>；[C] 股票 <in>

▲ I have to do my share of housework every day.
我每天都必須做我的那一份家務。

---

19. **size** [saɪz] n. [C][U] 尺寸，大小 <of>；[C] 尺碼

▲ What is the size of the TV set?
這臺電視機的尺寸是多大？

size [saɪz] v. 標定⋯的大小

▲ Each of the crabs is sized, weighed, and priced.
每隻螃蟹都被標定大小、秤重並標價。

---

20. **sound** [saʊnd] n. [U][C] 聲音 [同] noise

▲ Sound travels slower than light. 聲音傳導得比光慢。

---

21. **stop** [stɑp] v. (使) 停止；阻止 <from> (stopped | stopped | stopping)

▲ Willie stopped to help Elaine carry the heavy bag.
Willie 停下去幫忙 Elaine 提沉重的袋子。

💡 stop by (sth) 順道拜訪⋯

stop [stɑp] n. [C] 停止；車站

▲ The train came to a sudden stop. 火車突然停止。

---

22. **thin** [θɪn] adj. 薄的 [反] thick；瘦的 [反] fat (thinner | thinnest)

▲ Freda shivered with cold in her thin silk shirt.
Freda 穿著薄薄的絲質襯衫，冷得發抖。

💡 disappear/vanish into thin air 消失得無影無蹤

---

23. **today** [tə`de] adv. 今天；現今

▲ Ron couldn't go grocery shopping yesterday, but he will go today.

Ron 昨天無法去採買雜貨，但是他今天會去。

today [tə`de] n. [U] 今天

▲ Today is Mark's birthday. 今天是 Mark 的生日。

---

24. **wind** [wɪnd] n. [U][C] 風

▲ The wind is blowing at 10 miles per hour.

風正以每小時十英里的風速吹著。

wind [waɪnd] v. 彎彎曲曲，蜿蜒 <through>；使纏繞 <around> (wound | wound | winding)

▲ The stream winds through the forest.

小溪彎彎曲曲穿過森林。

---

25. **word** [wɝd] n. [C] 字，詞；簡短的談話 <of>

▲ Betty looked the Latin word up in a dictionary.

Betty 用字典查這個拉丁字的意思。

💡 eat sb's words 承認自己說錯話｜without a word 不發一言｜in a word 簡而言之

Unit 19

1. **another** [ə`nʌðɚ] adj. 再一個的；另外的

▲ Would you like to have another cup of tea?

你要不要再來一杯茶？

💡 one another 互相｜one after another 一個接一個

another [ə`nʌðɚ] pron. 再一個；另一回事，不同的人或

事物

▲ The woman finished her coffee and asked for another. 女子喝光了她的咖啡並再要了一杯。

2. **boy** [bɔɪ] n. [C] 男孩

▲ Jimmy is a five-year-old boy.
Jimmy 是個五歲的男孩。

3. **care** [kɛr] n. [U] 注意，小心 <with>；照顧

▲ The road was icy, so all the drivers drove with care.
道路結冰，所以所有的駕駛都小心駕駛。

💡 take care 保重 ｜ take care of... 照顧…

care [kɛr] v. 關心 <about>；在乎，在意 <about>

▲ The mother cared about her son so much that she hated to see him hurt.
那位媽媽如此關心她的兒子，以致於不想見到他受傷。

4. **common** [`kɑmən] adj. 共同的 ； 普通的 ， 常見的 [反] rare

▲ English serves as the common language of the world.
英文是世界的共同語言。

💡 common knowledge 常識

common [`kɑmən] n. [C] 公地，公用草地

▲ The locals have the great need for the use of the commons. 當地人很需要使用公用草地。

💡 have sth in common 有相同…

5. **difficult** [`dɪfə,kəlt] adj. 困難的，艱難的 [反] easy

▲ It is not easy to answer the difficult question.
要回答這個困難的問題並不容易。

---

6. **everyone** [`ɛvrɪ͵wʌn] **pron.** 每個人 [同] everybody

▲ The teacher gathered everyone together to take a group photograph.
老師把每個人集合在一起拍一張團體照。

everybody [`ɛvrɪ͵bɑdɪ] **pron.** 每個人 [同] everyone

▲ Everybody at the party was singing and dancing.
每個人在派對上都又唱又跳。

---

7. **free** [fri] **adj.** 自由的;免費的

▲ The country set some political prisoners free.
這個國家釋放了一些政治犯。

free [fri] **v.** 使自由,釋放 [同] release;使免於,使擺脫 <from>

▲ Finally, the terrorists agreed to free all the hostages.
最後,恐怖分子同意釋放所有人質。

🔮 free sb from sth 使…擺脫…

free [fri] **adv.** 自由地;免費地

▲ With all the charges against him dropped, the suspect walked free from court.
嫌犯因對他所有的指控都被撤銷而當庭獲釋。

🔮 for free/free of charge 免費地

---

8. **like** [laɪk] **prep.** 像;例如

▲ Danny looks very much like his father.
Danny 長得很像他爸爸。

like [laɪk] v. 喜歡 [反] dislike

▲ Claire likes fish, but she hates shrimp.

　Claire 喜歡吃魚，但她討厭吃蝦。

like [laɪk] n. [C] 喜好 (usu. pl.)

▲ Everyone has his or her own likes and dislikes.

　人各有好惡。

---

9. **quite** [kwaɪt] adv. 相當地；完全地，徹底地

▲ The weather is quite cold today. 今天天氣相當冷。

---

10. **same** [sem] adj. 相同的，一樣的 (the ～) <as>

▲ Your feet are the same size as mine.

　你的腳和我的腳一樣大。

same [sem] pron. 同樣的人或事物 (the ～)

▲ You treat me badly, so I will do the same to you someday.

　你待我不好，所以有一天我也會同樣回報你。

same [sem] adv. 同樣地 (the ～)

▲ The teacher treats all the students the same.

　這位老師對待所有的學生都一視同仁。

---

11. **shape** [ʃep] n. [C][U] 外形，形狀 <in>

▲ A rugby is oval in shape. 橄欖球是橢圓形的。

　💡 in the shape of sth 以…的形式｜in (good) shape 健康；狀況良好

---

12. **she** [ʃi] pron. 她

▲ When Della came, she brought some food and

drinks. Della 來的時候帶了一些食物和飲料。

her [hɚ] pron. 她的

▲ Jenny asked her son to clean the bathroom.

Jenny 要她兒子去打掃浴室。

hers [hɚz] pron. 她的 (所有物)

▲ Elva and I both have cars, but hers is an electric one.

Elva 和我都有車，但她的是電動車。

herself [hɚ`sɛlf] pron. 她自己

▲ The old lady talked to herself in a low voice.

那老婦人低聲地自言自語。

---

13. **sign** [saɪn] n. [C] 招牌，告示；跡象，徵兆 <of> [同]
indication

▲ What does that sign say? 那個告示牌上寫些什麼？

sign [saɪn] v. 簽署，簽字；示意 <to, for> [同] signal

▲ The patient has to sign a consent form before the
operation. 手術之前，這位病人得簽一份同意書。

---

14. **simple** [`sɪmpl] adj. 簡單的；樸素的

▲ The novel was written in simple English.

這本小說以簡易的英文寫成。

---

15. **sometimes** [`sʌm‚taɪmz] adv. 有時

▲ Sometimes Martin drinks coffee, and sometimes he
drinks tea. Martin 有時喝咖啡，有時喝茶。

---

16. **south** [saʊθ] n. [U] 南方，南部 (also South) (abbr. S)
(the ～)

▲ The sailors are sailing to the south now.

水手們現在正朝著南方航行。

south [savθ] **adj.** 南方的，南部的 (also South) (abbr. S)

▲ The south coast of the island is covered with palms.

這個島的南岸都是棕櫚樹。

south [savθ] **adv.** 朝南，向南 (abbr. S)

▲ Wild geese usually fly south before the winter comes. 野雁通常在冬天來臨前向南飛。

---

17. **space** [spes] **n.** [C][U] 空間；太空

▲ These magazines take up too much space on the shelf. 這些雜誌占了書架太多空間。

space [spes] **v.** 把…以一定間隔排列

▲ The five utility poles are spaced 20 feet apart.

這五個電線桿之間各相距二十英尺。

---

18. **sure** [ʃʊr] **adj.** 確定的，肯定的 <about, of> [同] certain

▲ Glen may come, but no one is sure about it.

Glen 也許會來，但沒有人確定。

💡 for sure 肯定的

sure [ʃʊr] **adv.** 當然

▲ "Would you please show me the way to the meeting room?" "Sure."

「可否麻煩告訴我會議室怎麼走？」「當然。」

---

19. **teacher** [ˋtitʃɚ] **n.** [C] 教師

▲ The teacher teaches English in a senior high school.

這位教師在一間高中教英文。

20. **town** [taʊn] n. [C] 城鎮
   ▲ The old couple live in a small town near the sea.
   這對老夫婦住在靠海的一個小鎮裡。

21. **try** [traɪ] v. 試圖，設法；嘗試 (tried | tried | trying)
   ▲ The girl tried to write with her left hand.
   那個女孩試圖用左手寫字。
   💡 try for sth 試圖獲得… | try sth on 試穿…
   try [traɪ] n. [C] 嘗試 (pl. tries)
   ▲ Let's give the recipe a try. 我們來試試這道食譜吧。

22. **understand** [ˌʌndɚˈstænd] v. 了解；理解，體諒
   (understood | understood | understanding)
   ▲ Gwen explained her idea again and again, but no one
   understood what she was talking about. Gwen 一次又
   一次解釋她的想法，但沒人了解她在說什麼。

23. **usually** [ˈjuʒʊəlɪ] adv. 通常地，經常地 [同] generally
   ▲ Jean usually gets up at 7 a.m.
   Jean 通常在早上七點起床。

24. **which** [hwɪtʃ] pron. 哪個
   ▲ Which is your hat, this one or that one?
   哪一頂是你的帽子，這頂還是那頂？
   which [hwɪtʃ] adj. 哪個
   ▲ Which street leads to the train station?

哪條街通往火車站？

25. **while** [hwaɪl] conj. 在…的時候；雖然 [同] although

▲ Mr. and Mrs. White were watching TV while their children were asleep.

White 夫婦在他們的孩子們睡覺時看電視。

while [hwaɪl] n. [sing.] 一會兒，一段時間

▲ Helen kept her friends waiting for a long while.

Helen 讓她的朋友們等了好一會兒。

while [hwaɪl] v. 消磨 (時光)，輕鬆地度過 <away>

▲ Steve whiled away the summer days fishing and hiking. Steve 以釣魚、健行輕鬆地度過夏日。

Unit 20

1. **again** [əˋgɛn] adv. 又，再一次；復原

▲ The book was so good that Mina wanted to read it again. 這本書好看到讓 Mina 想再讀一次。

🟡 once again 再次

---

2. **allow** [əˋlaʊ] v. 允許，准許 [同] permit；使有可能 [同] permit

▲ Eating and drinking are not allowed in the MRT trains and stations. 捷運車廂與站內禁止飲食。

---

3. **am** [ˋeˋɛm] adv. 上午 (also a.m.)

▲ The old man usually gets up at 6 am.

這位老先生通常早上六點起床。

4. **best** [bɛst] adj. 最好的，最優秀的 (the ～)

▲ Jack is by far the best player on the team.
　Jack 是這隊最優秀的球員。

best [bɛst] adv. 最好地

▲ Janice works best under pressure.
　Janice 有壓力時工作效率最好。

♥ had best + V 最好

best [bɛst] v. 擊敗，戰勝

▲ In two rounds, the boxer bested his opponent.
　那位拳擊手兩個回合內就擊敗了他的對手。

best [bɛst] n. [sing.] 最好的人或事物 (the ～)

▲ Most parents want the best for their children.
　多數父母都想把最好的東西給他們的孩子。

5. **can** [kæn] aux. 能，會；有可能

▲ The little girl can read and write.
　這個小女孩會讀也會寫。

♥ cannot help but + V = cannot help + V-ing 不得
　不… | cannot...too... 無論…也不為過；越…越好

can [kæn] n. [C] 罐 <of>

▲ Please bring me two cans of beer.
　請帶給我兩罐啤酒。

can [kæn] v. 將…裝罐 [同] tin (canned | canned |
canning)

▲ The fishermen canned the fish on the ship.

漁夫們在船上把魚裝罐。

6. **carry** [`kærɪ] v. 提，搬；攜帶 (carried │ carried │ carrying)

　▲ The box is too heavy for the girl to carry.
　　這個箱子太重，女孩搬不動。

　♥ carry on (sth) 繼續 │ carry sth out 執行…

7. **early** [`ɝlɪ] adj. 早期的，初期的 [反] late；提早的 [反] late (earlier │ earliest)

　▲ The rooster crowed in the early morning.
　　公雞在清晨啼叫。

　early [`ɝlɪ] adv. 在早期，在初期 [反] late；提早地 [反] late

　▲ Cathy woke up early in the morning.
　　Cathy 早上很早醒來。

8. **fact** [fækt] n. [C] 事實

　▲ People don't want rumors; tell them the facts.
　　人們不想聽傳言，告訴他們事實。

　♥ in fact 其實，事實上

9. **few** [fju] adj. 少數的，少許的 [反] many；一些

　▲ Only few people came to the party.
　　只有少許人來參加派對。

　♥ quite a few 相當多

　few [fju] pron. 少數的人或事物 <of> [反] many；一些人或事物 <of>

▲ Very few of the candidates come from foreign countries. 很少候選人來自國外。

10. **game** [gem] **n.** [C] 遊戲；比賽
   ▲ Tic-tac-toe is a fun game. 井字遊戲是有趣的遊戲。

11. **go** [go] **v.** 去 <to>；去 (參加) <to> (went｜gone｜going)
   ▲ The housewife goes to the market to buy food.
   這位家庭主婦去市場買食物。
   💡 go back to 追溯｜go by (時間等) 逝去
   go [go] **n.** [C] 嘗試 [同] try (pl. goes)
   ▲ Keith has never done that before, but he would like to give it a go.
   Keith 以前從沒做過那個，但是他想要試試。

12. **heat** [hit] **n.** [U] 熱，高溫
   ▲ The sun gives the world heat and light.
   太陽給這世界熱和光。
   heat [hit] **v.** (使) 變熱，(使) 變暖 <up>
   ▲ Joan heated up some water for coffee.
   Joan 加熱一些水來沖咖啡。

13. **ice** [aɪs] **n.** [U] 冰
   ▲ Water turns into ice at 0°C. 水在攝氏零度會結成冰。

14. **often** [ˋɔfən] **adv.** 經常 [同] frequently
   ▲ How often does Lewis go jogging?

Lewis 多久慢跑一次？

15. **other** [ˋʌðɚ] adj. 其他的，另外的；不同的，別的
▲ The soldiers have no other choice but to obey.
士兵們沒有其他的選擇，只能服從。
💡 other than 除了｜in other words 換句話說
other [ˋʌðɚ] pron. 另一個 (the ～)
▲ Mandy has two brothers. One is a lawyer, and the other is a doctor.
Mandy 有兩個兄弟。一個是律師，而另一個是醫生。

16. **own** [on] adj. 自己的
▲ Nicky wants to have his own room.
Nicky 想要有自己的房間。
own [on] pron. 自己 <of>
▲ Nicky wants to have a room of his own.
Nicky 想要有自己的房間。
💡 (all) on sb's own 獨自
own [on] v. 擁有
▲ Nellie owns this computer company.
Nellie 擁有這家電腦公司。

17. **race** [res] n. [C] 賽跑，速度競賽；種族，人種
▲ Paul won the championship in the running race.
Paul 在賽跑中得到冠軍。
race [res] v. (使) 參加比賽，與…比賽 <against>；(使) 快速移動或行進
▲ Paula used to race (against) her sister when they were

little. Paula 小時候常和妹妹賽跑。

18. **sing** [sɪŋ] v. 唱歌 <to> (sang｜sung｜singing)

▲ The mother sang a lullaby to the baby.
那個母親給寶寶唱了一首催眠曲。

19. **stay** [ste] v. 停留，留下；保持 (狀態)

▲ The colleagues stayed after work to play basketball.
同事們下班後留下來打籃球。

💡 stay away from... 遠離，避開…｜stay behind 留下不
走｜stay in 不出門｜stay out 在外過夜；晚歸｜stay
out of sth 不介入…｜stay up 熬夜

stay [ste] n. [C] 停留 <in> (usu. sing.)

▲ Randy met his future wife during his stay in Mexico.
Randy 在墨西哥停留期間遇見他未來的妻子。

20. **sunny** [ˋsʌnɪ] adj. 晴朗的，陽光普照的 [同] bright；樂觀
開朗的

▲ It is sunny today. 今天陽光普照。

21. **taste** [test] n. [C][U] 味道 <of> [同] flavor；(個人的) 愛
好，興趣 <in>

▲ The child doesn't like the taste of ginger.
這個孩子不喜歡薑的味道。

taste [test] v. 嘗…的味道

▲ The cook tasted the soup and found it was a bit salty.
廚師嘗了湯的味道並發現有點鹹。

22. **then** [ðɛn] adv. 然後；那時

▲ Steve watched TV and then went to bed.

Steve 看完電視，然後上床睡覺。

then [ðɛn] adj. 那時的

▲ Molly wanted to buy a van, but her then boyfriend preferred a truck.

Molly 想買廂型車，但她那時的男友比較喜歡卡車。

23. **traffic** [`træfɪk] n. [U] 交通；非法交易 <in>

▲ The traffic is heavy on the street now.

現在街上交通繁忙。

traffic [`træfɪk] v. 非法交易 (trafficked | trafficked | trafficking)

▲ Two men were arrested for trafficking in drugs.

兩個男子因非法交易毒品而被捕。

24. **visit** [`vɪzɪt] v. 拜訪，參觀

▲ Sandra visits her grandparents once in a while.

Sandra 偶爾拜訪她的祖父母。

visit [`vɪzɪt] n. [C] 拜訪，參觀 <from>

▲ Yesterday, Timmy had a visit from his uncle.

昨天，Timmy 的叔叔來看他。

💡 pay sb a visit 拜訪⋯

25. **west** [wɛst] n. [U] 西方，西部 (also West) (abbr. W) (the ~) <in>

▲ The sun set in the west. 太陽西下了。

west [wɛst] adj. 西方的，西部的 (also West) (abbr. W)

▲ The ride starts on the west coast of Taiwan and ends

on the east coast. 這趟騎行始於臺灣西岸，終至東岸。

west [wɛst] adv. 朝西，向西 (abbr. W)

▲ The house faces west. 這棟房子面向西方。

Unit 21

1. **ask** [æsk] v. 詢問 <about>；要求 <for>

   ▲ Helen asked the tour guide about the history of the tower. Helen 詢問導遊關於這座塔的歷史。

2. **bored** [bord] adj. 感到無聊的，感到厭煩的 <with>

   ▲ Melody is getting bored with her job and thinking of quitting it.

   Melody 對她的工作感到厭煩，正考慮要辭職。

3. **cent** [sɛnt] n. [C] 分 (一美元的百分之一)

   ▲ The pear is one dollar and twenty-nine cents per pound. 這梨一磅是一元二十九分。

4. **copy** [ˋkɑpɪ] n. [C] 複印；本，份 (pl. copies)

   ▲ Jayden made a copy of his report before handing it to his teacher. Jayden 把報告交給老師之前先複印一份。

   copy [ˋkɑpɪ] v. 複印；仿效 (copied | copied | copying)

   ▲ Copy this document and send it to Chris, please.
   麻煩請複印這份文件，然後寄給 Chris。

5. **drum** [drʌm] n. [C] 鼓

   ▲ Darren plays the drum in the band.
   Darren 在樂隊中擔任鼓手。

drum [drʌm] v. (使) 敲打 (drummed | drummed | drumming)

▲ The heavy rain kept drumming loudly against the window. 滂沱大雨不斷地大聲敲打窗戶。

💡 drum sth into sb 反覆向…灌輸…

6. **foot** [fʊt] n. [C] 腳；英尺 (abbr. ft) (pl. feet)

▲ Ducks have webbed feet. 鴨子的腳有蹼。

foot [fʊt] v. 支付 (帳單或費用)

▲ Whenever Nina and her boyfriend go to a restaurant, it is always her boyfriend that foots the bill.

每次 Nina 和她男友去餐廳吃飯時，總是她男友付帳。

7. **glasses** [ˋglæsɪz] n. [pl.] 眼鏡 [同] spectacles

▲ My father put on his glasses to read the newspaper. 我的父親戴上眼鏡看報紙。

8. **goodbye** [ˌɡʊdˋbaɪ] n. [C] 道別，告別

▲ The student went home after saying goodbye to his teacher. 這學生向老師道別後就回家了。

9. **homework** [ˋhom͵wɝk] n. [U] 功課，作業

▲ Willie always does his homework before dinner. Willie 總是在吃晚餐前做功課。

10. **hospital** [ˋhɑspɪtl] n. [C] 醫院

▲ The injured man was taken by ambulance to hospital. 那名受傷的男子被救護車送到醫院。

11. **mad** [mæd] adj. 發瘋的 ；生氣的 <at, with> (madder | maddest)

▲ Richard must be mad to spend so much money on the antique.

Richard 一定是瘋了才會花那麼多錢在那古董上。

12. **medium** [`midɪəm] adj. 中等的；(肉) 中等熟度的

▲ Does the T-shirt come in medium?

這件 T 恤有中等大小的嗎？

13. **meeting** [`mitɪŋ] n. [C] 會面；會議

▲ I've not seen Diana for more than ten years since our last meeting. 自從我們上次會面以來 ，我已經超過十年沒見過 Diana 了。

💡 call/attend/chair a meeting 安排 / 參加 / 主持會議

14. **O.K.** [o`ke] adj. 同意的 (also OK, okay) <with, by> [同] all right；不錯的，令人滿意的

▲ I'll go on vacation if it is O.K. with my boss.

如果我老闆同意的話，我就會去渡假。

O.K. [ˌo`ke] adv. 還不錯 (also OK, okay)

▲ Everything has gone O.K. so far.

一切到目前為止還算不錯。

O.K. [ˌo`ke] n. [sing.] 同意 ，批准 (also OK, okay) (the ~)

▲ Sophia got the O.K. to leave early today.

Sophia 今天獲准可以早退。

O.K. [ˌo`ke] v. 同意 ，批准 (also OK, okay) (O.K.'d |

O.K.'d | O.K.'ing)

▲ To my surprise, the manager O.K.'d my plan.
令我驚訝的是，經理同意我的計畫。

---

15. **piano** [pɪˋæno] n. [C] 鋼琴

▲ Carol can play the piano very well.
Carol 鋼琴彈得很好。

---

16. **question** [ˋkwɛstʃən] n. [C] 問題 [反] answer

▲ If you have any questions, you may raise your hand.
如果你有任何問題可以舉手。

💡 without question 毫無疑問

question [ˋkwɛstʃən] v. 詢問，盤問

▲ The police are questioning the suspect.
警方正在偵訊嫌犯。

---

17. **sale** [sel] n. [C][U] 出售；降價銷售

▲ The sale of guns is illegal in the country.
販賣槍枝在這個國家是違法的。

---

18. **send** [sɛnd] v. 送，郵寄；派遣 (sent | sent | sending)

▲ Henry sent his mother a card on Mother's Day.
Henry 在母親節那天送他媽媽一張卡片。

---

19. **sofa** [ˋsofə] n. [C] 沙發 [同] couch

▲ Kayla was so tired that she fell asleep on the sofa.
Kayla 非常累以致於在沙發上睡著了。

---

20. **thousand** [ˋθauzn̩d] n. (數字) 千 (pl. thousand,

thousands)

▲ After the police officer requested information, thousands of letters poured in.
警官要求提供線索後，數以千計的信湧入。

thousand [ˋθauznd] adj. 千

▲ There are more than one thousand applicants for the job. 那份工作的申請人超過一千個。

---

21. **tooth** [tuθ] n. [C] 牙齒 (pl. teeth)

▲ Jim is used to brushing his teeth after each meal.
Jim 習慣在每餐飯後刷牙。

---

22. **trouble** [ˋtrʌbl] n. [C][U] 問題，麻煩；[U] 險境，困境

▲ The disabled sometimes have trouble finding jobs.
身心障礙者有時找工作很困難。

trouble [ˋtrʌbl] v. 使困擾，使憂慮

▲ Jill looks absent-minded; there seems to be something troubling her.
Jill 看起來心不在焉，似乎有某事困擾著她。

---

23. **voice** [vɔɪs] n. [C][U] 聲音，嗓音；意見的表達

▲ The teacher raised his voice because of the noise from the road.
由於馬路上傳來的噪音，老師提高了他的音量。

---

24. **wave** [wev] n. [C] 波浪；(情緒等的) 突發 <of>

▲ We watched the waves crashing against the shore.
我們看著海浪拍擊海岸。

wave [wev] v. 揮手 <to, at>

▲ At the sight of her boyfriend, Jessie smiled and waved to him.

Jessie 一看到她的男友便對他微笑揮手。

25. **worry** [ˋwɝɪ] v. (使) 擔心 <about> (worried | worried | worrying)

▲ More and more consumers are worrying about food safety. 越來越多消費者擔心食安問題。

worry [ˋwɝɪ] n. [C][U] 擔憂，煩惱

▲ Try to forget your worries and relax.

試著忘掉你的煩惱，放輕鬆。

Unit 22

1. **breakfast** [ˋbrɛkfəst] n. [C][U] 早餐

▲ You should eat a full breakfast before starting on your journey. 你應在啟程前好好享用一頓早餐。

breakfast [ˋbrɛkfəst] v. 吃早餐 <on>

▲ Juan breakfasted on bread and milk this morning.

Juan 今天早上早餐吃麵包配牛奶。

2. **bright** [braɪt] adj. 明亮的 [反] dull；(顏色) 鮮豔的

▲ Anna was born on a bright summer morning.

Anna 在晴朗的夏天早晨出生。

💡 look on the bright side (of things) 看事物的光明面

bright [braɪt] adv. 明亮地

3. **cheese** [tʃiz] n. [U] 起司，乳酪
▲ Bobby ate a lot of cheese for protein.
Bobby 吃很多起司以補充蛋白質。

4. **corner** [ˋkɔrnɚ] n. [C] 街角；角落 <on, in>
▲ Vera's house is on the corner of Maple Street and Sixth Avenue.
Vera 的家在楓樹街和第六大道的轉角處。
💡 (just) around/round the corner 在路口；即將到來

5. **duck** [dʌk] n. [C] 鴨子；[U] 鴨肉
▲ The duck and its ducklings are swimming in the little pond. 那隻鴨子和其小鴨在小池中游水。
duck [dʌk] v. (為避免被擊中或發現而) 低頭或彎腰 <down>
▲ The girl ducked down in order not to be hit by the ball. 那女孩低頭以免被球打到。
duckling [ˋdʌklɪŋ] n. [C] 小鴨
▲ In the fairy tale, the ugly duckling turned into a swan in the end. 在這個童話故事中，醜小鴨最後變成天鵝。

6. **grandfather** [ˋgræn͵faðɚ] n. [C] (外) 祖父
▲ Emily named her son after her grandfather in memory of him.
Emily 以她祖父之名為兒子命名，以紀念他。

7. **hobby** [ˋhɑbɪ] n. [C] 嗜好 (pl. hobbies)

▲ William's hobby is reading and collecting comic books. William 的嗜好是看和收集漫畫。

8. **honey** [ˈhʌnɪ] n. [U] 蜂蜜

▲ The cook spread the lamb chops with honey before grilling them. 那位廚師在烤羊排之前先塗蜂蜜。

9. **hour** [aʊr] n. [C] 小時

▲ The bank clerk works eight hours a day.
那名銀行行員一天工作八個小時。

10. **lake** [lek] n. [C] 湖泊

▲ Ella used to swim in the lake in her childhood.
Ella 小時候常在那個湖裡游泳。

11. **magic** [ˈmædʒɪk] adj. 魔法的；魔術的

▲ The princess became an old woman after the witch put a magic spell on her.
公主在女巫對她施魔咒後變成一位老婦人。

magic [ˈmædʒɪk] n. [U] 魔法；魔術

▲ It was said that the old man was able to use magic to cure ill people.
據說那名老人能使用魔法治癒生病的人。

💡 work like magic 非常有效

12. **minute** [ˈmɪnɪt] n. [C] 分鐘；片刻，一會兒

▲ The movie will start in ten minutes, so we have to hurry up.
電影再過十分鐘就要開始了，所以我們要快點。

💡 the last minute 最後一刻

---

13. **moon** [mun] n. [sing.] 月亮 (the ～)

▲ The moon rose at 6:30 p.m. tonight.
今晚月亮在晚上六點半升起。

💡 once in a blue moon 很少地

---

14. **o'clock** [ə`klɑk] adv. …點鐘

▲ Debra goes to bed at ten o'clock every night.
Debra 每晚十點鐘上床睡覺。

---

15. **picnic** [`pɪknɪk] n. [C] 野餐

▲ Since it's a sunny day, why don't we go on a picnic?
既然今天天氣晴朗，我們何不去野餐？

picnic [`pɪknɪk] v. 去野餐 (picnicked | picnicked | picnicking)

▲ There are a lot of families picnicking in the park.
有很多家庭正在公園野餐。

---

16. **read** [rid] v. 閱讀；讀出，朗讀 (read | read | reading)

▲ Harper enjoys reading romantic novels at leisure.
Harper 喜愛在閒暇時讀浪漫小說。

reader [`ridɚ] n. [C] 讀者

▲ The author impressed readers with his creative imagination.
那名作者以其充滿創意的想像力讓讀者印象深刻。

---

17. **seat** [sit] n. [C] 座位；席位

▲ "Is this seat occupied?" "No, please have a seat."

「這位子有人坐嗎?」「沒有,請坐。」

seat [sit] v. 給⋯安排座位

▲ After the guests were seated, the dinner began.
客人就座後,晚餐就開始。

---

18. **somewhere** [ˋsʌmˌhwɛr] adv. 在某處

▲ I can't find my umbrella; I must have left it somewhere.
我找不到我的雨傘,我一定是把它留在某處了。

---

19. **sugar** [ˋʃʊgɚ] n. [U] 糖

▲ Stella likes to drink coffee without sugar.
Stella 喜歡喝咖啡不加糖。

---

20. **useful** [ˋjusfəl] adj. 有用的,有助益的 [反] useless

▲ The website provides several useful tips for building muscles. 這網站提供一些鍛鍊肌肉的有用訣竅。

useless [ˋjuslɪs] adj. 無用的 [反] useful

▲ I find the information in the book completely useless.
我覺得這本書裡的資訊完全無用。

---

21. **visitor** [ˋvɪzɪtɚ] n. [C] 參觀者,遊客

▲ The tourist attraction is full of visitors all year round.
那個旅遊景點一年到頭都有絡繹不絕的遊客。

---

22. **watch** [wɑtʃ] v. 觀看,注視;小心,留意

▲ The boy watched as the snake swallowed a frog.
男孩觀看蛇吞下青蛙。

💡 watch over sth 照看⋯

watch [wɑtʃ] n. [C] 手錶；[U][sing.] 觀察，監視 <on, over> (pl. watches)

▲ My watch keeps good time. 我的手錶很準確。

---

23. **weak** [wik] adj. 虛弱的；懦弱的，無決斷力的

▲ Mary is getting weaker because of breast cancer.
Mary 因乳癌而日漸虛弱。

weakness [`wiknɪs] n. [U] 虛弱 <in>；[C] 缺點 (pl. weaknesses)

▲ The disease may cause weakness in legs.
這個疾病可能會造成腿部無力。

---

24. **wonderful** [`wʌndɚfəl] adj. 美好的，愉快的 [同] great

▲ Violet and her family had a wonderful time in France.
Violet 和家人在法國度過了一段很美好的時光。

---

25. **write** [raɪt] v. 寫；(給…) 寫信 <to> (wrote | written | writing)

▲ Ben wrote a note to remind himself to pay the phone bill. Ben 寫紙條以提醒自己要繳電話帳單。

🦚 write sth down 寫下…

Unit 23

1. **bear** [bɛr] v. 忍受 [同] stand；負載 [同] hold (bore | born, borne | bearing)

▲ The patient couldn't bear the pain and asked for a painkiller. 那病人痛得受不了而要求止痛藥。

bear [bɛr] n. [C] 熊

▲ There are many bears living in that forest.
那座森林裡住著許多熊。

---

2. **bus** [bʌs] n. [C] 公車 <by> (pl. buses)

▲ Todd went to the science museum by bus.
Todd 搭公車去科博館。

---

3. **chance** [tʃæns] n. [C] 機會 [同] opportunity；[C][U] 可能性

▲ Mr. Clark goes fishing whenever he gets the chance.
Clark 先生一有機會就去釣魚。

💡 take a chance 冒險

chance [tʃæns] v. 冒險

▲ We should find a shelter instead of chancing our luck in the thunderstorm.
我們應該找個遮蔽處，而不是在暴風雨中冒險。

---

4. **clerk** [klɝk] n. [C] 職員；店員 [同] salesclerk

▲ If you need any help, please contact me at the clerks' office.
如果你需要幫助，可以打電話到職員辦公室給我。

---

5. **cross** [krɔs] n. [C] 十字圖案；十字架

▲ The red cross on the map shows where our destination is. 地圖上的紅十字代表我們的目的地。

cross [krɔs] **v.** 穿越，越過；使交叉

▲ Be careful when you cross the road.
過馬路時要小心。

🔆 cross sb's fingers 祈求好運

---

6. **error** [ˋɛrɚ] **n.** [C][U] 錯誤 <in>

▲ The teacher pointed out the typing errors in Dorothy's report.
老師指出 Dorothy 報告中的打字錯誤。

---

7. **guess** [gɛs] **v.** 猜測，推測

▲ I don't know the answer, so I will just guess.
我不知道答案，所以我只能去猜。

🔆 guess at sth 猜測… | I guess... 我認為…

guess [gɛs] **n.** [C] 猜測，推測

▲ Take a guess at how much the coat cost.
猜看看這件大衣多少錢。

---

8. **housewife** [ˋhaʊsˌwaɪf] **n.** [C] 家庭主婦 [同] homemaker (pl. housewives)

▲ Is it fair that a housewife has to do all the housework without being paid?
家庭主婦要做所有的家事又沒有薪水，這公平嗎？

---

9. **interview** [ˋɪntɚˌvju] **n.** [C] 面試；採訪

▲ Amelia will have a job interview two days later.
Amelia 兩天後有求職面試。

interview [ˋɪntɚˌvju] **v.** 對…進行面試；採訪

▲ Graham will be interviewed for the job.

Graham 將接受這個工作面試。

___

10. **key** [ki] adj. 極重要的，關鍵性的

▲ You are missing the key point in my presentation.

你沒抓到我報告的要點。

key [ki] n. [C] 鑰匙；祕訣 <to>

▲ Molly is looking for her car key everywhere in the house. Molly 正在房子四處找她的車鑰匙。

key [ki] v. 用鍵盤輸入 (訊息) <in>

▲ Zoe keyed in the code to get a discount on her order.

Zoe 輸入代碼以讓她訂購的東西打折。

___

11. **laugh** [læf] v. 笑

▲ The girls were laughing loudly in the café.

這些女孩們在咖啡店裡放聲大笑。

laugh [læf] n. [C] 笑，笑聲

▲ The teacher's joke raised a laugh in the whole class.

老師的笑話引起全班哄堂大笑。

___

12. **milk** [mɪlk] n. [U] 乳，牛奶

▲ Cole drinks a glass of milk every morning.

Cole 每天早上都喝一杯牛奶。

___

13. **neck** [nɛk] n. [C] 脖子，頸；領口，衣領

▲ Yvonne wore a scarf around her neck.

Yvonne 在脖子上圍了一條圍巾。

___

14. **officer** [ˋɔfɪsɚ] n. [C] 軍官；警官 [同] police officer

▲ Soldiers must obey their officers. 士兵必須服從長官。

15. **parent** [`pɛrənt] n. [C] 父母中的一人

▲ Ryder grew up in a single-parent family.
Ryder 在單親家庭中長大。

parents [`pɛrənts] n. [pl.] 父母親

▲ Naomi lost her parents in the earthquake.
Naomi 在地震中失去雙親。

16. **polite** [pə`laɪt] adj. 有禮貌的 [反] impolite, rude

▲ It is not polite to ask people about their age or income. 詢問別人的年齡或收入很沒禮貌。

politely [pə`laɪtlɪ] adv. 有禮貌地 [反] impolitely

▲ The gentleman always talks to ladies politely.
這位紳士對女士說話總是很有禮貌。

politeness [pə`laɪtnɪs] n. [U] 禮貌 [反] impoliteness

▲ The host's politeness made me feel a little uncomfortable. 主人客氣得令我覺得有點不自在。

17. **relative** [`rɛlətɪv] adj. 比較的；有關的 <to>

▲ Thomas is considering the relative merits of the insurance schemes.
Thomas 正在權衡這些保險方案彼此的優點。

relative [`rɛlətɪv] n. [C] 親戚 [同] relation

▲ Amy is a relative on my mother's side.
Amy 是我母親那邊的親戚。

relatively [`rɛlətɪvlɪ] adv. 相對地

▲ Although the eco-friendly car costs more, it

consumes relatively less fuel.

雖然這臺環保車比較貴，但它相對地比較省油。

---

18. **sheep** [ʃip] **n.** [C] 羊，綿羊 (pl. sheep)

▲ The sheep are raised for their fine soft wool.

飼養這些綿羊是為了取其優良又柔軟的羊毛。

---

19. **sore** [sor] **adj.** 疼痛的 <from>

▲ Chuck's shoulders were sore from carrying the heavy backpack all day.

Chuck 因為一整天背著這沉重的背包而肩膀疼痛。

sore [sor] **n.** [C] 瘡

▲ The stray dog is covered with sores.

這隻流浪狗身上布滿了瘡。

---

20. **topic** [ˋtɑpɪk] **n.** [C] 主題，話題 <of>

▲ The arrival of the new baby has been the main topic of conversation in our house for weeks. 新生嬰兒的來臨是我們家這幾個禮拜以來主要的話題。

---

21. **wake** [wek] **v.** 醒來 <up>；喚醒 (woke | woken | waking)

▲ It was almost noon when Samantha woke (up).

Samantha 醒來時已經近中午了。

💡 wake sb up 叫醒… | wake up to sth 開始意識到…

---

22. **wet** [wɛt] **adj.** 溼的 <with>

▲ The leaves are still wet with rain.

葉子因雨水仍是溼溼的。

wet [wɛt] v. 把⋯弄溼 (wetted | wetted | wetting)

▲ Shelly wetted the handkerchief with some water.
Shelly 用一些水把手帕浸溼。

23. **yard** [jɑrd] n. [C] 碼；院子

▲ A yard is equal to approximately 91 centimeters.
一碼大約是九十一公分。

24. **yellow** [`jɛlo] adj. 黃色的

▲ The leaves turned yellow in autumn.
這些葉子在秋天變成黃色。

yellow [`jɛlo] n. [C][U] 黃色

▲ Yellow made Poppy look young and lively.
黃色讓 Poppy 看起來年輕、有活力。

yellow [`jɛlo] v. (使) 變黃

▲ The wallpaper had yellowed and needed to be
replaced. 這些壁紙已經變黃，需要更換了。

25. **zoo** [zu] n. [C] 動物園

▲ There are about 800 species of animals in the zoo.
這個動物園裡有大約八百種動物。

Unit 24

1. **action** [`ækʃən] n. [U] 行動；[C] 行為

▲ You should take action to solve the problem as soon
as possible. 你應該盡快採取行動解決這個問題。

2. **add** [æd] v. 添加，增加 <to>；相加

▲ Clark added a little sugar to his tea.
Clark 在茶裡加了些許糖。

💡 add up to sth 合計為…

---

3. **afternoon** [ˌæftɚˋnun] n. [C][U] 下午

▲ My grandfather always takes a nap in the afternoon.
我爺爺在下午總是會小憩一下。

---

4. **airplane** [ˋɛrˌplen] n. [C] 飛機 [同] plane

▲ The airplane will be taking off in ten minutes.
飛機將在十分鐘後起飛。

---

5. **begin** [bɪˋgɪn] v. 開始；著手 (began | begun | beginning)

▲ The conference will begin at 2:30 p.m. tomorrow.
會議將在明天下午兩點三十分開始。

💡 to begin with 剛開始的時候；首先

beginning [bɪˋgɪnɪŋ] n. [C] 開頭，開端 (usu. sing.)

▲ The chairman will give a speech at the beginning of the workshop. 主席在研討會一開始會先演講。

---

6. **cap** [kæp] n. [C] (有帽舌的) 便帽；蓋子 [同] top

▲ The driver tipped his baseball cap to greet me.
司機微舉他的棒球帽向我打招呼。

cap [kæp] v. 覆蓋…的頂部 (capped | capped | capping)

▲ The mountain is capped with snow.

這山的山頂被雪覆蓋。

---

7. **cloud** [klaʊd] n. [C] 雲；陰影

▲ The dark clouds in the sky indicate it's going to rain.
天空中的烏雲意味著快下雨了。

---

8. **cup** [kʌp] n. [C] (帶有柄的) 杯子；獎盃

▲ A cup of hot tea can make you warm on a cold day.
一杯熱茶能讓你在寒冷的天氣暖和起來。

💡 not be sb's cup of tea 非…所好

---

9. **dance** [dæns] n. [C] 舞蹈；(正式的) 舞會

▲ The audience clapped the dance group's performance
enthusiastically. 觀眾為這舞蹈團體的表演熱烈鼓掌。

dance [dæns] v. 跳舞 <to>

▲ As soon as Rosa heard her favorite song, she started
to dance to it.
Rosa 一聽到她最喜愛的歌曲就隨著音樂跳舞。

---

10. **evening** [ˋivnɪŋ] n. [C][U] 傍晚，晚上

▲ Isaac will leave for Paris this evening.
Isaac 今晚出發前往巴黎。

---

11. **hate** [het] v. 憎恨 [反] love

▲ Most people hate to be criticized.
大部分的人討厭被批評。

hate [het] n. [U] 憎恨 [同] hatred [反] love

▲ Racism always arouses blind and bitter hate.

種族主義總是激起盲目痛苦的仇恨。

12. **I** [aɪ] pron. 我 (第一人稱單數主格)

▲ I am a high school student. 我是中學生。

me [mi] pron. 我 (I 的受格)

▲ Uncle Tom gave me a watch as a Christmas gift.
Tom 叔叔給我一只手錶作為耶誕禮物。

my [maɪ] pron. 我的 (I 的所有格)

▲ My parents always encourage me to pursue my dreams. 我的父母總是鼓勵我去追求夢想。

mine [maɪn] pron. 我的 (所有物)

▲ Winnie's new smartphone is the same as mine.
Winnie 新買的智慧型手機跟我的一樣。

myself [maɪˋsɛlf] pron. (反身代名詞) 我自己

▲ I always tell myself to live at the present moment.
我總是告訴我自己要活在當下。

💡 (all) by myself 單獨；獨自

13. **invite** [ɪnˋvaɪt] v. 邀請；請求

▲ The firm invited some pop singers to perform at their year-end party.
這間公司邀請一些流行歌手在他們的尾牙表演。

inviting [ɪnˋvaɪtɪŋ] adj. 吸引人的

▲ The cabin by the lake looks inviting.
那間湖濱小屋看起來很吸引人。

14. **leg** [lɛg] n. [C] 腿

▲ Austin broke his leg while playing basketball.

Austin 在打籃球時摔斷腿。

---

15. **medicine** [ˈmɛdəsn̩] n. [C][U] 藥物;[U] 醫學
   ▲ The patient was told to take the medicine after each meal. 這病人被叮嚀每餐飯後要吃藥。

---

16. **mouse** [maʊs] n. [C] 老鼠;滑鼠 (pl. mice)
   ▲ Natalie fainted at the sight of a mouse.
   Natalie 一看見老鼠就昏倒了。

---

17. **net** [nɛt] n. [C][U] 網子,網狀物
   ▲ The fisherman tried to cast a net and catch some fish.
   漁夫試著撒網捕一些魚。
   net [nɛt] v. 用網捕 (netted | netted | netting)
   ▲ Mr. Fox netted a lot of fish this morning.
   Fox 先生今天早上用網子捕了很多魚。

---

18. **pen** [pɛn] n. [C] 筆
   ▲ Could you lend me a ballpoint pen?
   你可以借我一枝原子筆嗎?
   pen [pɛn] v. 用筆寫 (penned | penned | penning)
   ▲ The guest penned a thank-you card to the host.
   這客人寫了一張感謝卡給主人。

---

19. **please** [pliz] v. 取悅
   ▲ Eason tried everything possible to please his girlfriend. Eason 想盡一切辦法討好女友。

---

20. **remember** [rɪˈmɛmbɚ] v. 想起;記得

▲ Kelly can't remember the exact place where she and her husband first met.

Kelly 想不起來她和她丈夫第一次見面的確切地點。

remembrance [rɪ`mɛmbrəns] n. [U] 紀念，懷念

▲ The monument was erected in remembrance of the soldiers killed in the war.

這個紀念碑的豎立是為了緬懷在戰爭中喪生的軍人。

---

21. **row** [ro] n. [C] 一排，一列

▲ Emily grinned, showing a row of white teeth.

Emily 咧嘴笑，露出一排潔白的牙齒。

row [ro] v. 划 (船)

▲ I'll row you across the river. 我會划船送你到對岸。

---

22. **skirt** [skɝt] n. [C] 裙子

▲ Judy wore a white T-shirt and a pink skirt today.

Judy 今天穿了一件白色 T 恤和粉色裙子。

---

23. **sorry** [`sɔrɪ] adj. 感到抱歉的 <for>；難過的，惋惜的

▲ I am very sorry for my carelessness.

我對我的疏忽感到抱歉。

---

24. **touch** [tʌtʃ] n. [C] 觸摸 (usu. sing.)

▲ Nina screamed when feeling a cold touch on her back.

Nina 覺得有冰涼的東西觸碰她的背而尖叫出來。

🔔 keep in touch (with sb) (和⋯) 保持聯絡

touch [tʌtʃ] v. 觸摸；感動

▲ Nick touched the cup to see if it was hot.
Nick 觸摸杯子看看它是不是燙的。

25. **zero** [ˋzɪro] **n.** [C][U] (數字) 零 [同] nought；[U] 零度
▲ Five minus five equals zero. 五減五等於零。

Unit 25

1. **afraid** [əˋfred] **adj.** 害怕的 <of> [同] scared；擔心的
▲ The kid is afraid of being alone in the house.
這孩子害怕自己待在家裡。

2. **ant** [ænt] **n.** [C] 螞蟻
▲ Jamie found it interesting to watch ants moving objects. Jamie 覺得看螞蟻搬東西很有趣。

3. **anything** [ˋɛnɪˏθɪŋ] **pron.** 任何事物
▲ Nicole helped the poor woman without asking for anything in return.
Nicole 幫助這個貧窮的婦人而不求任何回報。
💡 or anything 或是其他什麼類似的

4. **apartment** [əˋpɑrtmənt] **n.** [C] 公寓
▲ Vincent rented an apartment near his office.
Vincent 在辦公室附近租了一間公寓。

5. **arm** [ɑrm] **n.** [C] 手臂
▲ The mother took her baby in her arms.

這位母親將嬰兒抱在懷中。

arm [ɑrm] v. 為…提供武器裝備 <with>

▲ The army was armed with the latest chemical weapons. 那支軍隊配備最新的化學武器。

6. **below** [bɪ`lo] adv. 在下面 [反] above

▲ The climbers found a lake far below.
登山客發現下方深處有一個湖。

below [bɪ`lo] prep. (位置) 在…之下；低於 [反] above

▲ The sun went below the horizon. 太陽落到地平線下。

7. **card** [kɑrd] n. [C] 卡片；紙牌

▲ Paige lost her credit card during her trip in Japan.
Paige 在日本旅遊時遺失了信用卡。

8. **cousin** [`kʌzn] n. [C] 堂 (表) 兄弟姊妹

▲ I like all of my family members except for my cousin, George.
我喜歡所有的家庭成員，除了我的表弟 George 之外。

9. **dangerous** [`dendʒərəs] adj. 危險的

▲ A little learning is a dangerous thing.
【諺】學藝不精反誤事。

10. **date** [det] n. [C] 日期；約會

▲ The closing date for the job application is October 31st. 應徵這份工作的截止日期是十月三十一日。

date [det] v. 在…標明日期；與…約會 [同] go out with

▲ The report is dated April 5th.

這份報告的日期是四月五日。

11. **exciting** [ɪkˋsaɪtɪŋ] **adj.** 令人興奮的，刺激的
    ▲ I think it is exciting to watch horror movies at midnight. 我覺得半夜看鬼片很刺激。

12. **headache** [ˋhɛd͵ek] **n.** [C] 頭痛；令人頭痛的事
    ▲ Shane has got a bad headache, so he will be absent from work today.
    Shane 頭痛得很厲害，所以他今天不會去上班。

13. **inch** [ɪntʃ] **n.** [C] 英寸
    ▲ Eli's feet are nine inches long. Eli 的腳有九英寸長。

14. **king** [kɪŋ] **n.** [C] 國王，君主 (also King)
    ▲ Once upon a time, there lived a king and his daughter in the castle.
    很久以前，有一個國王和他女兒住在那城堡裡。

15. **lion** [ˋlaɪən] **n.** [C] 獅子
    ▲ *The Lion King* is one of the most famous Disney animated films.
    《獅子王》是迪士尼最有名的動畫電影之一。

16. **mistake** [mɪˋstek] **n.** [C] 錯誤 <in>
    ▲ Melvin found some spelling mistakes in the document. Melvin 發現這份文件有一些拼字錯誤。
    💡 by mistake 錯誤地
    mistake [mɪˋstek] **v.** 誤認 <for> (mistook | mistaken |

mistaking)

▲ It was embarrassing for Polly to mistake Mike for his brother. Polly 將 Mike 誤認為是他哥哥，真是尷尬。

17. **nobody** [`no͵bɑdɪ] pron. 沒有人

▲ It seems that nobody lives in this house.
這間房子好像沒人住。

nobody [`no͵bɑdɪ] n. [C] 小人物，無名小卒 (pl. nobodies)

▲ The wealthy man won't allow his daughter to marry a nobody. 那名富人不允許女兒嫁給無名小卒。

18. **noisy** [`nɔɪzɪ] adj. 吵雜的，喧鬧的 [反] quiet

▲ Mrs. Hanks was sleepless due to her noisy neighbors.
Hanks 太太因為吵雜的鄰居而睡不著。

19. **pie** [paɪ] n. [C][U] 派，餡餅

▲ My mother is baking an apple pie in the kitchen.
我的母親正在廚房烤蘋果派。

♥ pie in the sky 不切實際的事

20. **police** [pə`lis] n. [pl.] 警方，警察當局 (the ∼)

▲ Oliver reported his stolen car to the police.
Oliver 向警方報案車子失竊。

police [pə`lis] v. 在⋯部署警力，維持⋯的治安

▲ The president's visit to the Middle East was heavily policed. 總統出訪中東有嚴密部署的警力。

21. **round** [raʊnd] adj. 圓形的

▲ The girl with a round face and brown hair is my cousin. 那個圓臉、棕髮的女孩是我表妹。

round [raʊnd] n. [C] 一系列的事件 <of>

▲ The two countries decided to conduct another round of peace talks as soon as possible.

這兩個國家決定要盡快進行另一輪的和平會談。

round [raʊnd] adv. 四處，到處 [同] around

▲ After Danny checked in at the hostel, the clerk showed him round.

Danny 在旅社登記入住後，職員就帶他到處看看。

round [raʊnd] prep. 在…周圍，圍繞 [同] around

▲ There is a high wall round Mr. Marshall's house.

Marshall 先生家四周有高聳的圍牆。

round [raʊnd] v. 繞過

▲ The runner rounded the corner and headed for the finish line. 這位跑者繞過轉角後就直奔終點線。

---

22. **rule** [rul] n. [C] 規則 (usu. pl.)；[U] 統治 (期) <under>

▲ Those who break the school rules will be punished.

違反校規的人會被處罰。

rule [rul] v. 統治，治理；支配，操控

▲ The king ruled his country with an iron fist.

那國王以鐵腕政策治理國家。

---

23. **smoke** [smok] n. [U] (燃燒所產生的) 煙，煙霧

▲ There is no smoke without fire. 【諺】無風不起浪。

smoke [smok] v. 抽菸

▲ Noah was fined for smoking in public.

Noah 因為在公眾場合抽菸而被罰款。

24. **spell** [spɛl] v. 拼寫 (spelt, spelled | spelt, spelled | spelling)

▲ The little boy has difficulty spelling words.

這小男孩在拼寫字方面有困難。

25. **whose** [huz] pron. 誰的

▲ I don't know whose jacket this is.

我不知道這是誰的夾克。

Unit 26

1. **agree** [əˋgri] v. 贊同 <with, about, on>；同意 [反] refuse

▲ Everyone in the meeting agreed with the chairperson on the matter.

會議上的每個人都贊同主席對這事件的看法。

agreement [əˋgrimənt] n. [U] 意見一致；[C] 協定，協議

▲ The strike will go on because the bus drivers and the management didn't reach agreement. 由於公車司機和資方沒有達成共識，罷工會繼續進行。

2. **apple** [ˋæpḷ] n. [C][U] 蘋果

▲ An apple a day keeps the doctor away.

【諺】每日一蘋果，醫生遠離我。

3. **aunt** [ænt] n. [C] 姑媽；姨媽；伯母；嬸嬸；舅媽

▲ Aunt Emily always brings me a gift whenever she visits us. Emily 姑媽每次拜訪我們都會帶禮物給我。

4. **banana** [bə`nænə] n. [C][U] 香蕉
   ▲ These bananas are not mature and still look green.
   這些香蕉還沒熟，看起來仍是綠色的。

5. **baseball** [`bes`bɔl] n. [C][U] 棒球 (運動)
   ▲ John often plays baseball with his friends on weekends. John 通常在週末會跟朋友打棒球。

6. **bicycle** [`baɪˌsɪkl̩] n. [C] 腳踏車 <by> [同] bike
   ▲ Henry goes to school by bicycle every day.
   Henry 每天都騎腳踏車上學。

7. **cat** [kæt] n. [C] 貓
   ▲ A cat has nine lives. 【諺】貓有九條命。

8. **cry** [kraɪ] v. 哭 <over, about>；叫喊 <out> (cried | cried | crying)
   ▲ It's no use crying over spilt milk. 【諺】覆水難收。
   cry [kraɪ] n. [C] 叫喊
   ▲ We heard a cry for help and ran to take a look.
   我們聽到呼救聲就跑去查看。

9. **dead** [dɛd] adj. 死的，死亡的；沒電的
   ▲ Five gangsters were shot dead in the shooting.
   五名歹徒在槍擊事件中被射殺身亡。

10. **driver** [`draɪvɚ] n. [C] 司機，駕駛員

▲ The taxi driver was fined for running a red light.
這名計程車司機因為闖紅燈而被罰款。

11. **festival** [ˈfɛstəvl] n. [C] 慶典；節日

▲ The local people are holding a festival to celebrate the holiday. 當地人正舉行慶典來慶祝這個假日。

12. **hill** [hɪl] n. [C] 小山丘；斜坡

▲ On the hill stood a historic castle.
在那山丘上聳立一座有歷史意義的城堡。

13. **kid** [kɪd] n. [C] 小孩

▲ The kid was kidnapped by a man in a blue coat.
那小孩被一個穿藍色外套的男子綁架了。

kid [kɪd] v. (與某人) 開玩笑 [同] joke (kidded | kidded | kidding)

▲ You won the lottery? You're kidding!
你中樂透？你是在開玩笑吧！

14. **kitchen** [ˈkɪtʃɪn] n. [C] 廚房

▲ There is an oven, a refrigerator, and a dishwasher in the kitchen. 廚房裡有烤箱、冰箱和洗碗機。

15. **mark** [mɑrk] n. [C] 痕跡；記號

▲ The dog left some dirty marks on the carpet.
那隻狗在地毯上留下汙漬。

mark [mɑrk] v. 做記號；給…評分

▲ Ian marked the important passage in the book.

Ian 把書中重要段落標上記號。

16. **note** [not] n. [C] 便條；[pl.] 筆記 (~s)

▲ The note on the door says that the store will be closed this Wednesday.
門上的便條紙寫著商店本週三會休息一天。

note [not] v. 注意，留意

▲ Please note that smoking is not allowed in the building. 請注意在這棟建築物裡禁止吸菸。

17. **orange** [`ɔrɪndʒ] adj. 橙色的，橘色的

▲ You look great in that orange dress.
你穿那件橘色洋裝很好看。

orange [`ɔrɪndʒ] n. [C] 柳橙；[C][U] 橙色，橘色

▲ Terry had a sandwich and a glass of orange juice for breakfast. Terry 早餐吃三明治配一杯柳橙汁。

18. **pack** [pæk] n. [C] 一包；一群 (狼、犬)

▲ Mike bought a pack of cigarettes in the convenience store. Mike 在便利商店買了一包菸。

pack [pæk] v. 打包 (行李)；塞滿，擠進 <into>

▲ Rosalie is packing clothes for her business trip.
Rosalie 正在為她的出差打包衣物。

19. **pink** [pɪŋk] adj. 粉紅色的

▲ Molly tied up her hair with a pink ribbon.
Molly 用粉紅色緞帶繫頭髮。

pink [pɪŋk] n. [C][U] 粉紅色

▲ The little girl dressed in pink looks adorable.
那個穿著粉紅色衣服的小女孩看起來很可愛。

20. **popcorn** [`pɑpˌkɔrn] n. [U] 爆米花

▲ Grace never sees a movie without a tub of popcorn.
Grace 每一次看電影都會吃一桶爆米花。

21. **ruler** [`rulɚ] n. [C] 統治者；尺

▲ The king was not a good ruler; he ruled the country with an iron fist.
這國王不是好的統治者，他以鐵腕手段統治國家。

22. **sick** [sɪk] adj. 生病的 <with>；想吐的

▲ Kim was sick with the flu, so she didn't go to work yesterday. Kim 得流感生病了，所以她昨天沒去上班。
🔎 be sick of... 對…厭煩的

23. **soup** [sup] n. [C][U] 湯

▲ This is my family recipe for delicious chicken soup.
這是我做美味雞湯的家傳食譜。

24. **stair** [stɛr] n. [C] (樓梯的) 梯級；[pl.] 樓梯 (～s)

▲ Ellie sat on the top stair, reading a book.
Ellie 坐在樓梯的最上面一階看書。

25. **win** [wɪn] v. 獲勝 [反] lose；贏得 [同] gain (won | won | winning)

▲ Our school team won by a score of eight to six.
我們校隊以八比六的比數獲勝。

💡 win sb/sth back 重新贏得⋯

win [wɪn] n. [C] 勝利 [反] defeat

▲ The home team has had five wins and two losses so far. 主場球隊目前五勝二敗。

Unit 27

1. **arrive** [əˋraɪv] v. 抵達，到達 <at, in>；到來 [同] come

   ▲ A party of tourists just arrived at the five-star hotel.
   一個觀光團剛抵達這五星級飯店。

2. **ball** [bɔl] n. [C] 球；舞會

   ▲ It was a pity that the fielder failed to catch the ball.
   外野手未能接到球，真可惜。

   💡 hit/kick/throw a ball 擊 / 踢 / 丟球

   ball [bɔl] v. 把⋯弄成球型

   ▲ David balled his fists angrily while having a quarrel with the rude man.
   David 和這個無禮的男子吵架時生氣地緊握拳頭。

3. **basket** [ˋbæskɪt] n. [C] 籃子；籃框

   ▲ Evelyn put some apples in the basket.
   Evelyn 將一些蘋果放在籃子裡。

4. **basketball** [ˋbæskɪt‚bɔl] n. [C][U] 籃球 (運動)

   ▲ Ken played basketball to relieve his pressure from schoolwork. Ken 打籃球來抒解課業壓力。

5. **bird** [bɝd] n. [C] 鳥

▲ The early bird catches the worm.
【諺】早起的鳥兒有蟲吃。

6. **bite** [baɪt] n. [C] 咬的一口；一點點食物

▲ Ariel took a bite of the pear and found it rotten.
Ariel 咬了一口梨子後發現它腐爛了。

bite [baɪt] v. 咬 (bit | bitten | biting)

▲ The dog has bitten a hole in my sleeve.
那隻狗把我的袖子咬了一個洞。

7. **couch** [kaʊtʃ] n. [C] 沙發 [同] sofa

▲ Jenson enjoys lying on the couch and using his smartphone. Jenson 喜歡躺在沙發上玩智慧型手機。

💡 couch potato 一直在看電視的人

couch [kaʊtʃ] v. 以 (某種方式) 表達

▲ The document that was couched in legal jargon confused me. 這份充滿法律術語的文件讓我很困惑。

8. **decide** [dɪˋsaɪd] v. 決定；選定 <on>

▲ Jane decided to go to New Zealand for summer vacation. Jane 決定暑假時要去紐西蘭。

9. **doll** [dɑl] n. [C] 洋娃娃

▲ The little girl carries her doll wherever she goes.
小女孩走到哪裡都帶著她的洋娃娃。

10. **excited** [ɪkˋsaɪtɪd] adj. 感到興奮的 <about>

▲ Jessie is getting excited about her trip to Bali.

Jessie 對於她的峇里島之旅感到興奮。

---

11. **fill** [fɪl] **v.** 裝滿 <with>；充滿…感覺 <with>

▲ Before Toby ordered his meal, the waiter filled his glass with water.

在 Toby 點餐之前，服務生將他的杯子裝滿水。

fill [fɪl] **n.** [U] 需要的量，可應付的量

▲ I have had my fill of Wendy's complaints.

我已經受夠了 Wendy 的抱怨。

---

12. **item** [ˋaɪtəm] **n.** [C] 項目；一則 (新聞)

▲ Did you check all the items on the shopping list?

你核對過購物清單上所有的項目了嗎？

---

13. **kiss** [kɪs] **n.** [C] 吻

▲ Max gave his girlfriend a kiss before leaving.

Max 在離開之前吻了他女友。

kiss [kɪs] **v.** 吻，接吻 <on>

▲ The girl kissed her father on the cheek.

那女孩親吻她父親的臉頰。

---

14. **lead** [lid] **v.** 領導；領先 (led | led | leading)

▲ Sam is regarded as the perfect person to lead the research team.

Sam 被認為是領導這個研究團隊的最佳人選。

🍃 lead to sth 導致… | lead sb on 誤導…

lead [lid] **n.** [sing.] 領先；示範，榜樣

▲ The New York Knicks were in the lead in the last

three minutes. 紐約尼克隊在最後三分鐘時領先。

---

15. **noise** [nɔɪz] n. [C][U] 噪音 [同] sound

▲ Don't make so much noise. Your father is sleeping.
不要製造那麼多噪音。你父親在睡覺。

noisily [ˋnɔɪzɪlɪ] adv. 吵鬧地

▲ Several girls chatted noisily in the coffee shop.
一些女孩在咖啡店裡吵鬧地聊天。

---

16. **package** [ˋpækɪdʒ] n. [C] 包裹 [同] parcel ; 小包 [同] packet

▲ Freya received a package from her best friend yesterday. Freya 昨天收到她好友寄的包裹。

---

17. **page** [pedʒ] n. [C] (書或報章雜誌的) 頁，版

▲ The answers are given on the last page of the book.
答案在這本書的最後一頁。

---

18. **pipe** [paɪp] n. [C] 管子；菸斗

▲ The water pipe burst and flooded the kitchen.
水管爆裂而造成廚房淹水。

pipe [paɪp] v. 用管子輸送

▲ The oil is piped from the wells to the port.
石油透過管線從油井輸送到港口。

---

19. **pool** [pul] n. [C] 小水塘；游泳池 [同] swimming pool

▲ After the rain, there were many small pools of rainwater in the field. 雨後原野上有許多小雨水坑。

pool [pul] v. 集合 (資金、資源)

▲ The residents pooled their money to help the stray dogs. 居民把錢湊在一起以幫助流浪狗。

20. **present** [ˋprɛznt̩] adj. 出席的 <at, in> [反] absent；現在的

▲ Lola's whole family was present at her graduation ceremony. Lola 全家人都出席她的畢業典禮。

present [ˋprɛznt̩] n. [U] 現在；[C] 禮物

▲ At present, Joanna is working as a nurse in a local hospital. Joanna 目前在當地的醫院當護士。

present [prɪˋzɛnt] v. 授予，贈送 <with>；呈現，展現 <with>

▲ The actor was presented with an award to recognize his contribution to the film industry.
那名演員被頒獎以認可他對電影業的貢獻。

21. **salad** [ˋsæləd] n. [C][U] 沙拉

▲ The steak is served with a mixed salad.
這牛排有搭配一份什錦沙拉。

22. **sight** [saɪt] n. [U] 視力 [同] vision；[U][sing.] 看見

▲ Melanie lost her sight in an accident.
Melanie 在一場意外中喪失了視力。

🍃 at first sight 第一眼

sight [saɪt] v. 看到，發現

▲ The fisherman sighted some sea turtles laying their eggs on the beach. 漁夫發現一些海龜在沙灘上產卵。

23. **stupid** [ˋstjupɪd] adj. 笨的，愚蠢的 [同] silly

▲ The dog is too stupid to learn tricks.
那隻狗太笨學不會把戲。

24. **supermarket** [ˋsupɚˏmɑrkɪt] n. [C] 超市

▲ The supermarket is having a sale to attract more customers.
那間超市正在舉辦特賣活動以吸引更多的顧客。

25. **wrong** [rɔŋ] adj. 錯誤的，不對的 [反] right

▲ It is wrong to tell a lie. 說謊是不對的。

wrong [rɔŋ] adv. 錯誤地，不對地 [反] right

▲ Everything went wrong with Mike after he divorced his wife. Mike 和太太離婚後諸事不順。

wrong [rɔŋ] n. [U] 不正確；[C] 不公平的行為 [反] right

▲ It's parents' duty to teach their children how to tell right from wrong.
父母有責任教導孩子如何分辨是非。

wrong [rɔŋ] v. 冤枉，不公正地對待

▲ We should try to forgive those who have wronged us.
我們應試著原諒那些不公正對待我們的人。

Unit 28

1. **bag** [bæg] n. [C] 袋子，提袋

▲ I always bring my own reusable shopping bag when going grocery shopping.

我去買雜貨時都會自備環保購物袋。

---

2. **band** [bænd] n. [C] 樂團；細繩，帶

▲ The well-known rock band will give a concert tour in Asia. 這個知名搖滾樂團將在亞洲做巡迴演出。

---

3. **bat** [bæt] n. [C] 球棒；蝙蝠

▲ My dad bought me a baseball bat as my birthday present. 我父親買棒球棒給我當生日禮物。

bat [bæt] v. 用棒擊球 (batted | batted | batting)

▲ The spectators cheered loudly as Ryan batted three runners home. 當 Ryan 打擊出去使三名跑者回本壘得分時，觀眾大聲喝采。

---

4. **bath** [bæθ] n. [C] 沐浴；浴缸 [同] bathtub

▲ The mother is giving her baby a bath.
這位母親正在給嬰兒洗澡。

---

5. **beach** [bitʃ] n. [C] 沙灘 <on>

▲ In summer, my friends and I used to play on the beach all day long.
我和朋友們過去習慣夏天整天在沙灘上遊玩。

beach [bitʃ] v. 把船從水裡拖到岸上

▲ With special equipment, the workers succeeded beaching the boat near the rocks.
工人運用特別的器具成功把船拖到海灘的礁石附近。

---

6. **blind** [blaɪnd] adj. 失明的；盲目的

▲ Ken went blind at an early age. Ken 在年幼時失明。

💡 be blind to sth 沒有注意到…；對…視而不見

blind [blaɪnd] v. 使失明；蒙蔽 <to>

▲ Tommy was blinded in a car crash.
　Tommy 在一場車禍中失明。

---

7. **busy** [ˋbɪzɪ] adj. 忙碌的 <with>；熱鬧的 (busier | busiest)

▲ Samantha is busy with her homework.
　Samantha 正忙著做作業。

---

8. **cute** [kjut] adj. 可愛的 (cuter | cutest)

▲ What a cute puppy it is! 好可愛的小狗！

---

9. **die** [daɪ] v. 死 <from, of> (died | died | dying)

▲ Tina died from breast cancer at the age of 58.
　Tina 在五十八歲時死於乳癌。

---

10. **ear** [ɪr] n. [C] 耳朵

▲ Cover your ears if the sounds of the fireworks are too loud. 如果煙火太大聲就把耳朵摀起來。

---

11. **factory** [ˋfæktrɪ] n. [C] 工廠 (pl. factories)

▲ The chemical factory was fined for dumping toxic waste into the river.
　這化學工廠因為傾倒有毒廢棄物到河裡而被罰款。

---

12. **flower** [ˋflauɚ] n. [C] 花

▲ In her free time, Sophia enjoys planting flowers in the garden. Sophia 喜歡在閒暇時在花園裡種花。

flower [ˋflauɚ] **v.** 開花

▲ Sakura and tulips both flower in spring.
  櫻花和鬱金香都是在春天開花。

---

13. **jacket** [ˋdʒækɪt] **n.** [C] 夾克，短外套

▲ Michael often wears a leather jacket during winter.
  Michael 冬天通常都穿皮外套。

---

14. **kite** [kaɪt] **n.** [C] 風箏

▲ The weather is nice; let's go out to fly a kite.
  天氣很好，我們外出放風箏吧。

---

15. **lucky** [ˋlʌkɪ] **adj.** 幸運的，走運的 [同] fortunate [反]
  unlucky (luckier | luckiest)

▲ The baby was very lucky to survive the big fire.
  這名嬰兒很幸運在大火中倖存下來。

---

16. **nose** [noz] **n.** [C] 鼻子

▲ It is rude to pick your nose in front of others.
  在別人面前挖鼻孔是很無禮的。

---

17. **paint** [pent] **n.** [U] 油漆；[pl.] 顏料 (～s)

▲ Harvey gave the fence two coats of paint.
  Harvey 替籬笆上了兩層油漆。

  paint [pent] **v.** 在…上刷油漆；(用顏料) 畫

▲ After brief discussion, we decided to paint our living
  room blue. 經簡短討論後，我們決定把客廳漆成藍色。

---

18. **pair** [per] **n.** [C] 一雙，一對

▲ Daisy bought a pair of earrings to go with her evening dress.

Daisy 買了一對耳環，以搭配她的晚禮服。

💡 in pairs 成對

19. **pm** [ˌpiˈɛm] adv. 下午 (also p.m.)

▲ The plane is scheduled to take off at 3:40 pm.

這班飛機預定在下午三點四十分起飛。

20. **pot** [pɑt] n. [C] 罐，壺，盆

▲ The hostess made a pot of tea for her guests.

女主人為她的客人沖了一壺茶。

pot [pɑt] v. 將 (植物) 栽入盆中 (potted | potted | potting)

▲ Patty is busy potting the seedlings in the backyard.

Patty 正在後院忙著將幼苗栽在花盆中。

21. **shake** [ʃek] v. 搖動；發抖 (shook | shaken | shaking)

▲ The gas explosion shook the whole building.

瓦斯爆炸震動整幢大樓。

💡 shake hands with sb 與…握手

shake [ʃek] n. [C] 搖動，震動

▲ Rebecca said no with a shake of her head.

Rebecca 搖了一下頭說不。

22. **sharp** [ʃɑrp] adj. 銳利的 [反] blunt；急遽的，突然的 [同] steep

▲ Please hold the sharp knife carefully.

請小心拿好那把銳利的刀。

sharp [ʃɑrp] adv. 準時地

▲ The magic show started at 7:00 p.m. sharp.
魔術表演在晚間七點準時開始。

---

23. **sleep** [slip] n. [U] 睡眠；[sing.] (一段時間的) 睡眠

▲ Elliot got pimples for lack of sleep.
Elliot 因為缺乏睡眠而長痘痘。

sleep [slip] v. 睡，入睡 (slept | slept | sleeping)

▲ Some experts say that it's healthy to sleep eight hours a night.
有些專家說每晚睡足八個小時才健康。

---

24. **tape** [tep] n. [C] 錄音帶；[U] 膠帶 [同] Scotch tape

▲ Luca has a large collection of the singer's tapes.
Luca 大量收集這個歌手的錄音帶。

---

25. **throat** [θrot] n. [C] 喉嚨

▲ I have a sore throat and need to see a doctor.
我喉嚨痛，需要去看醫生。

💡 clear sb's throat 清喉嚨

Unit 29

1. **bed** [bɛd] n. [C][U] 床

▲ Finlay goes to bed at ten o'clock every night.
Finlay 每晚十點就上床睡覺。

💡 make the bed 整理床鋪

2. **bedroom** [ˈbɛdˌrum] **n.** [C] 臥室

▲ There're four bedrooms in Ross's house.
Ross 的房子有四間臥室。

3. **beside** [bɪˈsaɪd] **prep.** 在⋯旁邊

▲ The queen, who stood beside the king, waved to the crowd. 皇后站在國王旁邊，向群眾揮手。

4. **bottle** [ˈbɑtl] **n.** [C] 瓶子；一瓶的量

▲ Recycling plastic bottles can help save the Earth.
回收塑膠瓶可以幫助拯救地球。

bottle [ˈbɑtl] **v.** 裝瓶

▲ The beer is bottled in the factory.
啤酒是在這個工廠裝瓶的。

5. **careful** [ˈkɛrfəl] **adj.** 小心的 <with, about>

▲ Please be careful with these china plates.
請小心這些瓷盤。

6. **catch** [kætʃ] **v.** 抓住；撞見，發現 (caught | caught | catching)

▲ Aaron caught his cellphone before it fell to the ground. Aaron 在手機掉到地上前先接住它。

💡 catch up 達到同樣的水準，跟上；補做

catch [kætʃ] **n.** [C] 接球；(魚的) 捕獲量 (pl. catches)

▲ Good job! It's a nice catch! 做得好！球接得漂亮！

7. **dear** [dɪr] adj. 親近的 <to>

▲ My cousin Lisa is very dear to me.

我的表妹 Lisa 跟我很親近。

dear [dɪr] n. [C] 親愛的

▲ It's great to see you again, my dear.

再見到你實在是太棒了，親愛的。

dear [dɪr] adv. 高價地

▲ The overseas investment cost the company dear.

海外投資讓這間公司損失慘重。

8. **dollar** [`dɑlɚ] n. [C] (美國、加拿大或澳洲等的貨幣單位) 元

▲ The generous lady donated five thousand dollars to the orphanage.

這位慷慨的女士捐獻五千美元給孤兒院。

9. **email** [`imel] n. [C][U] 電子郵件 [同] e-mail, electronic mail

▲ You can make hotel reservations by phone or email.

你可打電話或用電子郵件來訂旅館。

email [`imel] v. 寄送電子郵件 [同] e-mail

▲ The students are required to email their reports to the teacher by the end of June.

學生們必須在六月底前把報告用電子郵件寄給老師。

10. **everything** [`ɛvrɪˌθɪŋ] pron. 每件事，一切

▲ Everything is ready; we can set out now.

一切都準備好了，我們可以出發了。

---

11. **farm** [fɑrm] n. [C] 農場

▲ My father-in-law runs a dairy farm in the country.
我岳父在鄉下經營乳牛農場。

farm [fɑrm] v. 耕作 (土地)

▲ The Simpsons have been farming the land since 1932. Simpson 家族自從 1932 年開始就一直耕種這片土地。

---

12. **funny** [ˈfʌnɪ] adj. 好笑的；奇怪的，難以理解的
(funnier | funniest)

▲ Kia made funny faces to make the girl laugh.
Kia 做出好笑的鬼臉讓這女孩笑。

---

13. **joke** [dʒok] n. [C] 笑話，玩笑 <about>

▲ Ewan likes to make jokes about the government officials. Ewan 喜歡拿政府官員開玩笑。

💡 play a joke on sb 開⋯的玩笑

joke [dʒok] v. 開玩笑，說笑話

▲ You are going to marry Lily? You must be joking!
你即將要跟 Lily 結婚？你在開玩笑吧！

---

14. **lamp** [læmp] n. [C] (尤指帶燈罩的) 燈

▲ Turning on the bedside lamp, Nora started to read a novel. 打開床頭燈後，Nora 開始看小說。

---

15. **mail** [mel] n. [U] 信件；郵政 (系統) [同] post

▲ Charlie gets a lot of junk mail every week.

Charlie 每週都會收到一大堆垃圾郵件。

mail [mel] v. 郵寄 <to> [同] post

▲ My grandfather mailed a bottle of homemade wine to me. 我爺爺寄了一瓶自製的葡萄酒給我。

---

16. **pin** [pɪn] n. [C] (尤指固定布料用的) 大頭針，別針

▲ It was so quiet here that I could hear a pin drop.
這裡如此安靜，我連一根針掉落都聽得見。

pin [pɪn] v. (用別針等) 釘住 <on> (pinned | pinned | pinning)

▲ The teacher pinned some photos to the bulletin board. 老師將一些照片釘在布告欄上。

---

17. **plate** [plet] n. [C] 盤子；一盤的量 [同] plateful

▲ You put too much food on my plate.
你在我的盤子上放太多食物了。

---

18. **pond** [pɑnd] n. [C] 池塘

▲ Meredith grows some water lilies in the pond.
Meredith 在池塘裡種一些睡蓮。

---

19. **potato** [pə`teto] n. [C][U] 馬鈴薯 (pl. potatoes)

▲ Emma chose steak and mashed potatoes for the main course. Emma 選擇牛排和馬鈴薯泥當主菜。

---

20. **pretty** [`prɪtɪ] adv. 相當，非常

▲ This refrigerator is pretty old; I think we should buy a new one.
這臺冰箱很老舊了，我覺得我們應該買一臺新的。

pretty [ˋprɪtɪ] **adj.** 漂亮的 (prettier | prettiest)

▲ Patrick couldn't help asking the pretty girl about her name. Patrick 忍不住詢問那位美女的名字。

---

21. **shorts** [ʃɔrts] **n.** [pl.] 短褲

▲ It's improper to visit a museum in shorts and slippers. 穿短褲和拖鞋去參觀博物館是不適當的。

---

22. **smile** [smaɪl] **n.** [C] 微笑，笑容

▲ Jasmine entered the room with a big smile on her face. Jasmine 臉上滿是笑容地進入房間。

smile [smaɪl] **v.** 微笑 <at>

▲ The salesclerk smiled at the customers in the store. 售貨員對著店裡的顧客微笑。

---

23. **speak** [spik] **v.** 講話，談話 <to, with>；(會) 講 (某種語言) (spoke | spoken | speaking)

▲ I'll speak to the manager about this proposal later. 我稍後會跟經理談到關於這個提案的事。

---

24. **taxi** [ˋtæksɪ] **n.** [C] 計程車 [同] cab, taxicab

▲ To catch the flight, Zara took a taxi to the airport. 為了趕飛機，Zara 搭計程車去機場。

---

25. **vegetable** [ˋvɛdʒtəbl̩] **n.** [C] 蔬菜；植物人

▲ The study shows that eating more fresh fruit and vegetables can make people healthier. 這份研究顯示多吃新鮮的蔬果會讓人們更健康。

Unit 30

1. **bee** [bi] **n.** [C] 蜜蜂
   ▲ A swarm of bees flew around the flowers in the garden. 一群蜜蜂在花園的花朵間穿梭。

2. **belong** [bɪˋlɔŋ] **v.** 屬於 <to>
   ▲ The villa by the lake belongs to Mr. Mitchell.
   湖邊的別墅屬於 Mitchell 先生所有。

3. **bowl** [bol] **n.** [C] 碗；一碗的量
   ▲ Bob found a crack in the bowl and asked the waiter to bring him another one.
   Bob 發現碗裡有個裂縫，就請服務生拿另一個給他。

4. **box** [bɑks] **n.** [C] 箱子；一箱的量
   ▲ Amy made a doghouse out of an empty cardboard box. Amy 用空的紙箱做了一間狗屋。
   box [bɑks] **v.** 裝箱 <up>；打拳擊
   ▲ Megan boxed up some old magazines to recycle.
   Megan 將一些舊雜誌裝箱回收。

5. **clothes** [kloz] **n.** [pl.] 衣服
   ▲ Andy attended his sister's wedding in his best clothes.
   Andy 穿上他最好的衣服去參加他姊姊的婚禮。

6. **cook** [kʊk] **v.** 煮，烹調
   ▲ Beatrice is cooking curried chicken for lunch.

Beatrice 正在煮咖哩雞當午餐。

cook [kʊk] n. [C] 廚師

▲ The restaurant is popular because they have good cooks. 那間餐廳很受歡迎是因為他們有很棒的廚師。

---

7. **desk** [dɛsk] n. [C] 書桌；服務臺

▲ During the test, you can only have erasers and pencils on your desk.

考試期間，你桌上只能放橡皮擦和鉛筆。

---

8. **envelope** [ˋɛnvə͵lop] n. [C] 信封

▲ Betty sealed the envelope and then addressed it.

Betty 把信封好，然後寫上姓名地址。

---

9. **fire** [faɪr] n. [C][U] 火

▲ The strong wind made the fire quickly spread to other wooden houses.

強風讓火勢快速地蔓延到其他的木造房子。

fire [faɪr] v. 發射 <at>；開除 [同] sack

▲ The policeman fired two shots at the robber before he ran away. 警察在搶匪逃走前對他開兩槍。

---

10. **forget** [fəˋgɛt] v. 忘記；忘記做 (forgot | forgotten | forgetting)

▲ It was embarrassing for Hugo to forget his client's name. Hugo 忘記客戶的名字，真是尷尬。

---

11. **friend** [frɛnd] n. [C] 朋友

▲ A friend in need is a friend indeed.

【諺】患難之交才是真朋友。

💡 make friends with sb 和⋯交朋友

---

12. **grandmother** [ˋgrænˏmʌðɚ] n. [C] (外) 祖母

▲ My grandmother is good at making apple pie.
我祖母很擅長做蘋果派。

---

13. **juice** [dʒus] n. [C][U] 汁，液

▲ Lisa squeezed some lemon juice on the roast fish.
Lisa 在烤魚上擠一些檸檬汁。

---

14. **lawyer** [ˋlɔjɚ] n. [C] 律師

▲ You had better consult a lawyer before you sign the
contract. 你在簽合約前最好先請教律師。

---

15. **map** [mæp] n. [C] 地圖 <on>

▲ Could you show me the location of the zoo on this
map? 你能告訴我動物園在地圖上的位置嗎？

💡 put sth on the map 使⋯出名

map [mæp] v. 繪製⋯的地圖

▲ The geographer planned to map the new island he
had just discovered.
這位地理學家計劃要幫新發現的島嶼繪製地圖。

---

16. **planet** [ˋplænɪt] n. [C] 行星

▲ The Earth is one of the planets circling around the
Sun. 地球是繞行太陽的行星之一。

---

17. **pleasure** [ˋplɛʒɚ] n. [C] 樂事；[U] 快樂，愉悅

▲ It is a pleasure to talk to you. 和你談話真愉快。

18. **prepare** [prɪˋpɛr] v. 準備 <for>

▲ Ashley has been preparing for her upcoming wedding for three months.
Ashley 為她即將到來的婚禮準備了三個月了。

19. **quick** [kwɪk] adj. 迅速的；敏捷的

▲ Ben had a quick glance at the front page before going to work. Ben 上班前迅速瞄一下頭版新聞。

quick [kwɪk] adv. 快速地 [同] quickly, fast

▲ The company always responds to their customers' questions quick.
這間公司總是很快地回應顧客的問題。

20. **rabbit** [ˋræbɪt] n. [C] 兔子

▲ Victoria is considering keeping a pet rabbit.
Victoria 正在考慮要養寵物兔。

21. **shoulder** [ˋʃoldɚ] n. [C] 肩膀

▲ Someone patted Dora on the shoulder when she was speaking on the phone.
Dora 在講電話時有人拍她的肩膀。

22. **snow** [sno] n. [U] 雪

▲ Snow fell heavily while Steve was driving home.
Steve 開車回家時雪下得很大。

snow [sno] v. 下雪

▲ It snowed heavily; as a result, many people were late

for work. 雪下得很大，因此很多人上班遲到。

23. **street** [strit] n. [C] 街道
▲ The narrow street was crowded with pedestrians.
這狹窄的街道擠滿了行人。

24. **terrible** [ˈtɛrəbl] adj. 糟糕的，可怕的 [同] horrible,
awful
▲ All of the flights were delayed because of the terrible
storm. 所有的班機因為這可怕的暴風雨而延誤了。

25. **video** [ˈvɪdɪo] n. [C] 錄影帶，影片；[U] 錄影 <on>
▲ How about renting a video and watching it tonight?
要不要租個影片今晚看？
video [ˈvɪdɪo] v. 錄下，錄製
▲ Bella videoed her daughter's birthday party.
Bella 將她女兒的生日派對錄影下來。
video [ˈvɪdɪo] adj. 錄影的
▲ Ms. Clarke has prepared a variety of video materials
for her English classes. Clarke 老師為她的英文課準
備了各式各樣的影片材料。

Unit 31

1. **bell** [bɛl] n. [C] 鐘，鈴
▲ The bell rang at the end of the class.
課堂結束時鈴響了。

2. **bench** [bɛntʃ] n. [C] 長凳 (pl. benches)

▲ We sat on the park bench, feeding the pigeons.
我們坐在公園的長凳上餵鴿子。

3. **brown** [braʊn] adj. 棕色的，褐色的

▲ Nancy's boyfriend has light brown hair and dark blue eyes. Nancy 的男友有淺棕色的頭髮和深藍色的眼睛。

brown [braʊn] v. (把食物) 炒成褐色

▲ The cook browned the meat before adding the carrots. 廚師加入紅蘿蔔前先把肉炒成褐色。

brown [braʊn] n. [C][U] 棕色，褐色

▲ My math teacher was dressed in dark brown today.
我的數學老師今天穿深棕色的衣服。

4. **butter** [ˋbʌtɚ] n. [U] 奶油

▲ To make the dish, the first step is to melt butter in a pan. 要做這道菜，首先就是在鍋子裡融化奶油。

butter [ˋbʌtɚ] v. 在⋯上塗奶油

▲ The father buttered toast for his children.
這位父親幫他的孩子在吐司上塗奶油。

5. **correct** [kəˋrɛkt] adj. 正確的 [同] right [反] incorrect

▲ Ida looked confused because she was not sure which answer was correct.

Ida 看起來很困惑，因為她不確定哪個答案是正確的。

correct [kəˋrɛkt] v. 改正，糾正

▲ The student was asked to correct the spelling errors in his homework.

這學生被要求改正作業裡的拼字錯誤。

6. **dictionary** [ˋdɪkʃənˏɛrɪ] n. [C] 字典 (pl. dictionaries)
   ▲ Matilda looked the word up in a Chinese-English dictionary. Matilda 用漢英字典查這個字。

7. **else** [ɛls] adv. 其他
   ▲ Who else is coming to the ball tonight?
   還有誰會來今晚的舞會？

8. **eraser** [ɪˋresə] n. [C] 橡皮擦
   ▲ Hank rubbed out his pencil sketch with an eraser.
   Hank 用橡皮擦擦去他的鉛筆素描。

9. **foreign** [ˋfɔrɪn] adj. 外國的
   ▲ The exchange program enables many foreign students to learn Chinese in Taiwan.
   這個交換計畫讓很多外國學生在臺灣學中文。

10. **fork** [fɔrk] n. [C] 叉子
    ▲ Westerners normally eat with a knife and fork.
    西方人通常用刀叉吃東西。

11. **grade** [gred] n. [C] 等級；分數
    ▲ The store is well-known for selling high-grade tea.
    這間店以販售高級茶而聞名。
    grade [gred] v. 把…分級；給…打分數
    ▲ The mangoes are graded according to size.
    這些芒果是根據大小尺寸分級的。

12. **habit** [`hæbɪt] n. [C][U] 習慣

▲ Poppy has got into the habit of drinking some wine before going to bed.

Poppy 已經養成睡前喝點紅酒的習慣。

🔴 form/develop a habit 養成習慣

13. **kick** [kɪk] v. 踢

▲ Jake was kicked in the shin while playing soccer.

Jake 踢足球的時候被踢到腳脛。

🔴 kick sb out 開除…

kick [kɪk] n. [C] 踢;極大的樂趣 [同] thrill

▲ Fred was in a bad mood, so he gave the door several kicks. Fred 心情不好,所以踹了門好幾下。

14. **lip** [lɪp] n. [C] 嘴唇

▲ Carol moved her lips but didn't make a sound.

Carol 的雙唇動了動,但沒有發出聲音。

15. **meet** [mit] v. 相遇,初次見面;會面 (met | met | meeting)

▲ It was in the library that Samuel first met his wife.

Samuel 就是在這間圖書館與他妻子初次相見。

🔴 meet sb halfway 遷就…

16. **pocket** [`pakɪt] n. [C] 口袋

▲ Ella took a few coins out of her coat pocket.

Ella 從她的外套口袋裡拿出一些硬幣。

pocket [`pakɪt] v. 裝入口袋;私吞

▲ Teddy went out after pocketing his keys and wallet.
Teddy 把鑰匙和皮夾放入口袋後就外出了。

17. **proud** [praʊd] **adj.** 驕傲的，自豪的 <of> [反] ashamed

▲ The couple are very proud of their son's achievements.
這對夫妻對兒子的成就感到很驕傲。

18. **rainbow** [`ren͵bo] **n.** [C] 彩虹

▲ A rainbow appeared in the sky when the rain
stopped. 雨停時天空出現一道彩虹。

19. **ride** [raɪd] **n.** [C] (騎車或乘坐車輛的) 行程

▲ Could you give me a ride to the train station?
你能載我去火車站嗎？

ride [raɪd] **v.** 騎，乘 (rode | ridden | riding)

▲ Gary will ride the 10:30 train to London.
Gary 將搭乘十點半開往倫敦的火車。

20. **singer** [`sɪŋɚ] **n.** [C] 歌手

▲ The folk singer frequently performs in restaurants.
這位民謠歌手常常在餐廳裡表演。

21. **sir** [sɝ] **n.** [C][sing.] 先生 (also Sir)

▲ What can I do for you, sir?
先生，有什麼我能為您服務的嗎？

22. **straight** [stret] **adv.** 直接，立刻；坦誠地

▲ Ralph went straight home after school.
Ralph 放學後就直接回家。

straight [stret] adj. 直的；直率的，坦誠的 <with>

▲ The little girl used a ruler to draw a straight line.

這小女孩用尺畫直線。

straight [stret] n. [C] 異性戀者 [反] gay

▲ Everyone should be treated equally whether they are straights or gays.

無論是異性戀或同性戀者，都應該被平等對待。

23. **ticket** [ˈtɪkɪt] n. [C] 票，券 <to, for>；罰單

▲ Joan reserved two plane tickets to New York online.

Joan 在網路上預訂兩張到紐約的機票。

24. **twice** [twaɪs] adv. 兩次；兩倍

▲ Melody goes to yoga twice a week.

Melody 每週上兩次瑜伽課。

25. **weekend** [ˈwikˌɛnd] n. [C] 週末 <on>

▲ The Fletcher family went skiing on the weekend.

Fletcher 一家人在週末去滑雪。

weekend [ˈwikˌɛnd] v. 度週末

▲ Seth is going to weekend in a beach resort.

Seth 即將要在海灘渡假勝地度過週末。

Unit 32

1. **belt** [bɛlt] n. [C] 皮帶，腰帶

▲ When you see the light on, please fasten your seat

belt. 看到此燈亮時，請繫上安全帶。

belt [bɛlt] **v.** 用帶子束緊

▲ Nick belted his trench coat in the doorway.
Nick 在門口把他的風衣腰帶束緊。

---

2. **block** [blɑk] **n.** [C] 街區；一大塊

▲ My cousin's house is two blocks away.
我表哥家離這裡有兩條街遠。

block [blɑk] **v.** 阻擋，妨礙

▲ The mountain path was blocked because of a landslide. 山道因為土石流而阻塞不通。

💡 block sth off 封閉… | block sth up 堵塞，塞住

---

3. **celebrate** [ˈsɛlə,bret] **v.** 慶祝

▲ Independence Day is celebrated on July 4th in the United States. 美國在七月四日慶祝獨立紀念日。

---

4. **cellphone** [ˈsɛlfon] **n.** [C] 行動電話，手機 [同] cellular phone, mobile phone

▲ Nowadays, nearly everyone owns a cellphone.
現今，幾乎每個人都擁有一支手機。

---

5. **cover** [ˈkʌvɚ] **v.** 覆蓋，遮蔽 <with>；涉及，涵蓋

▲ The desk was covered with dust. 書桌上滿是灰塵。

cover [ˈkʌvɚ] **n.** [C] 覆蓋物；(書或雜誌的) 封面

▲ Nina kept her computer under a plastic cover.
Nina 用塑膠套蓋住她的電腦。

---

6. **dirty** [ˈdɝti] **adj.** 骯髒的 (dirtier | dirtiest)

▲ My brother's room was full of dirty clothes and socks. 我弟弟的房間充滿髒的衣服和襪子。

dirty [ˋdɝtɪ] v. 弄髒 (dirtied | dirtied | dirtying)

▲ The kid dirtied his clothes in the art class.
這孩童在美術課時把衣服弄髒。

---

7. **enter** [ˋɛntɚ] v. 進入；參加 (比賽等)

▲ Paula entered the classroom with an anxious look on her face. Paula 滿臉愁容走進教室。

---

8. **foreigner** [ˋfɔrɪnɚ] n. [C] 外國人

▲ The public transportation in Tokyo makes it easy for foreigners to tour around the city.
東京的大眾運輸系統讓外國人在該城市觀光更容易。

---

9. **gift** [gɪft] n. [C] 禮物 [同] present；天賦 <for> [同] talent

▲ Mr. Brown gave his son a gift for his birthday.
Brown 先生給他兒子一個生日禮物。

---

10. **hang** [hæŋ] v. 懸掛 (hung | hung | hanging)；施以絞刑 (hanged | hanged | hanging)

▲ A portrait of the president was hung on the wall.
一幅總統的肖像被掛在牆壁上。

---

11. **hot** [hɑt] adj. 炎熱的；辛辣的 [反] mild (hotter | hottest)

▲ It's very hot inside the house; could you turn the air conditioner on? 室內好熱，你可以開一下冷氣嗎？

---

12. **hotel** [hoˋtɛl] n. [C] 旅館，飯店

▲ Sam stayed at a five-star hotel with a stunning ocean view. Sam 住在一間有迷人海景的五星級飯店。

13. **knock** [nɑk] v. 敲 <on, at>；碰倒，撞倒 <over>

▲ Be sure to knock on the door before you enter the manager's office. 進經理的辦公室前，一定要先敲門。

💡 knock sb out 把…打昏

knock [nɑk] n. [C] 敲門聲 <on, at>；(重重的) 一擊

▲ A loud knock on the door woke the baby.
大聲的敲門聲吵醒了嬰兒。

14. **lovely** [ˋlʌvlɪ] adj. 美麗的，漂亮的；愉快的 (lovelier | loveliest)

▲ Ariel looks lovely in this pink dress.
Ariel 穿上這件粉色洋裝看起來很漂亮。

15. **party** [ˋpɑrtɪ] n. [C] 宴會，派對；黨派 (pl. parties)

▲ We will throw a dinner party to welcome the new manager. 我們要舉行晚宴歡迎新來的經理。

party [ˋpɑrtɪ] v. (在派對上) 狂歡 (partied | partied | partying)

▲ Those young people partied until midnight.
那些年輕人在派對上狂歡到半夜。

16. **pull** [pʊl] v. 拉，拖 [反] push；抽走，移走 <off>

▲ The little boy pulled the door open and ran outside.
小男孩拉開門後就往外跑出去。

💡 pull over 把車停在路邊

pull [pʊl] n. [C] 拖，拉 [反] push

▲ Please give the rope a hard pull. 請用力拉一下繩子。

17. **queen** [kwin] n. [C] 王后，女王 (also Queen)

▲ Elizabeth was crowned Queen Elizabeth II at the age of 27.

伊莉莎白在二十七歲時被加冕為伊莉莎白二世女王。

18. **repeat** [rɪ`pit] v. 重複；跟著唸 <after>

▲ We should try not to repeat our mistakes.
我們應該試著不犯相同的錯誤。

19. **rose** [roz] n. [C] 玫瑰

▲ Jackson gave his wife a bunch of red roses on their wedding anniversary.

Jackson 在結婚紀念日時給他太太一束紅玫瑰。

20. **slim** [slɪm] adj. 苗條的 [同] slender；微小的 [同] slender (slimmer | slimmest)

▲ The actress tried hard to stay slim.
那位女演員努力保持苗條。

21. **string** [strɪŋ] n. [C][U] 細線；[C] 一連串 [同] series

▲ Freya used sticks, tape, a piece of cloth, and a ball of string to make a kite.

Freya 用木條、膠帶、一塊布和一團細線來做風箏。

22. **sweet** [swit] adj. 甜的；友善的，貼心的

▲ Polly ordered a cup of black tea to go with the sweet

chocolate cake.

Polly 點了一杯紅茶搭配這塊甜的巧克力蛋糕。

---

23. **tidy** [ˋtaɪdɪ] adj. 整潔的 [同] neat [反] untidy, messy (tidier | tidiest)

▲ Jessie always keeps her room neat and tidy.

Jessie 總是保持房間整潔。

tidy [ˋtaɪdɪ] v. 整理，收拾 <up> (tidied | tidied | tidying)

▲ Eva ordered her son to tidy up his room immediately.

Eva 命令她兒子馬上去整理房間。

---

24. **wife** [waɪf] n. [C] 妻子 (pl. wives)

▲ Bill became depressed after his wife passed away.

Bill 在妻子過世後變得消沉。

---

25. **window** [ˋwɪndo] n. [C] 窗戶；(商店的) 櫥窗

▲ The thief entered the house through the broken window. 小偷從破掉的窗戶進入屋內。

♥ open/close a window 打開 / 關閉窗戶

Unit 33

1. **answer** [ˋænsɚ] n. [C] 答案 <to>；答覆 [同] response

▲ Gavin worked out the answer to the math problem in a short time. Gavin 很快就解出這道數學題的答案。

answer [ˋænsɚ] v. 回答，回應；接電話

▲ When Tara's boyfriend proposed to her, she answered "Yes!" right away.

當 Tara 的男友跟她求婚時，她立刻說：「好！」

---

2. **boat** [bot] n. [C] 小船

▲ Rory is learning how to row a boat.

Rory 正在學如何划船。

🌢 be in the same boat (as sb) (和…) 處於同樣的困境

---

3. **boring** [ˋborɪŋ] adj. 無聊的，乏味的

▲ Bart fell asleep halfway through the boring speech.

Bart 在這無聊的演講中途睡著了。

---

4. **chair** [tʃɛr] n. [C] 椅子 <on, in>；主席

▲ Some guests sat on the chairs outside to wait for their tables. 有些客人坐在外面的椅子上候位。

chair [tʃɛr] v. 主持 (會議等)

▲ The debate will be chaired by Willie.

辯論會將由 Willie 主持。

---

5. **chicken** [ˋtʃɪkən] n. [C] 雞；[U] 雞肉

▲ Don't count your chickens before they are hatched.

【諺】勿打如意算盤。

---

6. **crazy** [ˋkrezɪ] adj. 荒唐的 [同] mad ；惱怒的 (crazier | craziest)

▲ It was crazy to go mountain climbing on a stormy day. 在暴風雨的天氣去爬山很荒唐。

7. **dress** [drɛs] n. [C] 洋裝 (pl. dresses)

▲ Ivy looked sexy in the low-cut evening dress.
Ivy 穿這件低胸晚禮服看起來很性感。

dress [drɛs] v. 穿衣，給…穿衣；穿…的服裝 <in>

▲ Joe got dressed and ran to catch the bus.
Joe 穿上衣服後就跑去趕公車。

💡 dress up 盛裝；假扮

8. **fly** [flaɪ] v. (鳥類等) 飛 ；(乘飛機) 飛行 <to> (flew | flown | flying)

▲ The eagle flew away after catching its prey.
老鷹抓住獵物後就飛走了。

fly [flaɪ] n. [C] 蒼蠅 (pl. flies)

▲ Numerous flies buzzed around the dead bird.
許多蒼蠅圍繞著死掉的鳥嗡嗡叫。

9. **frog** [frɑg] n. [C] 青蛙

▲ A lot of frogs live by that lake. 很多青蛙住在那湖邊。

10. **happen** [ˋhæpən] v. 發生 <to> [同] occur；碰巧 <to>

▲ Oscar looked upset. What happened to him?
Oscar 看起來很生氣。他發生了什麼事？

💡 happen on/upon... 偶然發現…

11. **hundred** [ˋhʌndrəd] n. (數字) 一百 ；很多 ，大量 (pl. hundred, hundreds)

▲ The stereo set cost Allen nearly eight hundred dollars. 這音響組花了 Allen 將近八百美元。

hundred [ˈhʌndrəd] adj. 一百個的

---

12. **hungry** [ˈhʌŋgrɪ] adj. 飢餓的；渴望的 <for> [同] eager
    (hungrier | hungriest)
    ▲ The poor people in Africa often go hungry.
    那些非洲的窮人常常挨餓。

---

13. **husband** [ˈhʌzbənd] n. [C] 丈夫
    ▲ Abby believes that Tom will make a good husband
    and father. Abby 相信 Tom 會是個好丈夫和好父親。

---

14. **lemon** [ˈlɛmən] n. [C][U] 檸檬
    ▲ Violet put a slice of lemon in her black tea.
    Violet 在紅茶裡加了一片檸檬。

---

15. **mine** [maɪn] n. [C] 礦坑，礦井
    ▲ A gold mine was discovered in the mountains.
    在山裡發現了金礦井。
    mine [maɪn] v. 開採
    ▲ The workers have mined much coal in the area.
    工人在這區域開採了許多煤礦。

---

16. **perhaps** [pəˈhæps] adv. 也許，可能 [同] maybe
    ▲ My pet rabbit behaved strangely. Perhaps I should
    take it to the vet.
    我的寵物兔舉止很怪異。也許我應該帶牠去看獸醫。

---

17. **push** [pʊʃ] v. 推，推動 [反] pull；逼迫，促使
    ▲ The kid pushed the shopping cart around the store.

這孩子推著購物車在店裡四處走。

push [puʃ] n. [C] 推 (pl. pushes)

▲ Casey gave the girl a push, and she fell to the ground.
Casey 把女孩推倒在地上。

---

18. **reporter** [rɪˋportɚ] n. [C] 記者

▲ Finch works as a reporter for a local newspaper.
Finch 在地方報社當記者。

---

19. **rice** [raɪs] n. [U] 米 (飯)

▲ The farmers had a good crop of rice this fall.
農夫們今年秋天稻米大豐收。

---

20. **sit** [sɪt] v. 坐 (下)；位於 (sat | sat | sitting)

▲ Sylvia sat on the sofa, listening to classical music.
Sylvia 坐在沙發上聽古典樂。

---

21. **square** [skwɛr] n. [C] 正方形；廣場

▲ All sides of a square are the same.
正方形的四個邊都相等。

square [skwɛr] adj. 正方形的

▲ This room is not square but rectangular.
這房間不是正方形的，而是長方形的。

---

22. **table** [ˋtebl̩] n. [C] 桌子

▲ Dean set the table while his wife was cooking dinner.
Dean 在他太太煮晚餐時擺放餐具。

💡 under the table 在暗地裡

---

23. **temple** [`tɛmpl] n. [C] 廟宇；太陽穴 (usu. pl.)

▲ Many tourists are fond of visiting the Greek temples.
很多遊客喜歡參觀希臘神殿。

---

24. **toilet** [`tɔɪlət] n. [C] 馬桶；廁所 [同] bathroom, restroom

▲ Don't forget to flush the toilet after using it.
用完馬桶後別忘了沖水。

---

25. **worker** [`wɝkɚ] n. [C] 工人 ；(某公司或組織的) 員工
(usu. pl.)

▲ The workers are loading the truck with bricks.
工人們正將磚塊裝上卡車。

Unit 34

1. **bathroom** [`bæθ,rum] n. [C] 浴室；廁所

▲ Nelson is taking a shower in the bathroom.
Nelson 正在浴室裡淋浴。

---

2. **borrow** [`baro] v. 借入 <from>

▲ Teresa borrowed some books from the library.
Teresa 從圖書館借了幾本書。

---

3. **boss** [bɔs] n. [C] 上司，老闆；主導者

▲ Our boss demanded that we finish the work by
Friday. 我們老闆要求我們在週五前完成工作。

boss [bɔs] v. 對⋯發號施令，把⋯差來遣去 <around>

▲ Stella likes to boss her brother around.

Stella 喜歡對她弟弟發號施令。

---

4. **climb** [klaɪm] **v.** 攀爬，攀登 <up, down>；(數量等) 攀升 <to> [同] go up

▲ The cat just climbed up the tree.
那隻貓剛剛爬上了樹。

climb [klaɪm] **n.** [C] 攀登 <up, down> (usu. sing.)；(數量等) 攀升

▲ The climb up the mountain took us about two hours.
上山花了我們約兩個小時。

---

5. **club** [klʌb] **n.** [C] 俱樂部；社團

▲ The country club charges a membership fee of $50.
這鄉村俱樂部收取五十美元的會費。

club [klʌb] **v.** 棒打 (clubbed | clubbed | clubbing)

▲ The dog that bit me was clubbed by my father.
咬我的狗被我父親打。

---

6. **dig** [dɪg] **v.** 挖掘；尋找，搜尋 <into> (dug | dug | digging)

▲ The child is digging a hole to plant a tree.
那孩子正在挖一個洞來種樹。

dig [dɪg] **n.** [C] 奚落，取笑；挖掘

▲ Graham enjoys having a dig at politicians.
Graham 喜愛奚落政客。

---

7. **engineer** [ˌɛndʒə`nɪr] **n.** [C] 工程師

▲ Mr. Lin's son works as a software engineer.

林先生的兒子擔任軟體工程師。

---

8. **ghost** [gost] n. [C] 鬼，幽靈
   ▲ The house is said to be haunted by the ghost of a woman. 據說這間房子有女人的鬼魂出沒。

---

9. **giant** [ˋdʒaɪənt] adj. 巨大的
   ▲ Wesley is a man of giant strength. Wesley 力大無比。
   giant [ˋdʒaɪənt] n. [C] 巨人；(成功有影響力的) 大公司
   ▲ The seven-foot basketball player looks like a giant.
   這七英尺的籃球選手看起來像個巨人。

---

10. **hello** [həˋlo] n. [C] 你好 (用於問候或打招呼)
    ▲ I think we should say hello to our new neighbor.
    我覺得我們應該要跟新鄰居打招呼。

---

11. **insect** [ˋɪnsɛkt] n. [C] 昆蟲
    ▲ Nicholas killed the insects with insecticide.
    Nicholas 用殺蟲劑殺死昆蟲。

---

12. **jeans** [dʒinz] n. [pl.] 牛仔褲
    ▲ Payton has more than fifty pairs of jeans.
    Payton 有超過五十條的牛仔褲。

---

13. **letter** [ˋlɛtɚ] n. [C] 信 <from>；字母
    ▲ Fanny got a letter from her pen pal today.
    Fanny 今天收到筆友的來信。
    💡 answer a letter 回信

---

14. **lonely** [ˋlonlɪ] adj. 孤獨的 [同] lonesome (lonelier |

loneliest)

▲ Spending time with friends helps us avoid being lonely. 和朋友來往能幫助我們免於孤獨。

---

15. **monkey** [ˋmʌŋkɪ] n. [C] 猴子

▲ The climber noticed a monkey sitting in the tree.
登山客注意到有一隻猴子坐在樹上。

💡 make a monkey (out) of sb 使…出醜，愚弄…

16. **pig** [pɪg] n. [C] 豬 [同] hog

▲ Jack makes a living by keeping pigs.
Jack 以養豬為生。

pig [pɪg] v. 狼吞虎嚥 <out> (pigged | pigged | pigging)

▲ The hungry boy pigged out on hamburgers and fries.
這飢餓的男孩狼吞虎嚥地吃漢堡和薯條。

17. **quarter** [ˋkwɔrtɚ] n. [C] 四分之一；(時間) 十五分鐘

▲ Albert walked a quarter of a mile to the train station.
Albert 走了四分之一英里的路到火車站。

18. **robot** [ˋrobɑt] n. [C] 機器人

▲ Japan is a leading producer of industrial robots.
日本是工業用機器人的主要生產國。

19. **shirt** [ʃɝt] n. [C] (尤指男式) 襯衫

▲ The long-sleeved shirt is made from pure cotton.
這件長袖襯衫是由純棉製成。

20. **sky** [skaɪ] n. [C][U] 天空 <in> (pl. skies)

▲ Ivan often uses his telescope to observe the stars in the sky. Ivan 常用他的望遠鏡觀察天上的星星。

21. **strange** [strendʒ] adj. 罕見的，奇怪的 [同] odd；不熟悉的，陌生的 (stranger | strangest)

▲ There are many strange animals and birds in Australia. 在澳洲有許多罕見的鳥獸。

22. **thick** [θɪk] adj. 厚的 [反] thin；濃的 [同] dense

▲ Betty spread a thick layer of jam on the toast.
Betty 在吐司上抹上一層厚的果醬。

thicken [ˋθɪkən] v. (使) 變厚或濃 [反] thin

▲ The chef added flour to thicken the sauce.
主廚添加麵粉以讓醬汁變濃稠。

23. **throw** [θro] v. 丟，投 <at, to> (threw | thrown | throwing)

▲ The angry mob threw stones at the police.
憤怒的暴民向警察丟擲石頭。

throw [θro] n. [C] 投，擲

▲ To our surprise, Hank's first throw was over fifty meters.
令我們驚訝的是，Hank 的第一投超過五十公尺。

24. **tonight** [təˋnaɪt] adv. 今晚

▲ Barbara will go out on a date tonight.
Barbara 今晚要外出約會。

tonight [təˋnaɪt] n. [U] 今晚

▲ We are looking forward to tonight's soccer game.
我們很期待今晚的足球賽。

25. **yesterday** [ˈjɛstɚde] adv. 昨天

▲ My friends and I watched a movie yesterday afternoon. 我和朋友昨天下午看了電影。

yesterday [ˈjɛstɚde] n. [U] 昨天；日前，往昔

▲ Steve and Lisa's wedding took place the day before yesterday. Steve 和 Lisa 的婚禮在前天舉辦。

Unit 35

1. **abroad** [əˈbrɔd] adv. 去 (在) 國外

▲ Traveling abroad is a good way to learn about other cultures. 到國外旅行是學習其他文化的好方法。

2. **bottom** [ˈbɑtəm] n. [C] 底部 (usu. sing.)；臀部 [同] backside

▲ The ship sank to the bottom of the sea after hitting an iceberg. 那艘船撞到冰山後就沉入海底。

bottom [ˈbɑtəm] adj. 底部的 [反] top

▲ You can find the book you want on the bottom shelf. 你可以在底部的書架找到你要的書。

bottom [ˈbɑtəm] v. 到達底部，降到最低點 <out>

▲ It seems that the oil prices have bottomed out. 油價似乎已經降到最低點了。

3. **bow** [baʊ] n. [C] 鞠躬

▲ The pianist gave a bow when her performance ended.
這鋼琴家在她表演結束時鞠躬。

bow [bo] n. [C] 弓

▲ The hunter shot an arrow from the bow.
那獵人用弓射箭。

bow [baʊ] v. 鞠躬 <to>

▲ The students bowed to their teacher respectfully.
學生們恭敬地向老師鞠躬。

---

4. **coat** [kot] n. [C] 大衣，外套；表面覆蓋的一層

▲ Melody went out without wearing a coat.
Melody 沒有穿外套就出門了。

coat [kot] v. 覆蓋…的表面 <with>

▲ The furniture in the deserted house was coated with
dust. 那廢棄屋子裡的家具上積了一層灰。

---

5. **comfortable** [ˋkʌmfɚtəbl̩] adj. 舒適的，舒服的；輕鬆自
在的

▲ The wooden chair is not comfortable to sit on.
這個木椅坐起來不舒服。

---

6. **daughter** [ˋdɔtɚ] n. [C] 女兒

▲ Mrs. White has two sons and one daughter.
White 太太有兩個兒子和一個女兒。

---

7. **dozen** [ˋdʌzn̩] n. [C] 一打，十二個 (abbr. doz.)；許多

▲ There are a dozen eggs in the container.

容器裡有十二顆蛋。

8. **farmer** [ˈfɑrmɚ] n. [C] 農民；農場主人
   ▲ The farmers had a poor harvest because of the drought. 農民因為乾旱而收成不好。

9. **girl** [gɝl] n. [C] 女孩；女兒 [同] daughter
   ▲ Every time Pete saw the girl, his heart raced.
   每一次 Pete 看到這女孩都會心跳加速。

10. **glad** [glæd] adj. 高興的 <about> (gladder | gladdest)
   ▲ Melvin's parents are glad about his success.
   Melvin 的父母非常高興他成功了。

11. **helpful** [ˈhɛlpfəl] adj. 有幫助的，有用的 <in>
   ▲ The website is helpful in learning social skills.
   這個網站對於學習社交技巧很有幫助。

12. **jump** [dʒʌmp] v. 跳躍 [同] leap；突然或快速行動
   ▲ The kids jumped up and down on the bed.
   孩子們在床上跳上跳下的。
   jump [dʒʌmp] n. [C] 跳躍 [同] leap
   ▲ The audience was amazed by the dancer's jumps.
   這舞者的跳躍讓觀眾驚奇。

13. **lazy** [ˈlezɪ] adj. 懶惰的 (lazier | laziest)
   ▲ Nicole is very diligent, while her brother is very lazy.
   Nicole 非常勤奮，然而她弟弟卻很懶散。

14. **lose** [luz] v. 失去；輸掉 (比賽等) [反] win (lost | lost | losing)

▲ Hundreds of people lost their jobs when the factory was closed down. 這間工廠關閉時有數百人失業。

---

15. **menu** [ˋmɛnju] n. [C] 菜單 <on>

▲ There are chicken, beef, and seafood on the menu. 菜單上有雞肉、牛肉和海鮮。

---

16. **Mr.** [ˋmɪstɚ] n. [U] (用在男子的姓或職稱之前) 先生 (also Mister)

▲ Mr. Grant has worked for the bank for ten years. Grant 先生在這銀行工作十年了。

---

17. **quiet** [ˋkwaɪət] adj. 安靜的；寡言的，話不多的

▲ The classroom was very quiet as the students took the exam. 學生們在考試時教室很安靜。

quiet [ˋkwaɪət] n. [U] 安靜

▲ Hebe desired to have some peace and quiet after a busy day. Hebe 渴望在忙碌的一天後擁有一些寧靜。

quiet [ˋkwaɪət] v. (使) 安靜 <down>

▲ Ben asked his children to quiet down and go to bed. Ben 要他的孩子安靜下來，然後上床睡覺。

---

18. **roll** [rol] v. 滾動 <off, into>；捲 <up>

▲ The egg rolled off the counter and broke on the floor. 這顆雞蛋滾落檯面，在地上破掉了。

roll [rol] n. [C] 一捲

▲ The supermarket offered a discount on paper towel
rolls. 這間超市的捲筒紙巾有折扣。

19. **shoe** [ʃu] **n.** [C] 鞋子

  ▲ Jasmine packed two pairs of shoes for her trip.
    Jasmine 為她的旅行打包兩雙鞋子。

  ♥ in sb's shoes 處於某人的境地

20. **shop** [ʃɑp] **n.** [C] 商店 [同] store

  ▲ The clothing shop is having a clearance sale.
    這間服裝店正在舉辦清倉大拍賣。

  shop [ʃɑp] **v.** 購物 <for> (shopped | shopped |
  shopping)

  ▲ I prefer to shop for clothes online because it is very
    convenient. 我偏好在網路上買衣服，因為很方便。

21. **snake** [snek] **n.** [C] 蛇

  ▲ The snake slowly swallowed the mouse.
    這條蛇慢慢地吞下老鼠。

  snake [snek] **v.** 蜿蜒伸展 [同] wind

  ▲ Pipes snaked all around the ceiling.
    天花板各處都鋪滿了管線。

22. **tail** [tel] **n.** [C] 尾巴

  ▲ The dog is wagging its tail at the little boy.
    那隻狗在對小男孩搖尾巴。

23. **tie** [taɪ] **n.** [C] 領帶；關係，聯繫 (usu. pl.)

  ▲ The groom and best man both dressed in a suit and

tie. 新郎和伴郎都是穿西裝打領帶。

tie [taɪ] v. 綁，繫 <to> [反] untie；平手 <with> (tied | tied | tying)

▲ The farmer tied his horse to a tree.
　農夫把他的馬拴在樹旁。

24. **towel** [taʊl] n. [C] 毛巾，紙巾

▲ Bennett wiped his body dry with a towel.
　Bennett 用毛巾把身體擦乾。

towel [taʊl] v. 用毛巾擦乾 <down>

▲ Ann quickly toweled her baby down after the bath.
　Ann 在沐浴後快速用毛巾把嬰兒擦乾。

25. **toy** [tɔɪ] n. [C] 玩具

▲ Brody has a large collection of toy cars.
　Brody 收集了大量的玩具車。

Unit 36

1. **actor** [ˈæktɚ] n. [C] 男演員

▲ Tom Hanks is one of my favorite actors.
　湯姆漢克斯是我最喜愛的男演員之一。

actress [ˈæktrɪs] n. [C] 女演員 (pl. actresses)

▲ The actress will star in a sci-fi movie.
　這女演員將主演一部科幻片。

2. **brave** [brev] adj. 勇敢的 [同] courageous (braver |

bravest)

▲ It was brave of Rory to save the old man from the burning house.

Rory 從失火的房子救出老人真是勇敢。

---

3. **butterfly** [ˋbʌtɚˏflaɪ] n. [C] 蝴蝶 (pl. butterflies)

▲ There are about 20,000 species of butterflies around the world. 全世界大約有兩萬種蝴蝶品種。

♥ have butterflies (in sb's stomach) …感到非常緊張

---

4. **collect** [kəˋlɛkt] v. 蒐集；收 (租金等)

▲ Dominic likes to collect stamps.

Dominic 喜歡蒐集郵票。

---

5. **convenient** [kənˋvinjənt] adj. 方便的 <for> [反] inconvenient

▲ Let's meet at the MRT station if it is convenient for you. 如果你方便的話，我們在捷運站碰面吧。

---

6. **dish** [dɪʃ] n. [C] 盤子；一盤菜 (pl. dishes)

▲ Nora and her husband take turns doing the dishes.

Nora 和她丈夫會輪流洗碗。

dish [dɪʃ] v. 分發 (菜) <out>

▲ The father dished the pasta out for his children.

這父親給孩子們分發義大利麵。

---

7. **draw** [drɔ] v. 畫；吸引 (興趣、注意) (drew | drawn | drawing)

▲ Kevin drew a pencil sketch of the city.

Kevin 畫了這城市的素描。

draw [drɔ] n. [C] 平局 [同] tie；抽獎

▲ The baseball game ended in a draw.
這場棒球賽最後雙方平手。

---

8. **feed** [fid] v. 餵養 <to>；(動物或嬰兒) 吃 (fed | fed | feeding)

▲ Anita likes to feed bread to the pigeons in the park.
Anita 喜歡餵麵包給公園裡的鴿子。

♥ feed on sth 以⋯為主食

feed [fid] n. [U] 飼料

▲ The website offers a wide range of animal feed.
這個網站販售各式各樣的動物飼料。

---

9. **gray** [gre] adj. 灰色的；灰白的

▲ Jacky often wears a gray T-shirt to work.
Jacky 時常穿著灰色的 T 恤去上班。

gray [gre] n. [C][U] 灰色

▲ The insurance sales agent is dressed in gray.
這保險業務員穿著灰色的衣服。

gray [gre] v. 頭髮變得灰白

▲ My mother is graying a little at the sides.
我母親的兩鬢有一點灰白了。

---

10. **hit** [hɪt] v. 打，擊 <on>；碰撞 [同] bang (hit | hit | hitting)

▲ The ball hit Jack on the head. 球打中了 Jack 的頭。

hit [hɪt] n. [C] 非常受歡迎的人或物；打，擊 <on>

▲ The pop singer's new album is a number one hit.
那流行歌手的新專輯是第一名的暢銷專輯。

🍐 be a hit with sb 受…歡迎

11. **holiday** [ˋhɑləˌde] n. [C][U] 假期；休假 [同] vacation

▲ Carrie planned to take a holiday on a tropical island.
Carrie 計劃要在熱帶島嶼渡假。

12. **leader** [ˋlidɚ] n. [C] 領袖，領導人

▲ Mr. Lee was elected as leader of the political party.
李先生被選為這政黨的領袖。

13. **lie** [laɪ] v. 躺 (lay | lain | lying)；說謊 <to> (lied | lied | lying)

▲ Ann is lying on the bed, thinking about her future.
Ann 正躺在床上思考她的未來。

lie [laɪ] n. [C] 謊言

▲ Miles promised that he wouldn't tell a lie again.
Miles 承諾他不會再說謊了。

🍐 white lie 善意的謊言

14. **miss** [mɪs] v. 未趕上，錯過；想念

▲ If you don't hurry, you will miss the train.
如果你不快一點，就趕不上火車了。

miss [mɪs] n. [C] 未擊中；(對年輕女子的稱呼) 小姐

▲ The last ball was a miss again, so the batter was struck out.
最後一球又未擊中，所以這名打者被三振出局。

15. **month** [mʌnθ] n. [C] 月分

▲ Mike and Judy got married last month.
Mike 和 Judy 上個月結婚了。

16. **Mrs.** [ˋmɪsɪz] n. [U] (用在已婚婦女的姓名之前) 太太，夫人

▲ Mrs. Brooks hired a nanny to help care for her children. Brooks 太太僱用保姆來幫忙照顧孩子。

17. **rainy** [ˋrenɪ] adj. 下雨的，多雨的 [同] wet (rainier | rainiest)

▲ Unfortunately, Joyce had five rainy days during her vacation. 不幸的是，Joyce 渡假期間有五天是下雨天。

18. **secretary** [ˋsɛkrəˏtɛrɪ] n. [C] 祕書 (pl. secretaries)

▲ The manager asked his secretary to arrange a meeting with Mark.
經理要求他的祕書安排和 Mark 的會面。

19. **smart** [smɑrt] adj. 聰明的 [同] clever [反] stupid

▲ The smart girl learns things very quickly.
這個聰明的女孩學東西很快。

20. **son** [sʌn] n. [C] 兒子

▲ Mr. Tyler's youngest son is a doctor.
Tyler 先生最小的兒子是醫生。

21. **spring** [sprɪŋ] n. [C][U] 春天；[C] 泉

▲ The flowers are coming into bloom with the coming

of spring. 隨著春天到來，花朵開始綻放了。

spring [sprɪŋ] v. 跳，躍 [同] leap (sprang | sprung | springing)

▲ Henry sprang out of bed when his mother came in.
當他母親進來時，Henry 立刻從床上跳起來。

---

22. **tall** [tɔl] adj. 高的

▲ Taipei 101 used to be the tallest building in the world. 臺北 101 曾經是世界上最高的建築物。

---

23. **tiger** [ˋtaɪgɚ] n. [C] 老虎

▲ People today see tigers in zoos rather than in the wild. 現今人們在動物園而不是野外看到老虎。

💡 paper tiger 紙老虎 (指外強中乾的敵人或國家)

---

24. **treat** [trit] v. 對待 <as, like>；治療 <for>

▲ The Murrays treat their pet dog as one of the family.
Murray 一家人把他們的狗當作家人看待。

treatment [ˋtritmənt] n. [U] 對待 <of>；[C][U] 治療，療法 <for, of>

▲ The social worker complained about the cruel treatment of the orphans.
社工抱怨孤兒們受到的殘酷對待。

---

25. **truck** [trʌk] n. [C] 卡車 [同] lorry

▲ Dust floated through the air after a truck sped past us.
卡車從我們旁邊呼嘯而過後，空氣中瀰漫著塵土。

Unit 37

1. **anybody** [ˋɛnɪ͵bɑdɪ] pron. 任何人 [同] anyone

   ▲ Can anybody tell me what I should do now?
   有任何人可以告訴我現在應該做什麼嗎？

   anyone [ˋɛnɪ͵wʌn] pron. 任何人 [同] anybody

   ▲ Don't reveal your secrets to anyone you don't trust.
   不要把祕密告訴任何你無法信任的人。

2. **brother** [ˋbrʌðɚ] n. [C] 兄弟

   ▲ Thomas is taller than his elder brother.
   Thomas 比他哥哥高。

3. **button** [ˋbʌtn̩] n. [C] 鈕扣

   ▲ A button was missing from my coat.
   我的外套掉了一顆鈕扣。

   button [ˋbʌtn̩] v. 扣上…的鈕扣 <up>

   ▲ Joan buttoned up her coat before going out.
   Joan 在出門前先扣上外套的鈕扣。

4. **cool** [kul] adj. 涼爽的；冷靜的

   ▲ Eason likes to read in the cool shade of a tree.
   Eason 喜歡在涼爽的樹蔭下讀書。

   cool [kul] v. (使) 冷卻；(感情) 冷淡下來 <off>

   ▲ Let the pumpkin pie cool for fifteen minutes before
   you cut it. 在你切南瓜派前，先讓它冷卻十五分鐘。

   💡 cool (sb) down/off (使) 冷靜下來

   cool [kul] n. [sing.] 涼爽；[U] 冷靜

▲ Mr. Owen took a walk in the cool of the early morning. Owen 先生在清晨的涼意中散步。

5. **dinner** [`dɪnɚ] n. [C][U] 晚餐；[C] 晚宴
   ▲ Harper had instant noodles for dinner.
   Harper 晚餐吃泡麵。

6. **elephant** [`ɛləfənt] n. [C] 大象
   ▲ The elephant is an enormous animal.
   大象是一種巨大的動物。

7. **except** [ɪk`sɛpt] prep. 除⋯之外 <for>
   ▲ Flora has been to all of the countries in Europe except for Greece.
   除了希臘外，Flora 去過歐洲所有的國家。
   except [ɪk`sɛpt] conj. 除⋯之外
   ▲ Nothing was decided except that some steps had to be taken at once.
   除了某些步驟必須立刻實行外，其他什麼都尚未決定。

8. **finger** [`fɪŋgɚ] n. [C] 指頭
   ▲ Hannah accidentally cut her finger while she was preparing dinner.
   Hannah 在準備晚餐時不小心切到手指。
   💡 point the finger at sb 指責⋯
   finger [`fɪŋgɚ] v. 用手指觸摸
   ▲ The kid fingered the candies in his pocket.
   這孩童用手指觸摸口袋裡的糖果。

9. **guitar** [gɪˋtɑr] n. [C] 吉他

▲ Winston is playing the electric guitar.
Winston 正在彈電吉他。

---

10. **honest** [ˋɑnɪst] adj. 誠 實 的 <with> [同] frank [反] dishonest

▲ To be honest with you, I don't think you would be good for this job.
坦白跟你說，我不認為你適合這個工作。

---

11. **horse** [hɔrs] n. [C] 馬

▲ Todd rides his horse in the fields on weekends.
Todd 週末會在田野間騎馬。

---

12. **lesson** [ˋlɛsn̩] n. [C] (一節) 課；教訓

▲ Maggie will start taking piano lessons next month.
Maggie 下個月會開始上鋼琴課。

---

13. **listen** [ˋlɪsn̩] v. 聽 <to>；聽從 <to>

▲ Listening to soft music can make me relax.
聽輕柔的音樂能讓我放鬆。

---

14. **Ms.** [mɪz] n. [U] 女士 (用於婚姻狀況不明或不願提及婚姻狀況的女子姓名之前)

▲ Ms. Carter is the CEO of the hotel chain.
Carter 女士是這連鎖飯店的執行長。

---

15. **noon** [nun] n. [U] 中午，正午 <at> [同] midday

▲ The workers have a one-hour lunch break at noon.

員工們在中午有一個小時的午休時間。

16. **price** [praɪs] n. [C][U] 價格；[sing.] 代價
   ▲ Jacky bought the leather jacket at half price.
   Jacky 以半價買了這件皮衣。
   price [praɪs] v. 給…定價 <at>
   ▲ The organic apples are priced at $4 each.
   這些有機蘋果每顆定價四美元。

17. **ring** [rɪŋ] n. [C] 圈；戒指
   ▲ Taiwan is located on the Pacific Ring of Fire.
   臺灣位於太平洋火環帶上。
   ring [rɪŋ] v. (使) 響起鈴聲 (rang | rung | ringing)
   ▲ Vicky rang the doorbell several times, but no one
   answered. Vicky 按門鈴好幾次，但是沒有人回應。

18. **shall** [ʃæl] aux. 將會 (與 I 或 we 連用)；表建議 (與 I 或 we 連用)
   ▲ I shall attend a national conference next Wednesday.
   我下週三將會參加一個全國性的會議。

19. **soldier** [ˋsoldʒɚ] n. [C] 士兵，軍人
   ▲ Thousands of soldiers lost their lives in the war.
   數千名士兵在這場戰爭中喪生。

20. **stand** [stænd] v. 站立；座落，位於 (stood | stood | standing)
   ▲ Fred stood there with his arms folded.
   Fred 雙臂交疊著站在那裡。

💡 stand up 起立 | stand up for sb/sth 支持…

stand [stænd] n. [C] (尤指公開的) 觀點;攤位 [同] stall

▲ The mayor didn't take a stand on the political issue.
市長對這個政治議題沒有公開表態。

---

21. **surprise** [sə`praɪz] n. [C] 意想不到的事物;[U] 驚訝

▲ Richard's friends intended to throw him a surprise
party for his birthday.
Richard 的朋友打算幫他辦個驚喜生日派對。

surprise [sə`praɪz] v. 使驚訝

▲ It surprised Erica that the doll looked like a real
baby. 這個娃娃看起來像真的嬰兒讓 Erica 很驚訝。

---

22. **tennis** [`tɛnɪs] n. [U] 網球

▲ The talented tennis player has won five
championships in the past ten years. 這位有天賦的網
球選手在過去十年已經贏得五座冠軍了。

---

23. **tip** [tɪp] n. [C] 尖端;小費

▲ Danny stood on the tips of his toes to hang the photo
on the wall. Danny 踮起腳尖將照片掛在牆上。

tip [tɪp] v. (使) 翻覆;給小費 (tipped | tipped | tipping)

▲ Watch out! Don't tip the milk jug!
小心!別打翻牛奶罐!

---

24. **T-shirt** [`ti‚ʃɜt] n. [C] T 恤 [同] tee shirt

▲ Guests in T-shirts and jeans are not allowed to enter
the posh restaurant.

穿著 T 恤和牛仔褲的客人不得進入這間高檔的餐廳。

25. **wait** [wet] **v.** 等候 <for>

▲ The spectators were waiting for the boxers to appear in the ring. 觀眾們正等候拳擊手上場。

💡 wait on sb/sth 服侍…；等候… | wait up 不眠地等待

wait [wet] **n.** [sing.] 等候

▲ The fans had a four-hour wait before they saw their idol. 粉絲等了四個小時才看到他們的偶像。

Unit 38

1. **bean** [bin] **n.** [C] 豆 (莢)

▲ Coffee beans are the seeds of coffee trees.
咖啡豆是咖啡樹的種子。

---

2. **cake** [kek] **n.** [C][U] 蛋糕

▲ Martha is good at making cakes and cookies.
Martha 很擅長做蛋糕和餅乾。

💡 be a piece of cake 輕而易舉的事

---

3. **cheap** [tʃip] **adj.** 便宜的 [反] expensive；廉價的

▲ The designer clothing is still not cheap in a sale.
這些名牌服裝在特價時仍然不便宜。

cheap [tʃip] **adv.** 便宜地，物美價廉地

▲ There were some boots going cheap in the store.
這間店有些靴子在廉價出售。

---

4. **count** [kaʊnt] v. 計數 <to>；很重要

▲ When you are angry, count to ten to relieve your anger. 當你生氣的時候，數到十來舒緩你的怒氣。

💡 count (up)on sb/sth 指望…，依賴…

count [kaʊnt] n. [C] 計數，計算

▲ The fireworks display will begin on the count of ten. 數到十時煙火秀將會開始。

5. **expect** [ɪkˋspɛkt] v. 預計；期望，期待

▲ We expect the experiment will be completed by Friday. 我們預計實驗將會在週五前完成。

6. **fail** [fel] v. 失敗，未能做到；不及格，未能通過考試 <in>

▲ It was a pity that the singer failed to go through to the final. 很可惜這歌手沒能進入決賽。

fail [fel] n. [C][U] 失敗；(考試) 不及格 <in> [反] pass

▲ Buck calls his girlfriend every night without fail. Buck 每晚必定會打電話給女友。

7. **fan** [fæn] n. [C] 迷；電風扇

▲ Maddox is a big fan of the Beatles. Maddox 是披頭四樂團的狂熱粉絲。

fan [fæn] v. 搧 (風) (fanned | fanned | fanning)

▲ Sawyer fanned himself with a leaflet. Sawyer 用傳單來幫自己搧風。

8. **garden** [ˋɡɑrdn̩] n. [C] 花園 [同] yard

▲ Ms. Smith grew some herbs in her garden.
Smith 女士在她的花園裡種了一些藥草。

garden [ˋgɑrdn̩] v. 從事園藝

▲ My father loves gardening in his free time.
我父親喜愛在閒暇時從事園藝。

9. **guy** [gaɪ] n. [C] 男人；[pl.] 大家，各位 (～s)

▲ I think Justin is a nice guy.
我覺得 Justin 是個不錯的人。

10. **hurt** [hɝt] v. 弄傷，受傷；感到疼痛 (hurt | hurt | hurting)

▲ The dancer hurt her knee in the performance.
這舞者在表演時膝蓋受傷。

hurt [hɝt] n. [C][U] (感情上的) 傷害，痛苦

▲ The woman felt a deep hurt after the divorce.
這婦人在離婚後感到很痛苦。

11. **join** [dʒɔɪn] v. 連接；參加

▲ Leo joined the two wires together by using tape.
Leo 用膠布把這兩條金屬線連接起來。

join [dʒɔɪn] n. [C] 接合處

▲ The wallpaper was glued so well that we could hardly see the joins.
這些壁紙被黏得很好，所以我們幾乎看不到接合處。

12. **lunch** [lʌntʃ] n. [C][U] 午餐

▲ When the clock struck twelve, the students started to have lunch.

當鐘聲在十二點響起時，學生們開始吃午餐。

lunch [lʌntʃ] v. 吃午餐 <on>

▲ Since Jessica was on a diet, she lunched on salad.
由於 Jessica 在節食，她午餐吃沙拉。

---

13. **married** [ˋmærɪd] adj. 已婚的

▲ Tristan has still not adjusted to married life.
Tristan 還不適應婚姻生活。

---

14. **mud** [mʌd] n. [U] 泥土，泥濘

▲ Irene's feet were stuck in the mud and couldn't move. Irene 的雙腳陷在泥濘中，動彈不得。

---

15. **pants** [pænts] n. [pl.] 褲子

▲ John ironed two shirts and three pairs of pants.
John 熨了兩件襯衫和三條褲子。

---

16. **radio** [ˋredɪ͵o] n. [C] 收音機；[U] 廣播節目

▲ Lauren turned on the radio the moment she got up.
Lauren 一起床就打開收音機。

radio [ˋredɪ͵o] v. 用無線電發送 <for>

▲ The sinking ship urgently radioed for help.
這艘在下沉的船緊急用無線電求救。

---

17. **root** [rut] n. [C] (植物的) 根；(問題的) 根源

▲ Carrots, onions, and ginger are root vegetables.
紅蘿蔔、洋蔥和薑都是根莖類蔬菜。

18. **shout** [ʃaʊt] v. 大聲叫喊 <at>

▲ Mary's husband often shouts at her.
Mary 的丈夫經常對她大吼大叫。

shout [ʃaʊt] n. [C] 叫喊聲 <of>

▲ The runner gave a shout of joy when crossing the
finish line. 這跑者跨過終點線時高聲歡呼。

---

19. **star** [stɑr] n. [C] 星星；明星

▲ The climbers saw numerous stars twinkling in the
sky. 這群登山客看見無數星星在天空閃爍。

star [stɑr] v. 主演，擔任要角 <in> (starred | starred |
starring)

▲ The young actor will star in the romantic movie.
這位年輕演員將在這部愛情片中擔任主角。

---

20. **surprised** [sə`praɪzd] adj. 感到驚訝的 <at, by>

▲ We were greatly surprised at Greg's fury.
我們對 Greg 的暴怒大感驚訝。

---

21. **teach** [titʃ] v. 教導，教授 (taught | taught | teaching)

▲ Mr. Grant taught history in the middle school.
Grant 先生在這間中學教歷史。

---

22. **theater** [`θiətə] n. [C] 劇院；[U] 戲劇

▲ People should turn their cellphones off when
watching a film in a movie theater.
人們在電影院看電影時應該要把手機關機。

---

23. **tired** [taɪrd] adj. 疲倦的；厭煩的

▲ Ezra began to feel tired as he neared the summit.
Ezra 接近山頂時就開始覺得疲累。

24. **uncle** [ˋʌŋkḷ] n. [C] 叔父，伯父，姨父，姑父，舅舅
▲ Uncle Frank is going to visit us at Christmas.
Frank 叔叔將會在耶誕節來拜訪我們。

25. **wall** [wɔl] n. [C] 牆 (壁)
▲ The Greeks built stone walls around the city.
希臘人在這城市四周築起石牆。

Unit 39

1. **beef** [bif] n. [U] 牛肉
▲ The Pearsons often have roast beef for lunch on
Sundays. Pearson 一家人週日中午通常吃烤牛肉。

2. **camp** [kæmp] n. [C][U] 營地；[C] 營
▲ Tim set up camp in the woods at dusk.
Tim 黃昏時在森林裡紮營。
camp [kæmp] v. 紮營，露營
▲ Let's camp by the lake tonight!
我們今晚就在湖邊露營吧！

3. **circle** [ˋsɝkḷ] n. [C] 圓圈；圈子，界
▲ The tourist used his fingers to form a circle to
indicate "OK."
這位遊客用手指形成圓圈以表示「沒問題」。

circle [`sɝkl] **v.** 盤旋；圈出

▲ A helicopter was circling above the roof.
　一臺直升機在屋頂上方盤旋。

---

4. **cow** [kaʊ] **n.** [C] 母牛，乳牛

▲ A herd of cows are eating grass in the field.
　一群乳牛正在草地上吃草。

---

5. **fine** [faɪn] **adj.** 健康的 [同] OK；優質的 (finer | finest)

▲ Roger felt fine after taking the medicine.
　Roger 吃了藥後身體就好了。

fine [faɪn] **adv.** 令人滿意地

▲ I'm not hungry, and a cup of tea would suit me fine.
　我不餓，一杯茶就夠了。

fine [faɪn] **v.** 處⋯以罰款 <for>

▲ Gloria was fined for speeding. Gloria 因超速被罰款。

fine [faɪn] **n.** [C] 罰款

▲ Levi faced a heavy fine for drunk driving.
　Levi 因酒駕而面臨高額罰款。

---

6. **floor** [flor] **n.** [C] 地面，地板；樓層

▲ The boys were playing chess on the floor.
　男孩們在地板上玩西洋棋。

floor [flor] **v.** 打倒在地

▲ Alfred was floored by the opponent's punch.
　Alfred 被對手的一拳打倒在地。

---

7. **gate** [get] **n.** [C] 大門；(機場的) 登機門

▲ The car went through the gate into the royal palace.
那輛車穿過了大門進入皇宮。

8. **ham** [hæm] n. [C][U] 火腿
   ▲ Ham and bacon are both made out of pork.
   火腿和培根都是豬肉做的。

9. **height** [haɪt] n. [C][U] 高度 <in>
   ▲ Calvin is six feet in height. Calvin 身高六英尺。

10. **joy** [dʒɔɪ] n. [U] 喜悅；[C] 樂事，樂趣
   ▲ Lucy wept for joy when she first heard her baby saying "mommy."
   Lucy 第一次聽到她的孩子叫「媽咪」時喜極而泣。

11. **loud** [laʊd] adv. 大聲地 [同] loudly
   ▲ Elsa asked the tour guide to speak louder so that she could hear him.
   Elsa 要求導遊講大聲一點，這樣她才可以聽見他的話。
   loud [laʊd] adj. 大聲的 [反] quiet
   ▲ Allen was annoyed by his roommate's loud music.
   Allen 被他室友大聲的音樂聲給惹惱。

12. **mathematics** [ˌmæθəˈmætɪks] n. [U] 數學 [同] math
   ▲ Mathematics is a required course in senior high school. 數學是高中的必修課程。

13. **moment** [ˈmomənt] n. [C] 片刻；時刻，時機
   ▲ Wait a moment; I need to answer the call.

等一下，我需要接個電話。

14. **nice** [naɪs] **adj.** 美好的；好心的 (nicer | nicest)

▲ Joe and his family spent a nice vacation in the ski resort. Joe 和家人在滑雪勝地度過美好的假期。

15. **pencil** [ˋpɛnsl] **n.** [C] 鉛筆

▲ Violet is drawing with colored pencils.
Violet 正用色鉛筆在畫圖。

🕯 in pencil 用鉛筆寫

16. **rain** [ren] **n.** [U] 雨

▲ We usually get a lot of rain in summer.
我們這裡夏天通常多雨。

rain [ren] **v.** 下雨

▲ It rained heavily while Dennis was driving to work.
Dennis 開車去上班時正在下大雨。

17. **rope** [rop] **n.** [C][U] 繩索，粗繩

▲ The man was tied to the tree with a rope.
這名男子被人用繩索綁在樹上。

18. **shower** [ˋʃaʊɚ] **n.** [C] 淋浴；陣雨

▲ Brandon takes a shower every morning.
Brandon 每天早上都會淋浴。

shower [ˋʃaʊɚ] **v.** 沖澡；(某物) 蜂擁而至 <on>

▲ Jessie heard her father showering and singing.
Jessie 聽到她爸爸邊沖澡邊唱歌。

19. **station** [`steʃən] n. [C] 車站；(提供某種服務的) 站，局
   ▲ Our house is located within walking distance of the train station. 我們家在火車站的步行範圍內。

20. **teenager** [`tinˌedʒɚ] n. [C] 青少年
   ▲ The rock singer is popular with teenagers.
   這位搖滾歌手深受青少年喜愛。

21. **toe** [to] n. [C] 腳趾頭
   ▲ Bob stood on his toes to reach for the book.
   Bob 踮起腳尖取書。

22. **tomato** [tə`meto] n. [C] 番茄 (pl. tomatoes)
   ▲ Marian picked up some tomatoes from her yard.
   Marian 從她的園子裡採摘一些番茄。

23. **total** [`totl] adj. 總的；完全的
   ▲ Jeff counts the total calories he eats every day.
   Jeff 會計算他每天吃下的卡路里總數。
   total [`totl] n. [C] 總數 <in>
   ▲ These paintings are worth approximately five million dollars in total. 這些畫的總值約為五百萬美元。
   total [`totl] v. 總計
   ▲ Our debts totaled $80,000 this year.
   我們今年的債務總計為八萬美元。

24. **uniform** [`junəˌfɔrm] n. [C][U] 制服 <in>
   ▲ The pupils have to wear school uniforms to school.

這些小學生們必須穿學校制服上學。

25. **welcome** [ˈwɛlkəm] v. 歡迎，迎接 [同] greet
    ▲ The couple welcomed their guests at the door.
    這對夫妻在門口歡迎客人。
    welcome [ˈwɛlkəm] adj. 受歡迎的
    ▲ Michelle didn't feel welcome at the party.
    Michelle 覺得自己在派對中不受歡迎。
    welcome [ˈwɛlkəm] n. [sing.] 歡迎
    ▲ The host family gave Ivan a warm welcome.
    寄宿家庭熱烈地歡迎 Ivan。

Unit 40

1. **blow** [blo] v. 吹；吹走 <off, away> (blew | blown | blowing)
    ▲ The wind was blowing hard all night. 整夜風都很大。
    💡 blow sth down 吹倒… | blow away 吹走

2. **carrot** [ˈkærət] n. [C][U] 胡蘿蔔
    ▲ Julia made the soup with carrots and onions.
    Julia 用胡蘿蔔和洋蔥來煮湯。

3. **clock** [klɑk] n. [C] 時鐘
    ▲ Asher set the alarm clock before going to bed.
    Asher 睡覺之前先設定鬧鐘。

4. **define** [dɪˈfaɪn] v. 給…下定義，解釋 <as>

▲Happiness is often defined as being content with what one has had.
幸福通常被定義為對自己擁有的東西感到滿足。

5. **finish** [ˈfɪnɪʃ] v. 完成；結束
▲Carlos couldn't play online games until he finished his homework. Carlos 完成作業才可以打線上遊戲。
💡 finish sth off 完成… | finish with sth 不再使用…
finish [ˈfɪnɪʃ] n. [C] 結束，結局
▲The basketball game was a close finish.
這場籃球賽結束時比分相近。
💡 from start to finish 從頭到尾

6. **fool** [ful] n. [C] 傻子，笨蛋 [同] idiot
▲I'm a fool to believe Ethan's honeyed words.
我真是個笨蛋，竟然相信 Ethan 的甜言蜜語。
💡 make a fool of sb 使…出洋相 | act/play the fool 裝瘋賣傻
fool [ful] v. 愚弄，欺騙 <into>
▲Carol was fooled into believing that Lucas was very rich. Carol 被欺騙而相信 Lucas 很有錢。

7. **glove** [glʌv] n. [C] 手套
▲The bride and groom both wore a pair of white gloves. 新娘和新郎都戴一雙白手套。
💡 fit...like a glove (尺寸) 非常合適…

8. **hat** [hæt] n. [C] 帽子

▲ Miranda would wear a straw hat when she walks in the sun. Miranda 在太陽底下行走時會戴草帽。

---

9. **hen** [hɛn] n. [C] 母雞
   ▲ The hen laid two eggs this morning.
   這隻母雞今天早上下了兩顆蛋。

---

10. **knee** [ni] n. [C] 膝蓋
   ▲ Mandy fell off her bike and scraped her knee.
   Mandy 從腳踏車上摔下來且擦傷了膝蓋。
   💡 on sb's knees 跪著 | drop to sb's knees 跪下 | bring sb/sth to their knees 打敗…
   knee [ni] v. 用膝蓋撞擊
   ▲ Alice kneed the robber in the belly.
   Alice 用膝蓋撞擊搶匪的肚子。

---

11. **maybe** [ˋmebɪ] adv. 也許 [同] perhaps
   ▲ Maybe the world will be ruled by robots someday.
   也許將來有一天這個世界會被機器人統治。

---

12. **meal** [mil] n. [C] 餐
   ▲ Most people worldwide have three meals a day.
   世界各地大部分的人一天吃三餐。
   💡 a light/heavy meal 簡單的 / 豐盛的一餐

---

13. **notice** [ˋnotɪs] v. 注意到
   ▲ Have you noticed anything unusual recently?
   你最近有注意到任何不尋常的事嗎？
   notice [ˋnotɪs] n. [C] 告示；[U] 注意，關注

▲ The assistant put up a notice on the bulletin board.
助理把告示貼在公布欄上。

---

14. **nurse** [nɝs] n. [C] 護士，護理人員

   ▲ The nurses are taking care of injured people in the hospital. 護士們正在醫院裡照顧傷者。

   nurse [nɝs] v. 看護，照顧

   ▲ The mother nursed her sick baby back to health.
   這母親照顧她生病的嬰兒恢復健康。

---

15. **photograph** [ˋfotə͵græf] n. [C] 照片 (also photo)

   ▲ The father took a photograph of his little daughter.
   這位父親幫他小女兒拍照。

   🔮 color/black-and-white/digital photograph 彩色 / 黑白 /
   數位照片

   photograph [ˋfotə͵græf] v. 照相，攝影

   ▲ The model sat on the grass to be photographed.
   這位模特兒坐在草地上被拍照。

---

16. **room** [rum] n. [C] 房間，室；[U] 空間

   ▲ The job applicants will be interviewed in the meeting room. 這些求職者將會在會議室被面試。

   🔮 make room for sb/sth 騰出空間給…

   room [rum] v. 合租 <with>

   ▲ I roomed with Samantha at college.
   我上大學時和 Samantha 合租。

---

17. **sad** [sæd] adj. 傷心的 <about> [反] happy；令人遺憾的

(sadder | saddest)

▲ Sylvia was sad about the death of her pet cat.

Sylvia 對於愛貓的死亡感到傷心。

18. **sister** [ˋsɪstɚ] n. [C] 姊姊，妹妹

▲ The twin sisters have different personalities—one is shy, and the other is outgoing.

這對雙胞胎姊妹個性不同——一個害羞，一個外向。

19. **telephone** [ˋtɛləˌfon] n. [C] 電話 [同] phone

▲ Would you mind my using your telephone?

你介意我使用你的電話嗎？

🕯 talk on the telephone 講電話

telephone [ˋtɛləˌfon] v. 打電話給… [同] call, phone

▲ Edward telephoned the bank for more details of the car loan. Edward 打給銀行詢問關於車貸的更多細節。

20. **thank** [θæŋk] v. 感謝 <for>

▲ The old man thanked Rachel for helping him cross the road. 這老人感謝 Rachel 幫助他過馬路。

thank [θæŋk] n. [pl.] 謝意，感謝 <to> (～s)

▲ I don't know how to express my thanks to you.

我不知如何表達對你的感謝。

🕯 thanks to... 幸虧…，由於…

21. **tomorrow** [təˋmɔro] adv. (在) 明天；(在) 未來

▲ We'll clean up the local beach tomorrow morning.

我們明天早上要去當地的海灘淨灘。

tomorrow [tə`mɔro] n. [U] 明天；未來

▲ Please turn the music down; I'm studying for tomorrow's test.
請把音樂關小聲一點，我在準備明天的考試。

---

22. **tool** [tul] n. [C] 工具，器具

▲ The basic tools are usually designed for right-handed people. 基本的工具通常都是為右撇子設計的。

---

23. **violin** [ˌvaɪə`lɪn] n. [C] 小提琴

▲ Perry has learned playing the violin since childhood.
Perry 從孩提時代就開始學小提琴。

---

24. **walk** [wɔk] v. 走；遛 (狗等動物)

▲ The backpacker walked three miles to the hotel.
這背包客走了三英里的路到旅館。

💡 walk away (從困境中) 一走了之 | walk away with sth 輕鬆獲 (獎) | walk out (因不滿) 退場

walk [wɔk] n. [C] 步行，行走

▲ My grandparents take a walk in the park every morning. 我的祖父母每天早上都去公園散步。

---

25. **wise** [waɪz] adj. 明智的 [同] sensible；聰明的 (wiser | wisest)

▲ It was wise of Cindy to think twice before making the decision. Cindy 做這決定前再三考慮真是明智。

---

26. **wish** [wɪʃ] v. (表達與現在或過去事實相反的狀況) 希望，但願；祝福

▲ Nolan wishes his parents could buy him a new smartphone.

Nolan 希望他父母可以買一支新的智慧型手機給他。

wish [wɪʃ] n. [C] 希望；(靠魔術實現的) 願望

▲ The priest expressed his wish for world peace.

這位神父表達了世界和平的願望。

💡 fulfill sb's wish 實現…的願望 | get sb's wish 如願以償

---

27. **yes** [jɛs] adv. 是的，好的 [反] no

▲ Eric said "yes" to all of the questions.

Eric 對所有的問題都說「是」。

yes [jɛs] n. [C] 贊成票，投贊成票的人 (pl. yeses) [反] no

▲ The results show that the noes are leading the yeses.

結果顯示投反對票的人超過贊成的人。

yeah [ˈjɛə] adv. (口語用法) 是的，好的

▲ "Would you like some more coffee?" "Yeah, sure."

「你要再來點咖啡嗎？」「好的，當然。」

NOTE 🖉

Unit 1

1. **basic** [ˋbesɪk] adj. 基礎的，基本的
   ▲ Food and water are basic needs for survival.
   食物和水是生存的基本需要。

2. **battle** [ˋbæt!] n. [C][U] 戰鬥 <in>；鬥爭 <against>
   ▲ The soldiers fought bravely in battle.
   士兵們在戰鬥中英勇作戰。
   battle [ˋbæt!] v. 戰鬥 <over>；鬥爭，奮鬥 <with>
   ▲ The two countries have battled over the borders for years. 這兩個國家為邊境戰鬥了數年。

3. **bit** [bɪt] n. [C] 小片；少量，少許 <of>
   ▲ The glass dropped on the ground and broke to bits.
   玻璃杯掉到地上，破成碎片。

4. **channel** [ˋtʃæn!] n. [C] 路徑，管道 <of>；頻道 <to>
   ▲ It is necessary for the government to establish channels of communication with the public.
   政府建立和大眾溝通的管道是必要的。
   channel [ˋtʃæn!] v. 把…導入，將…投入 <into> [同] direct
   ▲ The country channeled aid into poor countries.
   這國家將援助投入貧窮國家。

5. **china** [ˋtʃaɪnə] n. [U] 瓷器，瓷製品
   ▲ Amelia always enjoys her afternoon tea with delicate

china cups and plates.

Amelia 總是用精緻的瓷杯及瓷盤享用下午茶。

6. **customer** [ˈkʌstəmɚ] n. [C] 顧客

▲ We have regular customers that come to the store every day. 我們有每天都來店裡的老主顧。

7. **ending** [ˈɛndɪŋ] n. [C] 結局

▲ The love story has a happy ending.
這愛情故事有圓滿的結局。

8. **especially** [ɪˈspɛʃəlɪ] adv. 特別，尤其 [同] particularly；專門，特地 <for>

▲ You must pay attention especially to the next part.
你一定要特別注意聽下面這個部分。

9. **following** [ˈfɑləwɪŋ] adj. 接著的 [反] preceding；下列的，下面的

▲ Adolf will arrive in Taipei this Saturday and leave the following Monday.
Adolf 這週六會抵達臺北並會在下一個週一離開。

following [ˈfɑləwɪŋ] prep. 在…之後 [反] before

▲ Following the ceremony, there will be a party.
在典禮之後會有一場派對。

following [ˈfɑləwɪŋ] n. [sing.] 接下來，下面 (the ～)

▲ The following is an extract from the famous speech.
接下來是出自這著名演講的一段摘錄。

10. **furniture** [ˈfɝnɪtʃɚ] n. [U] 家具

▲ The couple needs to buy some furniture for their new house. 這對夫妻需要為他們的新家買一些家具。

11. **huge** [hjudʒ] adj. 巨大的，極大的 [同] enormous (huger | hugest)

▲ Shirley was blamed for making a huge blunder. Shirley 犯了極大的錯誤而被責備。

12. **introduce** [ˌɪntrə`djus] v. 介紹 <to>；引進 <into>

▲ Mr. Austin, may I introduce my uncle to you? Austin 先生，容我向您介紹我叔叔？

13. **means** [minz] n. [C] 方法，手段 (pl. means)；[pl.] 金錢，財富

▲ The scientist explained his theory by means of graphs. 那科學家藉由圖表來解釋他的理論。

💡 by no means 絕不 | by all means 當然可以

14. **nervous** [`nɝvəs] adj. 緊張的 <about>

▲ Danny was very nervous about the entrance exam. Danny 對於入學考試感到非常緊張。

15. **per** [pɚ] prep. 每

▲ The speed limit here is sixty-five miles per hour. 這裡的速限是每小時六十五英里。

16. **perfect** [`pɝfɛkt] adj. 完美的 [反] imperfect；最適合的 <for> [同] ideal

▲ The dancer's performance was perfect; she made no mistakes at all.

那位舞者的表現是完美的，她完全沒犯錯。

perfect [pɚˋfɛkt] v. 使完美，改善

▲ The player practiced hard to perfect his skills.

這位球員努力練習以使他的技術更完美。

perfect [ˋpɚfɛkt] n. [sing.] 完成式 (the ～)

▲ The perfect is the form of a verb showing an action that has happened in the past.

完成式是顯示動作已經發生在過去的動詞形式。

---

17. **progress** [ˋprɑgrɛs] n. [U] 進步，進展 <in>

▲ The country has made great progress in controlling the pandemic.

這個國家在控制疫情方面有很大的進展。

progress [prəˋgrɛs] v. 進步，改進 [反] regress；進行

▲ The student's English is progressing rapidly.

這個學生的英文正快速地進步。

---

18. **quality** [ˋkwɑlətɪ] n. [C][U] 品質 <of> (pl. qualities)

▲ The goods that are made in Japan are of high quality.

日本製的產品品質很好。

---

19. **rapid** [ˋræpɪd] adj. 快速的

▲ Gary was walking at a rapid pace. Gary 快步行走。

---

20. **region** [ˋridʒən] n. [C] 地區，區域 <of> [同] area

▲ This is a farming region of the country.

這裡是該國的農業區。

---

21. **sense** [sɛns] n. [C] 感官；[sing.] 感覺 <of>

▲ The five senses are sight, hearing, smell, taste, and touch. 五種感官是視覺、聽覺、嗅覺、味覺和觸覺。

sense [sɛns] v. 意識到，感覺到

▲ Alex sensed there was something wrong with his car. Alex 意識到他的車子出了問題。

22. **skin** [skɪn] n. [C][U] 皮膚

▲ The farmer often works in the sun, so he has rough dark skin.

這農夫經常在太陽下工作，所以他的皮膚粗糙黝黑。

💡 wet/soaked/drenched to the skin 溼透的

23. **suggest** [səg`dʒɛst] v. 提議，建議；暗示 [同] indicate

▲ Paul suggested that his friend (should) spend a week with him. Paul 建議他的朋友應該和他一起待一週。

24. **thus** [ðʌs] adv. 因此，所以

▲ Andrew failed all his tests. Thus, he couldn't graduate.

Andrew 考試全部不及格。因此，他畢不了業。

25. **willing** [`wɪlɪŋ] adj. 願意的，樂意的 <to>

▲ Brad is thankful that his neighbor is willing to help him. Brad 很感謝他的鄰居願意幫他。

●━━━━━━━━━━━◆━━━━━━━━━━━●

Unit 2

1. **behave** [bɪ`hev] v. 行事，表現 [同] act；舉止端正 [反]

misbehave

▲ Although Daniel is twenty years old, he still behaves like a child.

雖然 Daniel 二十歲，他的行為舉止仍然像個孩子。

2. **beyond** [bɪˋjɑnd] prep. 在⋯的那一邊；超過

▲ Beyond the mountain there is a village.

在山的那一邊有一座村落。

beyond [bɪˋjɑnd] adv. 在更遠處

▲ From the top of the building, you can see the lake and the hills beyond. 從這棟建築物的頂部，你可以看見湖泊和在更遠處的山丘。

3. **billion** [ˋbɪljən] n. [C] 十億 <of>

▲ The wealthy man has billions of dollars.

這名富人擁有數十億美元。

4. **blanket** [ˋblæŋkɪt] n. [C] 毛毯；[sing.] 覆蓋層

▲ The father wrapped his daughter in a blanket.

這個父親用毛毯裹住他的女兒。

blanket [ˋblæŋkɪt] v. 覆蓋 <in>

▲ The city is often blanketed in thick fog.

這個城市常常被籠罩在濃霧中。

5. **conflict** [ˋkɑnflɪkt] n. [C][U] 衝突，分歧 <over>；戰鬥，戰爭

▲ Stacy was in conflict with her boyfriend over the wedding. Stacy 和男友因婚禮的事而起衝突。

conflict [kən`flɪkt] v. 抵觸，衝突 <with>

▲ Carol's ideas conflicted with mine.
Carol 的想法和我的衝突。

---

6. **degree** [dɪ`gri] n. [C][U] 程度 <to>；[C] 度數 (abbr. deg.)

▲ We can trust Clark to a high degree.
我們對 Clark 的信任程度極高。

💡 by degrees 逐漸地 | to a degree 在某種程度上

---

7. **delicious** [dɪ`lɪʃəs] adj. 美味的

▲ The cake was so delicious that Della ordered one more. 這蛋糕如此美味，以致於 Della 又點了一份。

---

8. **enemy** [`ɛnəmɪ] n. [C] 敵人 (pl. enemies)

▲ The bossy manager made lots of enemies in the company. 那專橫的經理在公司裡樹敵無數。

---

9. **field** [fild] n. [C] 田地，牧場；領域 <of>

▲ There is a lot of corn growing in the field.
田地上種了很多玉米。

---

10. **gather** [`gæðɚ] v. 聚集；收集

▲ A large crowd gathered in the square.
一大群人聚集在廣場。

---

11. **importance** [ɪm`pɔrtn̩s] n. [U] 重要性 <of>

▲ Recycling is a matter of great importance.
資源回收是極重要的事情。

---

12. **manager** [`mænɪdʒɚ] n. [C] 經理

   ▲ Duncan is a marketing manager in the computer company. Duncan 是該電腦公司的行銷經理。

13. **nor** [nɔr] conj. 也不

   ▲ Samuel can neither ride a scooter nor drive a car. Samuel 既不會騎機車也不會開車。

14. **pleasant** [`plɛzn̩t] adj. 宜人的，令人愉快的 [同] nice

   ▲ It was a pleasant evening; everyone had a good time. 這是個令人愉快的夜晚，每個人都過得很愉快。

15. **pride** [praɪd] n. [U] 自豪；自尊 (心)

   ▲ Watching her son accept the award, Betty felt a sense of pride. 看著她兒子領獎，Betty 感到自豪。

   ♥ take pride in sb/sth 為⋯自豪

   pride [praɪd] v. 為⋯而自豪，以⋯為傲 <on>

   ▲ Elliot prides himself on always arriving on time. Elliot 對自己總是準時到達而感到自豪。

16. **puppy** [`pʌpɪ] n. [C] 小狗，幼犬

   ▲ Jerry gave his son a puppy. Jerry 送給他兒子一隻小狗。

17. **refuse** [rɪ`fjuz] v. 拒絕

   ▲ Ivy refused the man's offer to help her. Ivy 拒絕男子要幫忙她的提議。

18. **safety** [`seftɪ] n. [U] 安全

▲ Everyone has to follow road safety rules.
每個人都必須遵守道路安全規範。

---

19. **single** [ˋsɪŋgl] adj. 單一的;單身的,未婚的

▲ Felix didn't say a single word in the meeting.
Felix 在會議中不發一語。

single [ˋsɪŋgl] n. [C] 單曲

▲ The band's new single is popular with young people.
這樂隊的新單曲受到年輕人喜愛。

single [ˋsɪŋgl] v. 選出,挑出 <out>

▲ Mr. Smith singled out Marian's poem and asked her
to read it aloud to the class. Smith 老師選出 Marian
的詩並讓她大聲朗讀給全班聽。

---

20. **society** [səˋsaɪətɪ] n. [C][U] 社會 (pl. societies)

▲ The criminal is considered to be a danger to society.
這名罪犯被認為對社會是個危險。

---

21. **such** [sʌtʃ] adj. 這樣的

▲ Such behavior is not acceptable in this school.
這樣的行為在這所學校是不被接受的。

💡 such as 例如

such [sʌtʃ] pron. 如此,這樣

▲ Everybody thought Steve a loser, but he proved not
to be such. 每個人都認為 Steve 是個失敗者,但他證
明事實並非如此。

---

22. **surface** [ˋsɝfəs] n. [C] 表面 <on> ; (狀況或人的) 表面

\<on\>

▲ The moon has a lot of craters on its surface.
月球表面有很多坑洞。

surface [ˋsɝfəs] v. 浮出水面；顯露，浮現

▲ The submarine surfaced before coming into the port.
潛水艇在進港前浮出水面。

23. **therefore** [ˋðɛr͵for] adv. 因此，所以

▲ My brother is 20 and therefore eligible to vote in the presidential election.
我哥哥二十歲，因此有資格在總統大選中投票。

24. **whenever** [hwɛnˋɛvɚ] conj. 每當，無論何時

▲ Whenever you need my bicycle, you can borrow it.
無論你何時需要我的腳踏車，你都可以借用它。

whenever [hwɛnˋɛvɚ] adv. 無論何時

▲ Monica will read the book in a spare moment this Saturday or whenever.
Monica 在這週六或無論何時的空閒時間會讀這本書。

25. **wire** [waɪr] n. [C][U] 金屬線；[C] 電線

▲ Alisa used copper wire to make earrings.
Alisa 用銅線製作耳環。

Unit 3

1. **accident** [ˋæksədənt] n. [C] 意外，事故 \<in\>

▲ Greg's leg was broken in a traffic accident.

Greg 的腿在一次交通事故中斷了。

💡 by accident 偶然地，意外地

2. **attend** [ə`tɛnd] n. v. 出席，參加；定期去

▲ More than one hundred guests attended the church wedding. 超過一百位賓客出席這場教堂婚禮。

3. **bill** [bɪl] n. [C] 帳單；議案，法案

▲ Hank always pays his bills on time.

Hank 總是準時繳帳單。

bill [bɪl] v. 給…開立帳單 <for>

▲ The hotel guest is billed for the three-day stay.

這位飯店住客被開立了三天住宿的帳單。

4. **border** [`bɔrdə] n. [C] 邊境，邊界 <between>

▲ The illegal drug trade was found along the border between Mexico and the United States.

這起非法毒品交易在墨西哥和美國的邊界被發現。

border [`bɔrdə] v. (與某國) 接壤；環繞 <with>

▲ France borders Germany, Switzerland, and Italy in the east. 法國與德國、瑞士和義大利在東邊接壤。

5. **cause** [kɔz] n. [C] 原因，起因 <of>

▲ A lighted match was the cause of the big fire.

一根點著的火柴是這大火的起因。

cause [kɔz] v. 造成，導致

▲ The typhoon caused a lot of damage to the houses in the town.

颱風對鎮上房子造成很大的損壞。

6. **challenge** [ˋtʃæləndʒ] n. [C][U] 挑戰，難題；質疑
   \<from>
   ▲ Global warming is one of the greatest challenges humans face today.
   全球暖化是現今人類面對的最大挑戰之一。

   challenge [ˋtʃæləndʒ] v. 質疑，懷疑；(比賽) 挑戰 \<to>
   ▲ The author's view is strongly challenged by human rights defenders.
   那作者的觀點受到人權捍衛者的強烈質疑。

7. **diamond** [ˋdaɪmənd] n. [C][U] 鑽石
   ▲ Vivian has a very expensive diamond necklace.
   Vivian 有一條很昂貴的鑽石項鍊。

8. **diet** [ˋdaɪət] n. [C][U] (日常) 飲食；[C] 節食
   ▲ Having a balanced diet is good for your health.
   均衡飲食對你的健康有益。

   diet [ˋdaɪət] v. 節食
   ▲ Don't pass me the cake; I'm dieting.
   別遞蛋糕給我，我正在節食。

9. **direct** [dəˋrɛkt] adj. 直接的 [反] indirect；直達的 [反] indirect
   ▲ The soldier had direct contact with the base by radio.
   這士兵用無線電直接和基地聯絡。

   direct [dəˋrɛkt] v. 把…集中，把…對準 \<to>；管理

▲ The teacher asked the students to direct their attention to what he was going to say.

老師要學生們把注意力集中在他要說的事情上。

direct [dəˋrɛkt] adv. 直接地 [同] directly ; 直達地 [同] directly

▲ The angry customer wanted to talk to the manager direct. 生氣的顧客想直接跟經理講話。

10. **favor** [ˋfevɚ] n. [C] 幫助；[U] 支持，贊同

▲ Jasper helped Paula when she was in trouble, and he indeed did her a great favor. Jasper 在 Paula 有困難時幫了她，他真的幫了她一個大忙。

favor [ˋfevɚ] v. 贊同，支持 <over>；偏袒，偏愛

▲ The boss favored this plan over the others.
老闆支持這個計畫勝於其他的。

11. **generous** [ˋdʒɛnərəs] adj. 慷慨的，大方的 [反] mean

▲ The generous man is always willing to give money to the poor. 這慷慨的男子總是願意捐錢給窮人。

12. **government** [ˋgʌvɚmənt] n. [C] 政府 (usu. sing.)

▲ The government should take efficient steps to reduce crime rates. 政府應該採取有效的措施來降低犯罪率。

13. **include** [ɪnˋklud] v. 包含，包括

▲ The customer wants to know if the price includes tax.
顧客想知道這個價錢是否含稅。

14. **marriage** [ˋmærɪdʒ] n. [C][U] 婚姻，結婚

▲ Rosa's first marriage was not a very happy one.
Rosa 的第一次婚姻並不是很幸福。

---

15. **obvious** [`abvɪəs] adj. 明顯的

▲ The solution to this riddle is so obvious that even a kid can solve it.

這個謎語的解答如此明顯，甚至孩童都能解答。

---

16. **particular** [pəˋtɪkjələ] adj. 特別的 <of>；特定的

▲ Environmental protection is a matter of particular importance. 環保是特別重要的議題。

💡 in particular 特別，尤其

---

17. **port** [port] n. [C][U] 港口 <in>

▲ All the ships in port were destroyed by the bombing.
港口內的船隻都被炸毀了。

---

18. **realize** [`riə͵laɪz] v. 實現；明白，意識到

▲ People have to work hard to realize their dreams.
人們必須努力以實現他們的夢想。

---

19. **regard** [rɪˋgɑrd] n. [U] 尊敬，尊重 <for>；考慮 <for>

▲ The team had high regard for the talented player.
球隊很敬重這位有天賦的球員。

regard [rɪˋgɑrd] v. 認為 <as>

▲ People regard Lenny as the best of the violinists.
人們認為 Lenny 是最棒的小提琴手。

---

20. **schedule** [`skɛdʒʊl] n. [C] 計畫表；時刻表 [同] timetable

▲ The family made a schedule for their vacation.
這家人訂了一個渡假計畫表。

schedule [`skɛdʒʊl] v. 安排，排定 <for>

▲ The baseball game is scheduled for tomorrow.
棒球賽排定明天舉行。

---

21. **self** [sɛlf] n. [C][U] 自我，自己 (pl. selves)

▲ After the accident, Ava is no longer her usual self.
意外過後，Ava 不再是平常的樣子了。

---

22. **symbol** [`sɪmbl] n. [C] 象徵，標誌 <of>；符號 <for>

▲ The cross is the symbol of Christianity.
十字架是基督教的象徵。

---

23. **tiny** [`taɪnɪ] adj. 極小的 (tinier | tiniest)

▲ The bug was so tiny that no one saw it.
那隻蟲非常小以致於沒人看到牠。

---

24. **university** [ˌjunə`vɝsətɪ] n. [C][U] 大 學 (pl. universities)

▲ People go to university to get a degree in a certain field. 人們上大學以取得特定領域的學位。

---

25. **used** [juzd] adj. 用過的；習慣的 <to>

▲ Mason likes to collect used stamps.
Mason 喜歡收集用過的郵票。

💡 be/get used to sth/V-ing 習慣 (做)…

Unit 4

1. **active** [ˋæktɪv] adj. 活躍的 [反] inactive；積極的 <in>
   ▲ The 80-year-old lady still leads an active life.
   這八十歲的老婦人生活依然活躍。

2. **average** [ˋævrɪdʒ] adj. 平均的；普通的，一般的
   ▲ The average age of women having their first baby has risen. 女性懷第一胎的平均年齡已經上升。
   average [ˋævrɪdʒ] n. [C] 平均數 <of>；[C][U] 一般水準，平均水準
   ▲ The average of 7, 10 and 16 is 11.
   七、十和十六的平均數為十一。
   💡 below/above average 低 / 高於一般水準
   average [ˋævrɪdʒ] v. 平均數是，平均為
   ▲ Many salesclerks average 10 hours a day.
   許多銷售員平均一天工作十個小時。

3. **base** [bes] n. [C] 底部，底座 [同] bottom；基地
   ▲ This glass has a heavy base. 這玻璃杯有厚底座。
   base [bes] v. 把…設為總部 <in>
   ▲ The international company is based in Singapore.
   這間跨國公司總部在新加坡。

4. **being** [ˋbiɪŋ] n. [C] 生命，生物；[U] 存在
   ▲ There are many kinds of beings living on earth.
   有很多不同種的生物住在地球上。

5. **brand** [brænd] n. [C] 品牌 <of>
   ▲ Ethel doesn't like this brand of perfume.
   Ethel 不喜歡這個品牌的香水。

6. **brilliant** [ˋbrɪljənt] adj. 明亮的；傑出的，出色的
   ▲ The girls decided to have a picnic in the brilliant sunshine. 女孩們決定在明亮的陽光下野餐。

7. **claim** [klem] n. [C] 聲明，說法；索款，索賠 <for>
   ▲ The man made claims that he was innocent.
   這男子聲稱他是無辜的。
   claim [klem] v. 主張，聲稱；認領
   ▲ Irene claimed that she was the best in her class.
   Irene 聲稱她是班上最棒的。

8. **daily** [ˋdelɪ] adj. 每天的
   ▲ The researcher keeps a daily record of the temperature. 這研究人員每天記錄溫度。
   daily [ˋdelɪ] adv. 每天地
   ▲ Traffic accidents happen daily. 交通事故每天發生。
   daily [ˋdelɪ] n. [C] 日報 (pl. dailies)
   ▲ The daily is printed and sold every day except on Sundays.
   這份日報除了星期天之外，每天印刷並販賣。

9. **direction** [dəˋrɛkʃən] n. [C] 方向；[pl.] 指路 (~s)
   ▲ The tourists used the map to see the direction they should go. 觀光客用地圖看他們該前往的方向。

10. **ease** [iz] n. [U] 安逸，舒適；容易，不費力 <with>

▲ Rick dreamed of living a life of ease.
Rick 夢想過著安逸的生活。

ease [iz] v. 減輕，緩解

▲ The soft music will help to ease the stress.
這輕柔的音樂會幫助緩解壓力。

---

11. **final** [`faɪnl] adj. 最後的

▲ The two projects are in their final stages and will be completed soon.
這兩個案子在最後階段了，很快就會完成。

final [`faɪnl] n. [C] 決賽

▲ The team will do their best to reach the final and win it. 這支隊伍會盡全力進入決賽並獲勝。

---

12. **function** [`fʌŋkʃən] n. [C][U] 功能 <of>

▲ The doctor is doing research on the function of the brain. 這位醫生正在研究腦部的功能。

function [`fʌŋkʃən] v. 運轉，運作 [同] operate

▲ The machine is not functioning properly.
這部機器運轉不正常。

---

13. **glue** [glu] n. [C][U] 膠水

▲ The boy used glue to join the two pieces of paper together. 這男孩用膠水把兩張紙黏在一起。

glue [glu] v. 用膠水黏 <to> [同] stick (glued | glued | gluing, glueing)

▲ Lisa glued the stamp to the envelope.

Lisa 用膠水把郵票黏在信封上。

---

14. **instance** [ˋɪnstəns] n. [C] 實例 <of>
   ▲ The historian gave several instances of the tyrant's cruelty. 歷史學家提出好幾個這位暴君殘忍的實例。
   💡 for instance 例如

---

15. **nation** [ˋneʃən] n. [C] 國家
   ▲ Norway is one of the most developed nations in the world. 挪威是世界上最先進的國家之一。

---

16. **ocean** [ˋoʃən] n. [C] 海洋，大海 (the ~)
   ▲ Some people played on the beach, while others went swimming in the ocean.
   一些人在沙灘上玩，而一些人在海裡游泳。

---

17. **official** [əˋfɪʃəl] adj. 官方的，正式的；官員的，公務的
   ▲ Mandarin has been the official language of Taiwan since 1945.
   自從 1945 年起，國語就一直是臺灣的官方語言。
   official [əˋfɪʃəl] n. [C] 官員
   ▲ The prosecutor is a government official whose duty is to investigate crimes.
   檢察官是負責調查犯罪的政府官員。

---

18. **primary** [ˋpraɪˏmɛrɪ] adj. 主要的 [同] main
   ▲ His daughter's health is the father's primary concern.
   女兒的健康是這父親主要關心的事。

19. **prize** [praɪz] n. [C] 獎（品）

▲ Samuel won first prize in the speech contest.
Samuel 在演講比賽中得了第一名。

prize [praɪz] v. 重視，珍視

▲ Maggie prized her family above everything.
Maggie 重視她的家庭勝於一切。

20. **purpose** [ˋpɝpəs] n. [C] 目的 <of>

▲ The purpose of the study is to reveal the problems of drug abuse.
該項研究的目的是要揭示濫用毒品的問題。

💡 on purpose 故意地

21. **relationship** [rɪˋleʃən͵ʃɪp] n. [C] 關係，關聯 <between>；感情關係

▲ The relationship between smoking and lung cancer has been shown by many studies.
很多研究已顯示出吸菸和肺癌的關聯。

22. **religion** [rɪˋlɪdʒən] n. [U] 宗教信仰；[C] 宗教

▲ Freedom of religion is a fundamental human right.
宗教自由是一種基本人權。

23. **sensitive** [ˋsɛnsətɪv] adj. 易被冒犯的，敏感的 <to, about>；善解人意的，體貼的 [反] insensitive

▲ Amanda is sensitive to criticism; she always takes what others say personally. Amanda 對於批評很敏感，她總是將別人說的話對號入座。

24. **sex** [sɛks] **n.** [U] 性；[C] 男性，女性

▲ In Asia, sex education is a sensitive issue.
在亞洲，性教育是個敏感的議題。

25. **tradition** [trə`dɪʃən] **n.** [C][U] 傳統

▲ It has long been a Chinese tradition to eat rice dumplings on the Dragon Boat Festival.
端午節吃肉粽是一項悠久的中國傳統。

Unit 5

1. **address** [ə`drɛs] **v.** 在 (信封等) 上寫姓名或地址 <to>；應付，處理

▲ This letter is addressed to Trevor.
這封信是署名給 Trevor 的。

address [ə`drɛs] **n.** [C] 住址；演講

▲ Ezra wrote a name and address on the envelope.
Ezra 在信封上寫了名字和住址。

2. **beauty** [`bjutɪ] **n.** [U] 美，美貌；[C] 美人 (pl. beauties)

▲ Beauty is only skin-deep. 【諺】美貌是膚淺的。

3. **belief** [bɪ`lif] **n.** [sing.][U] 相信，信仰 <in>；[C] 信念，看法

▲ With a strong belief in God, the priest rose above many difficulties.
因為對上帝的堅定信仰，這牧師克服了很多困難。

4. **calm** [kɑm] v. 使平靜，使鎮靜 <down>

▲ Paula tried to calm her son down but in vain.

Paula 試著讓她兒子鎮靜下來，但是無效。

calm [kɑm] adj. 冷靜的；平靜的 (calmer | calmest)

▲ Alvin was quite angry half an hour ago, but he feels calmer now.

Alvin 半小時前相當生氣，但他現在覺得比較冷靜了。

calm [kɑm] n. [sing.][U] 寧靜，安詳

▲ The old lady got up early to enjoy the morning calm.

老婦人早起以享受早晨的寧靜。

---

5. **coast** [kost] n. [C] 海岸 <of>

▲ There are many islands off the west coast of Scotland. 蘇格蘭西海岸外有許多島嶼。

---

6. **commercial** [kə`mɝʃəl] adj. 商業的，商務的；營利性的

▲ The building is built for commercial use; it's not a residential building.

這棟建築是為商業用途而建的，它不是住宅大樓。

commercial [kə`mɝʃəl] n. [C] (電視或廣播裡的) 廣告

▲ Most people would switch to other channels during commercials. 許多人在廣告時會轉臺。

---

7. **deer** [dɪr] n. [C] 鹿 (pl. deer)

▲ While deer hunting is quite common in some western countries, it is considered by many people to be a cruel activity. 雖然在一些西方國家獵鹿極為普遍，許

多人卻認為這是殘忍的活動。

---

8. **emphasize** [ˋɛmfəˌsaɪz] v. 強調 [同] stress
   ▲ Traffic safety cannot be emphasized enough.
   交通安全再怎麼強調也不為過。

---

9. **energy** [ˋɛnɚdʒɪ] n. [U] 能量，能源；精力，活力
   ▲ Clean energy is produced through the methods that
   do not release greenhouse gases.
   清潔能源是由不排放溫室氣體的方式生產出來的。

---

10. **escape** [ɪˋskep] v. 逃走，逃脫 <from>；避開
   ▲ The prisoner escaped from prison last night.
   那犯人昨晚越獄了。
   escape [ɪˋskep] n. [C][U] 逃脫，逃離
   ▲ The driver had a narrow escape in the car accident.
   這司機在車禍中死裡逃生。

---

11. **fix** [fɪks] v. 修理；使固定，安裝 <to>
   ▲ The mechanic fixed the old car.
   技師修好了這輛舊車。
   fix [fɪks] n. [sing.] 受操縱的事
   ▲ People suspected that the election was a fix and
   refused to accept the results.
   人們懷疑選舉受操縱並拒絕接受結果。

---

12. **found** [faʊnd] v. 創立 [同] establish；把…基於 <on>
   ▲ The elementary school was founded in 1950.

這所小學於 1950 年創立。

13. **guard** [gɑrd] n. [C] 守衛，警衛；[U] 看守

▲ There was a guard posted at the entrance.

入口處設了一個守衛。

💡 be under guard 在警衛保護下

guard [gɑrd] v. 看守

▲ Two night watchmen guarded the factory.

兩名守夜警衛看守工廠。

14. **industry** [`ɪndəstrɪ] n. [U] 工 業；[C] 行 業 (pl. industries)

▲ Heavy industry uses large machines to produce large goods, such as ships and trains.

重工業利用大型機械生產大型商品，像是船和火車。

15. **major** [`medʒɚ] adj. 主要的 [反] minor

▲ Air pollution is a major problem in the city.

空氣汙染是這城市主要的問題。

major [`medʒɚ] n. [C] 主修科目

▲ What was Bill's major in college?

Bill 在大學的主修科目是什麼？

major [`medʒɚ] v. 主修 <in>

▲ The student wants to major in computer science at college. 這學生想在大學主修電腦科學。

16. **network** [`nɛt,wɝk] n. [C] 網狀系統 <of>；網路

▲ The country has an excellent network of railroads.

這個國家有良好的鐵路網。

network [ˋnɛtˌwɝk] **v.** 使 (電腦) 連網

▲ The software allows the researchers to network their computers. 這個軟體使研究人員的電腦可以連網。

---

17. **peak** [pik] **n.** [C] 山頂；最高點，高峰 <at> (usu. sing.)

▲ After a long climb, the climber finally reached the snow-capped peak.

攀爬許久後，這登山客終於到達白雪皚皚的山頂。

peak [pik] **v.** 達到頂峰，達到最大值

▲ Our sales were down in 2019 but peaked the next year.

我們的銷售量在 2019 年下跌，但隔年便達到頂峰。

---

18. **private** [ˋpraɪvɪt] **adj.** 私人的 [反] public ； 私立的 [反] public

▲ The rich man owns a private jet.
這位富人擁有一架私人飛機。

💡 in private 非公開的，私下的

---

19. **receive** [rɪˋsiv] **v.** 得到 [同] get；收到 <from>

▲ The government should make sure that all the children in the country receive a good education.
政府應該確保國內所有孩童都得到良好教育。

---

20. **scare** [skɛr] **v.** (使) 害怕，(使) 驚恐 [同] frighten

▲ The thunder scared the life out of the little girl.
雷聲把小女孩嚇得半死。

scare [skɛr] n. [sing.] 驚恐

▲ Maggie got a scare when she saw the snake.
Maggie 看到蛇時嚇了一跳。

21. **seek** [sik] v. 尋找；尋求，要求 (sought | sought | seeking)

▲ The climber sought shelter from rain in the cave.
登山客在山洞裡找到避雨處。

22. **shelf** [ʃɛlf] n. [C] 架子 <on> (pl. shelves)

▲ The librarian put the book on the top shelf.
圖書館員把這本書放到最上面的架子。

23. **style** [staɪl] n. [C][U] 方式 <of>；[C] 風尚，潮流 [同] fashion

▲ Brian likes the British style of living.
Brian 喜歡英國的生活方式。

💡 be in/out of style 正在 / 退流行

style [staɪl] v. 設計

▲ This dress is styled to suit any occasion.
這件洋裝的設計適合任何場合。

24. **traditional** [trə`dɪʃənl] adj. 傳統的

▲ It is traditional to throw rice on the newlyweds.
將米粒灑向新婚夫婦是一項傳統。

25. **travel** [`trævl] n. [U] 旅行

▲ Travel was slow and dangerous in old times.
旅行在古時既費時又危險。

travel [ˋtrævl̩] **v.** 旅行 <to>；行進

▲ Tessa wishes to travel to Iceland one day.
　Tessa 希望有一天去冰島旅行。

Unit 6

1. **advice** [ədˋvaɪs] **n.** [U] 忠告，建議 <on>

▲ The patient should take the doctor's advice on his
　health. 這病人應該接受醫生對他健康的忠告。

---

2. **bother** [ˋbɑðɚ] **v.** 費心做；使擔心，使焦急

▲ The actor didn't even bother to answer the reporter's
　question. 這演員甚至懶得回答記者的問題。

bother [ˋbɑðɚ] **n.** [U] 麻煩 [同] trouble

▲ Alison refused all help because she didn't want to
　give her friends any extra bother. Alison 拒絕所有的
　幫忙，因為她不想給朋友造成額外的麻煩。

---

3. **capital** [ˋkæpətl̩] **n.** [C] 首都；[U] 資本，資金

▲ The capital of New Zealand is Wellington.
　紐西蘭的首都是威靈頓。

capital [ˋkæpətl̩] **adj.** 大寫字母的

▲ The brand's logo is a capital "W."
　這品牌的標誌是一個大寫的 "W" 字母。

---

4. **century** [ˋsɛntʃərɪ] **n.** [C] 世紀 (pl. centuries)

▲ There were many important inventions in the
　twentieth century.

二十世紀有許多重大的發明。

5. **complex** [kəm`plɛks] adj. 複雜的 [同] complicated [反] simple

▲ Betty was confused about the complex plot of the movie. Betty 對電影複雜的情節感到困惑。

complex [`kɑmplɛks] n. [C] 綜合大樓；情結，心理負擔 <about>

▲ The old train station was transformed into a new shopping complex.
這棟舊火車站被改建為新的購物中心。

6. **contain** [kən`ten] v. 包含，容納

▲ This dictionary contains about 40,000 headwords.
這本字典包含大約四萬個詞條。

7. **continue** [kən`tɪnjʊ] v. (使) 繼續；(中斷後) 再繼續 [同] resume

▲ Though Cindy felt tired, she still continued working.
雖然 Cindy 覺得疲憊，她仍繼續工作。

8. **couple** [`kʌpl] n. [sing.] 一對 ；幾個 <of> [同] a few ； [C] 夫妻，情侶

▲ The clerk asked the customer to wait for a couple of minutes. 店員要求顧客等幾分鐘。

couple [`kʌpl] v. 連接，結合 <to>

▲ The restaurant car is coupled to the sleeping car.
這餐車被連接上臥鋪車廂。

9. **encourage** [ɪn`kɝɪdʒ] **v.** 鼓勵 <in> [反] discourage

▲ Emma encouraged her son in his ambition to become a doctor. Emma 鼓勵她兒子想成為醫生的志向。

encouragement [ɪn`kɝɪdʒmənt] **n.** [U] 鼓勵 [反] discouragement

▲ With her father's support and encouragement, Lillian eventually achieved her goal. 有了父親的支持和鼓勵，Lillian 最終達成了她的目標。

---

10. **flight** [flaɪt] **n.** [U] 飛行 <in>；[C] 航班

▲ The hunter shot down a bird in flight.
這獵人射殺了一隻正在飛行的鳥。

---

11. **forward** [`fɔrwəd] **adj.** 向前的 [反] backward

▲ The driver slammed on the brakes to stop any forward movement.
司機突然猛踩剎車以避免再向前移動。

forward [`fɔrwəd] **adv.** 向前；有進展地，前進地 (also forwards) [反] backward, backwards

▲ Danny leaned forward, whispering something in Carol's ear. Danny 向前傾身，在 Carol 耳邊低語。

💡 look forward to V-ing 期待⋯

forward [`fɔrwəd] **n.** [C] 前鋒

▲ In a football match, a forward is a player whose job is to attack and score goals.
在美式足球比賽中，前鋒是負責進攻和得分的球員。

forward [`fɔrwəd] **v.** 轉寄 (郵件等) <to> [同] send on

▲ Please forward Edmund's mail to his new address.
請把 Edmund 的郵件轉寄到他的新地址。

12. **handle** [ˋhændl̩] v. 應付，處理；拿，搬動

▲ The military official handled the crisis very well.
那名軍事人員將危機處理得很好。

handle [ˋhændl̩] n. [C] 把手，柄

▲ The handle of the frying pan came loose.
這煎鍋的柄鬆了。

13. **instead** [ɪnˋstɛd] adv. 作為替代

▲ There was no milk left, so we drank juice instead.
已經沒有牛奶了，所以我們喝果汁作為替代。

💡 instead of sb/sth 作為…的替代；而不是

14. **male** [mel] adj. 男性的，雄性的 [反] female

▲ The school used to admit only male students.
這所學校以前只收男學生。

male [mel] n. [C] 男性，雄性 [反] female

▲ It is reported that the suspect is a young white male.
據報導，嫌犯是一名年輕白人男性。

15. **medical** [ˋmɛdɪkl̩] adj. 醫學的，醫療的

▲ Medical care has been greatly improved today.
現今醫療保健已大有進步。

16. **memory** [ˋmɛmərɪ] n. [C][U] 記性 <for>；[C] 回憶 <of> (usu. pl.)

▲ Melissa has a good memory for faces.

Melissa 擅長記人的面孔。

💡 in memory of sb 為了紀念…

---

17. **northern** [ˋnɔrðɚn] **adj.** 在北部的，從北部的 (also Northern) (abbr. N)

▲ It rains a lot during the winter in the northern part of Taiwan. 臺灣北部地區冬天多雨。

18. **organization** [ˏɔrgənəˋzeʃən] **n.** [C] 組織，機構；[U] 組織，籌劃 <of>

▲ The United Nations is an international organization. 聯合國是一個國際組織。

19. **pose** [poz] **v.** 造成，引起 <for, to>；擺姿勢 <for>

▲ The increasing cost of living posed many problems for the elderly. 生活費上漲對老年人造成許多問題。

pose [poz] **n.** [C] 姿勢 <in>

▲ The man is sitting in a relaxed pose. 這男子以輕鬆的姿勢坐著。

20. **propose** [prəˋpoz] **v.** 提議，建議 <to>；提名，推薦 <for>

▲ The sales manager proposed an alternative plan to the boss. 業務經理向老闆建議了個替代方案。

21. **saw** [sɔ] **v.** 鋸 (sawed | sawed, sawn | sawing)

▲ The lumberman sawed the log in half. 伐木工把原木鋸成一半。

saw [sɔ] **n.** [C] 鋸子

▲ The carpenter used a saw to cut wood.
木匠用鋸子切割木頭。

22. **seem** [sim] v. 似乎

▲ Susan looked pale; she seemed to be sick.
Susan 看起來很蒼白，她似乎病了。

23. **seldom** [ˋsɛldəm] adv. 很少 [同] rarely

▲ Although David is a Christian, he seldom goes to church. 雖然 David 是基督徒，但他很少去教堂。

24. **shoot** [ʃut] v. 射殺；開槍 <at> (shot | shot | shooting)

▲ The robber was shot dead at the scene of the crime.
那名搶匪在犯罪現場被射殺。

shoot [ʃut] n. [C] 芽，苗；拍攝

▲ The farmer planted the seeds one week ago, and now tender green shoots start to appear.
農夫一週前種下種子，現在嫩嫩的綠芽開始出現。

25. **weight** [wet] n. [C][U] 重量 <by>；[U] 體重

▲ This grocery store sells fruit by weight.
這家雜貨店論重量賣水果。

💡 in weight 重量上 | gain/lose weight 增 / 減重

Unit 7

1. **alive** [əˋlaɪv] adj. 活 (著) 的；有活力的

▲ The earthquake victim was buried alive.

那位地震受難者被活埋。

2. **ancient** [`ɛnʃənt] adj. 古代的 [反] modern；古老的，年
代久遠的 [反] new

▲ Ancient Rome was an important civilization that
once ruled most of Europe.
古羅馬是一個曾經統治大部分歐洲的重要文明。

3. **avoid** [ə`vɔɪd] v. 避免，防止；避開

▲ In Japan, people tend to avoid standing out from the
crowd. 在日本，人們傾向避免與眾不同。

4. **chain** [tʃen] n. [C][U] 鏈條，鍊子；[C] 一連串，一系列
<of>

▲ Diane has a silver chain around her wrist.
Diane 手腕上有一條銀鍊子。

chain [tʃen] v. 用鏈條拴住 <up>

▲ The dangerous dog ought to be chained up.
那條危險的狗應用鏈條拴住。

5. **charge** [tʃɑrdʒ] n. [C][U] 收費，費用 <for>；[U] 管理，
負責

▲ The charge for admission is ten dollars.
入場費是十美元。

charge [tʃɑrdʒ] v. 收費 <for>；指控，告告 <with>

▲ The store doesn't charge extra for delivery.
這家店不額外收運費。

6. **conversation** [ˌkɑnvɚˈseʃən] **n.** [C][U] 交談，談話 <with>

▲ Tracy had a short conversation with her friends after school. Tracy 放學後和她的朋友們小聊一下。

---

7. **danger** [ˈdendʒɚ] **n.** [U] 危險 <in>；[C] 威脅，危險因素 <to>

▲ As the injured climber was trapped in the mountains, his life was in danger.
由於受傷的登山客受困山區，他有生命危險。

---

8. **difference** [ˈdɪfərəns] **n.** [C][U] 差別，不同 <between> [反] similarity

▲ The only difference between the two cars is the color. 這兩部車子唯一的不同是顏色。

---

9. **difficulty** [ˈdɪfəˌkʌltɪ] **n.** [U] 困難，艱辛 <in>；[C] 問題，難題 (usu. pl.) (pl. difficulties)

▲ The patient had difficulty (in) breathing.
這名病人呼吸困難。

---

10. **extra** [ˈɛkstrə] **adj.** 額外的

▲ Glen needed extra time and funds to carry out the project.
Glen 需要額外的時間和資金來進行這項企劃案。

extra [ˈɛkstrə] **adv.** 額外地

▲ If Judy works overtime, she will make $500 extra a month. 如果 Judy 加班，她一個月會額外多賺五百美元。

extra [ˋɛkstrə] n. [C] 另外收費的事物

▲ The price includes a main course and a dessert, but drinks are extras.

這價錢包含一份主餐和甜點，但飲料是另外收費的。

11. **force** [fors] n. [C] 部隊 (usu. pl.)；[U] 力量

▲ The president sent government forces to put down the rebellion. 總統派政府部隊去鎮壓叛亂。

force [fors] v. 強迫，迫使

▲ The mother urged her child to eat, but she couldn't force him to.

這媽媽催促她的孩子吃東西，但她無法強迫他吃。

12. **greet** [grit] v. 問候，迎接

▲ The singer was greeted by his fans at the airport.

那位歌手在機場受到他的歌迷迎接。

13. **hardly** [ˋhɑrdlɪ] adv. 幾乎不

▲ Victor was very busy and hardly noticed his wife was talking to him.

Victor 很忙，幾乎沒注意到他妻子在和他說話。

14. **likely** [ˋlaɪklɪ] adj. 很有可能的 [反] unlikely (likelier | likeliest)

▲ The train to Taichung is likely to arrive late.

開往臺中的火車很有可能會誤點。

likely [ˋlaɪklɪ] adv. 有可能地

▲ Jon will most likely be absent from the meeting.

Jon 很有可能會在會議上缺席。

---

15. **material** [mə`tɪrɪəl] n. [C][U] 材料，原料；布料 [同] fabric

▲ Iron is one material used in the production of steel.
鐵是製造鋼的一種材料。

---

16. **natural** [`nætʃərəl] adj. 自然的；正常的 [反] unnatural, abnormal

▲ An earthquake is a natural disaster. 地震是自然災害。

---

17. **origin** [`ɔrədʒɪn] n. [C][U] 起源，源頭 <of>；[pl.] 出身，血統 <of> (～s)

▲ The scientists tried to find out the origin of the virus.
科學家們試圖找出這病毒的源頭。

---

18. **painting** [`pentɪŋ] n. [C] 畫

▲ Many modern paintings are on display in the gallery.
有很多現代畫在這畫廊中展出。

---

19. **possibility** [,pɑsə`bɪlətɪ] n. [C][U] 可能 (性) <of> (pl. possibilities)

▲ There is little possibility of survival after the plane crash. 墜機後生還的可能性很小。

---

20. **regular** [`rɛgjələ-] adj. 定期的，固定的 [反] irregular；規律的 [反] irregular

▲ The bus runs at regular intervals from 6 a.m. to 10 p.m.

這班公車從早上六點到晚上十點有固定班次運行。

regular [ˋrɛgjələ] **n.** [C] 常客，老顧客

▲ Ariel is one of the regulars at the café; she goes there four times a week.

Ariel 是那家咖啡廳的常客之一，她一週去那裡四次。

---

21. **role** [rol] **n.** [C] 作用，任務 <in>；角色 <of> [同] part

▲ Bob's role in the team is to collect data.

Bob 在這團隊中的任務是收集數據。

22. **separate** [ˋsɛpərɪt] **adj.** 單獨的，不同的

▲ The chef uses separate cutting boards for different kinds of food.

這主廚用不同的砧板切不同種類的食物。

separate [ˋsɛpəˏret] **v.** (使) 分開 <from>

▲ Taiwan is separated from China by the Taiwan Strait.

臺灣和中國被臺灣海峽分開。

23. **silent** [ˋsaɪlənt] **adj.** 沉默的；寂靜的

▲ The foreign minister fell silent and made no comment. 外交部長陷入沉默，未作評論。

24. **speaker** [ˋspikə] **n.** [C] 講某種語言的人 <of>；演講者

▲ The teacher is a native speaker of English.

這位老師是一個以英語為母語的人。

25. **typhoon** [taɪˋfun] **n.** [C] 颱風

▲ Normally, three to four typhoons hit Taiwan every year.

每年通常有三到四個颱風侵襲臺灣。

Unit 8

1. **among** [ə`mʌŋ] prep. 在…中
   ▲ Fred saw his girlfriend among the crowd.
   Fred 在人群中看見他的女友。

2. **appearance** [ə`pɪrəns] n. [C][U] 外貌;[C] (公開) 露面
   ▲ More and more people today have plastic surgery to alter their physical appearances.
   現今有越來越多人進行整形手術來改變外貌。

3. **chief** [tʃif] adj. 最高級別的,首席的;首要的 [同] main
   ▲ The chief medical officer is the most senior government advisor on public health matters. 首席醫療官是政府在公共衛生事務方面最高級別的顧問。
   chief [tʃif] n. [C] 領導人;酋長
   ▲ Jackson was once a police chief.
   Jackson 曾是警察局長。

4. **comic** [`kɑmɪk] adj. 喜劇的 [反] tragic
   ▲ Is it a comic or a tragic play? 那是喜劇還是悲劇?
   comic [`kɑmɪk] n. [C] 漫畫 [同] comic book
   ▲ Many Taiwanese people enjoy reading Japanese comics. 許多臺灣人喜歡看日本漫畫。

5. **crowd** [kraʊd] n. [C] 人群,群眾 <of>

▲ There was a crowd of students waiting in front of the library. 有一群學生在圖書館前面等候。

crowd [kraʊd] v. 擠滿 <into>

▲ A lot of baseball fans crowded into the stadium.
許多棒球迷湧入體育場。

---

6. **describe** [dɪˋskraɪb] v. 描述

▲ The witness was asked to describe the bank robber.
目擊者被要求描述銀行搶匪的樣子。

---

7. **discovery** [dɪˋskʌvərɪ] n. [C] 被發現的事物；[U] 發現 <of> (pl. discoveries)

▲ Newton made many wonderful discoveries.
牛頓有許多傑出的發現。

---

8. **education** [ˌɛdʒəˋkeʃən] n. [sing.][U] 教育

▲ Ada received her education at home during childhood. Ada 小時候是在家裡接受教育。

---

9. **entire** [ɪnˋtaɪr] adj. 全部的，整個的 [同] whole

▲ The man was so hungry that he ate an entire turkey.
這男子太餓了而吃了一整隻火雞。

---

10. **event** [ɪˋvɛnt] n. [C] 事件；盛事

▲ The French Revolution is an important event in history. 法國大革命是歷史上重大的事件。

---

11. **figure** [ˋfɪgjɚ] n. [C] 數字 (usu. pl.)；[C] 人物

▲ The unemployment figures are worryingly high.

失業數字高得令人擔心。

figure [ˈfɪgjɚ] v. 認為；計算 [同] work out

▲ Carol figured that Andy wouldn't come because he was sick. Carol 認為 Andy 不會來，因為他生病了。

💡 figure sb/sth out 弄明白…；想出…

12. **further** [ˈfɝðɚ] adv. 更遠地；更進一步地

▲ The hiker was too tired to walk further.
這健行者太累而無法再走下去了。

further [ˈfɝðɚ] adj. 更多的，另外的

▲ Before making the decision, the manager needed further details. 經理在做決定前需要更多的細節。

further [ˈfɝðɚ] v. 改進，增進

▲ All nations should work together to further the cause of world peace.
所有國家應該一起努力來增進世界和平。

13. **independent** [ˌɪndɪˈpɛndənt] adj. 獨立的 <from>；自立的 <of> [反] dependent

▲ The United States became independent from Britain in 1776. 美國在 1776 年脫離英國獨立。

14. **instant** [ˈɪnstənt] adj. 立即的，立刻的 [同] immediate；速食的，即溶的

▲ The novel was such an instant success that the author rose to fame overnight.
這本小說立即獲得成功以致於作者一舉成名。

instant [ˈɪnstənt] n. [sing.] 瞬息，頃刻 <in>

▲ When the hunter fired his gun, the birds flew away in an instant. 獵人開槍時，鳥頃刻間飛走。

15. **peace** [pis] n. [sing.][U] 和平；[U] 平靜，安寧 <in>

▲ People hope world peace will last forever.
人們希望世界可以永久和平。

💡 make (sb's) peace with sb 與⋯和解

16. **pop** [pɑp] n. [U] 流行音樂；[C] 砰的一聲

▲ Claire loves various kinds of music such as pop, jazz, and funk. Claire 喜愛各種音樂，例如流行音樂、爵士樂和放克樂。

pop [pɑp] adj. 流行的

▲ The fans of the pop singer gathered in front of the hotel where he stayed.
這流行歌手的粉絲聚集在他下榻的旅館前面。

17. **population** [ˌpɑpjəˈleʃən] n. [C] 人口 (usu. sing.)

▲ The world's population is still increasing.
世界人口還在增加中。

18. **prove** [pruv] v. 證明，證實；結果是 (proved | proved, proven | proving)

▲ The suspect has to prove his innocence.
這個嫌疑人必須證明自己無罪。

19. **return** [rɪˈtɝn] v. 返回 <from> [同] go back；歸還，放回 <to> [同] give back

▲ What time will Arlen return from work?

Arlen 幾點會下班回家？

return [rɪˋtɝn] n. [sing.] 返回 <on>；歸還，放回 <of>

▲ On her return from the trip, Debby found that nobody was at home. Debby 旅行返家時，發現家裡都沒有人。

💡 in return (for sth) 作為 (⋯) 交換或回報

---

20. **shot** [ʃɑt] n. [C] 開槍，射擊；射門，投籃

▲ The police officer pulled out his gun and fired one shot. 這警官拔出他的槍後開了一槍。

---

21. **smooth** [smuð] adj. 光滑的 [反] rough；順暢的

▲ The baby's skin is as smooth as silk.
這嬰兒的皮膚像絲一般光滑。

smooth [smuð] v. (使) 平整

▲ The girl smoothed her dress and stepped forward.
這女孩撫平她的洋裝，然後往前走。

---

22. **success** [səkˋsɛs] n. [C][U] 成功 <in> [反] failure；[C] 成功的事物 [反] failure

▲ The business had much success in enhancing their public image.
這間公司在提升公眾形象方面極為成功。

---

23. **switch** [swɪtʃ] n. [C] 開關；徹底改變 <to> (usu. sing.)

▲ The room was dark, so Elaine turned on the light switch. 房間很暗，所以 Elaine 把電燈開關打開。

switch [swɪtʃ] v. 改變，調換 <to> [同] change

▲ I suggest we switch the meeting to Friday.

我建議我們把會面改到星期五。

24. **upon** [ə`pɑn] prep. 在…之上
▲ The gentleman wore a hat upon his head.
這名紳士頭上戴著一頂帽子。
💡 once upon a time 很久以前

25. **wild** [waɪld] adj. 野生的 [反] tame；未經開墾的
▲ The wild horse hasn't been tamed.
這匹野馬還沒被馴服。
wild [waɪld] adv. 撒野地，肆意胡鬧地
▲ The kids ran wild after their parents left the room.
孩子們在父母離開房間後肆意胡鬧。
wild [waɪld] n. [sing.] 荒野，荒地 (the ~) <in>
▲ Fewer and fewer tigers live in the wild these days.
現今越來越少的老虎生活在荒野。

Unit 9

1. **army** [`ɑrmɪ] n. [C] 陸軍，軍隊 (the ~) <in> (pl. armies)
▲ The general has served in the army for thirty years.
這位將軍在軍隊已服務了三十年。

2. **cancer** [`kænsɚ] n. [C][U] 癌
▲ The patient died of stomach cancer.
這病人死於胃癌。

3. **classical** [ˋklæsɪkl] adj. 古典的

▲ Do you prefer classical music or pop music?
你比較喜歡古典樂還是流行音樂？

---

4. **coin** [kɔɪn] n. [C] 硬幣

▲ The boys tossed a coin to decide who would go first.
男孩們丟銅板決定誰先走。

coin [kɔɪn] v. 創造，首次使用 (詞語)

▲ The expression was coined by the writer.
這個用語是由這位作者創造的。

---

5. **confident** [ˋkɑnfədənt] adj. 確信的；自信的，有信心的
<about>

▲ The manager is confident that the boss will accept
the proposal. 經理確信老闆會接受這個提案。

---

6. **current** [ˋkɝ·ənt] adj. 現時的，當前的 [同] present

▲ In the current economic situation, changing jobs may
not be a good idea.
就當前的經濟情勢，換工作可能不是好主意。

current [ˋkɝ·ənt] n. [C] 水流；氣流 <of>

▲ The swimmer was swept away by ocean currents.
游泳者被洋流沖走。

---

7. **display** [dɪˋsple] n. [C] 陳列，展示；表露 <of>

▲ The window display attracted many customers to go
into the shop. 這櫥窗陳列吸引很多顧客進店。

display [dɪˋsple] v. 陳列，展示；表露

▲ Many kinds of clocks were displayed in this shop.
這家店裡展示了許多種類的時鐘。

8. **dot** [dɑt] n. [C] 小圓點
▲ The shirt is white with black dots.
這件襯衫是白底黑點。

dot [dɑt] v. 在…上加點；散布 <with> (dotted | dotted | dotting)
▲ The teacher taught the little girl to dot her i's.
老師教小女孩在字母 i 上面加點。

9. **environment** [ɪn`vaɪrənmənt] n. [sing.] 自然環境 (the ~)；[C][U] 環境
▲ Some chemical factories polluted the environment.
一些化學工廠汙染自然環境。

10. **firm** [fɝm] n. [C] 公司，行號
▲ The two salesmen work for an electronics firm.
這兩個業務員為一家電子公司工作。

firm [fɝm] adj. 堅硬的 [反] soft；牢固的，穩固的 [同] secure
▲ Melody prefers a firm mattress to a soft one.
Melody 比較喜歡硬床墊勝過軟床墊。

firm [fɝm] v. 使 (土) 變硬，使 (土) 堅實
▲ The gardener firmed the soil around the new plant with his feet. 園丁用腳把新植物周圍的土壓實。

firm [fɝm] adv. 牢固地

11. **focus** [ˋfokəs] n. [sing.] (注意等的) 中心，焦點 <of>；
    [U] (圖像的) 清晰

    ▲ The conference is now the focus of everyone's
    attention. 這場會議是當前每個人注意的焦點。

    focus [ˋfokəs] v. 使集中 <on> [同] concentrate；調節 (鏡
    頭 等 的) 焦 距 <on> (focused, focussed | focused,
    focussed | focusing, focussing)

    ▲ The student tried to focus his attention on reading.
    這學生試著把注意力集中在閱讀上。

12. **growth** [groθ] n. [sing.][U] 生長；增長 [反] decline

    ▲ The pears have reached full growth.
    這些梨子已經成熟了。

13. **human** [ˋhjumən] adj. 人的，人類的

    ▲ Recent research has showed that eating too much
    salty food is bad for the human body.
    近期研究顯示吃太多高鹽分食物對人體有害。

    human [ˋhjumən] n. [C] 人，人類

    ▲ It's important to fix the damage that we humans have
    done to the Earth.
    解決我們人類對地球已造成的傷害是重要的。

14. **identity** [aɪˋdɛntətɪ] n. [C][U] 身分；[U] 特點，個性
    (pl. identities)

    ▲ The spy keeps his identity a secret.
    這名間諜隱藏他的身分。

💡 identity card (= ID card) 身分證

15. **instruction** [ɪn`strʌkʃən] n. [C] 指示，命令 (usu. pl.)；[pl.] 說明書 (～s)

▲ The general gave instructions that the soldiers had to get to the town by dawn.
將軍命令士兵們必須在破曉前抵達小鎮。

16. **instrument** [`ɪnstrəmənt] n. [C] 器械；樂器 [同] musical instrument

▲ Surgical instruments like scissors and clamps are used in general surgery. 外科手術器械像是剪刀和鉗子是在一般手術中使用的。

17. **personal** [`pɝsṇl] adj. 個人的；私人的

▲ The passengers were told to collect their personal belongings before leaving the aircraft.
乘客們被告知在離開飛機前要收好個人財物。

18. **prefer** [prɪ`fɝ] v. 較喜歡；寧可 <to> (preferred | preferred | preferring)

▲ Peter prefers beer to red wine.
比起紅酒，Peter 更喜歡啤酒。

19. **reality** [rɪ`æləti] n. [C][U] 現實，事實 (pl. realities)

▲ The dream of sending a man to the moon has become a reality. 把人送上月球的夢想已經成為事實。

💡 in reality 事實上，實際上

20. **royal** [`rɔɪəl] adj. 皇室的

▲ Prince William is a member of the British royal family. 威廉王子是英國皇室的成員。

royalty [ˋrɔɪəltɪ] n. [C] (專利) 使用費，(著作的) 版稅 (usu. pl.)

▲ The author donated half of the royalties from his new book to the charity.
這作者將其新書的一半版稅捐給慈善機構。

---

21. **similar** [ˋsɪmələ] adj. 相似的 <to> [反] different

▲ Guishan Island is similar to a turtle in shape.
龜山島的形狀與烏龜的形狀相似。

---

22. **soccer** [ˋsɑkə] n. [U] 足球 [同] football

▲ Ben enjoys playing soccer. Ben 喜歡踢足球。

---

23. **solve** [sɑlv] v. 解決 (問題等)；偵破

▲ Staying optimistic is the best way of solving a problem. 保持樂觀是解決問題最好的方法。

---

24. **target** [ˋtɑrgɪt] n. [C] (要達到的) 目標 [同] goal；(攻擊的) 目標

▲ Setting sales targets helps keep the team focusing on achieving their goals. 設定銷售目標幫助這團隊持續專注於達成他們的目標。

💡 meet/achieve/reach a target 達到目標

target [ˋtɑrgɪt] v. 以…為目標或對象 <at>

▲ The TV program is targeted at preschool children.
這電視節目以學齡前兒童為對象。

---

25. **value** [`vælju] n. [C][U] 價值，價格 <of>；[U] 重要性 <of>

▲ The value of gold was over $1,800 an ounce.
金價一盎司超過一千八百美元。

value [`vælju] v. 珍重，重視；給…估價 <at>

▲ The celebrity values privacy above anything else.
這名人把隱私看得比什麼都重要。

1. **chemical** [`kɛmɪkl̩] adj. 化學的

▲ H₂O is the chemical formula for water.
H₂O 是水的化學式。

chemical [`kɛmɪkl̩] n. [C] 化學製品

▲ The factory released toxic chemicals into the river.
這工廠排放有毒化學品進到河裡。

2. **childhood** [`tʃaɪld͵hʊd] n. [C][U] 童年 <since>

▲ Hayao Miyazaki has been interested in planes since childhood. 宮崎駿從小就對飛機感興趣。

3. **command** [kə`mænd] n. [C] 命令；[U] 指揮，控制

▲ The captain gave a command to abandon ship, and his crew obeyed it. 船長下令棄船，而他的船員都遵從了。

command [kə`mænd] v. 命令，要求

▲ The general commanded that the soldiers (should) follow him.

將軍命令士兵跟著他。

---

4. **connection** [kə`nɛkʃən] **n.** [C] 關聯 <between> [同] link；[C][U] 連接

▲ There is a connection between global warming and extreme weather. 全球暖化和極端氣候有關聯。

♥ in connection with sth 與⋯有關

5. **develop** [dɪ`vɛləp] **v.** (使) 發展，(使) 成長 <into>；開發

▲ The fishing village has developed into an international harbor. 這漁村發展成一個國際港口。

development [dɪ`vɛləpmənt] **n.** [U] 成長，發展

▲ Exercise is very important for child development. 運動對孩童成長很重要。

6. **effect** [ɪ`fɛkt] **n.** [C][U] 影響，效果 <on>

▲ The oil spill had a disastrous effect on the ocean. 漏油事件對海洋有災難性的影響。

effect [ɪ`fɛkt] **v.** 使發生，實現 [同] bring about

▲ The employees' efforts to effect change in the company's policy were unsuccessful. 員工們想改變公司政策的努力失敗了。

7. **expression** [ɪk`sprɛʃən] **n.** [C][U] 表達，表示 <of>；表情，神情

▲ Lucy decided to send Vincent a present as an expression of thanks for his help. Lucy 決定送 Vincent 一個禮物以表達感謝他的幫忙。

8. **favorite** [ˋfevrɪt] adj. 最喜歡的

▲ Blue is Gail's favorite color.

藍色是 Gail 最喜歡的顏色。

favorite [ˋfevrɪt] n. [C] 最喜愛的人或事物

▲ Clare is the teacher's favorite.

Clare 是老師最喜愛的學生。

---

9. **fit** [fɪt] v. 合身；放得進 <into> (fit, fitted | fit, fitted | fitting)

▲ This dress fits Gloria perfectly.

這件洋裝 Gloria 穿起來很合身。

fit [fɪt] adj. 健康的 [反] unfit；適合的 <for> [反] unfit (fitter | fittest)

▲ Hazel goes jogging every day to keep fit.

Hazel 每天慢跑健身。

fit [fɪt] n. [C] (情緒的) 突發 <of>

▲ The man has fits of depression now and then.

這男子有時會突然覺得憂鬱。

fit [fɪt] adv. 幾乎⋯地

---

10. **former** [ˋfɔrmɚ] adj. 以前的，舊時的；前任的 [同] ex-

▲ Uzbekistan was a member of the former Soviet Union. 烏茲別克曾是前蘇聯的一員。

---

11. **introduction** [͵ɪntrəˋdʌkʃən] n. [U] 採用，引進 <of>；[C] 介紹

▲ The company's profits have doubled since the introduction of the new technology.

公司的利潤自從引進這新科技後已翻倍了。

12. **iron** [ˈaɪən] n. [U] 鐵；[C] 熨斗
   ▲ Strike while the iron is hot.
      【諺】打鐵趁熱 (把握良機)。
   iron [ˈaɪən] v. 熨 (衣)，燙平 [同] press
   ▲ Colin has just ironed his shirts and pants.
      Colin 剛燙好他的襯衫和褲子。
   iron [ˈaɪən] adj. 強硬堅定的
   ▲ The leader is a man with an iron will and steely
      determination.
      這位領袖有鋼鐵般強硬堅定的意志與決心。

13. **judge** [dʒʌdʒ] n. [C] 法官；(比賽的) 裁判員，評審
   ▲ When the judge entered the courtroom, all the people
      stood up. 當法官進入法庭時，所有的人都起立。
   judge [dʒʌdʒ] v. 斷定，判斷
   ▲ Judy's parents taught her not to judge people by their
      looks. Judy 的父母教她不要以貌取人。

14. **limit** [ˈlɪmɪt] n. [C] 限制 <for>；極限 <of>
   ▲ There is no age limit for health insurance plans.
      參加健保計畫沒有年齡限制。
   limit [ˈlɪmɪt] v. 限制 <to>
   ▲ Each package tour is limited to 20 participants.
      每個套裝旅遊行程限二十個人參加。

15. **pain** [pen] n. [C][U] (身體上的) 疼痛 <in>；(心理上的)

痛苦 <of>

▲ John felt a pain in his left leg.
John 感到左腳一陣疼痛。

pain [pen] v. 使痛苦，使痛心

▲ It pained Eric to see the poor children begging on the streets. 看到窮孩子在街上乞討讓 Eric 痛心。

16. **production** [prə`dʌkʃən] n. [U] 生產，製造 <of>；產量 <in>

▲ Yeast is used in the production of bread.
酵母在製造麵包時被使用。

17. **proper** [`prɑpɚ] adj. 正確的；適當的 [反] improper

▲ Kevin showed his kid the proper way to brush teeth.
Kevin 教他孩子正確的刷牙方式。

18. **recover** [rɪ`kʌvɚ] v. 康復，恢復 <from>；找回

▲ Ken hopes his mother will recover from her illness soon. Ken 希望他母親早日從疾病中康復。

19. **sand** [sænd] n. [U] 沙；[C][U] 沙灘

▲ Walking along the beach, the girl had sand in her shoes. 沿著沙灘走，女孩的鞋子進沙了。

sand [sænd] v. (用砂紙) 打磨，磨光 <down>

▲ Before painting the bookshelf, the carpenter sanded it down thoroughly.
在粉刷書架之前，木匠先用砂紙把它徹底磨光。

20. **spelling** [`spɛlɪŋ] n. [U] 拼字，拼寫；[C] 拼法

▲ The teacher asked the student to correct his spelling mistakes. 老師要求這學生改正他的拼字錯誤。

21. **spirit** [ˋspɪrɪt] n. [sing.][U] 精神 <in> ；[pl.] 情緒 <in> (~s)

▲ The old lady feels young in spirit.
這老婦人精神上感覺年輕。

22. **support** [səˋport] n. [U] 支持 <of>；鼓勵 <of>

▲ The president lost the support of the people after the political scandal.
總統在政治醜聞後失去了人民的支持。

support [səˋport] v. 支持，贊成；養活

▲ The plan was supported by the participants in the meeting. 這計畫受到與會者的支持。

23. **tax** [tæks] n. [C][U] 稅

▲ The professional baseball player has to pay 40% tax on his income.
這位職業棒球選手須付 40% 的所得稅。

tax [tæks] v. 對…課稅

▲ The government taxes the rich to provide welfare services for the poor.
政府向富者課稅以提供貧者福利服務。

24. **war** [wɔr] n. [C][U] 戰爭 [反] peace

▲ A war broke out between the United States and Iraq.
美國與伊拉克之間爆發了戰爭。

25. **waste** [west] n. [sing.][U] 浪費 <of>；[U] 廢物，廢料

▲ The campaign is just a waste of time and money.
這活動只是浪費時間和金錢。

waste [west] v. 浪費 <on>；白費，未好好利用

▲ Mavis wasted a lot of time on video games.
Mavis 浪費很多時間在電玩上。

●━━━━━━━━━━━━━━━━●

Unit 11

1. **activity** [æk`tɪvətɪ] n. [C][U] 活動，行動；[C] (娛樂) 活動 (pl. activities)

▲ People are worried about growing gang activity in the city. 人們因城裡的幫派活動漸增感到擔心。

─────────────────────────────

2. **against** [ə`gɛnst] prep. 反對；對抗

▲ Several legislators voted against the bill.
幾位立法委員投票反對該法案。

─────────────────────────────

3. **clothing** [`kloðɪŋ] n. [U] 衣服

▲ Only two pieces of clothing can be taken into the fitting room at one time.
一次只能帶兩件衣服進入試衣間。

─────────────────────────────

4. **complete** [kəm`plit] adj. 完全的 [同] total；完整的 [同] whole [反] incomplete

▲ Nothing was achieved in the meeting; it was a complete waste of time.

會議中沒有達成任何事，這完全是浪費時間。

complete [kəm`plit] v. 完成；使完整

▲ The bridge took only 8 months to complete.
這座橋只花了八個月就完工了。

---

5. **curious** [`kjʊrɪəs] adj. 好奇的 <about>

▲ The students are curious about how life began.
學生們好奇生命是如何開始的。

---

6. **delivery** [dɪ`lɪvərɪ] n. [C][U] 運送，遞送 <of> (pl. deliveries)

▲ The delivery of mail has been delayed by the heavy snow. 大雪延誤了郵件的遞送。

---

7. **express** [ɪk`sprɛs] v. 表達，表示

▲ Nick expressed his opinions on the topic.
Nick 對這主題表達他的看法。

💡 express oneself 表達自己的想法或感受

express [ɪk`sprɛs] adj. 快遞的；特快的，直達的

▲ Evan sent the package by express mail.
Evan 用快遞寄包裹。

express [ɪk`sprɛs] adv. 用快遞

▲ Phoebe sent the important document express.
Phoebe 用快遞寄這份重要的文件。

express [ɪk`sprɛs] n. [C] 快車 (usu. sing.)；[U] 快遞 <by>

▲ The traveler took the Orient Express to cross Europe.

這旅客搭東方快車穿越歐洲。

---

8. **fear** [fɪr] n. [C][U] 害怕，懼怕

   ▲ The girl trembled with fear when she heard strange sounds in the house.

   當女孩聽到房子裡傳來怪聲音時，她害怕地發抖。

   💡 for fear (that).../of sth 以免…

   fear [fɪr] v. 害怕，懼怕

   ▲ Those brave soldiers didn't fear death.

   那些勇敢的士兵不怕死。

---

9. **folk** [fok] n. [pl.] 人們；父母，家屬 (~s)

   ▲ Ordinary folks can do extraordinary things.

   平凡人可以做不平凡的事。

---

10. **gain** [gen] v. 獲得 <from>；增加

    ▲ The student gained work experience from the internship program.

    這學生在實習計畫中獲得了工作經驗。

    gain [gen] n. [C] 收穫；[C][U] 增加 [反] loss

    ▲ No pains, no gains. 【諺】一分耕耘，一分收穫。

---

11. **golden** [`goldn̩] adj. 金色的；極佳的，非常有利的

    ▲ Hannah is a beautiful woman with golden hair.

    Hannah 是位有著金髮的美麗女子。

---

12. **latest** [`letɪst] adj. 最新的，最近的

    ▲ People can get access to the latest information on the Internet.

人們能在網路上接觸到最新的資訊。

13. **leaf** [lif] n. [C] 葉子 (pl. leaves)

▲ Some leaves turn yellow in autumn.

一些葉子在秋天變成黃色。

💡 turn over a new leaf 改過自新

14. **loss** [lɔs] n. [C][U] 失去，喪失 <of>；死亡 <of>

▲ The side effects of the medicine include headaches and loss of appetite.

這藥物的副作用包括頭痛和喪失食慾。

15. **mature** [mə`tjʊr] adj. 成熟的 [反] immature (maturer | maturest)

▲ The young man should be mature enough to deal with the problem.

這年輕人應該夠成熟可以處理這個問題。

16. **recent** [`risn̩t] adj. 最近的，近來的

▲ In recent months, people have taken to wearing face masks in public places.

最近幾個月，人們已開始在公共場所戴口罩。

17. **responsible** [rɪ`spɑnsəbl̩] adj. 負有責任的 <for>；作為原因的 <for>

▲ The bus driver should be responsible for the safety of the passengers on the bus.

公車司機應該負責車上乘客的安全。

18. **snack** [snæk] **n.** [C] 點心，零食

▲ Cathy often eats snacks between her main meals.
Cathy 常常在正餐之間吃點心。

snack [snæk] **v.** 吃零食

▲ To stay fit, Leila avoided snacking between meals.
為了保持身材，Leila 在餐與餐之間避免吃零食。

---

19. **sort** [sɔrt] **n.** [C] 種類 <of> [同] kind, type

▲ The little boy has all sorts of toys.
這小男孩有各種玩具。

♥ sort of 有點

sort [sɔrt] **v.** 把⋯分類 <into>

▲ May sorted the old letters into those to be shredded
and those to be kept.
May 把舊信件分類成要用碎紙機撕毀和要保留的。

---

20. **source** [sors] **n.** [C] 來源，出處 <of>；(消息等) 來源

▲ For many people, music is the source of endless
pleasure. 音樂對很多人來說是無限快樂之源。

---

21. **spider** [`spaɪdɚ] **n.** [C] 蜘蛛

▲ Most spiders spin webs. 大部分的蜘蛛織網。

---

22. **stick** [stɪk] **v.** 黏貼 <on>；插入 <into> (stuck | stuck |
sticking)

▲ Cole stuck a poster on the wall of his bedroom.
Cole 在他房間的牆上貼了一張海報。

♥ stick together 團結一致 | stick up 豎起

stick [stɪk] n. [C] 樹枝；手杖，拐杖

▲ The climbers collected some dry sticks to start a fire.
登山客們收集了一些乾樹枝來生火。

23. **task** [tæsk] n. [C] 工作，任務 [同] job

▲ Renee finished some tasks in the office today.
Renee 今天在辦公室完成了一些工作。

task [tæsk] v. 派給⋯任務 <with>

▲ The team was tasked with finding a solution to the problem. 這團隊被指派設法解決問題的任務。

24. **throughout** [θru`aʊt] prep. 遍及，到處；從頭到尾

▲ The disease spread throughout the world within a few months. 這疾病在幾個月內傳遍了全世界。

throughout [θru`aʊt] adv. 到處

▲ The laboratory is painted white throughout.
這實驗室到處都被漆成白色。

25. **toothbrush** [`tuθ͵brʌʃ] n. [C] 牙刷

▲ The boy used a toothbrush to clean his teeth.
這男孩用牙刷清潔他的牙齒。

Unit 12

1. **alone** [ə`lon] adv. 獨自地；單獨地，孤獨地 [同] by oneself

▲ Judy can't do the difficult job alone.

Judy 無法獨自做這個困難的工作。

alone [əˋlon] adj. 獨自一人的

▲ Being alone in a strange city can be frightening.
獨自一人在一個陌生的城市可能會令人害怕。

---

2. **building** [ˋbɪldɪŋ] n. [C] 建築物

▲ The big city has many tall buildings.
這個大城市有許多高的建築物。

---

3. **college** [ˋkɑlɪdʒ] n. [C][U] 學院，大學 [同] university

▲ Corey went to college after graduating from senior
high school. Corey 高中畢業後就去上大學。

---

4. **condition** [kənˋdɪʃən] n. [pl.] 條件，情況（～s）；
[U][sing.] 狀態，狀況

▲ Poor living conditions may lead to increased risk of
injury or disease.
生活條件差可能導致受傷或生病的風險增加。

condition [kənˋdɪʃən] v. 使習慣於，使適應

▲ In the past, women were conditioned to obey their
husbands. 女性在過去習慣於服從她們的丈夫。

---

5. **cycle** [ˋsaɪkl̩] n. [C] 週期，循環

▲ The caterpillar built a cocoon and entered a new
stage of its life cycle—the pupa.
毛毛蟲結繭並進入牠生命週期的新階段——蛹。

cycle [ˋsaɪkl̩] v. 騎腳踏車 [同] bike

▲ How about going cycling in the park?

到公園騎腳踏車如何？

---

6. **discover** [dɪ`skʌvɚ] v. 找到，發現

▲ The engineers discovered oil while they were digging in the desert. 工程師們在沙漠中挖掘時找到了石油。

---

7. **form** [fɔrm] n. [C] 種類，類型 <of>；形式

▲ Cycling is a cheap and popular form of transportation.

騎單車是一種便宜又受歡迎的交通類型。

💡 take the form of 以⋯形式出現

form [fɔrm] v. 成立；形成

▲ The organization was formed by a group of lawyers.

這組織是由一群律師所成立。

---

8. **general** [`dʒɛnərəl] adj. 大體的，大致的；總的，普遍的

▲ Sally spoke in general terms about the plan; she didn't know its full details.

Sally 大致講了一下這計畫，她不知道全部細節。

💡 in general 一般來說

general [`dʒɛnərəl] n. [C] 將軍

▲ A general is an officer of very high rank in the army.

將軍是陸軍中階級非常高的軍官。

---

9. **giraffe** [dʒə`ræf] n. [C] 長頸鹿

▲ A giraffe has a very long neck and long legs.

長頸鹿有很長的頸部和長腿。

---

10. **gold** [gold] n. [U] 金，黃金

▲ The bracelet is made of pure gold.

這手鐲是由純金打造。

gold [gold] adj. 金 (製) 的

▲ The wealthy man wears a gold watch at all times.

這有錢人總是戴著一只金錶。

11. **humble** [ˋhʌmbl̩] adj. 謙虛的 [反] proud；地位低下的，卑微的 (humbler | humblest)

▲ The humble man is not proud of his achievements.

這謙虛的男子不自傲於自己的成就。

12. **latter** [ˋlætɚ] adj. (兩者中) 後者的 [反] former；後面的，後半的

▲ Of the two words "modest" and "humble," the latter word is used more frequently. 在 "modest" 和 "humble" 這兩個字當中，後者這個字較常用。

13. **liberal** [ˋlɪbərəl] adj. 開放的，開明的

▲ The father has a liberal attitude toward his children's education.

這父親對孩子們的教育抱持著開放的態度。

14. **measure** [ˋmɛʒɚ] v. 測量；尺寸為⋯

▲ A mile is a unit for measuring distance.

英里是測量距離的單位。

measurement [ˋmɛʒɚmənt] n. [C] 尺寸；[U] 測量 <of>

▲ Before buying a bed, Stacey took measurements of her bedroom.

在買床之前，Stacey 先測量她臥室的尺寸。

15. **necessary** [ˋnɛsəˌsɛrɪ] adj. 必需的，不可或缺的
▲ It is necessary to dress formally for the interview.
穿著正式來參加這個面試是必需的。

16. **period** [ˋpɪrɪəd] n. [C] 一段時間 <of>；(人生中或歷史上的) 時期
▲ People with a cold should remain at home for a short period of time.
感冒的人應該在家裡待上一小段時間。

17. **president** [ˋprɛzədənt] n. [C] 總統；總裁，董事長
▲ In Taiwan, people elect their president every four years. 在臺灣，人們每四年選一次總統。

18. **rubber** [ˋrʌbɚ] n. [U] 橡膠
▲ Rubber can be used to make tires and boots.
橡膠可以用來做輪胎和靴子。

19. **southern** [ˋsʌðɚn] adj. 南方的，南部的 (also Southern) (abbr. S)
▲ The student who has lived in the south for years has a southern accent.
這位曾經在南方住了好幾年的學生有南方的口音。

20. **suitable** [ˋsutəbl̩] adj. 合適的 <for> [反] unsuitable
▲ The casual dress is not suitable for the formal party.
這件休閒的洋裝不適合正式的宴會。

21. **technology** [tɛk`nɑlədʒɪ] n. [C][U] 科技 (pl. technologies)

▲ Satellite technology makes it easier to track the locations of planes.
衛星科技讓追蹤飛機的位置變得容易許多。

22. **toward** [tə`word] prep. 向，朝；對於 [同] towards

▲ The dog ran toward its master. 這隻狗跑向牠的主人。

23. **typical** [`tɪpɪkl] adj. 典型的，有代表性的 <of>

▲ The colors of the painting, which are bright and lively, are typical of the artist's works. 這幅畫的顏色明亮又充滿活力，是這位藝術家的典型作品。

24. **unit** [`junɪt] n. [C] 單位 <of>；單元

▲ A word is a unit of language. 字是構成語言的單位。

25. **unless** [ən`lɛs] conj. 除非

▲ Unless the weather improves, the couple will have to postpone their trip.
除非天氣好轉，否則這對夫妻將得把他們的旅行延期。

Unit 13

1. **amount** [ə`maʊnt] n. [C][U] 數量 <of>

▲ The secretary had a large amount of work to do.
這祕書有大量的工作要做。

amount [ə`maʊnt] v. 合計，共計 <to>

▲ The loss amounted to a million dollars.

這損失共計一百萬美元。

2. **better** [ˋbɛtɚ] adj. 較好的 [反] worse；好轉的，康復的 [反] worse

▲ Francis' plan seems better than Toby's.

Francis 的計畫似乎比 Toby 的好。

better [ˋbɛtɚ] adv. 較好地 [反] worse

▲ Viola did the work better than anyone else.

Viola 這工作做得比誰都好。

🕯 had better 最好

better [ˋbɛtɚ] n. [U] (人或事物) 較好者 (the ～)

▲ Both of the shows are excellent, so it's difficult to decide which is the better.

兩個表演都很棒，所以很難決定哪個是較好的。

🕯 for better or (for) worse 無論好壞，不管怎樣

better [ˋbɛtɚ] v. 超過，勝過

▲ The athlete's record of Olympic gold medals hasn't been bettered yet.

這位運動員的奧運金牌數的紀錄尚未被超過。

3. **central** [ˋsɛntrəl] adj. 中心的，中部的

▲ Trafalgar Square is in the central part of London.

特拉法加廣場位於倫敦市的中心。

4. **consider** [kənˋsɪdɚ] v. 考慮；認為

▲ After considering the situation, Jenny made the

decision. 在考慮情況後，Jenny 做了決定。

---

5. **deliver** [dɪˋlɪvɚ] **v.** 運送，遞送 <to>；發表

▲ The package was delivered to the office this morning. 這包裹今天早上被遞送到辦公室。

---

6. **distance** [ˋdɪstəns] **n.** [C][U] 距離，路程；[sing.] 遠方

▲ The school is within walking distance of Lily's house. 學校到 Lily 家是走路就可以到的距離。

💡 keep sb's distance 保持距離

---

7. **download** [ˋdaʊnˌlod] **v.** 下載

▲ Downloading songs illegally will cause people a lot of trouble. 非法下載歌曲會帶給人們很多麻煩。

---

8. **guide** [gaɪd] **n.** [C] 準則，根據；嚮導，導遊

▲ Test scores are not always the best guide to assessment of ability.
考試成績不一定是評估能力的最好準則。

guide [gaɪd] **v.** 帶…參觀 <through> [同] lead；指引

▲ The professor guided her students through the museum. 這教授帶她的學生們參觀博物館。

---

9. **host** [host] **n.** [C] 主人，東道主；主持人

▲ The host poured tea for his guests.
這主人幫他的客人倒茶。

hostess [ˋhostɪs] **n.** [C] 女主人；女主持人

▲ The hostess asked her guests if they would like coffee.

女主人詢問她的客人是否想喝咖啡。

---

10. **ideal** [aɪˋdiəl] adj. 理想的，完美的 <for> [同] perfect
▲ The restaurant has excellent facilities, ideal for families with young children.
這餐廳有很棒的設施，對有小孩的家庭很理想。
ideal [aɪˋdiəl] n. [C] 理想 <of>
▲ Vivien eventually gave up her romantic ideal of love.
Vivien 最終放棄了她對愛情的浪漫理想。

---

11. **individual** [͵ɪndəˋvɪdʒʊəl] adj. 個人的，個體的；個別的，單獨的
▲ The dormitory has individual rooms.
這間宿舍有個人的房間。
individual [͵ɪndəˋvɪdʒʊəl] n. [C] 個人，個體
▲ Society is made up of individuals.
社會是由個人組成的。

---

12. **length** [lɛŋθ] n. [C][U] 長，長度 <in>
▲ The pole is thirty feet in length. 這竿子三十英尺長。
♥ at great length 長時間地 | go to great lengths to V 竭盡全力做…

---

13. **meaning** [ˋminɪŋ] n. [C][U] 意思，意義 <of>
▲ The teacher used some pictures to help the students understand the meaning of the word.
老師用一些圖片來幫助學生們了解這個字的意思。

---

14. **metal** [ˋmɛtl] n. [C][U] 金屬

▲ Gold is a precious metal. 黃金是一種貴金屬。

metal [ˋmɛtl̩] adj. 金屬製的

▲ The metal plate is used to collect solar energy.
這個金屬板是用來收集太陽能。

15. **novel** [ˋnɑvl̩] n. [C] 小說

▲ Wanda likes to read detective novels in her free time.
Wanda 在閒暇時喜歡看偵探小說。

novel [ˋnɑvl̩] adj. 新奇的

▲ Gerald often comes up with novel ideas.
Gerald 經常想出新奇的點子。

16. **positive** [ˋpɑzətɪv] adj. 樂觀的，正向的 [反] negative；
正面的，好的 [反] negative

▲ Positive thinking is an attitude that focuses on the
bright side of life.
正向思考是著重於生活光明面的一種態度。

positive [ˋpɑzətɪv] n. [C] 好的一面 [反] negative

▲ Before making the decision, Zoe weighed up the
positives and the negatives.
在做決定之前，Zoe 先權衡好壞面。

17. **project** [ˋprɑdʒɛkt] n. [C] 計畫，方案；作業，專題研究
<on>

▲ The government starts a project of building a new
dam. 政府開始一項興建新水庫的計畫。

18. **provide** [prəˋvaɪd] v. 提供 <for>

▲ The hotel provides a taxi ride to the airport for their guests. 這旅館為住客提供機場計程車接送服務。

19. **solution** [sə`luʃən] n. [C] 解決辦法 <to>

▲ It seemed too difficult to find a solution to that problem. 似乎難以找到解決那個問題的辦法。

20. **steel** [stil] n. [U] 鋼

▲ The window frame is made of stainless steel.
這窗框是不鏽鋼製成的。

steel [stil] v. 使…下決心，把心一橫 <to>

▲ The mother steeled herself to refuse her son's request. 這母親把心一橫拒絕兒子的請求。

21. **super** [`supɚ] adj. 極好的 [同] excellent

▲ All the classmates had a super time at the party.
所有同學在派對上玩得非常開心。

super [`supɚ] adv. 非常地

▲ Have you met Emma? She is super nice.
你見過 Emma 了嗎？她人非常地好。

22. **thought** [θɔt] n. [C] 想法 <on> [同] idea；[U] 考慮

▲ Sue asked her father if he had any thoughts on the matter. Sue 問她父親對這件事是否有任何想法。

💡 give thought to sth 仔細考慮… | on second thought 進一步考慮後

23. **universe** [`junə,vɝs] n. [sing.] 宇宙 (the ~) <in>

▲ Human beings are making efforts to look for other

intelligent life in the universe.

人類正努力找尋宇宙中其他有智慧的生命。

24. **usual** [`juʒʊəl] **adj.** 通常的，慣常的

▲ Despite the heavy snow, Glenn went to work at the usual time.

儘管下大雪，Glenn 還是在慣常的時間去上班。

25. **wood** [wʊd] **n.** [C][U] 木頭；[pl.] 森林 (the ~s) <in>

▲ The bridge is made of wood. 這橋是木製的。

Unit 14

1. **accept** [ək`sɛpt] **v.** 接受 [反] refuse；相信，接受 (不滿意的情況)

▲ Harry received an invitation but did not accept it.

Harry 收到邀請函，但沒接受邀請。

2. **approach** [ə`protʃ] **n.** [C] 方法，方式 <to>；[U] 接近 <of>

▲ The government needs a scientific approach to dealing with the problem.

政府需用科學的方式來處理這個問題。

approach [ə`protʃ] **v.** 接近；接洽，找…商談 <for>

▲ The plane is approaching the runway.

這飛機正接近跑道。

3. **blood** [blʌd] **n.** [U] 血，血液

▲ Blood runs in the veins. 血液在血管裡流動。

---

4. **climate** [`klaɪmɪt] n. [C][U] 氣候

   ▲ Alaska has a really cold climate. 阿拉斯加氣候嚴寒。

---

5. **cultural** [`kʌltʃərəl] adj. 文化的

   ▲ There are almost no cultural differences between the two countries. 這兩國幾乎沒有文化差異。

---

6. **culture** [`kʌltʃɚ] n. [C][U] 文化

   ▲ Herbal medicine has taken root in Chinese culture.
   草藥已經在中國文化中生根。

---

7. **decision** [dɪ`sɪʒən] n. [C] 決定

   ▲ The couple finally reached the same decision.
   這對夫妻最後達成一致的決定。

   ♥ make a decision 做決定

---

8. **department** [dɪ`pɑrtmənt] n. [C] (組織或機構中的) 系，部 <of>；(商店的) 部 (abbr. dept.)

   ▲ Cara graduated from the Department of Economics.
   Cara 是經濟系畢業的。

---

9. **effective** [ɪ`fɛktɪv] adj. 有效的 [反] ineffective

   ▲ The CEO took effective means to resolve this crisis.
   這執行長採取有效的方法來解決危機。

---

10. **evil** [`ivl̩] n. [C] 邪惡的事，罪惡的行為；[U] 邪惡 [反] good

   ▲ Some people believe that a cross can protect them

against evils of many kinds.
一些人相信十字架能保護他們對抗各種邪惡。
evil [`ivl] adj. 邪惡的 (eviler, eviller | evilest, evillest)
▲ The bad guy is full of evil thoughts.
這壞人充滿了邪惡的想法。

---

11. **historical** [hɪs`tɔrɪk!] adj. 歷史的
▲ Jerry is very interested in historical novels.
Jerry 對歷史小說很有興趣。

---

12. **imagine** [ɪ`mædʒɪn] v. 想像，設想
▲ Imagine (that) you are traveling to the moon.
想像一下你要去月球旅行。

---

13. **influence** [`ɪnfluəns] n. [C][U] 影響 <on>
▲ The poet had a great influence on other writers.
這個詩人對其他作家有很大的影響。
influence [`ɪnfluəns] v. 影響
▲ Several factors influenced Cherry's decision to refuse the job offer.
幾項因素影響 Cherry 決定拒絕這項工作邀約。

---

14. **liquid** [`lɪkwɪd] n. [C][U] 液體
▲ Both milk and juice are liquids.
牛奶和果汁都是液體。

---

15. **master** [`mæstɚ] n. [C] 大師 <at>；主人
▲ Shakespeare was a master at writing plays.
莎士比亞是寫劇本的大師。

master [ˋmæstɚ] v. 精通，掌握；征服 [同] overcome

▲ It takes practice to master a foreign language.
精通外語需要練習。

---

16. **method** [ˋmεθəd] n. [C] 方法，方式

▲ The teacher uses creative teaching methods to make learning more interesting.
這位老師使用有創意的教學方法，使學習更有趣。

---

17. **opinion** [əˋpɪnjən] n. [C][U] 意見，看法 <on>

▲ The local people expressed their opinions on the serious matter.
當地居民對這嚴重的事件表達他們的看法。

💡 in sb's opinion 依…看來

---

18. **post** [post] n. [C] 職位 [同] position；[U] 郵件 [同] mail

▲ Jacob got a post as a teacher in the small town.
Jacob 在這小鎮得到一份教師的職位。

post [post] v. 郵寄 [同] mail；派駐 <to>

▲ Cathy will post the letter on her way to work.
Cathy 在上班的路上會去寄信。

post [post] adv. 快速地

---

19. **record** [ˋrεkɚd] n. [C] 紀錄，記載 <of>；最高紀錄，最佳成績

▲ The scientist keeps a record of the changes in temperature. 這科學家紀錄氣溫的變化。

record [rɪˋkɔrd] v. 紀錄；錄音，錄影

▲ The old lady recorded every penny she spent.
這老婦人紀錄她花的每一分錢。

20. **sport** [sport] n. [C] 體育活動，運動

▲ Elaine enjoys all kinds of sports.
Elaine 喜歡各式各樣的運動。

sport [sport] v. 穿戴，裝飾

▲ George is sporting a T-shirt with a logo on it.
George 穿著一件上面有商標的 T 恤。

21. **stress** [strɛs] n. [C][U] 壓力，緊張 <under>；[U] 強調 <on> [同] emphasis

▲ The engineer is busy and under lots of stress; he has no time to relax.
這工程師忙碌又壓力大，他沒時間放鬆。

stress [strɛs] v. 強調，著重

▲ The doctor stressed the importance of early diagnosis and treatment. 這醫生強調早期診斷並治療的重要性。

22. **survival** [sə`vaɪvl] n. [U] 生存，存活

▲ The victim's survival is doubtful under the unfavorable circumstances.
在這種不利的情況下，這受害者是不太可能生還的。

23. **western** [`wɛstən] adj. 西方的，西部的 (also Western) (abbr. W)

▲ The Netherlands is a country in Western Europe.
荷蘭是位於西歐的國家。

western [ˋwɛstɚn] n. [C] 西部片

▲ The western is about the life in the west of the United States in the past.

這西部片是關於過去美國西部的生活。

---

24. **whole** [hol] adj. 全部的，整個的 [同] entire

▲ Bob spent his whole salary on that car.

Bob 把全部的薪水都花在那輛車上。

whole [hol] n. [C] 全部，整個 (the ～) <of> (usu. sing.)

▲ The whole of the vacation was ruined by the storm.

整個假期都被暴風雨給毀了。

🖢 as a whole 總體上

---

25. **youth** [juθ] n. [U] 年輕時期，青春 <in>；[C] 青年，小伙子

▲ In her youth, Freda's dream was to be a dancer.

Freda 年輕時的夢想是成為舞者。

Unit 15

1. **account** [əˋkaʊnt] n. [C] 報告 <of>；帳戶 (abbr. a/c, acct.) <with>

▲ The driver gave an account of the accident in detail.

這司機詳細報告那起事故。

🖢 on no account 無論如何絕不 | savings account 儲蓄帳戶

account [əˋkaʊnt] v. 解釋 <for> [同] explain；(在數量

上) 占 <for>

▲ How did Jacky account for his absence from the meeting? Jacky 如何解釋他缺席會議的原因？

---

2. **advance** [əd`væns] n. [C] 進步，進展 <in>；前進

▲ Recent advances in medicine are remarkable.
近日醫學的進步十分顯著。

💡 in advance (of sth) (在…之前) 事先，提前

advance [əd`væns] v. 進步；前進 <through>

▲ Mankind has advanced in knowledge but not in wisdom.
人類已在知識上有所進步，但在智慧方面並非如此。

---

3. **create** [krɪ`et] v. 創造；發明

▲ According to the Bible, it was God that created the world. 根據《聖經》，是上帝創造了世界。

---

4. **data** [`detə] n. [pl.][U] 資料，數據

▲ The scientist entered the research data into the spreadsheet. 這科學家把研究資料輸進試算表。

---

5. **director** [də`rɛktɚ] n. [C] 董事；導演

▲ The board of directors runs the trading company.
董事會經營著這家貿易公司。

---

6. **disease** [dɪ`ziz] n. [C][U] 病，疾病

▲ Avian flu is a fatal disease to birds and can deal a serious blow to the poultry industry.

禽流感是一種鳥類的致命疾病，能對家禽產業造成嚴重打擊。

---

7. **effort** [ˈɛfɚt] n. [C][U] 努力 <to>

▲ The student made an effort to improve his English pronunciation. 這學生努力要改善他的英文發音。

💡 in an effort to V 試圖⋯

---

8. **environmental** [ɪnˌvaɪrənˈmɛntl] adj. 環境的

▲ The international conference was held to discuss environmental issues.

這場國際會議是為了討論環境議題而舉辦。

---

9. **existence** [ɪgˈzɪstəns] n. [U] 存在

▲ It is believed that the universe came into existence about fifteen billion years ago.

一般相信宇宙大約在一百五十億年前成形。

💡 in existence 存在

---

10. **highly** [ˈhaɪlɪ] adv. 非常，極其

▲ Ethnic conflict is highly unlikely to occur in a society where people respect each other.

在人們互相尊重的社會中，種族衝突極不可能發生。

💡 speak/think highly of sb 對⋯評價很高

---

11. **image** [ˈɪmɪdʒ] n. [C] 形象；印象

▲ After the scandal broke, the company worked hard to improve its image.

在醜聞爆發出來後，這公司努力要改善其形象。

💡 be the (very/living/spitting) image of sb 長相酷似…

12. **improve** [ɪmˋpruv] v. 改善，提升
▲ Mandy studied hard to improve her math.
Mandy 用功念書以提升她的數學。

improvement [ɪmˋpruvmənt] n. [C][U] 改進，改善 <in>
▲ With the proper treatment, the doctor saw a great improvement in the patient's condition.
經過適當的治療，這醫生看到病人的狀況大大改善了。

13. **international** [ˌɪntɚˋnæʃnəl] adj. 國際的
▲ With over 190 countries as its members, the UN is an international organization. 有著超過一百九十個會員國，聯合國是一個國際性的組織。

14. **legal** [ˋlig!] adj. 合法的 [反] illegal；法律上的
▲ In Macau, gambling is completely legal.
在澳門，賭博是完全合法的。

15. **manage** [ˋmænɪdʒ] v. 經營，管理；設法做到
▲ Ivan is helping his father manage the family business. Ivan 正幫他父親經營家庭事業。

management [ˋmænɪdʒmənt] n. [U] 經營，管理；[sing.][U] 管理層，資方
▲ The company's financial problems are partly due to bad management.
這公司的財務問題部分是因為經營不善。

16. **mate** [met] n. [C] 夥伴；朋友

▲ Ian and his office mates went for a drink after work.
Ian 和他辦公夥伴們下班後去小酌一番。

mate [met] v. (使) 交配 <with>

▲ If you mate a horse with a donkey, you will get a mule. 如果你讓馬和驢交配，就會生出騾子。

17. **musician** [mju`zɪʃən] n. [C] 音樂家

▲ Beethoven was one of the greatest musicians in musical history.
貝多芬是音樂史上最偉大的音樂家之一。

18. **negative** [`nɛɡətɪv] adj. 負面的 [反] positive；消極的 [反] positive

▲ According to the study, early marriage has a negative effect on girls and their health.
根據研究，早婚對女孩和她們的健康有負面影響。

negative [`nɛɡətɪv] n. [C] (照片) 底片

▲ If you have the film developed, be sure to get back the negatives. 如果你去洗照片，一定要拿回底片。

19. **phrase** [frez] n. [C] 片語

▲ The phrase "all thumbs" means very awkward with one's hands.
"all thumbs" 這個片語是指某人的手很笨拙。

phrase [frez] v. 以⋯措辭表達

▲ The suspect tried to phrase his answer carefully.

這嫌犯試著措辭謹慎地回答。

20. **pressure** [`prɛʃɚ`] n. [C][U] 壓力 <under>
▲ Many students are under pressure from their parents to do well in studies.
很多學生在父母的壓力之下要在學習中表現出色。

pressure [`prɛʃɚ`] v. 強迫，對…施加壓力 <into, to> [同] pressurize
▲ The old man was pressured into lending his son lots of money. 這老人被迫借很多錢給他兒子。

21. **serve** [sɝv] v. 提供 (食物或飲料)；服務
▲ Dinner is served from 6 p.m. to 9 p.m.
晚餐從晚上六點到九點之間提供。
💡 serve sth up 提供 (食物)

22. **standard** [`stændɚd`] adj. 規範的；(語言) 標準的 [反] non-standard
▲ The factory paid the workers the standard rate.
這工廠付給工人規範的工資。
standard [`stændɚd`] n. [C][U] 標準，水準
▲ The teacher set high standards for his students.
這老師替他的學生們訂定了高標準。

23. **teens** [tinz] n. [pl.] 十幾歲 <in>
▲ The runner won his first gold medal in his early teens. 這位跑者在十幾歲出頭贏得他的第一面金牌。

24. **temperature** [`tɛmprətʃɚ`] n. [C][U] 氣溫；體溫

▲ Climate change causes a rise in the Earth's temperature. 氣候變遷造成地球氣溫上升。

25. **whom** [hum] pron. 誰

▲ Tony has two sons, one of whom will graduate from college this June.

Tony 有兩個兒子,其中一個今年六月要從大學畢業。

Unit 16

1. **affect** [ə`fɛkt] v. 影響

▲ Russia's war on Ukraine has greatly affected the world. 俄國對烏克蘭的戰爭對世界造成重大影響。

2. **aircraft** [`ɛr,kræft] n. [C] 飛機,航空器 (pl. aircraft)

▲ The pilot is now landing the aircraft.
駕駛員正在降落飛機。

3. **attention** [ə`tɛnʃən] n. [U] 注意,專注 <to>;關注

▲ Students must give their attention to their studies.
學生必須專注在課業上。

💡 draw sb's attention to 引起…的注意於…

4. **disappear** [,dɪsə`pɪr] v. 消失 <from> [同] vanish [反] appear;不見,失蹤 [同] vanish

▲ David watched the flying eagle until it disappeared from sight.

David 看著飛翔的老鷹，直到牠消失在視線中。

5. **expert** [ˋɛkspɝt] n. [C] 專家，內行人 <on, at, in>

▲ Jane Goodall is a world expert on chimpanzees.
珍古德是黑猩猩的世界級專家。

expert [ˋɛkspɝt] adj. 專家的，內行的 <at, in, on> [反]
inexpert

▲ The doctor is expert at plastic surgery.
這位醫生是整形外科的專家。

6. **factor** [ˋfæktɚ] n. [C] 因素 <in>

▲ Poverty is a major factor in crime.
貧窮是犯罪的主要因素。

7. **fair** [fɛr] adj. 合理的 [反] unfair；公平的 <with> [反]
unfair

▲ These workers are striving for a fair wage and
reasonable working hours.
這些工人在爭取合理的報酬和合理的工作時數。

fair [fɛr] n. [C] 露天遊樂會 [同] carnival, funfair；商品
展銷會

▲ At the fair, people can ride on large machines for fun
and play games to win prizes. 在這露天遊樂會，人們
可以坐大型機械玩樂和玩遊戲贏獎品。

fair [fɛr] adv. 公平地，公正地

▲ Jason won the championship fair and square.
Jason 是光明正大贏得冠軍的。

8. **female** [ˋfimel] **adj.** 女性的 [反] male

▲ Tsai Ing-wen is Taiwan's first female president.
蔡英文是臺灣第一位女性總統。

female [ˋfimel] **n.** [C] 女性 [反] male

▲ In the past, females were not allowed to vote.
在過去，女性不准投票。

9. **increase** [ɪnˋkris] **v.** 增加 <by, in> [反] decrease, reduce

▲ Ellen's salary increased by five percent this year.
Ellen 今年加薪 5%。

increase [ˋɪnkris] **n.** [C][U] 增加 <in> [反] decrease

▲ The organization reported an alarming increase in domestic violence.
該組織報告家庭暴力令人擔憂地增加。

♥ on the increase 正在增加

10. **indeed** [ɪnˋdid] **adv.** 確實

▲ Julia is old indeed, but she is always energetic.
Julia 確實老了，但她總是精力充沛。

11. **link** [lɪŋk] **n.** [C] 關聯 <between>；關係

▲ There is a link between smoking and lung cancer.
吸菸和肺癌有關聯。

link [lɪŋk] **v.** 使相關聯 <to, with>；連接 <to, with> [同] connect

▲ Vitamin D deficiency is linked to/with Alzheimer's disease. 缺乏維他命 D 與阿茲海默症有關。

12. **local** [ˈlokl̩] adj. 當地的，地方性的
   ▲ People can read local news in the local newspaper.
   人們在這地方報紙可以看到地方新聞。

   local [ˈlokl̩] n. [C] 本地人 (usu. pl.)
   ▲ The tourist asked the locals the best restaurant in town. 這觀光客詢問本地人城裡最好的餐廳。

13. **melody** [ˈmɛlədɪ] n. [C] 曲調，旋律 (pl. melodies)
   ▲ The song's melody is familiar, but Leo can't remember its lyrics.
   這首歌的旋律很熟悉，但 Leo 無法記得歌詞。

14. **minor** [ˈmaɪnɚ] adj. 次要的，較不重要的 [反] major
   ▲ This problem is of minor importance.
   這個問題是次要的。

   minor [ˈmaɪnɚ] n. [C] 未成年人
   ▲ Minors are not allowed to enter bars or nightclubs.
   未成年人不得進入酒吧或夜總會。

15. **nail** [nel] n. [C] 釘子 <into>
   ▲ The carpenter hammered a nail into the shelf.
   這木匠在架子上釘了一根釘子。

16. **patient** [ˈpeʃənt] n. [C] 病人
   ▲ The cancer patient has been taken good care of in the hospital. 這癌症病人在醫院一直受到良好照顧。

   patient [ˈpeʃənt] adj. 有耐心的 <with> [反] impatient

▲ Joyce is patient with her students, always trying out new ways to help them learn. Joyce 對她的學生很有耐心，總是嘗試新的方法來幫助他們學習。

17. **position** [pə`zɪʃən] n. [C] 姿勢；[C] 處境，狀況 <in> (usu. sing.)

▲ Zack sat in a comfortable position and started to read a book. Zack 以舒服的姿勢坐著並開始讀書。

💡 be in a/no position to V 能夠 / 無法做…

position [pə`zɪʃən] v. 放置

▲ Let's position the chairs in a circle.
讓我們把椅子排成一圈吧。

18. **prison** [`prɪzn̩] n. [C][U] 監獄 [同] jail

▲ The criminal was sent to prison for smuggling drugs.
這罪犯因為走私毒品而入獄。

19. **social** [`soʃəl] adj. 社會的；社交的

▲ Mental illness has become a serious social problem.
精神疾病已成為一個嚴重的社會問題。

20. **speech** [spitʃ] n. [C] 演講 <on>；[U] 說話能力

▲ The professor is giving a speech on AI technology.
這位教授正在做關於人工智慧科技的演講。

21. **step** [step] n. [C] 腳步；步驟

▲ The one-year-old baby could take a few steps.
這一歲的嬰兒能走幾步了。

step [stɛp] v. 走，跨步；踩 <on> [同] tread (stepped | stepped | stepping)

▲ The passenger stepped onto the platform.
這乘客走上了月臺。

---

22. **term** [tɝm] n. [C] 專門用語，術語 <for>；期限 <of>

▲ "Prognosis" is a medical term for predicting the likely development of a disease. 「預後」是一個醫學專門用語，意思是預測疾病可能的進程。

💡 in terms of sth 就…而言

term [tɝm] v. 把…稱為

▲ This kind of art is termed "abstract."
這種藝術被稱為「抽象派」。

---

23. **title** [`taɪtl̩] n. [C] 標題，名稱 <of>；稱謂，頭銜

▲ The author wrote a book under the title *Identity*.
這作家寫了一本書，書名是《認同》。

title [`taɪtl̩] v. 給 (圖書等) 起名

▲ The painter titled her new work *Silence*.
這畫家給她的新作品起名為《靜默》。

---

24. **user** [`juzɚ] n. [C] 使用者

▲ Road users should obey traffic rules.
道路使用者應遵守交通規則。

---

25. **wooden** [`wʊdn̩] adj. 木製的

▲ The wooden spoon is light and easy to carry.
這木製的湯匙又輕又容易攜帶。

Unit 17

1. **alarm** [ə`lɑrm] n. [C] 警報器；[U] 驚恐，擔憂

   ▲ When the fire alarm went off, many people ran toward the exit.

   當火災警報器響起時，許多人都跑向出口。

   💡 in alarm 驚恐地

   alarm [ə`lɑrm] v. 使恐懼，使擔憂

   ▲ Frank was alarmed by his son's high fever.

   Frank 為他兒子發高燒而擔憂。

---

2. **anger** [`æŋgɚ] n. [U] 憤怒

   ▲ Burning with anger, the woman slapped her husband.

   由於火冒三丈，這女人給她丈夫一記耳光。

---

3. **anywhere** [`ɛnɪˌhwɛr] adv. 任何地方 (also anyplace)

   ▲ Lester felt upset and didn't feel like going anywhere.

   Lester 覺得心煩意亂，任何地方都不想去。

---

4. **author** [`ɔθɚ] n. [C] 作者，作家 [同] writer

   ▲ The boy has read many children's books by that author. 這男孩讀過許多那位作家寫的童書。

   author [`ɔθɚ] v. 寫作

   ▲ The novel was authored by a historian.

   這本小說是一位歷史學家寫的。

---

5. **discuss** [dɪ`skʌs] v. 討論，談論 <with>

   ▲ The student discussed her thesis with her thesis

advisor. 這學生和指導教授討論她的論文。

6. **due** [dju] adj. 預計的 <to>；欠債的，應支付的 <to>
   ▲ The actress is due to play the role of a heroine in her next movie.
   這女演員預計在她下一部電影扮演女英雄的角色。
   💡 due to 因為
   due [dju] adv. 正對著
   ▲ These hikers are heading due north.
   這些健行者們朝正北方前進著。
   due [dju] n. [pl.] 會費 (~s) [同] fees
   ▲ As a member of the association, Karen has to pay her yearly dues. 身為這組織的成員，Karen 得繳年費。

7. **failure** [ˈfeljɚ] n. [C][U] 失敗 [反] success；[C] 失敗的人或事物 [反] success
   ▲ Failure is the mother of success.
   【諺】失敗為成功之母。

8. **feature** [ˈfitʃɚ] n. [C] 特色，特點 <of>；(報章雜誌的) 特寫 <on>
   ▲ The tower is the striking feature of the town.
   這座塔是這城鎮顯著的特色。
   feature [ˈfitʃɚ] v. 以…為特色
   ▲ The era features great technological progress.
   這個時代以偉大的科技進展為特色。

9. **feeling** [ˈfilɪŋ] n. [C] 感覺 <of>；[pl.] 情感，感情 (~s)

▲ A feeling of anger came over Nelson, so he shouted at his annoying friend. Nelson 突然感覺憤怒，因此對他惱人的朋友大吼大叫。

---

10. **lack** [læk] n. [sing.][U] 缺乏 <of> [同] shortage [反] surplus

▲ Mabel complains that her husband has a total lack of common sense. Mabel 抱怨她先生完全缺乏常識。

💡 for lack of sth 因缺乏…

lack [læk] v. 缺乏，缺少

▲ The team lacked time and money to finish the project. 這團隊缺乏時間和金錢去完成這個專案。

---

11. **maintain** [men`ten] v. 維持，保持；堅稱，斷言 [同] claim

▲ After graduating from junior high school, Patrick maintained contact with his classmates.
國中畢業後，Patrick 和他的同學們保持聯絡。

---

12. **match** [mætʃ] n. [C] 比賽；火柴

▲ The team has been practicing hard for the football match next month.
這支隊伍為了下個月的足球賽努力練習。

---

13. **mixture** [`mɪkstʃɚ] n. [C] 混合 <of>；[C][U] 混合物

▲ Quinn waited with a mixture of joy and anxiety.
Quinn 以喜悅和不安交織的心情等待著。

---

14. **musical** [`mjuzɪkl̩] adj. 音樂的

▲ How many musical instruments can the girl play?
這女孩會演奏多少樂器？

musical [`mjuzɪkl̩] **n.** [C] 音樂劇

▲ *Les Misérables* is one of the most famous musicals in the world. 《悲慘世界》是世上最有名的音樂劇之一。

15. **nearby** [`nɪr͵baɪ] **adj.** 附近的

▲ The tribal chief sent his son to a nearby village to ask for help. 這酋長派他兒子去附近的村落求助。

nearby [`nɪr͵baɪ] **adv.** 在附近

▲ Is there a post office nearby? 在這附近有郵局嗎？

16. **nearly** [`nɪrlɪ] **adv.** 將近 [同] almost

▲ It was nearly two o'clock in the morning when Norma came home. Norma 將近凌晨兩點回家。

💡 not nearly 遠不及，一點也不

17. **powerful** [`pauɚfəl] **adj.** 有權力的；有影響的，有渲染力的

▲ The president of the United States is one of the most powerful people in the world.
美國總統是世上最有權力的人之一。

18. **rare** [rɛr] **adj.** 罕見的，稀少的 [反] common (rarer | rarest)

▲ The giant panda is a rare species and is in danger of extinction. 大熊貓是種稀有物種並有滅絕的危險。

19. **speed** [spid] n. [C][U] 速度 <at>；[U] 快速，迅速 <with>

▲ The driver is driving at a speed of sixty miles per hour. 這駕駛正以時速六十英里行駛。

speed [spid] v. (使) 快速移動 (sped, speeded | sped, speeded | speeding)

▲ The ambulance sped down the street.
這輛救護車急駛過街道。

20. **state** [stet] v. 陳述，聲明

▲ The minister clearly stated his policy on education.
這位部長清楚地陳述他的教育政策。

statement [`stetmənt] n. [C] 陳述，聲明 <on>

▲ This morning, the mayor made a statement on the issue to the press.
今天早上，市長就此議題對媒體發表聲明。

21. **survive** [sɚ`vaɪv] v. 生存，倖存

▲ Two members of the crew survived the shipwreck.
兩位船員於船難中倖存。

22. **system** [`sɪstəm] n. [C] 系統；體制，制度

▲ The digestive system involves certain organs that turn food into energy.
消化系統包含某些轉化食物成能量的器官。

23. **tour** [tʊr] n. [C] 旅行，旅遊 <of>；參觀 <around>

▲ Ruth went on a three-day tour of Penghu.

Ruth 去澎湖旅行三天。

tour [tur] **v.** 旅行，旅遊

▲ During summer vacation, the family toured Canada.
  暑假時，這家人去加拿大旅行。

24. **trade** [tred] **n.** [U] 貿易 <between> [同] commerce；[C] 行業

▲ The trade between the two countries has increased.
  這兩國之間的貿易增加了。

trade [tred] **v.** 做買賣，進行交易 <with>；交換 <for> [同] swap

▲ The country traded with most of European countries.
  這個國家和大多數歐洲國家做買賣。

25. **vacation** [ve`keʃən] **n.** [C][U] 假期，休假 <on>

▲ Todd is on vacation in Italy at the moment.
  Todd 目前正在義大利渡假。

vacation [ve`keʃən] **v.** 渡假 <in, at>

▲ The Andersons are vacationing in the Maldives.
  Anderson 一家人正在馬爾地夫渡假。

Unit 18

1. **addition** [ə`dɪʃən] **n.** [U] 增加，添加 <of>；[C] 增加的人或事物 <to>

▲ The addition of salt greatly improved the flavor.
  添加鹽後味道好多了。

💡 in addition (to sth) 除 (⋯) 之外，還

2. **alike** [ə`laɪk] adv. 一樣地，相似地
▲ The two brothers were dressed alike.
這兩兄弟穿著相似。
alike [ə`laɪk] adj. 相同的，相像的
▲ The twins are exactly alike.
這對雙胞胎長得一模一樣。

3. **asleep** [ə`slip] adj. 睡著的 [反] awake
▲ The baby is sound asleep. 這小嬰孩正熟睡著。
💡 fall asleep 睡著

4. **attempt** [ə`tɛmpt] n. [C] 努力，嘗試 <to>
▲ The government has been making an attempt to encourage people to give birth.
政府持續試圖鼓勵人民生孩子。
attempt [ə`tɛmpt] v. 努力，嘗試 <to>
▲ Dylan attempted to stop smoking many times but failed. Dylan 屢次試圖戒菸但失敗。

5. **discussion** [dɪ`skʌʃən] n. [C][U] 談論，討論 <about>
▲ There has been enough discussion about the issue.
關於這個議題的討論已經夠多了。

6. **fashion** [`fæʃən] n. [C][U] 流行，時尚；流行款式
▲ Some people consider that miniskirts have gone out of fashion. 一些人認為迷你裙已經過時了。
💡 be in fashion 流行

fashion [ˋfæʃən] v. 製作 <from>

▲ The carpenter fashioned a shelf from pieces of wood.
這木匠用幾塊木頭製作了一個架子。

---

7. **flat** [flæt] adj. 平坦的；(輪胎等) 洩了氣的 (flatter |
flattest)

▲ The plain is (as) flat as a pancake. 這平原十分平坦。

💡 a flat refusal 斷然拒絕

flat [flæt] adv. 水平地

▲ The boy lay flat on his back, staring up at the sky.
這男孩平仰躺著，注視著天空。

flat [flæt] n. [C] 公寓 [同] apartment

▲ Alvin rent a two-bedroom flat near his office.
Alvin 在公司附近租了一間兩房的公寓。

---

8. **forest** [ˋfɔrɪst] n. [C][U] 森林

▲ The wildfire destroyed vast tracts of thick forest.
野火燒毀了廣大的密林地區。

---

9. **law** [lɔ] n. [U] (某國的) 法律 <under>；[C] (個別的) 法
規

▲ The use of nuclear weapons is illegal under
international law. 按照國際法，用核武是非法的。

💡 break the law 違反法律

---

10. **magazine** [ˌmægəˋzin] n. [C] 雜誌

▲ Vera has subscribed to several fashion magazines.
Vera 訂了幾本時裝雜誌。

---

11. **military** [ˋmɪləˌtɛrɪ] adj. 軍用的，軍隊的
   ▲ All the young men in the country must do military service. 這國家所有年輕男子都必須服兵役。
   military [ˋmɪləˌtɛrɪ] n. [C] 軍方，軍隊 (the ～) [同] the forces
   ▲ The military proposed an increase of 10% in defense spending. 軍方提議增加 10% 的國防預算。

12. **object** [ˋɑbdʒɪkt] n. [C] 物體；[sing.] 目標
   ▲ Don't move that object on the table.
   別移動桌上的那個物體。
   object [əbˋdʒɛkt] v. 反對 <to>
   ▲ The mother objected to her son's habit of smoking.
   這媽媽反對她兒子抽菸的習慣。

13. **occur** [əˋkɝ] v. 發生；出現 (occurred | occurred | occurring)
   ▲ A terrible car accident occurred on the road last night. 昨晚這條路上發生了可怕的車禍。
   💡 occur to sb (想法或主意) 出現在…腦中

14. **operate** [ˋɑpəˌret] v. 操作；動手術 <on>
   ▲ The worker doesn't know how to operate the machine. 這工人不知道如何操作這臺機器。

15. **produce** [prəˋdjus] v. 引起，使產生；生產，製作
   ▲ Climate change produced by global warming has a negative impact on coral reefs.

全球暖化所引起的氣候變遷對珊瑚礁有負面的影響。

produce [`prɑdjus] n. [U] 農產品

▲ The fresh organic produce is grown on a local farm.
這新鮮的有機農產品是在當地農場種植的。

---

16. **protect** [prə`tɛkt] v. 保護，防護 <from>

▲ You have to learn to protect yourself from harm.
你必須學習保護自己不受傷害。

---

17. **remove** [rɪ`muv] v. 移動，搬開 <from>；去除 <from>

▲ Cathy removed the painting from the wall and put it into a box. Cathy 移除牆上的畫並把它放進箱子。

---

18. **require** [rɪ`kwaɪr] v. 需要；要求

▲ Monkeypox requires physical contact to spread.
猴痘需要藉由身體接觸才能傳播。

requirement [rɪ`kwaɪrmənt] n. [C] 需要 <of> (usu. pl.)；要求，必要條件 <of>

▲ Taking minerals is important, but people rarely meet their daily requirement of what they need. 攝取礦物質很重要，但人們很少達到他們每日所需的量。

---

19. **spread** [sprɛd] v. 蔓延 <to>；散布 (spread | spread | spreading)

▲ The fire spread to the adjoining room in ten minutes.
大火在十分鐘內就蔓延到隔壁房間。

spread [sprɛd] n. [sing.] 擴散，蔓延 <of>

▲ The firefighters tried to prevent the spread of the fire.
消防隊員們試圖阻止火勢擴散。

---

20. **tone** [ton] n. [C] 語氣 <in>；[C][U] 音色，音質
   ▲ Annoyed with his son, the father replied in an angry tone. 被他兒子惹怒，這父親用生氣的語氣回答。

---

21. **trash** [træʃ] n. [U] 垃圾 [同] rubbish
   ▲ Daisy took out the trash before she left for work.
   Daisy 上班前先把垃圾拿出去丟。
   🔔 trash can 垃圾桶
   trash [træʃ] v. 搗毀，破壞
   ▲ Some protesters trashed shops and threw their goods onto the streets.
   一些抗議者搗毀商店並把商品丟到街上。

---

22. **trust** [trʌst] v. 信任 [反] distrust, mistrust；相信 [同] believe in, rely on
   ▲ The man is such a liar that no one trusts him.
   這男子是這樣一個騙子以致於沒人信任他。
   trust [trʌst] n. [U] 信任；信託，託管 <in>
   ▲ Peace is impossible without trust among nations.
   國家之間若無信任就不可能有和平。

---

23. **valuable** [ˋvæljəbl̩] adj. 值錢的，貴重的 [反] worthless；寶貴的
   ▲ The rich woman keeps her valuable jewelry in a safe in the bank. 這有錢的婦人將她貴重的珠寶存放在銀

行的保險箱裡。

24. **waist** [west] n. [C] 腰 (部)
▲ The supermodel has a tiny waist.
這超級模特兒的腰很細。

25. **within** [wɪðˋɪn] prep. 在 (時間) 之內；在 (範圍) 之內
▲ The client will be here within 10 minutes.
這客戶十分鐘之內會到。
within [wɪðˋɪn] adv. 在裡面，在內部 [反] outside
▲ Baron heard voices within, so he knocked on the door before entering the room.
Baron 聽到裡面有聲音，所以他在進房間之前先敲門。

Unit 19

1. **arrange** [əˋrendʒ] v. 安排，籌劃 <with>；排列
▲ Chad is arranging a monthly meeting with the manager. Chad 正與經理安排一個月一次的會議。
arrangement [əˋrendʒmənt] n. [C] 安排 (usu. pl.) <for>；[C][U] 約定 <with> [同] agreement
▲ Doris is making the arrangements for her birthday party. Doris 正在為自己的生日派對做安排。

2. **balance** [ˋbæləns] n. [U] (身體) 平衡；[sing.][U] (事物間) 平衡 <between> [反] imbalance
▲ The drunken man lost his balance and fell badly.

這酒醉男子失去平衡並重重跌倒。

balance [ˈbæləns] v. (使) 保持平衡 <on>；使⋯平衡

▲ The girl balanced a book on her head.
這女孩保持頭上書的平衡。

---

3. **bark** [bɑrk] n. [C] 吠叫聲

▲ The neighbors always complain that my dog has a loud bark. 鄰居們總抱怨我的狗的吠叫聲很大。

bark [bɑrk] v. 吠叫 <at>

▲ The dog barked furiously at the stranger.
這隻狗對陌生人狂吠。

---

4. **brain** [bren] n. [C] 腦；[C][U] 頭腦，智力 (usu. pl.)

▲ If a nerve cell of the brain is damaged, it will never recover its function.
如果腦神經細胞損傷，就無法恢復它的功能。

---

5. **company** [ˈkʌmpənɪ] n. [C] 公司 [同] firm, business；[U] 陪伴 (pl. companies)

▲ Darren works for a large computer company.
Darren 在一間大型電腦公司上班。

🔥 in sb's company/in the company of sb 與⋯一起

---

6. **contact** [ˈkɑntækt] n. [U] 聯絡，聯繫 <with>；接觸

▲ The control tower had lost contact with the pilot before the plane crashed.
塔臺在墜機前就和飛行員失去了聯絡。

🔥 make contact with sb 與⋯取得聯絡

contact [`kɑntækt] v. 聯絡，聯繫 <at>

▲ Customers may contact the bookstore by phone.
顧客們可以打電話聯絡這家書局。

7. **court** [kort] n. [C][U] 法院，法庭 <in>

▲ The man who was charged with murder appeared in court. 這名被控謀殺的男子出庭。

8. **edge** [ɛdʒ] n. [C] 邊緣 <of>；刀口，鋒利的邊緣

▲ Lisa sat on the edge of the bed, taking care of her sick son. Lisa 坐在床邊，照顧她生病的兒子。

🔅 on the edge of sth 瀕於⋯

edge [ɛdʒ] v. (使) 緩緩移動

▲ The old man edged his chair closer to the fire.
這老人把他的椅子緩緩移到火邊。

9. **flu** [flu] n. [U] 流行性感冒 [同] influenza

▲ The patient got the flu and felt very weak.
這病人得了流感而覺得很虛弱。

10. **formal** [`fɔrml] adj. 正式的，公開的 [反] informal

▲ The company sent the customer a formal written apology. 這公司對顧客發出正式書面的道歉。

11. **lower** [`loɚ] v. 降低

▲ Peter lowered his voice in order not to wake the sleeping baby.
Peter 降低他的音量以免吵醒正在睡覺的寶寶。

12. **mass** [mæs] n. [C] 大量，眾多 <of>；[sing.] (一) 大群 <of>

▲ A mass of dark clouds suddenly gathered in the sky.
大量的烏雲突然聚集在天空中。

13. **neither** [ˈniðɚ] adj. 兩者都不

▲ The student gave two answers, but neither one was right. 這學生給了兩個答案，但兩個都不對。

neither [ˈniðɚ] adv. 也不

▲ If Hannah won't go, then neither will her brother.
如果 Hannah 不去，那她弟弟也不去。

neither [ˈniðɚ] pron. 兩者都不 <of>

▲ Neither of Elton's parents knows where he is.
Elton 的父母兩人都不知道他的下落。

neither [ˈniðɚ] conj. 既不⋯(也不⋯)

▲ Darren is neither clever nor diligent.
Darren 既不聰明也不勤奮。

14. **offer** [ˈɔfɚ] v. 提供，給予；願意 (做)

▲ The company offered Lexi a good job, and she took it without a second thought.
這公司提供 Lexi 一份好工作，而她毫不猶豫接受了。

offer [ˈɔfɚ] n. [C] 提供，提議 <of>；出價，報價 <of>

▲ The girl refused the man's kind offer of help.
這女孩拒絕男子的好意幫忙。

15. **owner** [ˈonɚ] n. [C] 物主，所有人 <of>

▲ The pop singer is the owner of these sports cars.

這流行歌手是這些跑車的所有人。

16. **participate** [par`tɪsə‚pet] v. 參加 <in>
   ▲ Bill sprained his ankle, so he couldn't participate in the race. Bill 扭傷了腳踝，所以他不會參加賽跑。

17. **range** [rendʒ] n. [C] (一) 類、系列 <of> (usu. sing.)；[C] 範圍
   ▲ Jasper has a wide range of interests.
   Jasper 的興趣廣泛。
   range [rendʒ] v. (數量等) 範圍，幅度
   ▲ The prices of the potted plants range from $20 to $80. 這些盆栽的價格範圍介於二十到八十美元。

18. **rather** [`ræðɚ] adv. 相當
   ▲ This task was rather easy, and it was done without difficulty. 這工作相當簡單，輕易就完成了。
   🕯 rather than 而不是

19. **search** [sɝtʃ] n. [C] 搜索 <for> (usu. sing.)；(用電腦) 搜尋
   ▲ The storm hampered the search for the people trapped in the mountains.
   這暴風雨阻礙了搜索受困山區民眾的工作。
   🕯 in search of sth 尋找…
   search [sɝtʃ] v. 搜索，找尋 <for>；(用電腦) 搜尋 <for>
   ▲ The police officers are searching for the missing child. 警員們正在搜索失蹤的孩子。

20. **simply** [ˈsɪmplɪ] adv. 完全地，絕對地；只是 [同] just
   ▲ It is simply the best movie that I have ever seen.
      這絕對是我看過最棒的電影。

21. **stone** [ston] n. [U] 石材；[C] 石塊，石頭 [同] rock
   ▲ The old tower is made of stone, not wood.
      這座古老的塔是石造的，不是木製的。
   stone [ston] v. 向…投擲石塊
   ▲ The murderer was stoned to death.
      這殺人犯被人丟石塊擊斃。

22. **upper** [ˈʌpɚ] adj. 上面的，較高的 [反] lower
   ▲ The lower floors of the building were flooded while
      the upper floors remained intact.
      這棟建築的低樓層被水淹了，而較高的樓層完好無損。

23. **view** [vju] n. [C] 意見 <on> [同] opinion ；[C][U] 景色
      <of>
   ▲ The leaders exchanged views on the issue of
      terrorism. 領袖們就恐怖主義的議題交換意見。
   view [vju] v. 認為 <as> [同] see；觀看 <from>
   ▲ The country is viewed as a threat to international
      security. 這國家被認為是國際安全的一個威脅。

24. **whatever** [hwɑtˈɛvɚ] adj. 無論什麼樣的
   ▲ Liz would accept whatever help she could get.
      無論 Liz 可以受到什麼樣的幫助，她都會接受。
   whatever [hwɑtˈɛvɚ] pron. 任何…的事物；無論什麼

▲ Elsie may eat whatever she likes.
Elsie 可以吃任何她喜歡吃的東西。

25. wonder [`wʌndɚ] v. 想知道；驚訝 <at, about>
▲ Madge wonders who invented the television.
Madge 想知道誰發明了電視。

wonder [`wʌndɚ] n. [U] 驚訝 [同] awe；[C] 奇觀
▲ The tourists were filled with wonder when seeing the sight. 觀光客們看到那景象時非常驚訝。
💡 (it's) no/small/little wonder (that) 難怪

Unit 20

1. article [`ɑrtɪkl] n. [C] 文章，報導 <about, on>；物件 <of> [同] item
▲ There is an article about AIDS in today's paper.
今天報上有一篇關於愛滋病的報導。

2. available [ə`veləbl] adj. 可用的，可獲得的；有空的
▲ I'm sorry we don't have any single rooms available on June 1st. 抱歉我們六月一日沒有空的單人房。

3. basis [`besɪs] n. [U] 基礎，根據 <for>；[sing.] (行動) 方式 <on>
▲ The manager has no basis for his opposition.
這經理沒有反對的根據。

4. birth [bɝθ] n. [U] 分娩 <to>；[C][U] 出生

▲ Tina gave birth to twins this morning.

Tina 今天早上生了一對雙胞胎。

5. **cash** [kæʃ] n. [U] 現金

▲ Felix paid by credit card because he didn't have enough cash with him.

Felix 因為沒有足夠的現金在身上而用信用卡支付。

🕯 cash on delivery 貨到付款

cash [kæʃ] v. 兌現

▲ The businessman cashed a $100,000 check.

這商人兌現了一張十萬美元的支票。

6. **control** [kən`trol] n. [U] 控制 <of>；支配，掌控

▲ Drug abuse can make people lose control of their lives. 吸毒會讓人們對他們的生活失去控制。

control [kən`trol] v. 控制；掌控 (controlled | controlled | controlling)

▲ Further measures are taken to control the spread of the epidemic.

進一步的措施被採用來控制流行病的傳播。

7. **crisis** [`kraɪsɪs] n. [C][U] 危機 (pl. crises)

▲ During the financial crisis, many firms suffered great losses. 在金融危機期間，許多公司遭受重大的損失。

🕯 economic/financial/political crisis 經濟的 / 金融的 / 政治的危機 | in crisis 陷入危機

8. **damage** [`dæmɪdʒ] n. [U] 損害 <to>

▲ The earthquake caused a lot of damage to the village.
地震對這村莊造成了嚴重的損害。

damage [ˋdæmɪdʒ] **v.** 損害

▲ The crops were badly damaged by the storm.
暴風雨嚴重損害農作物。

9. **design** [dɪˋzaɪn] **n.** [C][U] 設計 <of>

▲ Nelly liked the design of the dress and bought it.
Nelly 喜歡這件洋裝的設計而買它。

design [dɪˋzaɪn] **v.** 設計

▲ The Louvre Pyramid is designed by a famous architect I. M. Pei.
羅浮宮金字塔是由知名建築設計師貝聿銘設計的。

10. **emotion** [ɪˋmoʃən] **n.** [C][U] 情緒，情感

▲ Gale couldn't hide his emotions anymore, so he began to cry.
Gale 無法再隱藏自己的情感，所以開始哭泣。

11. **football** [ˋfʊt͵bɔl] **n.** [U] 足球 [同] soccer ；橄欖球 [同] American football

▲ Tommy wants to become a football player in the future. Tommy 未來想成為一名足球員。

12. **goal** [gol] **n.** [C] 目標 [同] aim ；球門

▲ It takes hard work to achieve one's goal in life.
達成人生的目標需要努力。

13. **message** [ˋmɛsɪdʒ] **n.** [C] 訊息 <from, for, to>；[C] 要旨

(usu. sing.)

▲ The front desk clerk is taking a message from a caller. 這櫃檯職員正在幫一位來電者留訊息。

---

14. **model** [ˋmɑdḷ] n. [C] 模型 <of>；模特兒

▲ Terry is fond of making models of airplanes.
Terry 喜歡做飛機的模型。

model [ˋmɑdḷ] v. 當模特兒，穿戴…展示

▲ The young woman is modeling a dress by Chanel.
這位年輕女子正穿著香奈兒的洋裝展示。

---

15. **none** [nʌn] pron. 一點也沒有

▲ Nora expected to receive some cards from her friends, but none ever came.

Nora 期待她朋友送的卡片，但一封也沒收到。

none [nʌn] adv. 一點也不 <for>

▲ The rich man is none the happier for all his wealth.
這富人一點也不因為有錢而比較快樂。

---

16. **pattern** [ˋpætɚn] n. [C] 模式，形式；圖案，花樣

▲ The three murders followed the same pattern.
這三起謀殺案依循著相同的模式。

pattern [ˋpætɚn] v. 模仿 <after>

▲ The railway system is patterned after that used in Japan. 這鐵路系統是模仿日本使用的鐵路系統。

---

17. **personality** [͵pɝsṇˋælətɪ] n. [C][U] 個性，人格 (pl. personalities)

▲ Tracy is a woman with a strong personality; it's hard to talk her into doing this.

Tracy 是個性強勢的女性，要說服她做這件事很難。

---

18. **plain** [plen] adj. 明顯的 [同] obvious；樸素的 [同] simple

▲ The singer's devotion to music is plain to see.

這位歌手對音樂的投入顯而易見。

plain [plen] n. [C] 平原 (also plains)

▲ The plains of the Middle West provide most of America's grain. 中西部平原提供美國大部分的穀物。

19. **respect** [rɪ`spɛkt] n. [U] 敬重 <for>；尊敬 <with> [反] disrespect

▲ People admire the writer and have great respect for his works. 人們欽佩這位作家並敬重他的作品。

respect [rɪ`spɛkt] v. 敬重，尊敬 <for>

▲ People respect the scientist for her achievements.

人們敬重這位科學家的成就。

20. **result** [rɪ`zʌlt] n. [C][U] 結果，後果

▲ The players are waiting for the results to be announced. 選手們正在等待結果宣布。

♥ as a result of sth 因為…

result [rɪ`zʌlt] v. 發生，產生 <from>

▲ The accident resulted from the driver's carelessness.

這車禍起因於駕駛的疏忽。

21. **secret** [`sikrɪt] adj. 祕密的
   ▲ The castle has a secret passage to the graveyard.
   這城堡有一條通往墓地的祕密通道。
   secret [`sikrɪt] n. [C] 祕密
   ▲ Please don't reveal this secret to others.
   請勿向他人洩漏這個祕密。

22. **stage** [stedʒ] n. [C] (發展的) 階段，時期 <of>；舞臺
   ▲ The medicine is still in the early stages of development. 這藥物還在早期發展階段。
   stage [stedʒ] v. 舉辦，組織
   ▲ Some workers staged a hunger strike to protest against the unpaid leave.
   一些員工組織了一場絕食抗議，以抗議無薪假。

23. **supply** [sə`plaɪ] n. [C] 供應量 <of>；[pl.] 補給品 (pl. supplies)
   ▲ A plentiful supply of water was placed on board before the ship sailed for Oslo.
   在這艘船啟航去奧斯陸前，船上先裝了大量的水。
   supply [sə`plaɪ] v. 提供 <with>
   ▲ The military supplied the soldiers with sufficient food. 軍方提供士兵充足的食物。

24. **village** [`vɪlɪdʒ] n. [C] 村莊
   ▲ A village is usually smaller than a town.
   村莊通常比城鎮小。

25. **worse** [wɝs] adj. 更糟的；(病情) 更嚴重的

▲ The working conditions are getting worse and worse.
工作條件變得越來越糟了。

worse [wɝs] adv. 更壞，更糟

▲ The students did worse than they had expected in the
final exams. 學生們期末考試考得比他們預期的更糟。

worse [wɝs] n. [U] 更糟的事，更壞的情況

▲ These refugees had suffered some hardships, but they
didn't know that worse was to follow. 這些難民已經
遭遇了一些艱辛，但他們不知道更糟的還在後頭。

Unit 21

1. **absence** [ˈæbsn̩s] n. [C][U] 不在場 <in, during>；[sing.]
缺乏 [反] presence

▲ Don't speak ill of people in/during their absence.
不要在人們背後說他們的壞話。

2. **backward** [ˈbækwɚd] adj. 向後的 [反] forward

▲ Ben flew into a fury and walked away without a
backward glance. Ben 勃然大怒，頭也不回地走開。

backward [ˈbækwɚd] adv. 向後 (also backwards) [反]
forward, forwards

▲ The girl glanced backward over her shoulder to see
who was following her.
這女孩回頭掃了一眼，看誰在跟著她。

💡 backward and forward 來回地

3. **blackboard** [ˋblækˌbord] n. [C] 黑板
   ▲ Two students rubbed the blackboard clean for their teacher. 兩個學生幫老師把黑板擦乾淨。

4. **camel** [ˋkæml̩] n. [C] 駱駝
   ▲ A camel is a desert animal with either one or two humps. 駱駝是有一或兩個駝峰的沙漠動物。

5. **cockroach** [ˋkɑkˌrotʃ] n. [C] 蟑螂 (pl. cockroaches) (also roach)
   ▲ Many cockroaches live in the sewers.
   很多蟑螂住在下水道。

6. **corn** [kɔrn] n. [U] 玉米 [同] maize
   ▲ The farmers feed corn to their chickens.
   農夫們餵雞吃玉米。

7. **eastern** [ˋistən] adj. 東部的，東方的 (also Eastern) (abbr. E)
   ▲ Hualien City is a large city on the eastern shore of Taiwan. 花蓮市是臺灣東海岸的一大城市。

8. **edition** [ɪˋdɪʃən] n. [C] 版本
   ▲ A cheaper paperback edition of the novel will be published next month.
   這本小說下個月會出版較便宜的平裝版。

9. **electric** [ɪˋlɛktrɪk] adj. 用電的，電動的

▲ Since the room was cold, Bonnie turned on the electric heater. 因房間冷，Bonnie 打開了電暖器。

10. **freedom** [`fridəm] n. [C][U] 自由 <of>

▲ The dictator denied people's freedom of speech.
這獨裁者剝奪了人民的言論自由。

11. **guest** [gɛst] n. [C] 客人；(飯店的) 旅客

▲ The host invited 10 guests to the dinner party.
這主人邀請了十位客人參加晚宴。

12. **gun** [gʌn] n. [C] 槍

▲ The policeman pointed a gun at the armed robber.
這警員用槍指著武裝搶匪。

gun [gʌn] v. 用槍擊傷或擊斃 <down> (gunned | gunned | gunning)

▲ Two men were gunned down in the shooting incident. 兩名男子在這槍擊事件中被擊傷。

13. **listener** [`lɪsn̩ɚ] n. [C] (廣播) 聽眾；聽者

▲ The radio show is popular with young listeners.
這廣播節目受到年輕聽眾的歡迎。

14. **mix** [mɪks] n. [sing.] 組合；[C][U] 配料，混合料 [同] mixture

▲ Work stress and poor sleep are a deadly mix.
工作壓力和睡眠不足是一種致命的組合。

mix [mɪks] v. 混合；結合 <with>

▲ The cook mixed butter, eggs, and flour in the bowl.

這廚師在碗裡混合奶油、雞蛋和麵粉。

💡 mix sb/sth up 混淆⋯，把⋯弄錯

---

15. **narrow** [`næro] adj. 狹窄的 [反] wide

▲ The bridge is so narrow that only one person can cross it at a time.

這座橋如此地狹窄，以致於一次只能一個人通過。

narrow [`næro] v. (使) 變窄 [反] widen

▲ The road narrows and divides into two country lanes.
這條路變窄並分成兩條鄉間小路。

---

16. **papaya** [pə`paɪə] n. [C] 木瓜

▲ The papaya is a tropical fruit with orange flesh.
木瓜是一種有橘色果肉的熱帶水果。

---

17. **rent** [rɛnt] n. [C][U] 房租；租金 <for>

▲ The tenant pays the rent at the beginning of every month. 這房客每個月月初付房租。

rent [rɛnt] v. 租；出租 <to> [同] let

▲ Jason rented a car when traveling in the countryside.
Jason 在鄉間旅行時租了一輛車。

---

18. **reply** [rɪ`plaɪ] n. [C] 回答，回覆 [同] answer (pl. replies)

▲ Ken sent Mary three emails but received no reply.
Ken 寄了三封電郵給 Mary，但都沒收到回覆。

💡 in reply (to sth) 回覆 (⋯)

reply [rɪ`plaɪ] v. 回答 ，回覆 <to> (replied | replied | replying)

▲ Rose will find time to reply to her father's letter.
　Rose 會找時間回覆她父親的信。

---

19. **rocky** [ˋrɑkɪ] adj. 多岩石的 (rockier | rockiest)

　▲ The rocky trail is rough and difficult to hike.
　　這條石頭小徑崎嶇難行。

20. **satisfy** [ˋsætɪsˌfaɪ] v. 使滿意；滿足 (需要等) (satisfied | satisfied | satisfying)

　▲ It is impossible to satisfy everyone around you.
　　要使身邊每個人都滿意是不可能的。

21. **soap** [sop] n. [U] 肥皂

　▲ Sharon washed her hands with soap and water after using the bathroom.
　　上完廁所後，Sharon 用肥皂和水洗手。

　soap [sop] v. 在⋯上塗肥皂

　▲ The doctor soaped his hands and then rubbed his soapy hands.
　　這醫生在手上塗肥皂，然後搓了搓塗滿肥皂的手。

22. **subway** [ˋsʌbˌwe] n. [C] 地鐵 [同] underground

　▲ Let's take the subway; it's faster than a cab.
　　我們搭地鐵吧，比搭計程車快。

　underground [ˋʌndɚˌɡraʊnd] n. [sing.] 地鐵 (the ～) [同] subway

　▲ The London Underground is also called the tube due to the circular shape of its tunnels.

倫敦地鐵因為它圓形的隧道又稱為 tube。

metro [`mɛtro] n. [C] 地鐵，捷運 (pl. metros) [同] subway, underground

▲ Taipei Metro is regarded as a reliable subway system. 臺北捷運被認為是可信賴的地鐵系統。

23. **toothache** [`tuθ,ek] n. [C][U] 牙痛

▲ Stacey went to the dentist's because she had got toothache. Stacey 因為牙痛去看牙醫。

24. **truth** [truθ] n. [U] 實話 (the ~) [反] lie, falsehood, untruth；真實性 <in>

▲ The criminal was asked to stop lying and tell the truth. 這嫌犯被要求停止說謊並說實話。

25. **worth** [wɜθ] adj. 值…錢的；值得

▲ The bracelet is worth $50. 這手鐲值五十美元。

worth [wɜθ] n. [U] 價格，價值 <of>

▲ The flood destroyed $50,000 worth of medical equipment. 這水災毀了價值五萬美元的醫療設備。

Unit 22

1. **aid** [ed] n. [U] 幫助；[C] 輔助物

▲ The policeman came to Kyle's aid when he was lost in the town. 當 Kyle 在鎮上迷路時，警員前去幫助他。

💡 first aid 急救

aid [ed] v. 幫助，援助

▲ The volunteers worked hard to aid the flood victims.
這些義工們努力援助水患災民。

---

2. **badminton** [`bædmɪntən] n. [U] 羽毛球

▲ Playing badminton isn't difficult as long as people
watch the shuttlecock carefully.
只要人們仔細看球，打羽毛球並不難。

---

3. **blank** [blæŋk] adj. 空白的；茫然的

▲ The applicant signed his name in the blank space at
the bottom of the form.
這申請者在表格底部的空白處簽下他的名字。

blank [blæŋk] n. [C] 空白處，空格

▲ The guest filled in the blanks on the form and handed
it back to the clerk.
房客填好表格上的空白處並把它交還給職員。

---

4. **candle** [`kændl] n. [C] 蠟燭

▲ Teresa blew out the candle on the birthday cake.
Teresa 吹熄生日蛋糕上的蠟燭。

🕯 burn the candle at both ends 蠟燭兩頭燒；操勞過度

---

5. **combine** [kəm`baɪn] v. (使) 結合 <with>

▲ The painter combined red with blue to form the color
purple. 這畫家把紅色和藍色結合以形成紫色。

---

6. **cowboy** [`kaʊ͵bɔɪ] n. [C] 牛仔

▲ The cowboys rounded up the cattle in the field.

牛仔們將牧場上的牛趕在一起。

7. **elder** [ˈɛldɚ] n. [C] 較年長者，長輩
   ▲ Young children should be taught to respect the elders. 幼童應該被教導要尊敬長輩。
   elder [ˈɛldɚ] adj. 較年長的 [反] younger
   ▲ Who is the elder of the two brothers?
   這兩兄弟中誰較年長？

8. **electrical** [ɪˈlɛktrɪkl] adj. 與電有關的；用電的
   ▲ The electrical engineer's job is to design and make generators.
   這電氣工程師的工作是設計並製造發電機。

9. **employee** [ˌɪmplɔɪˈi] n. [C] 員工，受僱者 [同] worker
   ▲ Because of the economic crisis, more than half of the employees will be laid off.
   因為經濟危機，一半以上的員工會被解僱。

10. **friendship** [ˈfrɛndʃɪp] n. [C][U] 友誼
    ▲ The two men have formed a deep friendship since they were little. 這兩個男子從小就建立深厚友誼。

11. **gymnasium** [dʒɪmˈnezɪəm] n. [C] 體育館，健身房 (pl. gymnasiums, gymnasia) [同] gym
    ▲ The gymnasium has equipment for people to exercise their bodies and increase their strength.
    這健身房有讓人運動身體並增加體力的器材。

12. **haircut** [ˋhɛrˌkʌt] n. [C] 理髮

▲ Mr. Wang went to the barbershop to have a haircut.
王先生去理髮店理髮。

13. **manner** [ˋmænɚ] n. [sing.] 方法，方式 <of>；態度，舉止

▲ The girl did it after the manner of her father.
這女孩照她父親的方式做。

manners [ˋmænɚz] n. [pl.] 禮貌

▲ It's bad manners to point at people.
手指著別人是不禮貌的。

14. **motion** [ˋmoʃən] n. [U] 運行，移動 <of>；[C] 手勢，姿勢 <of> [同] gesture

▲ The rolling motion of the ship upset the sailor's stomach. 船搖搖晃晃讓這水手感到胃不舒服。

♥ in motion (車等) 在行進中

15. **ordinary** [ˋɔrdnˌɛrɪ] adj. 普通的，一般的

▲ It was just another ordinary day; nothing special happened.
那只是另一個普通的一天，沒特別的事發生。

16. **password** [ˋpæsˌwɝd] n. [C] 密碼

▲ Users need to enter their passwords to get access to the computer system.
使用者需要輸入密碼才能進入這個電腦系統。

17. **respond** [rɪ`spɑnd] v. 回應 <with> [同] react；回答，回覆 <to>

▲ The mother kissed the boy, and he responded with a smile. 這媽媽親了男孩，他回以一個微笑。

18. **restroom** [`rɛstrum] n. [C] 洗手間 [同] toilet

▲ During the long drive, Manton stopped at a fast food restaurant to use the restroom. 在開長途車期間，Manton 停在一家速食餐廳用洗手間。

19. **roof** [ruf] n. [C] 屋頂，頂部

▲ The pitched roof was built to withstand ice and snow. 這斜的屋頂是蓋來承受住冰雪的。

roof [ruf] v. 給 (建築物) 蓋屋頂 <with>

▲ The old cottage was roofed with thatch. 這古老的小屋以茅草蓋屋頂。

20. **scene** [sin] n. [C] (戲劇的) 一場；[sing.] 現場，地點

▲ In the opening scene, the princess was poisoned by a witch. 在戲劇的第一場，公主被巫婆所毒害。

21. **sock** [sɑk] n. [C] 短襪 (pl. socks)

▲ Ada put on a pair of socks and then her sneakers. Ada 穿上了一雙短襪和她的運動鞋。

22. **suppose** [sə`poz] v. 猜想 [同] presume；假定，假設

▲ Nash didn't answer the door, so his friend supposed that he was out.

Nash 沒有應門，所以他朋友猜想他出門了。

23. **trap** [træp] n. [C] 陷阱；圈套，詭計
   ▲ The hunter set a trap for foxes. 這獵人設陷阱抓狐狸。
   trap [træp] v. 困住 (trapped | trapped | trapping)
   ▲ The factory collapsed, and several workers were trapped in the rubble.
   這工廠倒塌，幾名工人被困在瓦礫堆下。

24. **umbrella** [ʌm`brɛlə] n. [C] (雨) 傘
   ▲ When it rained, Pierce put up his umbrella.
   下雨時 Pierce 撐起了他的傘。

25. **zebra** [`zibrə] n. [C] 斑馬
   ▲ The zebra looks like a horse but has black and white lines on its body.
   斑馬看起來像馬但有黑白條紋在身上。

Unit 23

1. **actual** [`æktʃʊəl] adj. 實際的
   ▲ The actual cost of building this stadium was much higher than the government had estimated.
   建造這運動場的實際費用比政府估計的高許多。

2. **aim** [em] n. [C] 目標；[U] 瞄準 <at>
   ▲ The young girl's aim is to become a lawyer.
   這年輕女孩的目標是成為一位律師。

aim [em] **v.** 打算，意圖 <at>；使…針對 (某人)，將 (某人) 定為…的對象 <at>

▲ The Olympic athlete aims at breaking the record.
這位奧林匹克運動員意圖要破紀錄。

3. **bake** [bek] **v.** 烘，烤

▲ Andy baked the cake at 160°C for 15 minutes.
Andy 以攝氏一百六十度烤蛋糕十五分鐘。

4. **branch** [bræntʃ] **n.** [C] 樹枝；分店，分支機構

▲ A bird perched on the tree branch with green leaves.
一隻鳥棲息在長綠葉的樹枝上。

branch [bræntʃ] **v.** 分岔

▲ The river branches three kilometers below the town.
這河流在城鎮下游三公里處分流。

5. **cartoon** [kɑr`tun] **n.** [C] 漫畫；卡通片，動畫片

▲ Henry enjoys reading the cartoons in newspapers.
Henry 喜歡看報紙上的漫畫。

cartoon [kɑr`tun] **v.** 畫漫畫

6. **compare** [kəm`pɛr] **v.** 比較，對比 <with>；將…比作 <to>

▲ Though this car is old, it is new compared with that one. 這輛車雖然舊，但和那輛車比較算是新。

7. **crayon** [`kreən] **n.** [C] 蠟筆，彩色粉筆

▲ The boy colored the picture with crayons.

這男孩用蠟筆給這幅圖上色。

---

8. **employ** [ɪmˋplɔɪ] **v.** 僱用 <as>；使用

▲ Robert was employed as a full-time clerk, which was his first job.

Robert 被僱用為全職店員，這是他的第一份工作。

employment [ɪmˋplɔɪmənt] **n.** [U] 受僱；僱用 <of>

▲ The two college graduates were offered employment in the sales department.

這兩個大學畢業生受僱於銷售部。

---

9. **engine** [ˋɛndʒən] **n.** [C] 引擎

▲ The car couldn't start because of the engine trouble.

這輛車發不動，因為引擎故障。

---

10. **equal** [ˋikwəl] **adj.** 相同的，相等的 <of>；平等的

▲ The two boxes are of equal size.

這兩個箱子大小相同。

💡 equal in 相同

equal [ˋikwəl] **v.** 等於；達到 (與過去) 相同的水準 (equaled, equalled | equaled, equalled | equaling, equalling)

▲ Two plus three equals five. 二加三等於五。

equal [ˋikwəl] **n.** [C] 相同 (重要等) 的人或事物

▲ The father treated all his children as equals.

這父親對他的孩子們一視同仁。

---

11. **fries** [fraɪz] **n.** [pl.] 炸薯條 [同] chips

▲ Rick ordered a hamburger and French fries.
Rick 點了一個漢堡和炸薯條。

---

12. **hall** [hɔl] n. [C] 大廳 [同] hallway ; 走廊 [同] corridor, hallway

▲ The guests left their coats in the entrance hall.
賓客們把他們的外套留在門廳。

---

13. **hamburger** [ˋhæmbɝɡɚ] n. [C] 漢堡 [同] burger

▲ Dora ordered a Coke to go with her hamburger.
Dora 點了一杯可口可樂配她的漢堡。

---

14. **mask** [mæsk] n. [C] 口罩，面罩；面具

▲ During the pandemic, people were required to wear face masks in public places.
在疫情期間，人們被要求在公共場合戴口罩。

mask [mæsk] v. 掩飾，掩蓋

▲ The widow's smile was meant to mask her deep sadness. 這寡婦的微笑是為了掩飾她深深的哀傷。

---

15. **motorcycle** [ˋmotɚˏsaɪkl] n. [C] 摩托車 [同] motorbike

▲ Some young people ride motorcycles without having driver's licenses. 有些年輕人無照騎摩托車。

---

16. **panda** [ˋpændə] n. [C] 熊貓

▲ Giant pandas are native to China, and they like to eat bamboo leaves. 大熊貓原產於中國，牠們喜歡吃竹葉。

---

17. **peaceful** [ˋpisfəl] adj. 安靜的，寧靜的；和平的

▲ Without her kids around, the mother enjoyed a peaceful afternoon.

小孩不在旁邊，這媽媽享受了一個安靜的下午。

18. **riches** [`rɪtʃɪz] **n.** [pl.] 財富，財產 [同] wealth

▲ Riches have wings. 【諺】錢財易散。

19. **runner** [`rʌnɚ] **n.** [C] 跑步者

▲ Bruno is a long-distance runner, and he will run the marathon.

Bruno 是個長距離跑者，他將參加這場馬拉松比賽。

20. **sample** [`sæmpl̩] **n.** [C] 樣本；樣品，試用品 <of>

▲ The scientist is analyzing the water samples collected from the river.

這科學家正在分析從河裡採集來的水樣本。

sample [`sæmpl̩] **v.** 品嘗

▲ Calvin sampled the cake and said it was delicious.

Calvin 品嘗了這蛋糕並說它好吃。

21. **selfish** [`sɛlfɪʃ] **adj.** 自私的

▲ Emma has no friends because she is selfish and mean. Emma 沒有朋友是因為她自私又刻薄。

22. **soda** [`sodə] **n.** [C][U] 汽水 (also soda pop) [同] pop

▲ Daniel likes ice cream soda most.

Daniel 最喜歡冰淇淋汽水。

23. **sweep** [swip] **v.** 清掃 [同] brush；(迅猛地) 帶走，捲走 (swept | swept | sweeping)

▲ The maid is sweeping the floor with a broom.
這女僕正在用掃帚清掃地板。

24. **tube** [tjub] n. [C] 管，管子

▲ Water passes through the plastic tube and flows to the lower tank. 水通過這塑膠管，流到下面的水箱。

25. **valley** [ˋvælɪ] n. [C] 山谷

▲ The climbers crossed a deep valley and then climbed a steep mountain.
登山者們穿過深谷，接著登上陡峭的山峰。

Unit 24

1. **adult** [əˋdʌlt] n. [C] 成年人

▲ Adults should be responsible for their own behavior.
成年人應為自己的行為負責。

adult [əˋdʌlt] adj. 成年的

▲ Frances spent most of her adult life in Paris.
Frances 成年後大多待在巴黎。

2. **appetite** [ˋæpə‚taɪt] n. [C][U] 胃口 (usu. sing.)

▲ The patient has lost some weight due to loss of appetite. 這病人因為失去胃口而瘦了一些。

3. **balcony** [ˋbælkənɪ] n. [C] 陽臺 (pl. balconies)

▲ The balcony has a view of the lake.

這陽臺可以看到湖景。

---

4. **brief** [brif] adj. 短暫的；簡短的

▲ Daisy made a brief visit to her aunt's house this morning. Daisy 今天早上短暫探望了她阿姨。

brief [brif] n. [C] 職責，任務簡介 (usu. sing.)

▲ The manager's brief is to come up with good ideas for the launch of new models.
這經理的職責是為新型號的上市想出好點子。

🌶 in brief 簡言之

brief [brif] v. 簡報 <on>

▲ The boss has been briefed on what to invest next.
這老闆已聽取了下一步該投資什麼的簡報。

---

5. **castle** [ˋkæsl̩] n. [C] 城堡

▲ The king and queen lived in that castle.
國王和王后住在那座城堡裡。

---

6. **conclude** [kənˋklud] v. 做出結論 <from>；(以…) 結束 <with>

▲ The scientist concluded from her research that plastic is a threat to humans. 這位科學家從她的研究做出塑膠對人類是威脅的結論。

---

7. **crow** [kro] n. [C] 烏鴉

▲ Some people believe that seeing a crow is a bad omen. 一些人認為看到烏鴉是不好的預兆。

---

8. **employer** [ɪmˋplɔɪɚ] n. [C] 僱主

▲ The manager needs to talk to Lily's last employer before deciding whether she can get the job.

在決定 Lily 是否能得到這份工作前，經理必須和她的上一位僱主談談。

---

9. **essay** [ˋɛse] n. [C] 短文，論文 <on>

▲ One requirement of the course is an essay on the history of the country.

這門課的要求之一是寫一篇關於國家歷史的論文。

---

10. **fee** [fi] n. [C] 費用

▲ The dentist demanded a high fee for Allen's treatment. 這牙醫要求 Allen 付高額的治療費。

---

11. **fry** [fraɪ] v. 油炒，油炸 (fried | fried | frying)

▲ Miranda used to fry chicken in hot oil, but now she likes to roast it in an oven. Miranda 過去習慣用熱油炸雞，但現在她喜歡用烤箱烤雞。

fry [fraɪ] n. [pl.] 魚苗

▲ The fishing nets can be dangerous to the fry, too.

這些魚網也可能對魚苗造成危險。

---

12. **handsome** [ˋhænsəm] adj. 英俊的 [同] good-looking；(數量) 可觀的 (handsomer | handsomest)

▲ Many girls were attracted by the handsome man.

許多女孩被這英俊的男子所吸引。

---

13. **heaven** [ˋhɛvən] n. [sing.] 天堂 (also Heaven) [同] paradise；[U] 開心極了

▲ It is said that the Devil was an angel, who was cast out from Heaven.

據說撒旦曾是天使，後來被逐出天堂。

💡 for heaven's sake 看在老天的分上

---

14. **mat** [mæt] n. [C] 墊子

▲ Before Eden entered the room, he wiped his shoes on the mat. Eden 進房間前先在墊子上擦鞋。

15. **notebook** [`not͵bʊk] n. [C] 筆記本；筆記型電腦 (also notebook computer)

▲ The student carried a notebook so that she could take notes in class.

這學生帶了一本筆記本好在課堂上做筆記。

16. **partner** [`pɑrtnɚ] n. [C] 配偶；合夥人

▲ Barbara often discusses her worries with her partner.

Barbara 通常會和她的配偶討論煩心事。

17. **peach** [pitʃ] n. [C] 桃子 (pl. peaches)

▲ Hedy likes all types of juicy fruit such as peaches.

Hedy 喜歡各種多汁的水果，例如桃子。

18. **rooster** [`rustɚ] n. [C] 公雞 [同] cock

▲ The rooster crowed loudly at sunrise.

這隻公雞在日出時大聲啼叫。

19. **sandwich** [`sændwɪtʃ] n. [C] 三明治 (pl. sandwiches)

▲ Alex made some ham sandwiches for breakfast.

Alex 做了一些火腿三明治當早餐。

sandwich [ˈsændwɪtʃ] v. 將⋯插在中間

▲ The notebook is sandwiched in between two novels.
這筆記本被插在兩本小說中間。

---

20. **score** [skor] n. [C] 得分，比數；分數，成績

▲ The latest baseball score is three to zero.
棒球賽最新的比數是三比零。

score [skor] v. 得 (分)；給⋯打分數 [同] mark

▲ The home team scored a goal at the start of the game.
地主隊在比賽一開始就得了一分。

---

21. **sheet** [ʃit] n. [C] 床單；一張 (紙) <of>

▲ The hotel changes the sheets in its rooms every day.
這家旅館每天都更換房間的床單。

---

22. **stamp** [stæmp] n. [C] 郵票 (also postage stamp)；戳記

▲ Hale stuck a 25-cent stamp on the envelope.
Hale 在信封上貼了一張二十五分的郵票。

stamp [stæmp] v. 跺 (腳)，重踩

▲ Finding his toy car broken, Tom stamped his foot angrily. Tom 發現他的玩具車壞掉時憤怒地跺腳。

---

23. **swim** [swɪm] v. 游泳 (swam | swum | swimming)

▲ It takes great strength to swim across the lake.
游過這座湖需要很大的體力。

swim [swɪm] n. [C] 游泳

▲ It is great to go for a swim on a hot day.

天熱時游泳很棒。

24. **turtle** [`tɝtl] n. [C] 龜，海龜
   ▲ Turtles symbolize longevity in Chinese culture.
   龜在中國文化中象徵長壽。

25. **victory** [`vɪktərɪ] n. [C][U] 勝利，獲勝 <over> (pl.
   victories) [反] defeat
   ▲ The army gained a glorious victory over its enemy.
   這軍隊輝煌戰勝敵人。

Unit 25

1. **ahead** [ə`hɛd] adv. 在前面 <of> [反] behind；未來，今
   後 <of>
   ▲ Ann sat two rows ahead of her friend.
   Ann 坐在她朋友前面兩排的位置。

2. **apply** [ə`plaɪ] v. 申請 <to, for>；適用 <to> (applied |
   applied | applying)
   ▲ The organization applied to the bank for financial
   aid. 這組織向銀行申請財務援助。

3. **balloon** [bə`lun] n. [C] 氣球
   ▲ Johnny let go of the balloon, and it floated up into
   the sky. Johnny 把氣球放掉，它飄上了天空。

4. **burn** [bɝn] v. 燃燒；燒毀 (burned, burnt | burned, burnt | burning)

▲ A fire is burning in the small fireplace.
火在小小的壁爐裡燃燒著。

♥ burn up 燒盡 | burn the candle at both ends 勞累過度

burn [bɝn] n. [C] 燒傷，燙傷

▲ The girl survived the fire but suffered serious burns.
這女孩在大火中存活下來，但嚴重燒傷。

5. **ceiling** [ˋsilɪŋ] n. [C] 天花板

▲ The lobby of the hotel has a high ceiling.
這飯店大廳的天花板很高。

♥ hit the ceiling 暴跳如雷

6. **courage** [ˋkɝɪdʒ] n. [U] 勇氣 [反] cowardice

▲ Jacob plucked up the courage to ask the girl out on a date. Jacob 鼓起勇氣約這女孩出去約會。

7. **deaf** [dɛf] adj. 耳聾的，失聰的 <in>

▲ The woman is deaf in her right ear, so she is unable to hear well. 這女子右耳聾，所以她聽得不清楚。

♥ turn a deaf ear (to sth) 不願聽 (…)

8. **empty** [ˋɛmptɪ] adj. 空的，無人的 (emptier | emptiest)

▲ The school was empty because everyone was on vacation. 學校空無一人，因為大家都放假了。

♥ do sth on an empty stomach 空腹做…

empty [ˋɛmptɪ] v. 清空，倒空 (also empty out)

(emptied | emptied | emptying)

▲ The cleaner emptied the garbage can, for it was too full. 因為垃圾桶太滿，所以清潔工把它清空。

---

9. **eve** [iv] n. [C] 前夕 (usu. sing.)

▲ We'll go to watch the firework display on New Year's Eve. 我們除夕會去看煙火秀。

---

10. **gardener** [ˋɡɑrdnɚ] n. [C] 園丁，花匠

▲ The gardener is pruning the trees in the yard.
這園丁正在庭院裡修剪樹木。

---

11. **highway** [ˋhaɪ͵we] n. [C] 主要幹道，公路

▲ The driver went on the highway to get to the city.
這駕駛走主要幹道進城。

---

12. **hike** [haɪk] n. [C] 長途健行

▲ The two friends set off on a 20-mile hike in the mountains.
這兩個朋友踏上了二十英里的山區長途健行。

hike [haɪk] v. 長途健行

▲ Dora and her family spent their night hiking around the lake. Dora 和家人晚上在湖邊健行。

---

13. **hunt** [hʌnt] v. 打獵，狩獵；搜尋 <for> [同] search

▲ The lion hunts at night and sleeps in the day.
這頭獅子晚上狩獵，白天睡覺。

hunt [hʌnt] n. [C] 打獵，狩獵；[C] 搜尋 <for> (usu. sing.)

▲ The man went on a fox hunt with his hounds.
這男子和他的獵狗去獵狐狸。

14. **midnight** [`mɪd,naɪt] n. [U] 午夜，子夜

    ▲ Mason stayed up studying until midnight.
    Mason 熬夜讀書直到午夜。

    💡 burn the midnight oil 熬夜工作

15. **obey** [o`be] v. 聽從，遵守 [反] disobey

    ▲ The students are asked to obey the school rules.
    學生們被要求要遵守校規。

16. **paste** [pest] n. [U] 醬，糊；[C][U] 麵團

    ▲ Since the cook didn't have any fresh tomatoes, he added some tomato paste into the sauce. 因為沒有任何新鮮番茄，廚師在醬汁裡加了一些番茄糊。

    paste [pest] v. (用漿糊) 黏，貼

    ▲ The notice was pasted to the front door.
    這告示被貼在大門上。

17. **pear** [pɛr] n. [C] 梨

    ▲ There is a pear tree in front of the house.
    這房子前面有一棵梨樹。

18. **rude** [rud] adj. 粗魯的，不禮貌的 [同] impolite [反] polite (ruder | rudest)

    ▲ It was rude of Jeff to ask the lady about her age.
    Jeff 問那女士的年齡是不禮貌的。

19. **scared** [skɛrd] **adj.** 害怕的，驚恐的 <of> [同] afraid
   ▲ Cindy has always been scared of cockroaches.
   Cindy 一直都害怕蟑螂。

20. **section** [ˋsɛkʃən] **n.** [C] 部分 <of>
   ▲ The tail section of the airplane was found in the sea.
   這飛機的尾翼部分在海裡被發現。

21. **shine** [ʃaɪn] **v.** 照耀，發光 (shone | shone | shining)；
   把⋯擦亮 [同] polish (shined | shined | shining)
   ▲ The sun is shining brightly in the cloudless sky.
   太陽在晴朗的天空明亮地照耀著。
   💡 shine through (品質等) 顯而易見
   shine [ʃaɪn] **n.** [sing.][U] 光彩，光澤
   ▲ The old wooden desk has a beautiful shine.
   那舊木桌有美麗的光澤。

22. **stranger** [ˋstrendʒɚ] **n.** [C] 陌生人
   ▲ Teresa tends to feel nervous in front of strangers.
   Teresa 在陌生人面前會顯得焦慮。

23. **swing** [swɪŋ] **n.** [C] 鞦韆；揮動 <at>
   ▲ The children are playing on the swings in the park.
   孩童們正在公園裡盪鞦韆。
   swing [swɪŋ] **v.** 晃動；轉動 (swung | swung | swinging)
   ▲ The hanging rope was swinging to and fro in the wind. 這垂掛的繩子在風中前後晃動。

24. **ugly** [ˈʌglɪ] adj. 醜陋的 [同] hideous [反] beautiful
(uglier | ugliest)

▲ The witch cast a spell on the prince, turning him into
an ugly toad.
女巫對王子施魔法，將他變成一隻醜陋的癩蛤蟆。

25. **wash** [wɑʃ] v. 清洗；洗 (身體的某部位)

▲ The dirty pants need washing. 這髒褲子需要清洗。

💡 wash sth away 沖走⋯

wash [wɑʃ] n. [C] 洗滌，洗澡 (usu. sing.)

▲ Lester gives his dog a wash every Saturday.
Lester 每週六都幫他的狗洗澡。

Unit 26

1. **altogether** [ˌɔltəˈgɛðɚ] adv. 完全；總共

▲ The picnic was altogether ruined by the rain.
這野餐完全被雨破壞了。

2. **appreciate** [əˈpriʃɪˌet] v. 理解，領會 [同] realize；感謝

▲ People don't appreciate the value of health until they
lose it. 人們直到失去健康才領會健康的重要。

3. **barbecue** [ˈbɑrbɪˌkju] n. [C] 烤肉 (會) (also barbeque)
(abbr. BBQ)

▲ The family had a barbecue in their yard.
這家人在院子裡辦烤肉會。

barbecue [ˋbɑrbɪˌkju] v. 用烤肉架燒烤 (also barbeque)

▲ Julie had some barbecued chicken for dinner.
  Julie 晚餐吃了些烤雞。

---

4. **cage** [kedʒ] n. [C] 籠子

▲ The zoo-keeper found the bear was still in the cage.
  動物園管理員發現這隻熊還在籠子裡。

cage [kedʒ] v. 關進籠子

▲ It is cruel to cage the elephant.
  把大象關進籠子很殘忍。

---

5. **centimeter** [ˋsɛntəˌmitɚ] n. [C] 公分 (abbr. cm)

▲ The pencil is fifteen centimeters long.
  這枝鉛筆十五公分長。

---

6. **cream** [krim] n. [U] 奶油；乳液，護膚霜

▲ Nelson would like some cream in his coffee.
  Nelson 想要在他的咖啡裡加一些奶油。

cream [krim] adj. 米黃色的

▲ The boy wore a cream-colored sweater.
  這男孩穿著一件米黃色的毛衣。

---

7. **debt** [dɛt] n. [C] 借款，欠款 <of>；[U] 負債 [反] credit

▲ Lisa has debts of 5,000 dollars, but she has no money
  to pay it off. Lisa 欠款五千美元，但她沒錢償還。

---

8. **entrance** [ˋɛntrəns] n. [C] 入口 <to> [反] exit；[U] 進入
  許可 <to>

▲ The main entrance to the supermarket is near the parking lot. 這超市的主要入口靠近停車場。

9. **exact** [ɪgˋzækt] adj. 確切的，精確的
   ▲ Bruce knows the meeting is in May, but he forgets the exact date.
   Bruce 知道會議是在五月，但他忘記確切的日期。

10. **goose** [gus] n. [C] 鵝 (pl. geese)
    ▲ All his geese are swans. 【諺】敝帚自珍。

11. **hip** [hɪp] n. [C] 臀部
    ▲ The jeans are a little tight across the hips.
    這牛仔褲臀部有點緊。

12. **hippopotamus** [͵hɪpəˋpɑtəməs] n. [C] 河馬 (pl. hippopotamuses, hippopotami) [同] hippo
    ▲ A hippopotamus is a large gray animal that lives near water. 河馬是一種住在水邊的大型灰色動物。

13. **ill** [ɪl] adj. 生病的，不舒服的 [同] sick (worse | worst)
    ▲ Maggie had flu, so she was ill in bed.
    Maggie 得了流感，所以她臥病在床。
    ill [ɪl] adv. 壞地，惡劣地
    ▲ Owen is negative about everything; he always takes things ill.
    Owen 對任何事都很消極，他總是往壞處想。
    💡 speak/think ill of sb 說…壞話 / 認為…不好
    ill [ɪl] n. [C] 問題，苦惱 (usu. pl.)

▲ The girl is too young to know the ills of life.
這女孩太年輕而不知人生的苦惱。

14. **mop** [mɑp] n. [C] 拖把
   ▲ Cindy is cleaning the kitchen floor with a mop.
   Cindy 正在用拖把拖廚房的地板。
   mop [mɑp] v. 用拖把拖 (mopped | mopped | mopping)
   ▲ Fiona asked her son to mop the bedroom floor.
   Fiona 要她兒子用拖把拖臥室地板。

15. **organ** [ˋɔrgən] n. [C] 器官
   ▲ The stomach is a digestive organ. 胃是消化器官。

16. **path** [pæθ] n. [C] 小路 , 小徑 <to> ; (達到…的) 途徑
   <to>
   ▲ People can follow this small path to the main road.
   人們可以順著這條小徑去到主要道路。

17. **pillow** [ˋpɪlo] n. [C] 枕頭
   ▲ The little boy laid his head on the pillow and listened
   to the bedtime story.
   小男孩的頭枕著枕頭並聽著床邊故事。

18. **sailor** [ˋselɚ] n. [C] 水手，船員
   ▲ The sailor navigated the boat toward the harbor.
   這水手駕船航向港口。

19. **screen** [skrin] n. [C] 螢幕
   ▲ The TV set has a 50-inch color screen.

這電視機有五十吋的彩色螢幕。

---

20. **selection** [sə`lɛkʃən] n. [sing.][U] 選擇，挑選 <of> ；
    [C] 可供挑選的東西 <of> (usu. sing.) [同] range
    ▲ The child wants to make his selection of toys.
    這孩子想自己挑選玩具。

21. **sleepy** [`slipɪ] adj. 睏倦的，打瞌睡的 (sleepier |
    sleepiest)
    ▲ Since Mandy didn't sleep well last night, she feels
    sleepy now. 由於 Mandy 昨晚沒睡好，她現在很睏。

22. **strawberry** [`strɔ͵bɛrɪ] n. [C] 草莓 (pl. strawberries)
    ▲ Tina made a cake with many fresh strawberries on
    top. Tina 做了一個上面有很多新鮮草莓的蛋糕。

23. **terrorist** [`tɛrərɪst] n. [C] 恐怖分子
    ▲ The U.S. president condemned the terrorist attacks in
    New York as "acts of war."
    美國總統譴責紐約的恐怖攻擊事件是「戰爭行為」。

24. **upstairs** [ʌp`stɛrz] adv. 在樓上，往樓上 [反] downstairs
    ▲ The company has another office upstairs.
    這公司在樓上有另一間辦公室。
    upstairs [ʌp`stɛrz] adj. 樓上的 [反] downstairs
    ▲ The bird flew in through the upstairs window.
    這隻鳥從樓上的窗戶飛了進來。
    upstairs [ʌp`stɛrz] n. [sing.] 樓上 (the ～)

▲ The family used the downstairs and rented out the upstairs. 這家人使用樓下並把樓上租出去。

25. **wealth** [wɛlθ] **n.** [U] 財富
   ▲ Wealth doesn't necessarily bring happiness.
   財富未必會帶來快樂。

Unit 27

1. **artist** [ˋɑrtɪst] **n.** [C] 藝術家
   ▲ Monet is one of the greatest artists of all time.
   莫內是有史以來最偉大的藝術家之一。

2. **bakery** [ˋbekərɪ] **n.** [C] 麵包店 (pl. bakeries)
   ▲ The bakery is well-known for its yummy bread and cakes. 這間麵包店以其美味的麵包和蛋糕聞名。

3. **barber** [ˋbɑrbɚ] **n.** [C] 理髮師
   ▲ A barber's job is to cut men's hair or shave them.
   理髮師的工作是幫男性剪髮或剃鬍。

4. **cancel** [ˋkænsl] **v.** 取消 (canceled, cancelled | canceled, cancelled | canceling, cancelling)
   ▲ Nydia canceled the appointment because of urgent business. Nydia 因急事取消了約會。

5. **chalk** [tʃɔk] **n.** [C][U] 粉筆
   ▲ The teacher wrote a sentence on the blackboard with a piece of chalk.

這老師用一枝粉筆在黑板上寫了一個句子。

chalk [tʃɔk] v. 用粉筆寫

▲ The students were chalking things on the walls.
學生們正用粉筆在牆壁上寫東西。

---

6. **cure** [kjʊr] n. [C] 治療方法 <for>；解決方法 <for>
▲ Doctors have not discovered a cure for the disease.
醫生們尚未發現該疾病的治療方法。

cure [kjʊr] v. 治癒 <of>
▲ The doctor cured the patient of his disease.
這醫生治好了病人的疾病。

---

7. **deny** [dɪˋnaɪ] v. 否認；剝奪 <to> (denied | denied | denying)
▲ The man denied the charge of murder and pleaded his innocence.
這男子否認謀殺的控告並辯白自己是無辜的。

---

8. **excite** [ɪkˋsaɪt] v. 使興奮，使激動
▲ The prospect of going abroad for further study excited the student. 出國深造的機會使這學生很興奮。

excitement [ɪkˋsaɪtmənt] n. [U] 興奮，激動
▲ There was growing excitement among the fans as they waited for the superstar to arrive.
當粉絲們等著超級巨星到來時，他們變得越來越興奮。

---

9. **eyebrow** [ˋaɪ͵braʊ] n. [C] 眉毛 [同] brow
▲ Michael has got very bushy eyebrows.

Michael 的眉毛很濃密。

💡 raise sb's eyebrows 揚起眉毛 (表示驚訝)

---

10. **grand** [grænd] adj. 壯麗的 [反] humble；偉大的，崇高的

   ▲ The couple looked at the grand view of the ocean.
   這對情侶看著大海的壯麗景色。

---

11. **hole** [hol] n. [C] 洞，坑

   ▲ The stranger peeped through a hole in the wall.
   這名陌生人從牆上的洞窺視。

---

12. **hurry** [ˋhɝɪ] v. 加快 [同] rush (hurried | hurried | hurrying)

   ▲ You will have to hurry or you will be late for school.
   你得快點，不然上學會遲到。

   hurry [ˋhɝɪ] n. [sing.] 匆忙，倉促 [同] rush

   ▲ Rory left in such a hurry that he forgot his keys.
   Rory 離開得太倉促，連他的鑰匙都忘了。

---

13. **independence** [ˌɪndɪˋpɛndəns] n. [U] 獨立 <from>；自主，自立

   ▲ India achieved independence from England without war. 印度未經戰爭便脫離英國獨立。

---

14. **mug** [mʌg] n. [C] 馬克杯；一大杯 <of>

   ▲ The mug is used for drinking coffee.
   這個馬克杯是用來喝咖啡的。

15. **pale** [pel] adj. 蒼白的；淺的，淡的 [反] deep [同] light
    (paler | palest)
    ▲ The mother turned pale after hearing the bad news.
    這母親聽了壞消息後臉色變蒼白。

16. **pizza** [`pitsə] n. [C][U] 披薩
    ▲ The Italian restaurant offers pasta and pizza.
    這家義大利餐廳供應義大利麵和披薩。

17. **plus** [plʌs] prep. 加 [反] minus
    ▲ Two plus three equals five. 二加三等於五。
    plus [plʌs] n. [C] 優勢，好處
    ▲ Some knowledge of English is a plus in today's
    world. 懂些英文在現今世界是一個優勢。
    plus [plʌs] adj. 有利的 [反] minus
    ▲ One plus point of the apartment is that it's near the
    MRT station. 這公寓的好處之一是靠近捷運站。

18. **salesperson** [`selz͵pɚsn̩] n. [C] 售貨員 (pl. salespeople)
    ▲ The salesperson always wears a smile on her face.
    這售貨員總是面帶微笑。
    salesman [`selzmən] n. [C] 男售貨員 (pl. salesmen)
    ▲ The car salesman showed the new car to the
    customer. 這男汽車售貨員向顧客展示新車。
    saleswoman [`selz͵wumən] n. [C] 女售貨員 (pl.
    saleswomen)
    ▲ The saleswoman is persuading Lily to buy the dress.

這女售貨員正在說服 Lily 買這件洋裝。

19. **secondary** [ˈsɛkənˌdɛrɪ] adj. 中等的，中學的；次要的 <to>

▲ The teenage girl is a secondary school student.
這位青少年是個中學生。

20. **settle** [ˈsɛtḷ] v. 解決；確定，決定

▲ The two countries tried to settle the dispute over the border region. 這兩國試圖解決邊境糾紛。

settlement [ˈsɛtḷmənt] n. [C] 協定 <of>；[U] 付清 (欠款) <of>

▲ Both sides entered into negotiations to reach a peaceful settlement of the conflict.
雙方開始談判以達成解決衝突的和平協定。

21. **slip** [slɪp] v. 滑倒 <on>；溜走 [同] slide (slipped | slipped | slipping)

▲ Be careful not to slip on the wet floor.
小心別在溼地板上滑倒了。

slip [slɪp] n. [C] 紙條 <of>；小錯誤

▲ Eli left a message for his daughter on a slip of paper.
Eli 在紙條上留了個訊息給他的女兒。

22. **sudden** [ˈsʌdṇ] adj. 突然的

▲ Everyone was very surprised by the sudden change.
這突然的變化讓每個人都很驚訝。

sudden [ˈsʌdṇ] n. [sing.] 突然

▲ All of a sudden, a strong earthquake struck the city.

突然間，這城市發生大地震。

---

23. **textbook** [ˋtɛkst͵bʊk] n. [C] 教科書，課本

▲ The tutor asked the student to open his biology textbook to page 37.

這家教要學生將生物課本翻到第三十七頁。

---

24. **vote** [vot] n. [C] (選) 票 ; [C] 投票 , 表決 <on> (usu. sing.) [同] ballot

▲ The proposal was approved, with 10 votes in favor and two against.

這提議被通過了，十票贊成，兩票反對。

vote [vot] v. 投票，選舉 <for>

▲ Willy hasn't decided whom to vote for at the election. Willy 還沒決定選舉要投票給誰。

---

25. **weigh** [we] v. 有…重；秤重

▲ Lawrence weighs 140 pounds.

Lawrence 有一百四十磅重。

Unit 28

1. **bar** [bɑr] n. [C] 酒吧；酒吧的吧檯

▲ The hotel bar serves alcoholic drinks such as wine and whiskey.

這飯店酒吧提供含酒精的飲料，例如紅酒和威士忌。

bar [bɑr] v. 禁止 <from>；阻擋 (barred | barred | barring)

▲ The government barred dissidents from returning to the country. 這政府禁止異議人士返國。

2. **basics** [`besɪks] n. [pl.] 基礎 <of>

▲ It is essential to learn the basics of English grammar. 學習英文文法的基礎是必要的。

3. **beat** [bit] v. 打敗，戰勝 [同] defeat；打 (beat | beaten | beating)

▲ Japan beat Korea and got to the final. 日本隊打敗韓國隊並進入決賽。

💡 beat around the bush 轉彎抹角

beat [bit] n. [C] (心臟) 跳動；節拍

▲ Susie put her head on the injured man's chest but felt no beat of his heart. Susie 把頭靠在受傷男子的胸膛，但感覺不到他的心跳。

4. **chase** [tʃes] n. [C] 追捕，追趕

▲ The TV news reported a police chase. 這電視新聞報導警察追捕。

chase [tʃes] v. 追捕，追趕 <after>；驅趕

▲ Fans chased after the actress, calling her name. 影迷們追著這位女演員跑，叫著她的名字。

5. **cheer** [tʃɪr] v. 歡呼，喝采

▲ The dancer performed so wonderfully that the audience all cheered for him.

這舞者表演得如此棒，以致於所有的觀眾都為他喝采。

💡 cheer up (使) 振作，(使) 高興起來

cheer [tʃɪr] n. [C] 歡呼聲，喝采聲 [反] boo

▲ Let's give the winner a big cheer.

讓我們為勝利者大聲歡呼吧。

---

6. **debate** [dɪ`bet] n. [C][U] 談論，討論 <over>；辯論會 <on>

▲ There has been a heated public debate over education. 大眾一直熱烈地談論著教育。

debate [dɪ`bet] v. 爭論，討論 <with>

▲ Tiffany debated with her friends on the matter.

Tiffany 和她朋友就這件事進行討論。

---

7. **depth** [dɛpθ] n. [C][U] 深度 <in> (usu. sing.)

▲ This pond is 10 feet in depth. 這池子有十英尺深。

---

8. **excuse** [ɪk`skjuz] v. 原諒，寬恕 <for>；免除 <from>

▲ Jimmy is excused for being late this time and won't be punished. Jimmy 這次遲到被原諒了，不會被處罰。

💡 excuse me 打擾一下；借過

excuse [ɪk`skjus] n. [C] 藉口，理由 <for>

▲ Albert didn't have a good excuse for being absent from work. Albert 曠職沒有正當理由。

💡 there is no excuse for sth 沒有藉口為…開脫

9. **fireman** [ˋfaɪrmən] n. [C] 男消防隊員 [同] firefighter (pl. firemen)

▲ Those firemen are trained to stop fire from burning. 那些男消防隊員受訓阻止火勢延燒。

firewoman [ˋfaɪr͵wʊmən] n. [C] 女消防隊員 [同] firefighter (pl. firewomen)

▲ The girl wants to be a firewoman to save lives from fire. 這女孩想當女消防隊員，在大火中拯救生命。

10. **hero** [ˋhɪro] n. [C] 英雄 (pl. heroes)

▲ The war hero is admired for his exceptional bravery. 這位戰爭英雄因無比的勇敢受人欽佩。

heroine [ˋhɛro͵ɪn] n. [C] 女英雄

▲ The lady is known as the heroine of the women's movement. 這女士以身為女權運動的女英雄著名。

11. **income** [ˋɪn͵kʌm] n. [C][U] 收入

▲ The banker has an income of $500,000 a year. 這銀行家年收入五十萬美元。

12. **ink** [ɪŋk] n. [U] 墨水

▲ The ballpoint pen ran out of ink. 這枝原子筆沒墨水了。

ink [ɪŋk] v. 給⋯上油墨

▲ Before printing on the paper, the printing plate was inked. 在印在紙上前，這印刷版先被上了油墨。

13. **insist** [ɪnˋsɪst] v. 堅稱；堅持 <on>

▲ The suspect insisted that he was innocent, but the police didn't believe him.

這嫌犯堅稱自己是清白的，但警方不相信他。

14. **naughty** [ˋnɔtɪ] adj. 頑皮的，不聽話的 [反] good (naughtier | naughtiest)

▲ The naughty boy likes to play tricks on others.

這頑皮的男孩喜歡對別人惡作劇。

15. **pardon** [ˋpardn̩] n. [C] 赦免

▲ The president granted the criminal a pardon, so he could go free. 總統赦免了這罪犯，所以他可以獲釋。

pardon [ˋpardn̩] v. 赦免；原諒 <for> [同] forgive

▲ The political prisoner was pardoned and released by the president. 這政治犯被總統赦免並釋放。

💡 pardon me 對不起，請原諒；請再說一遍

16. **platform** [ˋplæt͵fɔrm] n. [C] 月臺；講臺

▲ The train will depart from platform one.

這班火車將從第 1 月臺開出。

17. **poetry** [ˋpoɪtrɪ] n. [U] (總稱) 詩

▲ The poet dedicates her poetry to her beloved homeland. 這詩人將她的詩獻給她摯愛的祖國。

18. **scooter** [ˋskutɚ] n. [C] 小型機車 (also motor scooter)

▲ Brian got his scooter out, turned on the motor, and went off. Brian 牽出他的小型機車、發動並離開。

19. **shame** [ʃem] **n.** [sing.] 可惜，遺憾；[U] 羞愧

▲ It's a shame that our school team lost the game.
我們的校隊輸了比賽，真是遺憾。

shame [ʃem] **v.** 使蒙受差辱，使丟臉

▲ The waiter felt shamed by the way the rude customer treated him. 這服務生因粗魯顧客的對待而蒙受差辱。

20. **shock** [ʃɑk] **n.** [C] 令人震驚的事件或經歷 <to> (usu. sing.)；[sing.][U] 震驚

▲ The sudden death of the superstar came as a big shock to his fans.
這巨星的突然死亡讓他的粉絲倍感震驚。

shock [ʃɑk] **v.** (使) 震驚

▲ It shocked the workers that the factory could be closed down soon.
工廠將要關閉這件事讓工人們震驚。

21. **snail** [snel] **n.** [C] 蝸牛

▲ The snail moves slowly with its shell on its back.
這蝸牛背著殼慢慢移動。

22. **supper** [`sʌpɚ] **n.** [C][U] 晚餐 [同] dinner

▲ The family is used to having supper at 7 p.m.
這家人習慣在晚上七點吃晚飯。

23. **till** [tɪl] **conj.** 直到⋯為止 [同] until

▲ Claire lived with her parents till she got married.
Claire 直到結婚為止都跟父母一起住。

till [tɪl] **prep.** 直到⋯為止 [同] until

▲ The post office is open till 12 p.m. on Saturdays.
這郵局星期六開到中午十二點為止。

24. **waiter** [`wetɚ] n. [C] 服務生

▲ The waiter's job is to serve food and drinks in the restaurant.
這服務生的工作是在這餐廳端食物和飲料。

waitress [`wetrɪs] n. [C] 女服務生 (pl. waitresses)

▲ The guest asked the waitress for a refill.
這顧客向女服務生要求續杯。

25. **wheel** [hwil] n. [C] 輪子，車輪；方向盤 <at, behind>

▲ The front wheels of the car were worn away.
這車子的前輪磨損了。

Unit 29

1. **bathe** [beð] v. (給某人) 洗澡 [同] bath

▲ Before going to bed, Crystal bathed and washed her hair. 上床睡覺前，Crystal 洗澡和洗頭。

2. **biscuit** [`bɪskɪt] n. [C] 餅乾 [同] cookie

▲ The old couple has tea and biscuits at four o'clock every afternoon.
這對老夫婦每天下午四點喝茶、吃餅乾。

3. **blame** [blem] v. 責怪，歸咎於 <for>

▲ The adults didn't blame the little boy for making the

mistake. 大人們不怪小男孩犯錯。

blame [blem] n. [U] 責怪，歸咎

▲ People can't put the blame for the accident on the driver. 這件意外人們不能怪駕駛。

---

4. **cheat** [tʃit] v. 作弊；騙取 <out of>

▲ The student cheated in the exam by bringing crib sheets. 這學生帶小抄在考試中作弊。

cheat [tʃit] n. [C] 騙子，作弊者

▲ Eden is such a cheat that no one wants to play cards with him. Eden 是騙子，所以沒有人要跟他玩牌。

---

5. **classmate** [`klæs,met] n. [C] 同班同學

▲ Leo often plays basketball with his classmates after school. Leo 常和他的同班同學在放學後打籃球。

---

6. **dentist** [`dɛntɪst] n. [C] 牙醫

▲ Fitch needs to go to the dentist to have his teeth checked. Fitch 得去看牙醫檢查牙齒。

---

7. **detail** [`ditel] n. [C] 細節；[U] 詳細

▲ Grace is a careful worker and pays close attention to every detail.

Grace 是個仔細的員工，很注意每個細節。

💡 down to the smallest detail 非常詳細地

detail [`ditel] v. 詳細描述

▲ The news report detailed the events of the crime.

新聞報導詳細描述這犯罪事件。

---

8. **exist** [ɪgˋzɪst] v. 存在
   ▲ The scientist thinks that life exists on other planets.
   這位科學家認為其他星球上有生命存在。

9. **fisherman** [ˋfɪʃɚmən] n. [C] 漁夫 (pl. fishermen)
   ▲ The fisherman makes a living by catching fish.
   這漁夫靠捕魚為生。

10. **hop** [hɑp] v. (人) 單腳跳；(蛙等) 齊足跳 (hopped | hopped | hopping)
    ▲ The player sprained his ankle when he hopped during training. 這球員在訓練時單腳跳扭傷腳踝。
    hop [hɑp] n. [C] 短距離跳躍
    ▲ The girl cleared the puddle with a hop.
    這女孩跳過水坑。

11. **internal** [ɪnˋtɝnl] adj. 國內的 [同] domestic [反] external；(組織等) 內部的 [反] external
    ▲ Other countries have no right to interfere in the nation's internal affairs.
    其他國家無權干涉這國家的內政。

12. **Internet** [ˋɪntɚ͵nɛt] n. [sing.] 網際網路 (the ～) (also internet)
    ▲ The Internet is one of the most important inventions in the 20th century.
    網際網路是二十世紀最重要的發明之一。

13. **jam** [dʒæm] n. [C][U] 果醬；[C] 堵塞

▲ The jam is made from boiled fruit and sugar.

這果醬是用煮熟的水果和糖做的。

jam [dʒæm] v. 把 … 塞入 <into>；擠滿 <with>
(jammed | jammed | jamming)

▲ The clerk jammed the documents into the drawer.

這職員把文件塞進抽屜裡。

14. **necklace** [ˋnɛkləs] n. [C] 項鍊

▲ The woman wore a pearl necklace around her neck.

這女子在脖子上戴了一條珍珠項鍊。

15. **playground** [ˋpleˌgraʊnd] n. [C] 操場，運動場

▲ Some students ran and played in the playground
during the morning break.

一些學生在上午休息時間在操場上又跑又玩。

16. **poet** [ˋpoɪt] n. [C] 詩人

▲ Shakespeare was an English poet and playwright.

莎士比亞是一位英國詩人及劇作家。

17. **policeman** [pəˋlismən] n. [C] 男員警 [同] cop (pl.
policemen)

▲ The robber scuffled with a policeman and ran away.

這搶匪和一位男員警短暫扭打，然後跑了。

18. **seafood** [ˋsiˌfud] n. [U] 海鮮

▲ The restaurant offers various kinds of seafood such
as crabs and shrimps.

這餐廳提供各式各樣的海鮮，例如螃蟹和蝦子。

---

19. **shy** [ʃaɪ] adj. 害羞的 (shyer | shyest)

▲ Ann is too shy to speak English with foreigners.
Ann 太害羞而不敢跟外國人說英文。

---

20. **silence** [ˋsaɪləns] n. [U] 寧靜 <of> [同] quiet；[C][U] 沉默

▲ At midnight, a loud bang broke the silence of the night. 半夜，一聲巨響打破了夜晚的寧靜。

silence [ˋsaɪləns] v. 使安靜

▲ The teacher raised his hand to silence the students.
這老師舉起手讓學生們安靜。

---

21. **soybean** [ˋsɔɪˌbin] n. [C] 大豆 (also soya bean)

▲ The tofu is made from soybeans. 這豆腐是大豆做的。

---

22. **surf** [sɝf] v. 衝浪

▲ Young people go surfing, looking for adventure and excitement. 年輕人去衝浪，追求冒險和刺激。

♥ surf the Internet 上網

---

23. **tofu** [ˋtofu] n. [U] 豆腐

▲ Many vegetarians use tofu in cooking instead of meat. 許多素食者煮菜時用豆腐取代肉類。

---

24. **wallet** [ˋwɑlɪt] n. [C] 皮夾 [同] billfold

▲ A pickpocket stole Jared's wallet from his trouser pocket.

一個扒手從 Jared 的褲子口袋裡偷走他的皮夾。

---

25. **wolf** [wʊlf] n. [C] 狼 (pl. wolves)

▲ A pack of wolves chased the deer. 一群狼追逐著鹿。

Unit 30

1. **beard** [bɪrd] n. [C] 鬍鬚，山羊鬍

▲ The man wearing a thick beard is Wade's father.
留著濃密鬍鬚的男子是 Wade 的父親。

2. **board** [bord] n. [C] 布告板 <on>；板，木板

▲ The waiter chalked up the menu on a board in the restaurant. 這服務生在餐廳布告板上用粉筆寫菜單。

board [bord] v. (使) 上 (船、火車或飛機)；寄宿

▲ Flora boarded a plane to Taipei today.
Flora 今天搭上飛往臺北的飛機。

3. **calendar** [`kæləndɚ] n. [C] 日曆

▲ Gina marked important dates on the calendar.
Gina 在日曆上標記重要的日子。

4. **chess** [tʃɛs] n. [U] 西洋棋

▲ Ted enjoys playing chess with his friends in his free time. Ted 喜愛在空閒時和朋友下西洋棋。

5. **click** [klɪk] v. (使) 發出卡嗒聲；按一下 (滑鼠) <on>

▲ Two Lego blocks clicked together.

兩個樂高積木卡嗒一聲合在一起。

click [klɪk] n. [C] 喀啦聲

▲ The door suddenly shut with a click.
這門突然喀啦一聲關上了。

---

6. **dial** [`daɪəl] n. [C] 儀表盤；旋鈕，調節器

▲ The driver looked at the dial to check his speed.
這駕駛看一下儀表盤來查看他的速度。

dial [`daɪəl] v. 撥號 (dialed, dialled | dialed, dialled | dialing, dialling)

▲ Customers may dial the phone number to contact the store. 顧客可以撥這電話號碼來聯絡店家。

---

7. **division** [dɪ`vɪʒən] n. [C][U] 分開，分割 <of>；分歧，不和 <within>

▲ The partners made a fair division of the profits.
合夥人們公平地分利潤。

---

8. **expense** [ɪk`spɛns] n. [C][U] 支付，花費

▲ Mike bought the car at an expense of $50,000.
Mike 花費五萬美元買了這部車。

💡 at the expense of sth/sb 以⋯為代價，犧牲⋯

---

9. **flag** [flæg] n. [C] 旗幟

▲ People in Taiwan hang out national flags on Double Tenth Day. 臺灣人民在雙十節懸掛國旗。

---

10. **hunter** [`hʌntɚ] n. [C] 獵人，捕獵者

▲ The hunters are hunting deer and bears.

獵人們正在獵鹿和熊。

---

11. **jog** [dʒɑg] v. 慢跑 (jogged｜jogged｜jogging)

▲ Helen goes jogging every day to keep fit.
Helen 每天慢跑以保持身材。

jog [dʒɑg] n. [sing.] 慢跑

▲ Newman went for a jog along the riverbank.
Newman 沿著河岸慢跑。

---

12. **judgment** [`dʒʌdʒmənt] n. [C][U] 判斷；[U] 判斷力
(also judgement)

▲ Robert taught his daughter not to make hasty
judgments. Robert 教他女兒不要倉促下判斷。

---

13. **meter** [`mitɚ] n. [C] 公尺 (also metre) (abbr. m)；計量
器，儀表

▲ One meter is about 39.37 inches.
一公尺大約是三十九點三七英寸。

---

14. **needle** [`nidl] n. [C] 針

▲ The old lady couldn't put the thread through the eye
of the needle. 老婦人無法把線穿過針眼。

---

15. **poison** [`pɔɪzn] n. [C][U] 毒，毒藥

▲ The man killed himself by taking some poison.
這男子服毒自殺。

poison [`pɔɪzn] v. 在…裡下毒；使受汙染

▲ The agent killed the politician by poisoning his tea.

這特務在政客的茶裡下毒殺害他。

---

16. **pork** [pork] **n.** [U] 豬肉

▲ Muslims don't eat pork because it's considered unclean. 穆斯林不吃豬肉，因為它被視為不淨。

---

17. **postcard** [ˋpost͵kɑrd] **n.** [C] 明信片

▲ A postcard can be sent by post without an envelope. 明信片可以不用信封郵寄。

---

18. **seesaw** [ˋsi͵sɔ] **n.** [C] 翹翹板 [同] teeter-totter

▲ Those children are playing on the seesaw happily. 那些孩子正在開心地玩翹翹板。

---

19. **sidewalk** [ˋsaɪd͵wɔk] **n.** [C] 人行道 [同] pavement

▲ Riding motorcycles on the sidewalk is not allowed. 在人行道上騎機車是不被允許的。

---

20. **skilled** [skɪld] **adj.** 熟練的 <at> [反] unskilled

▲ The tailor is very skilled at making men's clothes. 這裁縫師製作男士服飾非常熟練。

---

21. **spoon** [spun] **n.** [C] 湯匙

▲ The patient is so weak that he can't even lift a spoon. 這病人虛弱到連一根湯匙都拿不動。

---

22. **swallow** [ˋswɑlo] **v.** 吞嚥，吞下

▲ Julia chewed her food well before she swallowed it. Julia 把食物細嚼後嚥下。

swallow [ˋswɑlo] **n.** [C] 燕子；吞嚥，吞下

▲ One swallow does not make a summer.

【諺】一燕不成夏;一事成功並非萬事大吉。

23. **trial** [ˋtraɪəl] **n.** [C][U] 審判;試驗

▲ The lawyer believed that the case would never go to trial. 律師相信這案件絕不會交付審判。

24. **watermelon** [ˋwɔtɚˏmɛlən] **n.** [C][U] 西瓜

▲ Watermelons are Perry's favorite fruit in summer.

西瓜是 Perry 夏天最喜歡的水果。

25. **workbook** [ˋwɝkˏbʊk] **n.** [C] 習題簿,練習簿

▲ The workbook contains questions and exercises.

這練習簿裡有問題和練習題。

Unit 31

1. **admit** [ədˋmɪt] **v.** 承認;招認 <to> [同] confess [反] deny (admitted | admitted | admitting)

▲ Ruby admitted breaking her sister's toy out of jealousy. Ruby 承認因嫉妒而弄壞妹妹的玩具。

2. **beer** [bɪr] **n.** [U] 啤酒

▲ The beer is made at a local brewery.

這啤酒是當地一家啤酒廠製造的。

3. **bone** [bon] **n.** [C] 骨頭

▲ Karen got a fish bone stuck in her throat.

Karen 被魚刺哽住喉嚨。

---

4. **character** [ˋkærɪktɚ] n. [C] 性格，個性 (usu. sing.)；
[C] 人物，角色

▲ Bruce has a quiet character and seldom expresses himself.
Bruce 的個性很文靜，很少表達自己的想法。

---

5. **childish** [ˋtʃaɪldɪʃ] adj. 幼稚的 [同] immature [反] mature

▲ Even though Laurel is an adult, she is still very childish. 雖然 Laurel 是成人，但她還是很幼稚。

---

6. **countryside** [ˋkʌntrɪ͵saɪd] n. [U] 鄉村 [同] the country

▲ Tony likes going to the countryside to get out of the noisy city. Tony 喜歡去鄉村，以離開吵鬧的城市。

---

7. **dialogue** [ˋdaɪə͵lɔg] n. [C][U] (戲劇等裡的) 對白；(團體或國家間的) 對話 <with> (also dialog)

▲ The dialogue in that film is very amusing.
那部影片的對白很有趣。

---

8. **domestic** [dəˋmɛstɪk] adj. 家庭的；國內的

▲ The housewife is busy with domestic chores.
這家庭主婦正忙於家務。

---

9. **fate** [fet] n. [C] 命運 (usu. sing.)；[U] 天意

▲ Even though the man suffered many hardships, he accepted his fate calmly. 雖然這男子歷經了很多艱

辛，但他平靜地接受他的命運。

---

10. **flow** [flo] n. [C] (液體等) 流動 <of> (usu. sing.)；
[C][U] (車) 流 (usu. sing.)

▲ The surfer swam against the flow of the sea.
這衝浪者逆著海流游泳。

flow [flo] v. (液體等) 流動；湧至 [同] pour, flood

▲ The river flows calmly into the sea.
這條河靜靜地流入海中。

---

11. **ignore** [ɪgˋnor] v. 忽略，不理會

▲ Lena ignored her parents' advice and insisted on
going her own way.
Lena 忽略她父母的勸告，堅持我行我素。

---

12. **joint** [dʒɔɪnt] adj. 共有的，共同的

▲ The rescue was a joint effort among several
countries. 這救援行動是數國共同的努力。

joint [dʒɔɪnt] n. [C] 關節；接合處

▲ With winter approaching, the old man's joints get
stiffer. 隨著冬天到來，老人的關節越發僵硬。

---

13. **lady** [ˋledɪ] n. [C] 女士 (pl. ladies)

▲ There is a young lady waiting at the front desk.
有一位年輕的女士在服務臺等待。

---

14. **mile** [maɪl] n. [C] 英里

▲ The train station is two miles away.

火車站在兩英里外。

15. **neighbor** [ˈnebɚ] **n.** [C] 鄰居

▲ Roy's neighbors complained about the loud noise from his party. Roy 的鄰居抱怨他的派對很吵。

16. **pound** [paʊnd] **n.** [C] 磅 (abbr. lb)；英鎊 (also pound sterling)

▲ The butter is sold by the pound.
這奶油是論磅來賣的。

17. **pray** [pre] **v.** 禱告，祈禱 <to, for>；祈求 <for>

▲ The priest knelt down and prayed to God for the victims. 這牧師跪下為受害者們向上帝祈禱。

18. **prince** [prɪns] **n.** [C] 王子

▲ The prince became king after his father died.
這王子在父親去世後成為了國王。

princess [ˈprɪnsɛs] **n.** [C] 公主 (pl. princesses)

▲ The king's favorite daughter was Princess Anna.
這國王最喜歡的女兒是 Anna 公主。

19. **select** [səˈlɛkt] **v.** 選擇，挑選 <from> [同] choose, pick

▲ The baby panda's name was selected from over 1,000 suggestions.

這熊貓寶寶的名字是從超過一千個建議中選出來的。

select [səˈlɛkt] **adj.** 挑選出來的

▲ Only a select few reporters are allowed to interview the president.

只有少數幾位挑選出來的記者被允許採訪總統。

20. **silver** [ˋsɪlvɚ] n. [U] 銀；銀器 [同] silverware
   ▲ That spoon is made of silver. 那根湯匙是銀製的。
   silver [ˋsɪlvɚ] adj. 銀製的；銀色的
   ▲ Helena always wears a silver ring on her little finger.
     Helena 的小拇指總是戴著銀製的戒指。

21. **soft** [sɔft] adj. 柔軟的 [反] hard；柔滑的 [反] rough
   ▲ Lying on the bed, Sam sunk into the soft mattress.
     Sam 躺在床上時陷入柔軟的床墊裡。

22. **stomachache** [ˋstʌməkˏek] n. [C][U] 胃痛
   ▲ Scott ate too much spicy food and had a bad
     stomachache. Scott 吃太多辛辣食物而胃痛得不得了。

23. **sweater** [ˋswɛtɚ] n. [C] 毛衣
   ▲ Polly is knitting a pink sweater for her daughter.
     Polly 正為她女兒織一件粉紅色的毛衣。

24. **upload** [ʌpˋlod] v. 上傳 [反] download
   ▲ It takes some time to upload the files.
     上傳這些檔案需要一些時間。

25. **weekday** [ˋwikˏde] n. [C] 平日，工作日
   ▲ Most people have to work on weekdays.
     大部分的人在平日要工作。

Unit 32 👈

1. **aloud** [ə`laʊd] adv. 出聲地，大聲地 [同] out loud
   ▲ The teacher asked Mason to read the paragraph aloud. 老師叫 Mason 把這段唸出來。

2. **beg** [bɛg] v. 乞求 <for>；乞討 <from> (begged | begged | begging)
   ▲ The criminal admitted his guilt and begged for forgiveness. 這罪犯認罪並乞求原諒。

3. **broad** [brɔd] adj. 寬的，寬廣的 [反] narrow；廣泛的
   ▲ This river is ten meters broad. 這條河十公尺寬。

4. **chopstick** [`tʃɑp,stɪk] n. [C] 筷子 (usu. pl.)
   ▲ Most Chinese people use chopsticks to eat food. 大部分的中國人用筷子進食。

5. **concern** [kən`sɝn] n. [U] 擔心，憂慮；[C][U] 關心 (的事)
   ▲ Tom's reckless driving is a cause for concern to his father. Tom 開車魯莽是讓他父親擔心的一個原因。
   concern [kən`sɝn] v. 與…有關，涉及；使擔心
   ▲ The first chapter concerns the poet's ancestry. 第一章與這詩人的家族史有關。
   💡 concern oneself with/about sth 關心；擔心

6. **curtain** [`kɝtn̩] n. [C] 簾，窗簾；(舞臺上的) 幕
   ▲ The sunlight was too bright, so Lillian closed the

curtains. 陽光太亮了，所以 Lillian 把窗簾拉上。

curtain [`kɝtn̩] **v.** (用簾子) 隔開 <off>

▲ The two brothers curtained off the bedroom to get some privacy.
這兩兄弟用簾子隔開臥室，以得到一點隱私。

---

7. **diary** [`daɪərɪ] **n.** [C] 日記 (pl. diaries) [同] journal

▲ Nelly keeps a diary to record what has happened every day. Nelly 寫日記以紀錄每天發生的事。

---

8. **doubt** [daʊt] **n.** [C][U] 懷疑，疑慮 <about>

▲ The police had serious doubts about the suspect's innocence. 警方嚴重懷疑這嫌犯的清白。

🍋 no/without doubt 無疑地 | be in doubt 不確定

doubt [daʊt] **v.** 懷疑

▲ Since Ted is sick, his friends doubt if he can come tonight.
由於 Ted 生病了，他的朋友懷疑他今晚是否能過來。

---

9. **fault** [fɔlt] **n.** [C] 過錯，過失 <for>；毛病，缺陷

▲ It is the driver's fault for the car accident.
是這駕駛的過失而造成了車禍。

🍋 at fault 有過錯，為…負責 | find fault with sb/sth 挑…的毛病

fault [fɔlt] **v.** 挑…的毛病

▲ The show is excellent and can't be faulted.
這表演絕佳，沒什麼好挑毛病的。

10. **foolish** [`fulɪʃ] adj. 傻的，愚蠢的 <of> [同] silly
▲ It is foolish of people to ignore the threat of climate change. 人們忽視氣候變遷的威脅是愚蠢的。

11. **impressive** [ɪm`prɛsɪv] adj. 令人印象深刻的
▲ The young actor's performance in the latest movie is really impressive.
這年輕演員在最新電影中的表現真的令人印象深刻。

12. **keeper** [`kipɚ] n. [C] 飼養員
▲ Adam is an elephant keeper at the zoo.
Adam 是這動物園裡的大象飼養員。

13. **lap** [læp] n. [C] (坐著時的) 大腿 <on>
▲ The baby was sitting on its mother's lap.
這寶寶坐在媽媽的腿上。

14. **minority** [maɪ`nɔrətɪ] n. [C] 少數 <of> [反] majority；[C] 少數群體 (usu. pl.) (pl. minorities)
▲ Only a minority of students passed the difficult test.
僅少數學生通過這困難的考試。

15. **nephew** [`nɛfju] n. [C] 姪子，外甥
▲ Ben is Maria's nephew; he is the son of her sister.
Ben 是 Maria 的外甥，他是她姊姊的兒子。

16. **prayer** [prɛr] n. [C] 祈禱文；[U] 祈禱，禱告 <in>
▲ The Catholic said his prayers before going to bed.
這天主教徒在上床睡覺前唸祈禱文。

17. **priest** [prist] **n.** [C] 牧師

▲ Graham plans to become a priest and work in the church of his hometown.

Graham 計劃要當牧師並在他家鄉的教堂裡工作。

18. **print** [prɪnt] **n.** [U] 印刷品，出版物；印刷字體

▲ Most of the late poet's works have got into print.

這已故詩人大部分的作品都出版了。

💡 be in/out of print (書) 仍可買到的 / 已絕版的

print [prɪnt] **v.** 印；印刷

▲ The teacher made some changes to the handout before printing it. 老師在印出講義前做了一些修改。

19. **servant** [`sɝvənt] **n.** [C] 僕人

▲ The old servant served his master devotedly.

這老僕人盡忠地服侍他的主人。

20. **skill** [skɪl] **n.** [C][U] 技能，技巧

▲ The carpenter's work requires a lot of skills.

這木匠的工作需要許多技巧。

21. **soil** [sɔɪl] **n.** [C][U] 泥土，土壤 [同] earth

▲ Watermelons grow very well in sandy soil.

西瓜在沙質的土壤裡生長良好。

22. **stream** [strim] **n.** [C] 小河，溪流；流動 <of>

▲ The hiker walked along a clear stream in the forest.

這健行者沿著森林裡清澈的溪流走著。

stream [strim] **v.** 流，流動 <out of> [同] pour

▲ Water streamed out of the leaky faucet.
水從漏水的水龍頭流出來。

23. **swimsuit** [`swɪmsut] n. [C] 泳裝

▲ Before going swimming, Polly changed into her swimsuit. 去游泳前，Polly 先換上她的泳裝。

24. **wedding** [`wɛdɪŋ] n. [C] 婚禮

▲ Helen and Bob's wedding will take place next Sunday. Helen 和 Bob 的婚禮將在下週日舉行。

25. **whale** [hwel] n. [C] 鯨

▲ The blue whale is the largest animal on earth.
藍鯨是世上最大的動物。

Unit 33

1. **angle** [`æŋgl] n. [C] 角，角度；觀點，立場

▲ The two streets meet at right angles.
這兩條街直角交會。

2. **beginner** [bɪ`gɪnɚ] n. [C] 初學者

▲ The book is difficult for beginners and too easy for advanced learners.
這本書對初學者是難的，對進階的學生又太簡單。

3. **brush** [brʌʃ] n. [C] 刷子

▲ Bruce used a brush to clean his sneakers.

Bruce 用刷子來清理他的球鞋。

brush [brʌʃ] v. 刷

▲ Before going to bed, the girl brushed her teeth.
上床睡覺前，這女孩先刷牙。

---

4. **clap** [klæp] v. 鼓 (掌)；拍 (手) (clapped | clapped | clapping)

▲ The audience clapped the dancer's excellent performance. 觀眾為舞者絕佳的演出鼓掌。

clap [klæp] n. [sing.] 霹靂聲 <of>

▲ The lightning flashed, and then a clap of thunder frightened the kids.
閃電一閃，然後雷聲把孩子們嚇了一跳。

---

5. **consideration** [kən͵sɪdə`reʃən] n. [U] 考慮，斟酌；[C] 考慮的事或因素

▲ After careful consideration, Ruth decided to buy a new car. 經過仔細考慮後，Ruth 決定買一輛新車。

💡 take sth into consideration 將⋯列入考慮

---

6. **dancer** [`dænsɚ] n. [C] 舞者

▲ Claire loves dancing and wants to be a ballet dancer in the future.
Claire 喜愛跳舞，她將來想做一名芭蕾舞者。

---

7. **disagree** [͵dɪsə`gri] v. 不同意，反對 <with, on> [反] agree；不一致 <with> [反] agree

▲ The couple had a quarrel because they disagreed with each other on the matter.

這對夫妻因為不同意彼此對這件事的看法而吵架。

disagreement [ˌdɪsə`grimənt] n. [C][U] 分歧，意見不合 <among> [反] agreement

▲ There are disagreements among the colleagues about the way to solve the problem.

同事之間對解決這問題的方式意見不合。

---

8. **dragon** [`drægən] n. [C] 龍

▲ The dragon is an imaginary creature that has wings and can breathe out fire.

龍是一種有翅膀並會噴火的虛構生物。

---

9. **fellow** [`fɛlo] n. [C] 人，傢伙

▲ We all like Christopher because he is a nice fellow.

我們都喜歡 Christopher，因為他是一個好人。

---

10. **forgive** [fə`gɪv] v. 原諒 <for> (forgave | forgiven | forgiving)

▲ Terry forgave his son for breaking his favorite vase.

Terry 原諒兒子打破了他最喜愛的花瓶。

---

11. **indicate** [`ɪndə,ket] v. 顯示；表明

▲ The study indicates that over 30% of the jobs in the country rely on tourism.

研究顯示這國家超過 30% 的工作依靠觀光業。

---

12. **ketchup** [`kɛtʃəp] n. [U] 番茄醬 (also catsup)

▲ Ketchup is made from tomatoes and spices.

番茄醬是用番茄和調味料做成的。

---

13. **lay** [le] v. 放置 [同] place；生 (蛋) (laid | laid | laying)

▲ May laid her hand on her son's shoulder to comfort him. May 把手放在兒子的肩上安慰他。

---

14. **mirror** [ˋmɪrɚ] n. [C] 鏡子 <in>

▲ Kate is looking at her reflection in the mirror.
Kate 正看著鏡中自己的影像。

mirror [ˋmɪrɚ] v. 反映 [同] reflect

▲ The mass media should try to mirror the opinions of ordinary people.
大眾傳播媒體應該試著反映一般民意。

---

15. **nerve** [nɝv] n. [C] 神經；[U] 勇氣，膽量

▲ The nerve damage caused the patient great pain.
神經損傷造成這病人劇烈疼痛。

---

16. **press** [prɛs] n. [sing.] 新聞界，記者 (the ~)；[C] 出版社

▲ The foreign minister will meet the press on Monday.
外交部長星期一將會見記者。

press [prɛs] v. 按，壓 [同] push；熨平，燙平 [同] iron

▲ The manager pressed the button to summon his assistant. 這經理按鈕叫喚他的助理。

---

17. **principle** [ˋprɪnsəpl] n. [C][U] 原則；[C] 原理

▲ The president sticks to her principles and continues the fight against racism.

這總統堅持她的原則並持續對抗種族歧視。

💡 in principle 原則上，基本上

---

18. **prisoner** [ˋprɪznɚ] n. [C] 犯人

▲ The prisoner is serving time for smuggling drugs.
這囚犯因走私毒品正在服刑。

---

19. **shark** [ʃɑrk] n. [C] 鯊魚

▲ The shark has sharp teeth and a pointed fin on its back. 鯊魚有鋒利的牙而且背上有尖尖的鰭。

---

20. **slide** [slaɪd] n. [C] 滑梯；下滑 <in> (usu. sing.) [反] rise

▲ Tom sat on his mother's lap and went down the slide together. Tom 坐在母親的大腿上，一起溜下滑梯。

slide [slaɪd] v. (使) 滑動，(使) 滑行 <across>；悄悄地走 <out of> (slid | slid | sliding)

▲ The skater slid across the frozen lake.
這溜冰者滑行過結冰的湖面。

---

21. **stretch** [strɛtʃ] n. [C] (土地或水域等的) 一片 <of>；(連續的) 一段時間 <of>

▲ The tourists took a boat trip across the lake, which was the biggest stretch of water there.
觀光客們搭船遊湖，這是那裡最大的一片水域。

stretch [strɛtʃ] v. 拉長；伸展 (身體)

▲ Henry stretched the elastic band too far and then it snapped. Henry 把橡皮筋拉得太長，然後它就斷了。

---

22. **strict** [strɪkt] adj. 嚴格的 <with, about> [反] lenient

▲ The teacher is strict with students about being punctual for her class.

這老師嚴格要求學生上她的課要準時。

---

23. **tale** [tel] **n.** [C] 故事，傳說

▲ The Taiwanese folk tale is about the indigenous people who fought against Japanese soldiers.

這臺灣民間故事是關於原住民對抗日本軍人的故事。

24. **whisper** [`hwɪspɚ] **n.** [C] 低語 <in>；傳聞，私下的議論 [同] rumor

▲ Cathy told her close friend the secret in a whisper.

Cathy 小聲對她密友說出這祕密。

whisper [`hwɪspɚ] **v.** 低語，小聲說話 <to>

▲ Mike whispered to Molly so that no one else could hear what he said.

Mike 對 Molly 小聲說話，好讓別人聽不到他說的話。

25. **whoever** [hu`ɛvɚ] **pron.** 無論誰

▲ Whoever finds my wallet will get NT$3,000 as a reward. 無論是誰找到我的皮夾，都可以得到新臺幣三千元的獎賞。

Unit 34

1. **anytime** [`ɛnɪ,taɪm] **adv.** 在任何時候

▲ The guest will get here anytime between 7 p.m. and 8:30 p.m.

這客人會在晚上七點到八點半之間到達這裡。

2. **boil** [bɔɪl] n. [sing.] 沸騰 (狀態)

▲ The cook brought the soup to the boil and added some salt. 這廚師把湯煮沸，然後加一些鹽。

boil [bɔɪl] v. 煮沸，燒開

▲ The host is boiling water to make tea.
這男主人正在燒開水泡茶。

---

3. **businessman** [ˋbɪznɪs͵mæn] n. [C] 商 人 (pl. businessmen)

▲ The shrewd businessmen were quick to find how to make big profits.
這些精明的商人很快發現如何賺取大筆利潤的方式。

---

4. **clever** [ˋklɛvɚ] adj. 聰明的 [同] intelligent, smart；狡猾的

▲ The clever girl is able to learn things quickly.
這聰明的女孩能夠快速學東西。

---

5. **contract** [ˋkɑntrækt] n. [C] 合約，契約 <with>

▲ Judy entered a two-year contract with this company.
Judy 和這公司簽訂了兩年的合約。

contract [kənˋtrækt] v. (使) 收縮，(使) 縮小 [反] expand

▲ When metal cools, it contracts. 金屬冷卻時會收縮。

---

6. **delay** [dɪˋle] n. [C] 延遲，延誤 <in>；[U] 耽擱 <without>

▲ The typhoon caused serious delays in flights.
這颱風造成班機嚴重延誤。

delay [dɪ`le] v. 延誤；延後 <for>

▲ The plane was seriously delayed by a storm.
這飛機因暴風雨而嚴重延誤。

7. **distant** [`dɪstənt] adj. 遙遠的，遠方的 <from>；冷漠的，不親近的

▲ It took Jack eight hours to take a boat to the distant island. Jack 花了八個小時搭船到那個遙遠的島嶼。

8. **drawing** [`drɔɪŋ] n. [C] 圖畫 <of>；[U] 繪畫

▲ The artist is doing a drawing of the castle.
這藝術家正在為這城堡畫一張畫。

9. **fog** [fɑg] n. [C][U] 霧 [同] mist

▲ The driver couldn't see the road because the fog was very thick. 因為霧很濃，這駕駛看不見路。

fog [fɑg] v. (因水氣等) 變得模糊 (also fog up) [同] mist up, steam up (fogged | fogged | fogging)

▲ Since the steam fogged the mirror, Willy couldn't see his reflection in it clearly. 由於蒸氣讓鏡子變得模糊，Willy 看不清他在鏡中的樣子。

10. **garlic** [`gɑrlɪk] n. [U] 大蒜

▲ Anna flavored the soup with some cloves of garlic.
Anna 用幾瓣大蒜給湯調味。

11. **journal** [`dʒɝnl] n. [C] 雜誌，期刊

▲ The professor's research paper was published in the academic journal last month.

這教授的研究論文上個月被發表在這學術期刊上。

12. **kilogram** [ˋkɪləˏgræm] n. [C] 公斤 (abbr. kg)

▲ Joe bought five kilograms of oranges in the supermarket. Joe 在超市買了五公斤的柳橙。

13. **lift** [lɪft] v. 舉起 (also lift up)；抬起 (肢體等) [同] raise (also lift up)

▲ The mover is strong enough to lift the heavy box.

這搬家工人夠強壯，可以舉起這沉重的箱子。

lift [lɪft] n. [C] 電梯 [同] elevator；搭便車 [同] ride

▲ The hotel guest took the lift to the tenth floor.

這飯店住客搭電梯到十樓。

14. **niece** [nis] n. [C] 姪女，外甥女

▲ Belle is Mr. Brown's niece; she is the daughter of his brother.

Belle 是 Brown 先生的姪女，她是他哥哥的女兒。

15. **painful** [ˋpenfəl] adj. 疼痛的；令人痛苦的 [反] painless

▲ Evan broke his arm, and it was painful to the touch.

Evan 摔斷手臂，碰到時很痛。

16. **printer** [ˋprɪntɚ] n. [C] 印表機

▲ The secretary used the laser printer to print documents.

這祕書用雷射印表機列印文件。

---

17. **protective** [prə`tɛktɪv] adj. 防護性的，保護的
   ▲ The workers have to wear protective clothing in the chemical factory.
   工人們在這化學工廠裡必須穿防護衣。

---

18. **pupil** [`pjupl] n. [C] 學生
   ▲ The child is a third-grade pupil in the elementary school. 這孩子是這間小學三年級的學生。

---

19. **shell** [ʃɛl] n. [C] 貝殼
   ▲ The girls collected beautiful shells on the beach.
   女孩們在沙灘上撿美麗的貝殼。

---

20. **somewhat** [`sʌm,hwɑt] adv. 有點，稍微
   ▲ The dress is somewhat expensive for Lora.
   這件洋裝對 Lora 來說有點貴。

---

21. **struggle** [`strʌgl] n. [C] 奮鬥，努力 <for>；掙扎
   ▲ Dr. King led African Americans in their struggle for equal rights. 金恩博士領導非裔美國人為平權而奮鬥。
   struggle [`strʌgl] v. 奮鬥，努力；打鬥 <with>
   ▲ The single mother struggled to raise her three kids.
   這單親媽媽努力撫養她的三個孩子。

---

22. **succeed** [sək`sid] v. 成功 <in>
   ▲ Sandy succeeded in passing the college entrance exam. Sandy 成功通過大學入學考試。

---

23. **teapot** [ˋtiˌpɑt] **n.** [C] 茶壺

▲ The tea set consists of a teapot and six teacups.
這茶具組由一個茶壺和六個茶杯組成。

---

24. **width** [wɪdθ] **n.** [C][U] 寬度 <in>

▲ The mountain road is five meters in width.
這條山路有五公尺寬。

---

25. **wine** [waɪn] **n.** [U] 葡萄酒

▲ Red wine is an alcoholic drink made from grapes.
紅酒是葡萄做的含酒精飲料。

Unit 35

1. **absent** [ˋæbsn̩t] **adj.** 缺席的 <from> [反] present

▲ The student has been absent from school for three
weeks. 這學生已缺課三星期了。

absent [æbˋsɛnt] **v.** 缺席 <from>

▲ The employee absented himself from the meeting
without a good excuse.
這員工沒有正當理由就缺席這場會議。

---

2. **anyway** [ˋɛnɪˌwe] **adv.** 無論如何，不管怎樣 (also
anyhow)

▲ The plan might not work, but the team decided to try
it anyway.
這計畫可能不可行，但不管怎樣這團隊決定試試。

---

3. **bookstore** [`buk,stor] n. [C] 書店

▲ The online bookstore sells all kinds of books.
這網路書店販賣各式各樣的書籍。

4. **cell** [sɛl] n. [C] 細胞

▲ The doctor didn't find any cancer cells in the patient's liver.
醫生並未在這病人的肝臟裡找到任何癌細胞。

5. **cloth** [klɔθ] n. [U] 布 (料);[C] 抹布

▲ This dress is made of the finest cotton cloth.
這洋裝是用最佳的棉布料製作的。

6. **crime** [kraɪm] n. [U] 違法行為,犯罪活動;[C] 罪,罪行

▲ The police were having a crackdown on street crime.
警方正在打擊街頭犯罪活動。

7. **divide** [dɪ`vaɪd] v. (使) 分開 ,(使) 分組 <into> ; 分隔 (also divide off)

▲ The teacher divided the students into six groups.
老師將學生們分成六組。

divide [dɪ`vaɪd] n. [C] 分歧 ,隔閡 <between> (usu. sing.)

▲ The divide between the rich and the poor is growing.
貧富分歧日趨擴大。

8. **downstairs** [daʊn`stɛrz] adv. 在樓下 [反] upstairs

▲ The bathroom of the two-story house is located downstairs.

這兩層樓房子的廁所位於樓下。

downstairs [daʊn`stɛrz] n. [sing.] 樓下 (the ～)

▲ The downstairs was rented to a bookseller.
樓下被出租給書商。

downstairs [daʊn`stɛrz] adj. 樓下的 [反] upstairs

▲ In summer, the downstairs rooms are hot and damp.
在夏天，樓下的房間又熱又潮溼。

9. **earn** [ɝn] v. 賺 (錢)；贏得

▲ Paul earned a living by teaching English.
Paul 以教英文維持生計。

10. **forth** [forθ] adv. (從某地) 外出，離開

▲ Amber set forth on her travel during summer vacation. Amber 暑假期間啟程去旅行。

11. **gentle** [`dʒɛntl̩] adj. 溫和的，和藹的 <with> [反] rough；徐緩的 (gentler｜gentlest)

▲ Gavin is gentle with people; he never hurts others' feelings. Gavin 對人溫和，他從不傷害別人的感情。

12. **justice** [`dʒʌstɪs] n. [U] 正義，公正 [反] injustice；司法，審判

▲ Harriet has a strong sense of justice; she always treats people fairly.
Harriet 是一個很有正義感的人，她總是公正待人。

13. **ladybug** [`ledɪˌbʌg] n. [C] 瓢蟲

▲ A ladybug is a small round beetle, usually with black spots. 瓢蟲是一種小小圓圓、通常有黑色斑點的甲蟲。

14. **load** [lod] **n.** [C] 負重，載重 <of>；工作量
▲ The truck is carrying a heavy load of timber.
這卡車裝載著大量的木材。

load [lod] **v.** 裝載 <into> (also load up) [反] unload
▲ The movers loaded the furniture into the truck.
搬家工人們把家具裝載到卡車裡。

15. **nod** [nɑd] **n.** [C] 點頭
▲ The gentleman greeted those ladies with a nod of the head. 這紳士向那些女士們點頭打招呼。

nod [nɑd] **v.** 點頭 (nodded | nodded | nodding)
▲ The manager nodded to show that she agreed.
這經理點頭表示她同意了。

💡 nod off 打瞌睡

16. **poem** [`poɪm] **n.** [C] 詩 <about>
▲ Ryan wrote a poem about the beauty of nature.
Ryan 寫了一首關於大自然之美的詩。

17. **pudding** [`pʊdɪŋ] **n.** [C][U] 布丁
▲ Lucy made a pudding for the Christmas dinner.
Lucy 為耶誕節晚餐做了一個布丁。

18. **punish** [`pʌnɪʃ] **v.** 處罰，懲罰 <for>
▲ The student was punished for cheating on the test.
這學生因為考試作弊而被處罰。

punishment [ˈpʌnɪʃmənt] n. [C][U] 處罰，懲罰 <as>

▲ Jeffery's parents grounded him for a week as a punishment.

Jeffery 的父母將他禁足一個星期作為處罰。

19. **puzzle** [ˈpʌzl̩] n. [C] 猜謎，智力遊戲；謎，令人費解的事 (usu. sing.)

▲ Freda spent many nights working on the jigsaw puzzle. Freda 花了好多個夜晚拼這個拼圖。

puzzle [ˈpʌzl̩] v. (使) 感到迷惑

▲ Kent was puzzled by the complicated math problem.

Kent 對這複雜的數學題感到迷惑。

20. **shopkeeper** [ˈʃɑpˌkipɚ] n. [C] 店主 [同] storekeeper

▲ The shopkeeper tried to attract more shoppers by giving out coupons.

這店主藉由送出優惠券來試圖吸引更多購物者。

21. **soul** [sol] n. [C] 靈魂

▲ Some people wonder whether the soul will leave the body at death.

有些人疑惑靈魂在死時是否會離開身體。

22. **suit** [sut] n. [C] 套裝，西裝

▲ The lawyer likes to wear dark suits.

這律師喜歡穿深色西裝。

suit [sut] v. 對⋯方便；適合，與⋯相稱

▲ If the time suits Harry, he will come to discuss the

details with us.

如果這時間對 Harry 方便，他會來和我們討論細節。

23. **tear** [tɪr] n. [C] 眼淚 (usu. pl.)

▲ The sad story moved everybody to tears.

這悲傷的故事讓每個人感動流淚。

tear [tɛr] v. (被) 撕掉，(被) 撕裂 (tore | torn | tearing)

▲ Feeling very angry, Ann tore the letters to pieces.

由於感到很生氣，Ann 把信撕成碎片。

💡 tear sb/sth apart 使⋯分離；把⋯撕開

24. **text** [tɛkst] n. [U] 正文 ; [C] (手機的) 簡訊 (also text message)

▲ This book contains too much text and too few pictures. 這本書正文太多且圖畫太少。

25. **windy** [ˋwɪndɪ] adj. 風大的，刮風的 (windier | windiest)

▲ The fishermen usually don't sail out to sea in windy weather. 漁夫們通常不在風大的天氣駕船出海。

Unit 36

1. **affair** [əˋfɛr] n. [C] 事務 ; 風流韻事 <with> [同] love affair

▲ Every day, the manager has lots of affairs to look after. 這經理每天有很多事務要處理。

2. **ape** [ep] n. [C] 猿，類人猿

▲ Apes, such as gorillas and chimpanzees, are similar to humans. 猿類，像是大猩猩和黑猩猩，和人類相似。

3. **bun** [bʌn] n. [C] 小圓麵包；圓髮髻 <in>

▲ The cook cut a bun in half to make a hamburger.
這廚師把小圓麵包切成兩半以做漢堡。

4. **cereal** [ˋsɪrɪəl] n. [C][U] 穀物食物

▲ Gina poured the breakfast cereal into her bowl and added some milk.
Gina 把早餐麥片倒進她的碗裡並加一些牛奶。

5. **cloudy** [ˋklaʊdɪ] adj. 多雲的 [反] clear (cloudier | cloudiest)

▲ It is cloudy today; many thick clouds gather over the sky. 今天天氣多雲，厚厚的雲聚集在天上。

6. **custom** [ˋkʌstəm] n. [C][U] 風俗，習俗

▲ It is the custom for Taiwanese people to celebrate Lunar New Year. 慶祝農曆新年是臺灣人的習俗。

7. **double** [ˋdʌbl] adj. 雙的；雙人的

▲ Drivers need to understand it is illegal to cross solid double white lines to change lanes.
駕駛應了解跨越雙白實線變換車道是違法的。

double [ˋdʌbl] v. 加倍

▲ Because Ida was very hard-working, her boss doubled her salary.

由於 Ida 工作很勤奮，她的老闆把她的薪水加了一倍。

double [ˋdʌbl̩] **n.** [C][U] 兩倍，雙份；[C] 雙人房

▲ This buyer offered Frank $10,000, but another one promised to give him double. 這買家向 Frank 出價一萬美元，但另一個買家承諾給他兩倍。

double [ˋdʌbl̩] **adv.** 雙層地，雙重地

▲ Larry wanted to see a doctor because he started seeing double. Larry 因為視力出現重影而想要去看醫生。

---

8. **drawer** [ˋdrɔɚ] **n.** [C] 抽屜

▲ Lily keeps her diary in the bottom drawer.
Lily 把她的日記放在最底層的抽屜。

---

9. **examination** [ɪgˌzæməˋneʃən] **n.** [C] 考試 [同] exam；[C][U] 檢查 <on>

▲ The student is preparing for the college entrance examination. 這學生正在準備大學入學考試。

---

10. **garbage** [ˋgɑrbɪdʒ] **n.** [U] 垃圾 [同] rubbish

▲ The truck comes to collect garbage every day.
這卡車每天來收垃圾。

---

11. **goat** [got] **n.** [C] 山羊

▲ These goats are kept on the farm to produce milk.
這些山羊被豢養在農場生產羊奶。

---

12. **lamb** [læm] **n.** [C] 小羊；[U] 羊羔肉

▲ The lamb followed the mother sheep wherever she went.

母羊到哪裡，這小羊就跟到哪裡。

lamb [læm] v. 生小羊

▲ The ewe is going to lamb next month.
這母羊下個月要生小羊。

---

13. **leadership** [`lidɚ,ʃɪp] n. [C][U] 領導；[U] 領導能力

▲ Under the CEO's leadership, the company began to thrive. 在這執行長的領導下，這公司開始生意興隆。

---

14. **lone** [lon] adj. 單獨的，獨自的 [同] solitary

▲ There was a lone figure standing on the deserted street. 有個人形單影隻地站在空蕩蕩的街道上。

---

15. **noodle** [`nudl] n. [C] 麵條 (usu. pl.)

▲ Katherine often eats instant noodles for lunch.
Katherine 中午常吃速食麵當午餐。

---

16. **policy** [`pɑləsɪ] n. [C] 政策，方針 <on> (pl. policies)

▲ The nation has adopted a strict policy on patents.
這國家採取嚴格的專利權政策。

---

17. **pumpkin** [`pʌmpkɪn] n. [C][U] 南瓜

▲ On Halloween, people make lanterns out of pumpkins. 人們在萬聖夜用南瓜做燈籠。

---

18. **quantity** [`kwɑntətɪ] n. [C][U] 量 <of> (pl. quantities)

▲ People should drink a large quantity of water when catching a cold. 感冒時，應該喝大量的水。

---

19. **rat** [ræt] n. [C] 老鼠

▲ On seeing a rat in the kitchen, Emily screamed loudly. Emily 一看到廚房裡的老鼠就大聲尖叫。

20. **shore** [ʃor] n. [C][U] 岸 <of>

▲ The old couple walked along the shore of a lake.
這對老夫妻沿著湖邊散步。

21. **sour** [saʊr] adj. 酸的 [反] sweet；酸臭的，酸腐的

▲ The plum is too sour and can't be eaten now.
這李子太酸，現在還不能吃。

sour [saʊr] n. [U] 酸味雞尾酒，沙瓦

▲ This whiskey sour is made from whiskey, lime juice, sugar, and ice.
這款威士忌沙瓦是用威士忌、萊姆汁、糖和冰做的。

sour [saʊr] v. (使) 令人不快，(使) 不友好；(使) 酸腐

▲ Mutual accusations have soured the relations between the two countries.
相互指控已讓這兩個國家關係惡化。

22. **terrorism** [ˈtɛrəˌrɪzəm] n. [U] 恐怖主義

▲ So far, the September 11 attacks have been the worst acts of terrorism the United States has experienced.
到目前為止，九一一攻擊是美國經歷過最糟糕的恐怖主義活動。

23. **thief** [θif] n. [C] 小偷 (pl. thieves)

▲ Two thieves broke into the store last night and stole some cash. 兩名小偷昨晚闖入商店，偷了一些現金。

24. **tissue** [ˋtɪʃʊ] n. [U] (細胞) 組織；[C] 面紙
   ▲ Many athletes have very little fat tissue.
   很多運動員的脂肪組織非常少。

25. **wing** [wɪŋ] n. [C] 翅膀
   ▲ The bird flapped its wings and flew away.
   這隻鳥拍拍翅膀飛走了。

Unit 37

1. **album** [ˋælbəm] n. [C] (音樂) 專輯；集郵冊，相冊
   ▲ The pop singer has just released her latest album.
   這流行歌手剛推出她的最新專輯。

2. **argue** [ˋɑrgju] v. 爭論，爭吵 <with, over>；主張，提出
   理由 <for>
   ▲ Julie argued with her friend over which movie to see.
   Julie 和她朋友爭論要看哪一部電影。
   argument [ˋɑrgjumənt] n. [C] 爭論，爭吵 <with, over>；理由，論點
   ▲ Dave had an argument with his wife over money.
   Dave 和妻子為錢而爭吵。

3. **burden** [ˋbɝdn̩] n. [C] 負擔，重擔 <of>；負荷 [同] load
   ▲ After his father died, Kent had to carry the heavy burden of supporting the whole family.
   Kent 在父親死後必須負起養全家的重擔。

burden [ˋbɝdn̩] **v.** 煩擾 <with>

▲ The actress was burdened with constant attention from her fans. 這女演員為影迷持續的關注所煩擾。

---

4. **chapter** [ˋtʃæptɚ] **n.** [C] 章，回；一段時期，階段 <in>

▲ This chapter deals with the Roman Empire.
這一章是講述羅馬帝國。

---

5. **cocoa** [ˋkoko] **n.** [U] 可可粉 (also cocoa powder)

▲ The baker added some cocoa to the dough to give it a chocolate flavor.
這烘焙師在麵團裡加了一些可可粉以增添巧克力味。

---

6. **depend** [dɪˋpɛnd] **v.** 依…而定，取決於 <on>；依賴，依靠 <on> [同] rely

▲ The rice harvest largely depends on the weather.
稻米的收成主要取決於天氣。

💡 it depends 視情況而定

---

7. **dove** [dʌv] **n.** [C] 鴿子

▲ Doves are symbols of peace, purity, and hope.
鴿子是和平、純潔和希望的象徵。

---

8. **dryer** [ˋdraɪɚ] **n.** [C] 烘乾機

▲ Iris took the wet clothes out of the washing machine and put them into the dryer.
Iris 把溼衣服從洗衣機拿出來，並把它們放進烘乾機。

---

9. **examine** [ɪgˋzæmɪn] **v.** 調查，審查 <for>；檢查

▲ The experts examined the wreckage for some clues about the crash.

專家們調查殘骸要找一些墜機的線索。

---

10. **gentleman** [ˋdʒɛntḷmən] n. [C] 先生；紳士 (pl. gentlemen)

▲ The waiter served a glass of champagne to the gentleman. 服務生為這位先生端上一杯香檳。

---

11. **gradual** [ˋgrædʒʊəl] adj. 逐漸的 [反] sudden

▲ There has been a gradual decrease in the death rate with the advanced medical technology.

有了先進的醫療技術，死亡率已逐漸降低。

---

12. **lane** [len] n. [C] 鄉間小路；巷

▲ A narrow country lane leads up the hill.

一條狹窄的鄉間小路通往山丘上。

---

13. **lend** [lɛnd] v. 借出，借給 <to> (lent | lent | lending)

▲ Mark didn't have any cash with him, so Tess lent NT$1,000 to him. Mark 身上沒有任何現金，所以 Tess 借了新臺幣一千元給他。

💡 lend (sb) a hand 幫助 (⋯) | lend an ear 傾聽

---

14. **mango** [ˋmæŋgo] n. [C] 芒果 (pl. mangoes)

▲ A mango is a tropical fruit with a thin skin and orange-yellow flesh.

芒果是一種皮薄、果肉橘黃的熱帶水果。

15. **nut** [nʌt] **n.** [C] 堅果

▲ Owen likes to eat nuts, such as walnuts and hazelnuts. Owen 喜歡吃堅果，像是核桃和榛果。

16. **praise** [prez] **n.** [U] 讚美，表揚 [反] criticism

▲ The strict teacher gives her students little praise.
這嚴厲的老師很少讚美她的學生。

praise [prez] **v.** 讚美，表揚 <for> [反] criticize

▲ The boy was praised for his honesty.
這男孩因為誠實而受到讚美。

17. **purple** [ˋpɝpl] **adj.** 紫色的 (purpler | purplest)

▲ The farmer is picking purple eggplants on the farm.
這農夫正在農田摘紫色的茄子。

purple [ˋpɝpl] **n.** [C][U] 紫色

▲ Purple is a mixture of red and blue.
紫色是紅色和藍色的混合。

18. **railroad** [ˋrel͵rod] **n.** [C] 鐵路，鐵道 [同] railway

▲ The railroad was built to connect the two cities.
這條鐵路被建來連接兩個城市。

19. **refrigerator** [rɪˋfrɪdʒə͵retɚ] **n.** [C] 冰箱 [同] fridge

▲ Lily put the vegetables and fruit in the refrigerator to keep them fresh. Lily 把蔬果放在冰箱以保鮮。

20. **shut** [ʃʌt] **v.** 關閉；停止營業 [同] close (shut | shut | shutting)

▲ Bill shut the door behind him and left.

Bill 關上身後的門並離開。

💡 shut (sth) off 關掉 (機器等) | shut up 閉嘴

shut [ʃʌt] adj. 關閉的，關上的 [同] closed

▲ Mina listened to the music with her eyes shut.
　Mina 閉著眼聽音樂。

---

21. **spot** [spɑt] n. [C] 地點，場所 <on>；斑點 [同] patch

▲ This garden is a perfect spot for a wedding banquet.
　這個花園是婚禮宴會的絕佳地點。

💡 on the spot 在現場；當場

spot [spɑt] v. 看見，注意到 (spotted | spotted | spotting)

▲ Jennifer spotted her boyfriend in the crowd.
　Jennifer 在人群中看見她的男友。

---

22. **thirsty** [ˋθɝstɪ] adj. 口渴的 (thirstier | thirstiest)

▲ John was so thirsty that he drank up a bottle of water in ten seconds.
　John 如此口渴以致於在十秒內喝完一瓶水。

---

23. **tongue** [tʌŋ] n. [C] 舌頭；語言

▲ The little girl ran her tongue over her lips when seeing the cake.
　這小女孩看到蛋糕時用舌頭舔了舔嘴唇。

💡 slip of the tongue 失言

---

24. **track** [træk] n. [C] 小道，小徑；足跡，車痕

▲ The adventurer followed the track through the jungle.

這冒險家順著小徑穿過叢林。

🕯 keep track of sb/sth 了解…的動態 / 紀錄…

track [træk] v. 跟蹤，追蹤 <to>

▲ The hunter tracked the bear to its den.
這獵人跟蹤那頭熊到牠的巢穴。

---

25. wool [wʊl] n. [U] 羊毛

▲ These sheep are mainly kept for their wool.
這些綿羊主要是養來取羊毛的。

Unit 38

1. ankle [ˈæŋkl̩] n. [C] 腳踝

▲ Oliver slipped and sprained his ankle.
Oliver 滑了一跤並扭傷腳踝。

---

2. arrow [ˈæro] n. [C] 箭

▲ The hunter shot an arrow at the deer.
這獵人朝鹿射了一箭。

---

3. burst [bɝst] n. [C] 爆裂，破裂；爆發 <of>

▲ There was a burst in the pipe, and water splashed everywhere. 管子爆裂，水噴濺得到處都是。

burst [bɝst] v. 爆炸，破裂；衝，闖 <into> (burst | burst | bursting)

▲ The bubble burst in the air. 這泡泡在空中破掉。

🕯 burst out crying/laughing 突然大哭 / 大笑

---

4. **chart** [tʃɑrt] n. [C] 圖表 [同] diagram

▲ The bar chart showed a decline in sales this year.

這長條圖顯示今年銷售額下降。

---

5. **cola** [`kolə] n. [C][U] 可樂，碳酸飲料

▲ Nicky likes all types of cola, such as Coke and Pepsi.

Nicky 喜歡各式碳酸飲料，像是可口可樂和百事可樂。

Coke [kok] n. [C][U] 可口可樂

▲ Coke is a registered trademark of the Coca-Cola Company. 可口可樂是可口可樂公司註冊的商標。

---

6. **description** [dɪ`skrɪpʃən] n. [C][U] 描述 <of>

▲ The witness gave a detailed description of the robber.

這目擊者對搶匪做了詳細的描述。

🔋 be beyond description 無法形容，難以描述

---

7. **drama** [`drɑmə] n. [C][U] 戲劇；戲劇性 (事件)

▲ *Friends* was once a famous television drama.

《六人行》曾是很有名的電視劇。

---

8. **dull** [dʌl] adj. 枯燥的，乏味的；(色彩等) 不鮮明的，晦暗的

▲ It was such a dull movie that some audience fell asleep.

這是如此枯燥的一部電影以致於一些觀眾睡著了。

dull [dʌl] v. 緩解，減輕

▲ The patient took some medicine to dull the pain.

這病人吃一些藥來緩解疼痛。

---

9. **exit** [ˋɛgzɪt] n. [C] 出口 ; 離開 ， 退場 <from> (usu. sing.)
▲ There are three emergency exits in the building.
這棟建築物有三個緊急出口。

exit [ˋɛgzɪt] v. 離開 <from>
▲ People exited the movie theater from the side door.
人們從側門離開電影院。

10. **govern** [ˋgʌvɚn] v. 治理，管理 [同] rule
▲ The principal governs the high school wisely.
這位校長睿智地管理這所中學。

11. **gram** [græm] n. [C] 公克 (also gramme) (abbr. g, gm)
▲ The bag of flour weighs 500 grams.
這袋麵粉重五百公克。

12. **lantern** [ˋlæntɚn] n. [C] 燈籠
▲ The kids hollowed pumpkins to make lanterns on Halloween. 孩子們在萬聖夜挖空南瓜做燈籠。

13. **liver** [ˋlɪvɚ] n. [C] 肝臟
▲ Paul's liver is damaged because of alcohol abuse.
Paul 的肝臟因為酗酒而損壞。

14. **marry** [ˋmærɪ] v. 娶 ， 嫁 ， (和…) 結婚 (married | married | marrying)
▲ Ralph asked his girlfriend to marry him.
Ralph 要他女友嫁給他。

15. **operator** [`ɑpəˌretɚ] n. [C] 接線生

▲ The caller asked the operator to put him through to Room 918. 來電者要求接線生幫他接通到 918 號房。

16. **principal** [`prɪnsəpl] adj. 最重要的，主要的 [同] main

▲ Rice is the principal food of Chinese people.
米飯是中國人的主食。

principal [`prɪnsəpl] n. [C] 校長

▲ The principal gave a speech to all the teachers and students this morning.
這校長今天早上對所有老師和學生演講。

17. **quiz** [kwɪz] n. [C] 問答遊戲，智力競賽；小考 (pl. quizzes)

▲ The history quizzes in the newspaper are difficult.
這報紙上的歷史問答遊戲很難。

18. **relation** [rɪ`leʃən] n. [C][U] 關係，關聯 <between> [同] relationship

▲ The study shows the relation between sugar and cancer cells. 這研究顯示糖和癌症細胞的關係。

💡 in relation to sth 關於…，涉及…

19. **rub** [rʌb] v. 揉搓，摩擦 (rubbed | rubbed | rubbing)

▲ The sleepy boy rubbed his eyes and yawned.
這睏倦的男孩揉眼睛並打哈欠。

rub [rʌb] n. [C] 擦，揉搓 (usu. sing.)

▲ Mandy gave the desk a good rub with a wet cloth.

Mandy 用溼抹布把桌子好好擦一遍。

20. **silly** [ˋsɪlɪ] **adj.** 傻的，愚蠢的 [同] foolish (sillier | silliest)

   ▲ It was silly of Samuel to trust such a liar.
   Samuel 傻到相信這樣一個騙子。

21. **steak** [stek] **n.** [C][U] 牛排

   ▲ The customer would like his steak medium-well.
   這位顧客的牛排想要七分熟。

22. **thunder** [ˋθʌndɚ] **n.** [U] 雷，雷聲

   ▲ There was thunder and lightning all night.
   整晚雷電交加。

   thunder [ˋθʌndɚ] **v.** 轟隆隆地移動

   ▲ The train just thundered past the platform.
   這火車剛轟隆隆地從月臺駛過。

23. **treasure** [ˋtrɛʒɚ] **n.** [U] 寶藏；[C] 珍寶，藝術珍品

   ▲ The pirates were digging for buried treasure.
   海盜們正在挖掘埋藏的寶藏。

   treasure [ˋtrɛʒɚ] **v.** 珍惜

   ▲ Marcia treasures the pocket watch her father gave her. Marcia 很珍惜父親給她的懷錶。

24. **upset** [ʌpˋsɛt] **adj.** 苦惱的，心煩的 <about, by>；生氣的 <with>

   ▲ Tony is very upset about the argument he had with his girlfriend yesterday.

Tony 因為昨天和他女朋友起爭執而非常苦惱。

upset [ʌpˋsɛt] v. 使苦惱；打亂，攪亂 (upset | upset | upsetting)

▲ The bad news upset Victor; he looked worried.

這壞消息使 Victor 苦惱，他看起來很擔心。

upset [ˋʌpsɛt] n. [C][U] 苦惱，心煩

▲ The emotional upset has affected Nicole since her father died.

自從 Nicole 的父親過世後，她內心一直心煩著。

---

25. **worm** [wɝm] n. [C] 蟲

▲ Chickens eat insects and worms like crickets and earthworms. 雞吃昆蟲和蟲，例如蟋蟀和蚯蚓。

worm [wɝm] v. 擠過，鑽過 <through>

▲ Polly wormed her way through the crowd to meet her friends. Polly 擠過人群，和朋友們碰面。

● ━━━━━━━━━━━━━━ ◆ ━━━━━━━━━━━━━━ ●

Unit 39

1. **arrival** [əˋraɪvl] n. [C][U] 抵達 <at, in> [反] departure；[U] 來臨 <of>

▲ Owing to the traffic jam, Eli's arrival at the town was delayed for an hour.

因為塞車，Eli 抵達這城鎮的時間延誤了一個小時。

---

2. **backpack** [ˋbæk͵pæk] n. [C] 背包

▲ Beth put her laptop in a backpack and took it to

school. Beth 把筆電放進背包帶去學校。

backpack [`bæk,pæk] v. 背包旅行 <around>

▲ Alex backpacked around Europe, camping or staying in youth hostels.

Alex 在歐洲各地背包旅行，露營或住青年旅館。

---

3. **cabbage** [`kæbɪdʒ] n. [C][U] 甘藍，捲心菜

▲ The cook made borscht soup with chopped cabbage and tomatoes. 廚師用切碎的捲心菜和番茄做羅宋湯。

---

4. **classic** [`klæsɪk] adj. 典型的，有代表性的；經典的

▲ The patient had all the classic symptoms of flu.

這病人有所有流感的典型症狀。

classic [`klæsɪk] n. [C] 經典之作

▲ *A Tale of Two Cities* by Charles Dickens is an all-time classic.

查爾斯狄更斯的《雙城記》是一部空前的經典之作。

---

5. **comb** [kom] n. [C] 梳子

▲ Renee used a comb to tidy and arrange her hair.

Renee 用梳子整理她的頭髮。

comb [kom] v. 用梳子梳

▲ Wayne is really untidy at home; he doesn't even comb his hair. Wayne 在家時很邋遢，他甚至不梳頭。

💡 comb sth out 梳理 (頭髮)

---

6. **desert** [`dɛzɚt] n. [C][U] 沙漠，荒漠

▲ The man rode a camel across the desert.

這男子騎著駱駝穿越這片沙漠。

desert [dɪˋzɝt] v. 拋棄，丟棄 [同] abandon

▲ The poor dog was deserted by its master and became a stray animal.

這隻可憐的狗被主人拋棄，成了一隻流浪動物。

---

7. **duty** [ˋdjutɪ] n. [C][U] 義務 [同] obligation；[C][U] 職務 (usu. pl.) (pl. duties)

▲ It is every citizen's duty to vote in an election.

選舉投票是每一個公民的義務。

💡 be on/off duty 上 / 下班

---

8. **eagle** [ˋigl] n. [C] 鷹

▲ The eagle swooped down and snatched a rabbit.

這隻老鷹俯衝下來抓了一隻兔子。

---

9. **fever** [ˋfivɚ] n. [C][U] 發燒；[sing.][U] 狂熱

▲ The patient had a high fever this morning, but he feels better now.

這病人今天早上發高燒，但他現在覺得好多了。

---

10. **grain** [gren] n. [U] 穀物；[C] 穀粒

▲ After the harvest finished, the grain was stored in the barn. 收割結束後，穀物被儲存在穀倉裡。

---

11. **grape** [grep] n. [C] 葡萄

▲ These grapes will be used for making red wine.

這些葡萄會被用來製作紅酒。

---

12. **lens** [lɛnz] n. [C] (照相機等的) 鏡頭；鏡片，透鏡 (pl. lenses)

▲ A wide-angle lens allows people to take photos with a wider view. 廣角鏡讓人們可以更寬廣的視野拍照。

---

13. **luck** [lʌk] n. [U] 運氣

▲ Some people believe the number 13 means bad luck.
一些人相信數字十三表示惡運。

♥ try sb's luck 碰運氣

---

14. **membership** [ˋmɛmbɚ͵ʃɪp] n. [U] 會員資格，會員身分 <in, of>

▲ If people don't pay the annual fee, they will lose their membership in the club.
如果人們不付年費，就會喪失這俱樂部的會員資格。

---

15. **pajamas** [pəˋdʒæməz] n. [pl.] 睡衣褲

▲ Mason changed into his pajamas before going to bed.
Mason 上床睡覺前先換上睡衣。

---

16. **promise** [ˋpramɪs] n. [C] 承諾，約定

▲ Emma is a woman of her word and never breaks her promise. Emma 是個信守諾言的人，從不食言。

♥ make/keep a promise 立下 / 信守承諾

promise [ˋpramɪs] v. 承諾，保證

▲ Ted promised to return the money by Monday.
Ted 承諾星期一還錢。

---

17. **raincoat** [ˋren͵kot] n. [C] 雨衣

▲ Because it was raining, the motorcyclist put on his raincoat. 因為正在下雨，這摩托車騎士穿上他的雨衣。

---

18. **repair** [rɪ`pɛr] n. [C][U] 修理 <to>

▲ The mechanic will make some repairs to the car.
這技工將修理這輛車。

💡 under repair 正在修理中

repair [rɪ`pɛr] v. 修理 [同] mend

▲ Alfred's coffee machine isn't working, so he has to get it repaired.
Alfred 的咖啡機壞了，所以他得將它送修。

---

19. **sail** [sel] v. 航行，行駛；啟航，開船 <for>

▲ The fishing boat sailed down the river.
這艘漁船往河下游航行。

sail [sel] n. [C] 帆

▲ A yacht with a white sail floated on the waters near the harbor.
一艘有白帆的遊艇浮在港口附近的海域上。

💡 set sail 啟航

---

20. **slipper** [`slɪpɚ] n. [C] 拖鞋

▲ It was rude of Zack to go to the restaurant in slippers.
Zack 穿拖鞋到餐廳是很不禮貌的。

---

21. **storm** [stɔrm] n. [C] 暴風雨

▲ As the severe storm struck the country, many places were flooded.

當這大暴風雨侵襲這國家時，很多地方被淹了。

storm [stɔrm] **v.** 猛衝 <into>

▲ The angry workers stormed into the factory.
憤怒的工人們衝進了這間工廠。

---

22. **tire** [taɪr] **v.** (使) 感到疲勞

▲ The energetic young man walked around all day without tiring.
這精力充沛的年輕人整天到處走也不會感到疲勞。

💡 tire of sb/sth 對⋯感到厭煩

tire [taɪr] **n.** [C] 輪胎

▲ The tire burst while Sally was driving her children to school.
Sally 正開車載她的孩子去學校時，車子爆胎了。

---

23. **triangle** [ˋtraɪˏæŋgl] **n.** [C] 三角形

▲ The pyramid has four sides, and three of them are triangles. 這金字塔有四面，其中三個面是三角形。

---

24. **wherever** [hwɛrˋɛvɚ] **adv.** 無論什麼地方，去任何地方

▲ The tourist wants to go on a tour in Cambridge, Oxford, or wherever.
這遊客想去劍橋、牛津或任何地方旅遊。

wherever [hwɛrˋɛvɚ] **conj.** 無論在哪裡，無論到哪裡

▲ Wherever the suspect is, the police will surely find him. 這嫌犯無論在哪裡，警方一定會找到他。

---

25. **wound** [wund] **n.** [C] 傷，傷口

▲ The victim died from a knife wound to his neck.
這受害者死於頸部刀傷。

wound [wund] v. 使受傷

▲ The explosion killed two people and wounded five others. 這起爆炸造成兩人死亡、其他五人受傷。

Unit 40

1. **bend** [bɛnd] v. 彎 (腰)，曲 (膝) <down> ; (使) 彎曲
   (bent | bent | bending)

   ▲ Jason bent down to pick up his pencil from the ground. Jason 彎腰將鉛筆從地上撿起來。

   bend [bɛnd] n. [C] 彎道，轉彎處 <in>

   ▲ There is a sharp bend in the road up ahead.
   前方道路有一個急轉彎。

2. **café** [kə`fe] n. [C] 咖啡廳 (also cafe)

   ▲ Ruby bought a cup of coffee and a simple meal at the café. Ruby 在這咖啡廳買了一杯咖啡和一個簡餐。

3. **coal** [kol] n. [U] 煤

   ▲ Ian put more coal into the stove to help the fire burn.
   Ian 放更多煤進爐子以幫助火燃燒。

4. **congratulation** [kən͵grætʃə`leʃən] n. [U] 祝賀 <on> ;
   [pl.] 祝賀，恭喜 (~s)

   ▲ Ruth sent Daniel a text of congratulation on his

promotion.

Ruth 發了一封簡訊給 Daniel 祝賀他的升官。

5. **drug** [drʌg] n. [C] 毒品;藥物

▲ The drug addict took cocaine and marijuana.

這毒品成癮者吸食古柯鹼和大麻。

drug [drʌg] v. 用藥麻醉 (drugged | drugged | drugging)

▲ The patient was drugged and soon lost consciousness.

這病人被打了麻醉劑就很快失去了意識。

6. **earring** [ˋɪr͵rɪŋ] n. [C] 耳環 (pl. earrings)

▲ Stella bought a pair of earrings in the store.

Stella 在這間店買了一對耳環。

7. **earthquake** [ˋɝθ͵kwek] n. [C] 地震

▲ Some buildings collapsed after the strong earthquake.

一些建築物在強震過後倒塌了。

8. **false** [fɔls] adj. 虛假的,偽造的;錯誤的 (falser | falsest)

▲ A person giving false evidence in court is committing an offence.

在法庭上做偽證的人是在犯罪。

9. **fox** [faks] n. [C] 狐狸 (pl. foxes)

▲ Some people think the businessman is as sly as a fox.

一些人認為這商人像狐狸一樣狡猾。

10. **guava** [ˋgwɑvə] n. [C] 番石榴

▲ A guava is a round tropical fruit with white flesh and hard seeds.

番石榴是一種圓形熱帶水果，果肉白且有堅硬的種子。

11. **lid** [lɪd] n. [C] 蓋子

▲ Felix helped his mother get the lid off the jar.

Felix 幫他母親把瓶蓋打開。

🔮 keep a lid on sth 防止…失控；保守祕密

12. **mention** [ˋmɛnʃən] v. 提及，談到 <to>

▲ Martin mentioned the plan to the manager, but it was not accepted.

Martin 跟經理提及這計畫，但它未被接受。

🔮 don't mention it 不客氣 | not to mention sth 更不必說…

mention [ˋmɛnʃən] n. [C][U] 提及，談到 <of> (usu. sing.)

▲ There was little mention of the accident in the papers. 報紙上幾乎沒有提及這起意外。

13. **mood** [mud] n. [C] 心情，情緒

▲ Listening to soft music usually puts Glenn in a good mood. 聽輕音樂通常讓 Glenn 心情好。

🔮 be in the mood for sth 有意要…

14. **pan** [pæn] n. [C] 平底鍋 [同] saucepan

▲ The cook used a pan to fry the eggs.

這廚師用平底鍋來煎蛋。

---

15. **reject** [rɪ`dʒɛkt] **v.** 拒絕，不接受 [反] accept；不錄用 [反] accept

▲ Andy stubbornly rejected his friend's offer of help.
Andy 固執地拒絕他朋友要幫他的提議。

---

16. **relate** [rɪ`let] **v.** 有關聯 <to> [同] connect；找到聯繫 <to>

▲ Eating habits highly relate to one's health.
飲食習慣和一個人的健康有高度關聯。

---

17. **review** [rɪ`vju] **n.** [C][U] 審查，審核 <under>；[C] 評論

▲ The deal was under review by the government banking regulators.
這項交易正在政府銀行監管員的審查中。

review [rɪ`vju] **v.** 審查，審核；評論

▲ Before making the decision, the committee had reviewed the current situation.
在做這決定之前，委員會已審查了當前的情勢。

---

18. **salty** [`sɔltɪ] **adj.** 鹹的 (saltier | saltiest)

▲ Eating too much salty food, such as bacon, isn't good for health.
吃太多像是培根這類鹹的食物對健康不好。

---

19. **snowy** [`snoɪ] **adj.** 下雪的，多雪的 (snowier | snowiest)

▲ It was snowy yesterday, and the road was buried under heavy snow this morning.

昨天下雪了，而今天早上這條路被埋在厚雪之下。

20. **strike** [straɪk] n. [C][U] 罷工 <on>；攻擊，突襲 <on>

▲ The workers have been on strike for more than a month. 工人們已經罷工超過一個月了。

strike [straɪk] v. 撞，擊；擊打 (struck | struck | striking)

▲ A ball struck the girl on the back of her head.
一顆球擊中這女孩的後腦。

♥ strike a balance (between...) (在…中) 求得平衡

21. **toast** [tost] n. [U] 吐司；[C] 敬酒，乾杯

▲ Vera is spreading butter on a piece of toast.
Vera 在一片吐司上塗奶油。

toast [tost] v. 舉杯為…敬酒 <with>；烤

▲ The wedding guests toasted the bride and groom with wine. 婚禮賓客們以紅酒舉杯為新娘新郎敬酒。

22. **trick** [trɪk] n. [C] 騙局，詭計；惡作劇

▲ The woman's tears were just a trick to win people's sympathy. 這女人的眼淚只是博取人們同情的詭計。

trick [trɪk] v. 欺騙，誘騙 <into>

▲ The bad guy tricked the old lady into signing the paper. 這壞人誘騙老婦人在文件上簽名。

23. **true** [tru] adj. 正確的，真實的 [反] false；真正的 [同] real (truer | truest)

▲ Is it true that the rock band is making a concert tour?

這搖滾樂團要做巡迴演唱是真的嗎？

💡 come true (夢想) 成真

true [tru] adv. 不偏離地，正中地

▲ The bullet flew fast and true to the target.

這子彈飛得很快且正中靶子。

true [tru] v. 裝準，擺正 <up>

▲ The worker trued the window frame up before he hung the windows.

這工人在掛上窗戶前，先把窗框裝準。

---

24. **worst** [wɝst] adj. 最差的，最糟的

▲ This is the worst bread Yvonne has ever eaten.

這是 Yvonne 吃過最糟的麵包。

worst [wɝst] adv. 最嚴重地，最糟地

▲ The global economy has been worst hit by the pandemic. 全球經濟受疫情打擊最為嚴重。

💡 worst of all 最糟的是

worst [wɝst] n. [sing.] 最壞的人或事，最糟的情況 (the ～)

▲ The flood last year is the worst that the country has suffered from.

去年的洪水是這國家遭受過最糟的一次。

---

25. **yam** [jæm] n. [C] 山藥

▲ A yam is a root vegetable which looks like a long potato. 山藥是一種看起來像長形馬鈴薯的根莖植物。

單字索引

單字索引

單字索引

單字索引

單字索引

單字索引

單字索引

單字索引

單字索引

Index

單字索引

單字索引

單字索引

基礎英文法養成篇

英文學很久,文法還是囧?
本書助你釐清「觀念」、抓對「重點」、舉一反三「練習」,
不用砍掉重練,也能無縫接軌、輕鬆養成英文法!

特色一:條列章節重點

每章節精選普高技高必備文法重點,編排環環相扣、循序漸進。

特色二:學習重點圖像化與表格化

將觀念與例句以圖表統整,視覺化學習組織概念,輕鬆駕馭文法重點。

特色三:想像力學文法很不一樣

將時態比喻為「河流」,假設語氣比喻為「時光機」,顛覆枯燥文法印象。

特色四:全面補給一次到位

「文法小精靈」適時補充說明,「文法傳送門」提供相關文法知識章節,觸類旁通學習更全面。

特色五:即時練習Level up!

依據文法重點設計多元題型,透過練習釐清觀念,融會貫通熟練文法

陳曉菁 編著

英語 *Make Me High* 系列

基礎英文字彙力 2000 隨身讀

彙　　整	三民英語編輯小組
責任編輯	何尉賢
美術編輯	陳欣妤

創 辦 人	劉振強
發 行 人	劉仲傑
出 版 者	三民書局股份有限公司 (成立於 1953 年)

三民網路書店
https://www.sanmin.com.tw

地　　址	臺北市復興北路 386 號　（復北門市）　(02)2500-6600
	臺北市重慶南路一段 61 號 (重南門市) (02)2361-7511

出版日期	初版一刷 2022 年 2 月
	三版一刷 2024 年 3 月
書籍編號	S871810
I S B N	978-957-14-7760-2

著作財產權人©三民書局股份有限公司
法律顧問　北辰著作權事務所　蕭雄淋律師
著作權所有，侵害必究
※ 本書如有缺頁、破損或裝訂錯誤，請寄回敝局更換。

三民書局